D1479301

rising silver mist

DISCLAIMER

The Gottwas are an invented tribe, loosely inspired by the Ojibwe people. I did not want to cause offense to Native Americans by writing about customs that aren't mine.

CHARACTERS

Adette: Taeewa's mate; the *bazash's* daughter

Adison Wood: Ace and Lily's mother; Linus's wife

Ace Wood: Linus's son; Maximus's grandson

Aylen: Nova's sister; Cat's aunt

Astra Sakar: half-fae; owns Astra's Bakery

Bee: Beatrice; owns Bee's Place; Blake's grandmother

Blake: Bee's grandson; Cat's friend

Borgo Lief: Ishtu's lover; Cruz's "adoptive" father

Cassidy (Cass): Cat's best friend in Rowan; Etta's daughter

Catori Price: main character

Chatwa: Iya's mother; twin sister to Holly's mother, Ley; hunter

Cruz Vega: fae; faux medical examiner; friends with the Woods family; Lily's fiancé; Lyoh & Jacobiah's son

Derek Price: Cat's father; Nova's husband

Elika: Negongwa's mate; Gwenelda's mother; Kajika's adoptive mother

Etta: real name is Cometta; part fae; daughter of Astra; sister to Stella

Faith Sakar: Stella's daughter; bad blood between her and Cat

Gregor: current fae wariff; soulless narcissist

Gwenelda: huntress; first to awaken; absorbed Nova's soul

Holly: Ley; half-mortal, half-fae; Jacobiah Vega's half-sister, Cruz's aunt

Ishtu: Kajika's mate; looked like Cat

Iya: Chatwa's daughter; Cat's great-grandmother

Jacobiah Vega: fae; former wariff; Cruz's father; killed by Lyoh Vega

Jimmy: Cass's brother; Etta's son

Kajika: Ishtu's ex-husband; Gwenelda's brother-in-law

Ley: Holly; Chatwa's "twin sister"; half-fae / half-human

Lily Wood: fae; mute; Ace's sister; Linus's daughter; Cruz's fiancée

Linus Wood: King of the fae

Lyoh Vega: Jacobiah's wife; Cruz's mother; killed her husband; killed Ishtu

Maximus Wood: Linus's father; ruthless, lawless, bloodthirsty leader

Menawa: Gwenelda's mate; Kajika's brother

Negongwa: revered leader of Gottwa Indians

Nova Price: Catori's mother; Derek's beloved wife

Satyana: Aylen's daughter; Shiloh's twin sister

Shiloh: Aylen's daughter; Cat's young cousin; Satyana's twin sister; has the sight

Silas: *lucionaga*

Stella Sakar: part fae; daughter of Astra; sister to Cometta (Etta)

Taeewa: Gwenelda's youngest brother; the 13th hunter

Tony: Aylen's husband

Woni: Iya's daughter; Nova's mother; Cat's grandmother

GOTTWA LANGUAGE

aabiti: mate
    abiwoojin: darling
    adsookin: legend
    baseetogan: fae world; Neverra; Isle of Woods
    bazash: half-fae, half-human
    bekagwe: wait for me
    chatwa: darkness
    debwe: truth
    gajeekwe: the king's advisor, like a minister
    gatizogin: I'm sorry
    Gejaiwe: the Great Spirit
    gassen: faerie dust
    gingawi: part hunter, part fae
    golwinim: Woods's guards, fireflies
    gwe: woman
    ishtu: sweetness
    kwenim: memory
    ley: light
    ma kwenim: my memory
    maagwe: come with me
    maahin: come forth
    Makudewa Geezhi: Dark Day
    manazi: book

mashka: tough
mawa: mine
meegwe: give me
meekwa: blood
Mishipeshu: water faeries, *Daneelies*
naagangwe: stop her
nockwad: mist
nilwa: defeater
pahan: faeries
tokwa: favor

FAELI LANGUAGE

adamans: glass flowers as tall as wheat stalks

alinum: rowan wood

astium: portal, door

calidum: lesser fae; *bazash*

caligo: mist

caligosubi: one who lives below the mist, aka marsh-dweller

caligosupra: one who lives above the mist, aka mist-dweller

calimbor: skytrees

captis: magnetize

clave: portal locksmith

cupola: cage of nightmares

Daneelies: water faeries, *Mishipeshu*

diles: venomous Neverrian creature, a cross between a frog and a crocodile

draca: first guard; wariff's protector (dragon-form)

Duobosi: coupling ceremony

enefkum: eunuch

fae: sky-dwellers

Forma: underground-dwellers, bodiless, *Unseelies*

Fias: child

gajoï: favor

Hareni: grotto

kalini: fire

lucionaga: faerie guards

Lustriums: clusters of stars

mallow: an edible plant, faerie weed; doesn't affect humans the same way it affects faeries, and hunters are immune

Massin: Your highness

Mea: mine

Mikos: Neverrian snake coated in sharp quills

Milandi: marvelous

Neverra: baseetogan; Isle of Woods

Obso: please

Potas: I can't

Plantae: plants

Quid est: Who is it?

Runa: Neverrian gondolas carried by faeries

Seelies: light faeries, *Fae*

Sepula: ceremony of the dead

stam: giant flat shells that bob in the glades

ti ama: I love you

Unseelies: dark faeries, bodiless, *Forma*

Vade: go

Valo: bye

Ventor: Hunter

Wariff: equal to *Gajeekwe*

To LIANA.

A BEAUTIFUL LIGHT THAT WENT OUT TOO SOON.

PART I
EARTH

PROLOGUE

I traced the braided gold band of my mother's engagement ring, running my fingertip against the chiseled planes of the inset rubies. Dad had given it to me two weeks before, and I hadn't taken it off since. Like gleaming pockets, the red stones held memories of my mother. Some days, those memories were painful and I fisted my hands; some days, they were joyful and I eagerly dove inside the red depths.

Tonight's memory was a joyful one.

"On my eighth birthday, I wanted sugar cookies instead of a cake. While Mom made the dough, I rifled through her box of cookie cutters and picked a ghost. She asked me, *why not a flower?* I reminded her that my name meant *spirit*. So ghosts were more accurate than flowers."

I held my ring up to the faint beam of light spilling from my desk lamp. The rubies winked at me.

"You should've seen my mother's face. She paled and sat me down, then explained that Catori didn't mean ghost; that it meant a powerful force, a supreme being. Which of course prompted me to say, *you named me God?*"

Mom had laughed.

She had the most wonderful laughter. It filled all of her, from her eyes to her mouth to her chest. I would've given anything to hear that sound again.

The warm fingers combing through my long black locks stilled. "Never has a name suited a person better."

"Are you making fun of me?"

The hand wrapped around the mass of my hair and tugged gently to pivot my head. "Cat, I may be endowed with an incredible sense of humor, but I do sometimes set it aside. I don't think your parents could've named you better. You're a force to be reckoned with." A crooked smile settled over Ace's lips. "Supremely sexy and powerfully addictive. A goddess in her own right."

I rolled my eyes. "I bet you can't say those things with a straight face."

"Am I not allowed to smile at my gorgeous girlfriend?"

I searched his eyes for humor but became sidetracked by their exquisiteness. There wasn't much I didn't like about Ace, but those eyes . . . those eyes completely undid me. Bluer and more brilliant than the iridescent veins in the opal pendant I abandoned at Holly's farmhouse the night I learned the hunters had killed her.

"And I can say it with a straight face." His hand released my hair, traveled down the side of my body, and settled on my hip where his other hand already rested. Applying the gentlest pressure, he pivoted my body to face his. "You are supremely sexy and powerfully addictive, Catori Price."

A shiver crackled through each one of my nerve endings. Yes, his hands were on me. And yes, the fire running through his veins heated my own blood. But it was more than that with Ace. His very presence turned me into a livewire.

I wasn't sure how I could ever have been immune to him. I often thought of our first encounter in the county jail, where he'd come to bail out his best friend Cruz Vega. The meeting—the handshake—felt like eons ago.

"What are you thinking about?"

"Laundry," I deadpanned.

"Really?" His eyes bored into mine. "My declaration made you think of laundry?"

I licked my lips that suddenly felt cracked as though I hadn't sipped water in days.

He watched my mouth, dark eyebrows slanted over his straight nose. The caged dust that girdled my neck like an inked rendition of barbed wire throbbed underneath my skin.

A second heartbeat.

I touched the pulsating flesh with my fingers. Even though Stella's confiscated dust was locked underneath my skin, I always worried it would leach into my throat and choke me, like it should've done when she'd unleashed it on me back in the hospital.

Ace lowered his face to my neck and kissed his way across my collarbone. When his lips brushed my knuckles, my hand sprang away. "Would you like me to get your mind off your very human tribulations?"

I shivered. Before I could speak, he kissed the thin skin sheltering the dust.

I forgot about Stella then. I forgot about my mother. About the meaning of my name. About the ghost cookies I'd baked. About my father sleeping across the hall from me. I forgot I was part faerie and part hunter, and that dating Ace was not only a terrible idea, but also a dangerous one.

His mouth skimmed my jaw. "Still thinking about laundry?"

"No." The word leaped out of me—hoarse, loud, rash.

He kissed my mouth, and the heady warmth that had enveloped my skin swathed my veins.

A long moment later, when our lips broke apart, my pulse felt like it had escaped my body and scattered across my bedroom.

"I want you to teach me to resist *captis*," I blurted out.

Ace's hands, which had slipped underneath my gray T-shirt some-time during our make-out session, stilled on the base of my spine. "Why?"

Ever since Mom died, stress limned everything in my life. I was terrified my father would find out that magic existed in our world and be punished for knowing. I feared my best friend Cass would be killed in the crossfire of the hunter/faerie war simmering in our town. I dreaded that Stella would return to Rowan and carve her dust out of my neck. I worried that Gwenelda and Kajika would plow my backyard to awaken the rest of their hunter family—my family. Not that I considered myself a hunter these days.

Neither did I consider myself a faerie for that matter.

I favored another term: human. I'd even gotten the word tattooed over the brand Cruz had seared into my flesh, the one that had morphed into a W for Wood—Ace's last name—and glowed each time my pulse hastened.

"Why do you want me to teach you to resist *captis?*"

I traced the faint white lines of the W, then balled my fingers into a slack fist and raised my gaze to Ace's. "In case a faerie other than yourself decides to use it on me."

His jaw ticked.

"I want to become stronger, Ace. Help me become stronger. Fighting something I can see is difficult enough. But fighting something invisible feels impossible. And yet I remember you telling me I resisted it a bit back in Detroit. The first time you used it on me. Were you stroking my ego, or did I really manage?"

"You really managed, but I don't know how you did it. I just *felt* you blocking me."

"Use it on me and tell me when you feel resistance, and I'll figure out what I'm doing."

His features were all hard lines.

I touched his brow to smooth it. "I'm not trying to resist *you.*"

With a gravelly sigh, his features loosened. "I hadn't even considered anyone else using it on you."

"I wouldn't want to imagine anyone seducing you either—with or without magic."

"That wouldn't happen."

"And yet, I find myself imagining this more often than I like. Ever since you told me faeries weren't monogamous—"

"I would never cheat on you, Cat."

I wanted to believe Ace, but it felt idealistic, romantic of him to say this, and stupid and naïve of me to trust it. We'd been together all of two weeks. What would happen in a couple months when I was no longer new and shiny?

Although the consideration rattled me, I shoved it away. Now wasn't the time to focus on potential risks. Now was the time to focus on real risks: faerie allure. "Please teach me."

His chest rose and fell.

"Think of all that time we'll have to spend practicing." I smiled to sweeten my demand.

"I don't like using it on you."

"Would you rather I ask someone else to teach me?"

His blue eyes ground into my black ones. "Absolutely not."

"So you'll do it?"

He loosed a heavy sigh. "Yes, but not today."

"Tomorrow?"

He kissed my nose, then the corners of my mouth. "You are supremely sexy, powerfully addictive, and incredibly"—he gave me that cocky grin of his—"*incredibly* stubborn."

"My father says he pities the man I'll marry. So consider yourself lucky you're already engaged."

His smile vanished. "I hope you don't believe him."

A blush crawled up my throat, snaked over my jaw. "I'm nineteen. Marriage is the furthest thing from my mind. Besides, maybe I'll never get married."

Unlike him . . .

Ace would marry soon. I wasn't sure when. I didn't want to know. Already the idea of him having a wife—albeit one he disliked—made my stomach roll. "Can we talk about something else? Anything else?"

"I don't love her."

I pressed my cheek against his shoulder. Even though I knew he didn't love Angelina, even though I had no reason to feel jealous, I did, and that terrified me more than almost everything else.

And the Great Spirit only knew what a feat that was, considering the actual dangers in my life.

1

THE NIECE

While Dad read the paper, I squeezed a lemon into his mug of Earl Grey. Ever since Lily told me acidic food repelled Unseelie spirits, I'd been filling my father's stomach with vinegar and citrus juice. Not that there were any Unseelie spirits roaming though Rowan.

Apparently, on the Night of Mist—which is the only night Unseelies can exit the *Hareni*, their underground home—none had made their way to a faerie portal. But there were hundreds of portals in Neverra. What if the faeries keeping watch over the magical doors had missed an Unseelie escaping?

Dad snorted, then shook his head.

I tipped one of my eyebrows up. "What?"

"This story in the paper. A Home Depot employee claims he was taking inventory and noticed a huge amount of missing stock, so he checked the security footage and saw *himself* tug crates out into the parking lot. He has no memory of doing this." Dad closed the newspaper, crinkling the Bible-thin sheets.

"Was he fired?"

"On the spot. That's why he went to the paper. To plead his case." Dad folded and refolded the broadsheets, then tossed them into the bin beneath the sink. "The lengths people will go to." He tunneled his hand through his pillow-mussed hair. "All that for iron rope and chains."

Lemon juice dripped between my fingers and onto my socks. "That's . . . that's what he stole?"

"Yes. Strange, huh?"

The crushed lemon rind slid through my fingers and landed with a wet plop on the tiled floor.

Iron.

Memory loss.

I'd bet anything hunters had influenced him to hand them iron chains before making the memory vanish from his mind.

"You okay, honey? You look a little pale."

"Fine." The word came out like a hiss.

Dad frowned.

I bent over to pick up the fallen lemon, which I tossed atop the newspaper way too hard.

"You sure?"

I nodded. "I should get going. I promised to meet Kajika at Bee's this morning."

Dad's blue eyes dimmed at the mention of the hunter's name. He wasn't a fan of Kajika. Dad thought him unstable and strange. The fact that he was covered in tattoos and muscles didn't help.

I rubbed my own marking. How would Dad react if he saw it?

Even though I'd begged Ace to reclaim his dust—dust to a faerie was the equivalent of a gun to a soldier—he'd refused to remove it from my neck, where it concealed Stella's dust from human eyes.

Dad watched my fingers.

I froze.

Could he see? Had Ace finally listened to me and withdrawn his dust?

"I don't like the looks of all those people who moved in with them."

My neck felt wooden. I managed a stiff nod. "I'm not a fan of that crowd either, but Kajika was Holly's nephew." He wasn't, but Dad still believed this.

Fact: Holly had descended from the Gottwa tribe, which had adopted Kajika and his brother a couple years before the massacre— the "Darkest Day"—that led the hunters to entomb themselves for two centuries in rowan wood caskets filled with spelled rose petals.

Out of the twelve graves, two were empty—Gwen's and Kajika's—

and one held an actual dead body—Gwen's mother. Dad and Aylen had dug up her grave, but before my aunt had had time to read the inscription, which would've brought the huntress back to life by stealing a human soul, Kajika and I had stopped the ritual. Exposed, the pink petals around the hibernating huntress's body had grayed and desiccated, releasing the magic that had preserved her.

That day, for the first and only time, I'd pitied Gwenelda. Even though she'd stolen my mother's soul—granted not on purpose—I never wished heartache on her. I wasn't vengeful, but I was resentful. I resented Gwenelda for creating new hunters with her blood. Those untrained savages believed I was their enemy and had attacked me with rowan wood arrows in my own backyard.

My chest burned at the memory. And then my brand lit up with Ace's W. I tried to even out my heart rate before he barreled into the house to check up on me.

Dad assumed we were friends—and he was okay with that. He liked Ace. He found him charming and thoughtful and generous. And like the rest of the world, he believed Ace was engaged and that his fiancée was pregnant with their child.

Angelina *was* pregnant, but not with Ace's child.

My phone vibrated in the back pocket of my jeans. I fished it out.

Ace: *R u OK?*

Yes.

Were you thinking about me?

I smiled, a feat considering how unsettled I felt about the news Dad had just read in the morning paper. *I never stop.*

Don't think about me too hard as I have a meeting with the council this morning. Gregor and Cruz's lovely mother have something important to tell us apparently.

Really?

Yeah. What are you up to?

Even though I didn't want to lie, I knew telling him I was going to call a meeting with Kajika would incense him. *Doing my nails. Curling my hair. Full body wax. The usual.*

Three dots lit up. I was expecting a smart-aleck comeback, but all I got was, *What are you actually doing?*

Nothing exciting. Don't worry.

I'm always worried.

Gotta go. Dad's looking at me funny.

"You want me to come with you to meet Kajika?" Concern contorted Dad's features. In the time since Mom died, tiny wrinkles had exploded over his face, crinkling the corners of his eyes and mouth. Grief and extreme weight loss had been rough on my father. "I was heading over to Bee's anyway. I wanted to check up on her, and then I have a meeting with Mr. Hamilton's niece."

"Mr. Hamilton has a niece?"

"'Parently he does."

Rowan was a small town where everyone knew everyone's business, and yet I had never once heard old Mr. Hamilton talk about family. And boy, could the man talk.

"Why are you meeting her?"

"She's a medical examiner."

My eyes widened. "Really?"

"She just moved here." Dad's gaze lowered to the tiled floor. "She—" He shoved a hand through his blond hair that seemed to have gotten lighter, bleached by grief. "She bought Blake's old place."

I gasped. "What?"

"Bee said she needed to put it on the market, and then Mr. Hamilton mentioned his newly-divorced niece was looking for a place to live, and well . . ."

A chill enveloped me. "I suppose it was a matter of time before someone took over his house."

Dad enfolded me in his arms. "Still hurts, huh?"

"So damn much."

I didn't think anything could hurt me after losing my mother, but losing my best friend . . . There were no words for what that had done to me.

LONG TIME

*W*hen Dad left the kitchen to get dressed, I called Kajika.

"Hi, Catori."

I hadn't heard his voice since before Stella attacked me. It sounded unfamiliar, brittle. Kajika was rough around the edges, but not his voice. His voice had always been smooth.

"Catori?" he repeated, softer this time.

I splayed my fingers on the wooden kitchen island, gaze fixed to the door that led down to the morgue. It used to be buttercup-yellow— Mom believed the cheery hue would tone down the creepiness of its destination—but I'd painted it white after her death. I'd tried to erase Mom, because every tiny trace of her cleaved my heart open wider.

"We need to talk," I finally said. "Can you meet me at Bee's in a half hour?"

"Come to the compound."

"And be ambushed by your *friends*? No thank you."

"They are not my *friends*. Besides, I have spoken to them, and they have sworn to never again hurt you."

Like I'd believe a bunch of crazed, dust-thirsty hunters. "Meet me at Bee's in thirty minutes. Alone."

"All right."

After hanging up, I finished tidying up the kitchen, put a load of laundry in the wash, and wrapped a scarf around my neck—the common mortal couldn't see the navy whorls printed on my skin, but Kajika wasn't a common mortal . . . he could see through faerie dust.

When I walked into Rowan's one and only inn ten minutes later, I made a beeline for Cass, who was frothing up milk behind the varnished wooden bar.

I took off my puffer vest and draped it over a barstool, then seated myself on top another. April had pushed away March days ago, warming the frozen earth. Buds had broken over branches like goosebumps and daffodils had pierced the ground and shot upward, splashing color over our monochrome town. Even the sky seemed bluer in the spring, but the air was still brisk.

Cassidy filled a mug with black coffee and set it in front of me before I could even ask.

Blue eyes darting through her dark brown bangs, Cass tipped her chin toward the back of the room. In a low voice, she whispered, "Check out the booth next to the window."

"Why?"

"Just do it." Nursing my mug of coffee, I swiveled on my stool.

Sheriff Jones sat in a corner booth with his dime-sized eyes on his breakfast date, a black-haired woman with high cheekbones and dark eyes who looked to be around his age. I spun back around.

"I think he's cheating on his wife. He keeps laughing at *everything* she says." She rolled her eyes. "Middle-aged people flirting are *so* gross."

"Says the girl with a penchant for middle-aged men." I folded my legs, then blew the steam off my coffee and dipped my lips inside.

"What are you talking about?"

"The guy back in Detroit."

"He was thirty-six."

"That's seventeen years older than you."

She smiled as she poured the warm milk into clear mugs, topped them with espresso, then plated two golden muffins from the white porcelain cake stand.

"Speaking of middle-aged people, how's the new cook doing?"

The woman was from Mullegon, the next town down the coast. Like Rowan, it was a small harbor town. Unlike Rowan, it had more than one main street, which wasn't to say it was busier, because it wasn't really. It just offered a bit more choice.

"She's handling the rushes pretty well. You should try her corn muffins." She heaved in a shaky breath. "They're almost as good as Blake's."

Blake's death had been as hard on her as it had been on me. After he'd been honorably discharged from the army, he'd come home and worked as a short-order cook in his grandmother's inn alongside Cass, who'd traded community college for a waitressing job. Her goal was to become a professional bartender once she turned twenty-one.

Which reminded me . . . "You're turning twenty in a month!"

Her eyes twinkled. "I know! I'm planning a kickass party. You think Ace and Lily would come?"

Cass was in awe of the Wood siblings. Although they gave few interviews and steered clear of paparazzi, their wealth and faces were no secret.

"I bet they'd come if you asked them," I told her.

She walked around the bar and seized her platter. "Can *you* ask them? Since you and Ace are—"

I widened my eyes. Cass was the only person who knew Ace and I were dating. She'd been so excited and not at all surprised. When I explained the bit about his fiancée carrying Linus's child, her jaw had gaped as wide as the *papier maché* mask we'd fashioned back in middle school for a class play.

She blew on her bangs and grimaced. "Sorry. I forget."

"Try not to. Small town. Big mouths."

She grinned, then scampered toward the sheriff's table just as the door jingled. It was my father. He wore jeans and a woolen navy sweater that made him look bulkier than he was. He'd started gaining back *some* weight, which wasn't saying much. At 6'4", filling out was a feat.

"Hey, Cat, did you see Mr. Hamilton?"

"Nope."

"Derek!" Sheriff Jones bellowed, gesturing Dad over.

Dad turned toward his high school friend. When he noticed the woman sitting with him, he frowned. "Hey, George."

"I've been keeping this lovely lady company until you arrived. Milly, meet Derek Price, greatest coroner in the state of Michigan and greatest guy in the tristate area."

Dad smiled. "Don't believe a word this guy says."

The brunette smiled, lifting her hand toward Dad, who shook it. "Pleasure to meet you, Derek."

Dad dragged a chair to the booth and sat.

After asking him if he wanted something to drink, Cass returned to me. "Okay. Now I'm confused. If she's not Jones's not-so-secret lover, who the heck is she?"

"She's Mr. Hamilton's niece."

The woman looked nothing like her uncle.

"Come again? Old Mr. Hamilton has family?"

"I know, right? I found out this morning."

"What's she doing in Rowan?"

"She just got divorced and decided to move to Rowan. She's a medical examiner."

"No way!"

"Yeah. Way."

"That's cray cray."

"Tell me about it."

Cass wrinkled her nose. "You think she lives with him?"

"No, she bought"—I swallowed, but it didn't take the bitter edge off what I was about to share—"Blake's old place."

With shaky fingers, Cass repositioned a corn muffin on the cake stand, slotted another in its place, and then piled another on top. Then she fixed the other side of the golden tower, which didn't need fixing. When she was done, she knuckled a tear out of her eye. "It's not like he's ever coming back."

No, Blake wasn't coming back.

Cass sniffled loudly. "Let's hope she leaves better tips than Mr. Hamilton."

"He leaves tips?"

"I got ten cents once."

A bark of laughter escaped me. I pressed my palm against my mouth to stifle the sound that had Dad turning around. "Cass. Joke," I croaked, between bursts of laughter.

Cass broke into a grin.

Tears dripped out of the corners of my eyes and traveled down my cheeks. I wiped them away, but more came. Cass handed me a paper napkin and grabbed one for herself. Each time our eyes would meet, we'd crack up all over again. Our nerves must've been severely shot if we were laughing this hard over a dime.

It wasn't until the door jingled that I sobered up.

Kajika had arrived.

3

THE CONFESSION

*K*ajika looked from me to Cass to my father then back to me. His expression was somber. Then again, his expression was *always* somber. The cadavers in our basement seemed downright cheerful compared to him.

"Catori, all is well?"

That almost got me laughing hysterically again. His speech sounded so olden. Kajika belonged to an era that no longer existed, an era when women wore petticoats and corsets, and Natives still lived in wigwams and traded pelts for black powder.

"Everything's fine," I finally said, shoving my hair off my face. It was as black as his, a black that looked almost blue in direct sunlight.

Cass stared at the hunter, then frowned at me. At least Dad was so absorbed by his conversation that he paid me no mind.

"What did you want to discuss?"

I gestured to the most isolated booth in the inn, then grabbed my vest and coffee and walked over. After we sat, Cass came by to take his order.

"Water, please."

Before leaving, Cass whispered excitedly, "Do you have any new fights coming up? I really enjoyed last week's."

My sip of coffee went down the wrong hole. I sputtered. "You're still fighting?" I wheezed out.

"I need the money. And fighting eases my temper." Eyes firmly planted on mine, he cocked his face to the side, and his slippery black hair fell across his forehead. "Better I fight in a ring than in real life."

"Yeah."

"To answer your question, Cassidy, I fight this Thursday. You are both welcome to come."

I cleared my throat. If he knew I was seeing Ace, he would most definitely rescind his invitation.

"I'll be there." Cass returned to the bar, filled a tall glass with ice cubes and water, then returned to our table to deposit it before Kajika. For a second, I thought she might take off her black waist apron and plop down on the wine-colored banquette next to me, but the sheriff beckoned her over.

Once she was gone, I said, "There was a perplexing article in the paper this morning."

"Perplexing?"

"Disturbing. Distressing."

His vocabulary—although padded by Blake's memory—dated back two hundred years, so some words eluded him.

"I know what perplexing means, Catori." He placed his forearms on the table. "Why did it *perplex* you so?"

"Home Depot. Iron chains. Ring a bell?"

He pulled his arms off the table and knotted them in front of him. "You know I do not steal."

"The employee who carried out the crates of iron had no memory of doing it. Perhaps it wasn't you, but only hunters"—I lowered my voice—"possess *influence*."

Kajika's eyes gleamed sharply. "I was not aware of this. Thank you for bringing it to my attention."

"You seriously had no clue?"

He shook his head. I searched his face for tells but found none. Maybe he hid them well, or maybe he really didn't know.

"Don't you control them?"

"Control them? I train them, yes, but I do not seek to control others. I leave that to Gwenelda."

"Well, either she's not doing a good job of it or—" I rocked forward in the booth, so that my whisper reached Kajika quicker. "Or she's planning an attack. Which would really screw up the fragile peace betw—"

"Peace?" His lips contorted into a scowl. "What peace would that be, Catori? Yesterday, the *golwinim* killed one of ours."

"They did? Who?" I secretly hoped it would be Alice. I'd only met her once, but I didn't like her. And my dislike of her had nothing to do with the fact that she'd had sex with Kajika. The hunter was allowed to have sex with whomever he wanted. I just didn't like her. She seemed wild and entitled.

"Tom. The former general."

My mind clicked on a memory. The night I'd returned from Detroit, a man wearing army fatigues flanked Gwenelda. That must've been Tom. "Why did they kill him?"

"Because they could."

"There must be more to it than that."

"Why must you always take their side?"

"I don't." *Did I?* "It just seems odd to me they eliminated him out of opportunity."

Kajika snorted. "For someone who spends much time with faeries, you do not appear well acquainted with them."

Heat engulfed my face. I pulled the scarf looser and began unwrapping it when I remembered why I was wearing it in the first place. I froze and began to loop it back around. I wasn't quick enough.

Kajika hooked a finger in the soft material and tugged it away from me. His eyes widened as they flashed up to mine. "You confiscated *gassen?*"

I bit my lip. Nodded. "Not on purpose, though."

He frowned.

Making my voice as faint as possible, I said, "I ran into Stella, and, well . . . she tried to asphyxiate me. Almost managed it, but then a nurse saw I was choking and cleared my airwaves with her scalpel, and my blood . . . it magnetized Stella's dust."

Although Kajika remained quiet, a vein throbbed furiously at his temple.

I shrugged. "At least now I know how it works."

He closed his eyes. When he opened them, they were almost black. "I will kill her."

"No, Kajika." I shook my head. "I didn't tell you about it to get revenge."

"That is twice that faeries attacked one of ours."

I winced. *One of theirs.*

"I thank *Gejaiwe* Stella failed, but I will not allow their crimes to go unpunished."

"Kajika—"

"Do not protect them," he growled, and his growl attracted unwanted attention.

"Let *me* punish her," I whispered. "You said you would teach me to fight, so teach me to fight."

Kajika studied me.

"And no, I will never use what you teach me against you. I swear it."

After a long while, he said, "Tomorrow morning. I will pick you up at nine o'clock."

"In the morning or at night?"

Kajika's face swung to the side, to the body looming over our table. The body I had failed to sense advancing our way.

"Why is Kajika picking you up at nine, Cat?"

I cringed.

Ace's timing was awful.

"What Catori and I do does not concern you, *pahan*," Kajika spit out.

Calling Ace *pahan*—the Gottwa term for faerie—was not a good idea. That was exactly the reason Kajika did it though, to irritate Ace. To think these two males had once agreed to work together to bring peace to their people seemed downright implausible.

Even though our booth was sort of secluded, it was in no way removed enough. Dad and the sheriff were leaning out of theirs to watch us.

Cass scampered our way. "'Morning, Ace."

Ace didn't acknowledge my friend. "Why is he picking you up at nine?"

Undeterred, Cass asked, "Coffee? Tea?"

"Ace, please . . ." I whispered. "Don't make a scene. I'll explain later."

"Why would you explain yourself to him, Catori?" Kajika asked.

"Maybe I should come back later," Cass said.

Ace dropped in next to me. I scooted away. He reached under the table. His hand settled on my knee. I jolted further away, stopping only when my back hit the brick wall.

"You are frightening her," Kajika said.

Ace raised one corner of his mouth in a half sneer, half smile. "I may provoke many feelings in Cat, but fright isn't one of them."

"Kajika agreed to teach me to fight," I blurted out, because it beat discussing the *feelings* Ace roused in me.

"Absolutely not," he said.

Kajika narrowed his dark gaze. "Because you believe you have a say in what she does?"

"I may not have a say in what she does"—Ace speared me with his incandescent blue eyes—"but I have a say in *who* she does it with."

Ace tried to put his hand on my thigh again, but I shifted away . . . again. Letting him put his hand on me felt wrong. It felt like a statement—one I didn't want to make right now.

My pulse accelerated. The W on my hand ignited, and then Ace's palm began to glow.

"Catori, why does Ace have a say on who you spend time with?"

"He doesn't."

I half-expected Ace to rise, to storm off, like he always did when he was angry, but he didn't move. He barely breathed.

Kajika studied my mark in charged silence. The last time I'd seen him, he'd asked why the V had morphed into a W, and I'd explained Lily had used magic to unlink me from her fiancé and pass my mark on to her brother. I pulled my hand under the table, but Ace didn't move his hand out of the hunter's sight. If anything, he fanned his fingers to make it more visible.

Anger honed Kajika's expression into an inflexible, tangible thing as stiff and sharp as one of his rowan wood arrows. It slid into my breastbone, remained lodged there.

"What would have happened to Stella if she had killed Catori?" Kajika's voice was as brittle as an arrow tip.

"I could've punished her as I saw fit," Ace answered.

"Could you have killed her?"

Ace nodded.

"And yet she took the risk to attack Catori? She either does not care for her life, or she did not know the meaning of your mark. *Or she did not fear retribution.*"

Ace went very still, whereas Kajika leaned forward.

"Would you have avenged Catori's death, Ace?"

The faerie's shoulders tightened so fast I could almost hear the vertebrae of his spine click into place. "She didn't die."

"That is not what I asked." Kajika shook his head just as Cass returned with a thick cream mug, which she deposited in front of Ace.

"I made you tea. You like it black, right?"

Ace didn't respond.

"Can I get anyone any—"

Kajika's eyes sank into Cass's and gleamed. "Leave and do not return until we call on you."

Although I wished Kajika hadn't used his influence on my friend, I was thankful he'd sent her away. Cass had a minute amount of faerie blood in her, but no knowledge of it. Knowledge of it would have consequences. What if she went to Neverra? What if she turned on me? What if—

"You should not trust Ace, Catori."

My throat went dry. I didn't dare look at Ace. Instead, I studied my mother's ring, spun it. I didn't want to doubt him.

"I have heard of your reputation," Kajika continued. "Your people believe you to be soft. Unfit to lead them."

A vein ticked in Ace's throat. "Glad to know what's said about me, but I must say, I'm surprised *my people* gossip with your people. And I'm surprised hunters are interested in fae gossip. Aren't you too busy raising a vengeful army to discuss Neverrian politics?"

"Neverrian politics are of much interest to us. We seek allies amongst your people. Preferably *strong* ones. Although I do not particularly trust Cruz, he has grown quite ruthless, has he not?"

Ace's eyes burned with fresh anger. They burned so bright I began to worry fire would spurt out of them. *Could it?* Or could fire only leak out of his fingers? I studied Ace's hands, watched for flames. None licked his skin.

"Why is Kajika picking you up at nine tomorrow, Cat?" Ace asked through gritted teeth.

"To teach me how to fight." I bit my lower lip. Why was I ashamed of this? Ace knew I wanted to become tougher. I released my lip.

"No," Ace said.

I shoved a lock of hair behind my ear. "It's not your choice. It's mine."

Hurt stretched over him. "I can teach you to fight. You don't need Kajika."

The texture of his voice splintered both my resolve and heart.

Kajika folded his arms and leaned back, the leather seat groaning beneath him. "Faeries do not know how to fight. At least, not fairly. But I suppose you *could* teach Catori dirty tricks."

Anger sheeted from Ace. His fingers rolled into a fist. Before I realized what it would look like, I wrapped my fingers around his. They burned gently in mine but did not ignite.

Kajika stared at our linked hands.

"In Gottwa tradition, only lovers or mothers hold another person's hand. Enemies do not touch each other, unless it is to kill. But I have observed humans hold friends' hands. Is Ace your friend or lover, Catori, because he certainly is not your child."

I let go of Ace's hand. "He's my friend."

Something flickered in Ace's expression. *Disappointment?*

"You should choose your friends more wisely." He rose. "I should get back to my clan. I will see you tomorrow, Catori." And then he was gone.

"Friend?" Ace asked.

"Would you have punished Stella?"

Ace cocked an eyebrow. "Is that why you demoted me to *friend*?" He spoke the word as though it tasted foul.

I pivoted to face him. "Would you?"

The lightbulb over our booth jeweled his eyes. "I would've done way worse than kill her."

4

BROKEN BONDS

"I don't want Kajika to teach you how to fight," Ace said, as I recovered from the shock of his declaration.

Was anything worse than death in Neverra?

"I want to be enough for you," he continued. "Is that unreasonable?"

"Kajika knows things you don't."

"I know many things."

"Do you know how I moved water?" I murmured.

"You were angry—"

"I've been angry since then, but never managed to move anything. When Stella attacked me, I was powerless."

"We could figure it out."

"Why do you want me to choose? Why can't I have both you and Kajika as instructors? You don't see me asking you to pick me over your fiancée."

"I don't have a choice in the matter," he responded stiffly. "You do."

"Why *can't* you break it off with her?"

"I could but then then I'd get barred from returning to Neverra. Which in and of itself wouldn't be so dire if I didn't actually need my home to survive. Remember when we spoke about changelings?"

I dug through my memory until the right conversation cropped up. They died.

"The fire in their veins," I whispered. "It extinguishes if they don't return to Neverra."

His face smudged with a cold smirk. "Pretty dire choices, huh?"

The hinges that held my jaw shut slackened. Broke.

He ran his finger underneath my chin. I jolted away.

Our booth was secluded, but we were still in public.

Ace's eyes narrowed. I tipped my head sideways, in the general direction of my father. I wasn't sure if Ace would believe that was the only reason I'd jerked away.

Not when I didn't believe it myself.

Kajika had planted a tiny seed of doubt in my mind. I hated him for doing it, but I also appreciated his concern. I trusted the hunter over almost everyone else in Rowan because he always voiced his true thoughts.

"Think we could go somewhere more private?" Ace asked.

"I have . . . I have stuff to do."

His mouth tightened. Although I could tell he wanted to challenge me, ask what *stuff* needed to be done, all he said was, "I have *stuff* to deal with too."

He rose so rigidly that my heartbeat shuddered in my ears. "Ace—"

"Maybe I'll see you tomorrow."

And then he was gone too.

I planted my elbows on the table and rested my face in my open palms. I wanted to both growl and cry. I did neither. I remained strangely silent, trying to sort through my emotions and thoughts.

Inhaling deeply, I raked my hair off my face and gathered my jacket and bag. Although I wanted to leave without speaking to anyone, that wasn't a possibility. Pasting on a smile, I stopped by Dad's table. "I'm heading home."

His gaze flashed to the inn windows. "Alone?"

"Yeah." I held my hand out toward the woman at his table. "You must be Milly." As she shook it, I added, "Welcome to our weird town."

The sheriff said, "*Charming* town," and Milly laughed.

"It's a pleasure to meet you." She let go of my hand. "Catori, right?"

"That's right."

"My uncle tells me you're a very bright girl. A doctor-in-training."

I was surprised Mr. Hamilton knew what I was studying. "I've put the doctor part on hold for a little while, but yeah, that's the plan."

"If you ever want to discuss medical school, I've been there. Done that," Milly said.

Mom had also been there, done that. Even though I felt a twinge of sadness, I said, "I might take you up on that. Dad's medical knowledge is limited to Pepto-Bismol and Band-Aids."

Dad said, "Hey," but grinned.

"I need to get to work, folks. Was a real pleasure meetin' you, Milly. If you need anything, you know where to find me." Sheriff Jones got up and put on his khaki jacket adorned with a shiny gold star. I bet he polished it every night. "You ain't allergic to nothin', are ya, Milly?"

"I don't eat red meat."

"That won't be a problem. We've got real good fish here in Michigan. Thursday night, then. Seven PM."

Milly smiled. "I'll be there."

"Derek?"

"I should be free. Unless Cat—"

"I have plans for Thursday." I didn't want to hold my father back.

"Then I'll be there. With a six-pack."

"Good man." Sheriff Jones smiled at me. "You watch out now, Catori. Those boys you hang out with seem like trouble."

Even though I wasn't made of faerie fire, I smoldered. "They're nice to me."

"Are they?" Dad asked.

"Yes." My cheeks flamed brighter.

Nineteen, Cat. You're nineteen. Act like it.

"Your daughter's a beautiful woman, Derek," Milly said. "Better get used to seeing her surrounded by boys."

I blinked at Mr. Hamilton's niece, while Dad grimaced.

"I don't think any father can get used to that."

I needed to put an end to this torturous topic. "Will you be home for lunch?"

"I was going to show Milly around. Unless you want me to come home for lunch?"

"I should finish reading this article on microbiology. I'm trying to keep up with my classes." I hadn't studied in months, but I wanted my father to feel free.

"Virology was my favorite," Milly said.

I used to think I lied to protect my father, but the truth was, I lied to protect myself. "I'd love to hear your thoughts once I read the paper."

Milly nodded eagerly.

"Enjoy your tour of Rowan," I said. Cass called out my name, and I went over to the bar where she was wiping down glasses.

Voice thankfully low, she said, "I swear I could smell the testosterone all the way over to here. Were they fighting over you? Is that it?"

"They're not. They're just fighting with each other."

Her eyebrows quirked up behind her bangs.

"How much do I owe you for the coffee?" I took my wallet out.

"Nothing. It's hot flavored water."

"Cass—"

"Your money's no good here."

I was about to put away my wallet, but unzipped it instead. I pulled out a dime and placed it on the bar. "Then the least I can do is leave you a tip."

Cass laughed. "Get out of here."

I tucked a five-dollar bill underneath the coin even though Cass insisted I take it back. And then I went home to my empty house.

5

THE SAP

*B*efore dawn crept over the horizon the following morning, a dream pulled me out of sleep. It was neither good nor bad. Only strange.

The air had smelled sweet in my dream. A fire crackled. Sap boiled in iron kettles. Patches of thin snow dappled the bare earth. Laughter whirred as soft as the flung-open wings of the blue bird I chased through a clearing. Words spilled out of my mouth as swiftly as my breaths. *Ishtu, maagwe!* I was excited. Thrilled by the sight of the bird. In a hurry to catch up with it, but how could I catch up with something that flew? And yet my footfalls were quick. Almost as quick as the bird's flight. I floated through the long grass.

Magena! Magena, bekagwe! a girl called to my dream-self. Black hair ribboned behind her like an inky stream, but the rest of her features were blurry, her body as ethereal as mist.

Had I dreamed of Ishtu?

Ishtu had been Kajika's mate. Apparently, I resembled her—too much. Kajika had been crazy about her and crazed with grief when the faeries had murdered her. Recently, he'd learned she'd had an affair with a faerie—Borgo Lief—and that had shattered him.

His perfect mate hadn't been so perfect after all.

If Borgo hadn't committed suicide with my poisonous blood—I shuddered at the memory of him exploding into ashes—I was certain Kajika would've ended the faerie's life.

Truth was, I was a little bitter toward Ishtu. I felt Kajika deserved better than a two-timing wife. He was tempestuous and prejudiced, but no one could fault him his loyalty.

I pushed Ishtu and Kajika out of my mind. Focused on the other parts I remembered. *Magena. Bekagwe. Maagwe.* I let the words roll off my tongue, tasted them.

I threw my legs over the side of the bed. In the beam of light spilling from my bathroom, I crept over to my closet and opened my sock drawer, where I kept the handwritten Gottwa and Faeli dictionary Holly had given me. The words weren't arranged alphabetically so it took me a while to locate them, but I found two. *Bekagwe*: wait for me. And *maagwe*: come with me. I didn't find *magena*.

I decided I would ask Kajika when he showed.

I pulled on leggings, a sports bra, a T-shirt, and a hoodie, then sent Ace another text message. He hadn't answered last night's message, but cell phones didn't have reception in Neverra—which was where I imagined he'd gone. I hated thinking he'd stayed on Earth, because that would mean he was avoiding me.

Had I been that hurtful? Our conversation swam through my mind, but I'd analyzed it so many times since yesterday that it had taken on a hazy quality.

I tugged my hair into a high ponytail that whipped my shoulder blades as I hopped down the stairs. I opened the fridge door and stared at the shelves, trying to decide what I wanted to eat. A flat glass bottle filled with amber liquid caught my eye. I unscrewed the cap and sniffed the maple syrup.

It smelled like my dream.

Gottwa history and traditions weren't completely foreign to me— my grandfather had filled my ears with stories of tribal life—but dreaming of simmering sap felt very specific. Gottwas had been famous for their maple sugar and syrup. They'd tap the trees around their camp during the spring and transform the sap into a prized commodity they could trade.

As I replaced the bottle, I wondered why I'd dreamed of maple syrup and Ishtu. *Ishtu* meant sweetness in Gottwa. Maybe that was the link?

I shut the fridge door hard. Jars rattled from the impact.

Since when did I analyze dreams? Mom used to do that. Dad sometimes did it. But me?

My mind was rational.

I was rational.

Or at least I was supposed to be.

I rammed the dream out of my mind.

While I waited for the clock's arms to mark nine o'clock, I pulled an article on virology up on my smartphone and read it, cramming my restless mind with concrete facts and useful information instead of baseless deliberations about two girls chasing a bird while their mothers boiled tree blood.

AT 8:58 AM, I opened the front door and scanned the horizon for the rusty gray pickup Kajika had inherited from Holly.

I waited.

Waited some more.

The iron wind chime tinkled over my head. I squinted up at it and thought again of my mother. Originally, Mom had suspended it over our door to protect us from evil spirits. I'd dismissed her superstition as an old wives' tale. The evil spirits had obviously not been kept out, since she died. The same day I'd repainted the yellow door, I ripped the wind chime from its hook and threw it out. Weeks later, when I learned iron affected faeries—like an electronic dog collar incensed a dog—I'd bought a new one and hung it.

I reached high and touched the longest metal tube.

Since Ace and I had started seeing each other, I'd tinkered with the idea of taking it down, but Ace convinced me to leave it up. In memory of my mother, but also because it could potentially deter *some* faeries from entering my house. Besides, as long as my bedroom windows were shut, the grating noise didn't bother him.

Something glinted in the distance. Shading my eyes, I caught sight of a car. It was big and gray, and coughed and clanked.

6

THE SPIRIT PLANE

I hopped down my porch stairs toward Kajika's cab.

He rested an elbow in the open window. "Your information was accurate." Purple shadows rimmed his eyes.

"My information?" I went around the front and settled in next to him.

"The theft."

"Oh." I wished I hadn't been right. "What did they need iron chains for?"

"To fence in Holly's property. They fear the faeries. Especially the *golwinim*." The *golwinim*—faerie guards in the bodies of brutal fireflies— were keeping tabs on the hunters. "Those pests never leave."

"Did you slice off any noses?" That was the Gottwa punishment for theft.

"Gwenelda promised she had compensated the employee generously."

But had she compensated the store? I decided not to ask. "So they're not planning on attacking faeries with the chains?"

"We defend ourselves. We do not attack."

The gray pickup barreled through the open gates of the cemetery so fast I tugged my seatbelt on.

Kajika wasn't wearing his—then again, only faeries could kill hunters, so I supposed he didn't fear car crashes. But then I noticed his seat belt flapped uselessly by his shoulder, ripped. "Had a disagreement with your seatbelt?"

He glanced at it. "It tore the night we drove back from the fighting ring."

I frowned. I'd been in the car with him, yet couldn't remember him ripping a seatbelt.

Suddenly, it came back to me.

Lily had shown up in the middle of the road. Kajika had jammed his foot against the brakes. His body had slammed against mine. I'd thought his seatbelt had come undone. That he'd toppled over me by accident.

It hadn't been an accident.

I blinked at him, then blinked at the road that flew past my window.

He'd thrown himself over me to protect me. Shame prickled the nape of my neck. I wasn't sure what I was ashamed of. Not understanding this before? I rubbed the patch of skin, but it did little to lessen the tingling. "Thank you."

After a long moment, Kajika asked, "For what?"

"For being kind to me when I don't always deserve it."

Silence stretched tightly between us. When after several long minutes he still hadn't said anything, I asked him what *magena* meant.

The car swerved a little. "Where did you hear the name Magena?"

So it was a name. Must have been the other girl's name. The one who was running alongside Ishtu. The one whose body I'd been in. "In my dream."

"You dreamed of Magena?"

"I dreamed I *was* Magena. Was this someone you knew?"

Tension crimped his brow. "Magena was Ishtu's oldest sister."

"In my dream, she was chasing after a blue bird." I didn't mention Ishtu had been with her. "Weird, huh?"

"She abhorred birds."

I frowned. *Abhorred?* "Not in my dream. The bird thrilled her."

His fingers clenched around the plastic steering wheel. "When she was young, she thought they were enchanting creatures. After Lyoh Vega murdered Ishtu, Magena reviled anything that flew. She developed a great talent with a bow and arrow, and spent her days walking the woods, spearing every animal with wings."

I imagined the blue bird plummeting from the sky, wings wide and still, an arrow stuck in its feathery breast, dark blood trickling over its small, soft body. The thought chilled me. I felt sad for Magena. Sad something cherished had turned into something loathed.

"Magena is one of the twelve." Kajika's deep voice startled me out of my thoughts. "She lies in one of the rose petal graves." The air blowing in through his open window ruffled the long strands of hair framing his face.

"She's buried in my backyard?"

He nodded.

I shuddered.

"Gottwas believed dreams were a separate plane on which spirits could interact with the living to deliver messages."

"You think her spirit"—I swallowed—"talked to me?" I whispered that last part. There was nothing rational about that, and yet I entertained the idea. I was losing my mind. "That's crazy."

I was crazy.

"Why?"

"She was chasing a bird. Happily chasing a bird while women boiled maple syrup."

"Maybe she is trying to show you how our life was before faeries tortured us and drove us underground. Or maybe she is trying to inform you of her readiness to awaken."

My heart pitched up my throat. "We're not waking any more up."

Kajika didn't answer.

"You promised."

"Did I?"

"Yes." Had he though? "You can't sacrifice people to bring back the hunters. Besides, you have a new clan now."

He snorted. "And what a clan that is."

"Please. Don't dig around my backyard. Don't kill people."

"I will not sacrifice your family or innocent humans."

"What about the not-so-innocent ones?"

His amber gaze skirted over me before returning to the road.

"You plan on waking them, don't you?"

His silence was all the answer I needed.

7

THE BARN

Kajika and I had both remained contemplative after discussing his buried family, so when he announced we'd arrived, it took me a second to realize where.

A red clapboard barn sprawled ahead of us, circled by tufts of wild grass and gray mud. It was the place where Kajika fought for money.

"It is vacant during the day." He got out of the truck, then hoisted a nylon duffle bag from the cargo bed.

I eyed the bag as I hopped out of the car. "What do you have in there?"

"Equipment."

"Like boxing gloves?"

"What would you need boxing gloves for? You do want to learn to fight faeries and defend yourself from hunters, correct?"

Right. Boxing gloves wouldn't be useful against supernatural offenders unless they were fire-proof. In that case, they could come in handy. I'd once had my fingers burned with faerie fire, and it had not been pleasant.

Mud sucked at my sneakers as I trod over to the entrance.

As Kajika pulled the enormous door open, paint flaked off the worm-eaten planks and fluttered into the spring breeze like pollen.

The air inside was as cold as the waves that lapped Rowan's shore at this time of year: bone-chilling. Chafing my arms with my palms, I trailed the hunter toward the ring.

"You spend a lot of time here?"

"Yes."

"Even though it's far away?"

"I habitually run here."

"In my dream, I was running fast."

"Has your speed increased?"

"Not that I'm aware of."

"Perhaps—"

"I haven't become a huntress, Kajika. No blue moon, remember?"

"Yet you moved water with your mind." His amber eyes hunted my face.

"But I don't know how I did it . . ."

He flicked on a switch, and strings of bare lightbulbs lit up the dusky interior that smelled of sour beer and damp hay.

"You let your mind reach out to its surroundings. That is how you did it."

My hands slid off my arms, settled back down along my sides. "I haven't done it since."

"You have tried again?"

"Yes, but nothing happened."

"It took my brother an entire night to figure out how to move the pinecones with his mind."

"How long did it take you?"

He smiled. There was something shameless about his smile. "It came to me swiftly. I believe it was because I had been impatient for the gift Negongwa bestowed upon me. Perhaps your mind's inability to reach out is due to your lack of excitement about your latent nature."

I bit my lip. "You think if I suddenly became okay with it, I could snap my fingers and things would move?"

"Snapping your fingers will not make anything move."

"It was a figure of speech."

He raised a dark eyebrow but didn't comment. Instead he tossed his bag on the floor, crouched and unzipped it. He took out a wooden bow and white arrows that were more ornate than the ones he'd given me in the past. These were fitted with iron tips and feathered fletching. I brushed my thumb over the dove-gray feathers. "Did you make these?"

"I no longer need to forage and hunt for food, or tan hides to make clothes, and few *pahans*, other than the *golwinim*, dare visit our world, so I have much spare time." He handed me the bow. "Have you ever used a bow, Catori?"

"Blake and I used to chase each other with plastic bows and suction darts. Does that count?"

He rolled his tall body back up. "It is the same principle, I suppose. Show me."

I nocked an arrow and extended my left arm while dragging the arrow back with my right hand. "Should I let go?"

"What is your target?"

There was a bale of hay on the other side of the barn. It was a large target, but it was far away. I tipped my chin toward it.

The second Kajika nodded, I closed one eye, took aim, and let the arrow soar. It arched and fell unceremoniously between me and my target. "Did I not pull back enough?"

"Your hands need to be at shoulder-height. And when you pull back, your shoulder blades should touch." He took a second bow from his bag, fit an arrow, and in the space of a heartbeat, let it fly. The arrow whispered through the air and landed smack in the bale's middle.

"Show off." I smiled.

His nostrils flared with a soft, amused snort. "I have had much practice. Your turn again."

I shot an arrow. It went farther than the last, but its path deviated from the straight line.

Kajika readjusted my stance. "Again."

Another arrow vibrated off my bow.

Better.

Not great though.

"Again. Anchor the string." He demonstrated. His arrow cut the air like a bullet.

I tried. Mine whizzed off, but still fell far from its mark.

"Again."

He must've spoken that single word two dozen times. By my umpteenth attempt, my arm muscles ached and my back was on fire. On the upside, I no longer thought it was cold.

"One last time, Catori. And really follow through. Same way you would if you were to throw a ball. Actually, put the bow down."

I lowered it. He handed me an arrow.

"Throw it."

Swiping my hoodie sleeve over my brow, I pulled my arm back. My joint throbbed and screamed.

"Now."

I hurled it with every last drop of strength I could muster, stumbling forward from the momentum. The arrow didn't go far.

"Did you feel that?"

"By that, you mean the horrible pain radiating through my shoulder?"

Concentration transformed into concern, grooving his forehead. "Are you in pain?"

Even though I felt as flimsy and useless as Kajika's seatbelt, I regretted admitting it. So I shrugged. "I was being dramatic. I'm fine."

His gaze absorbed the shakiness of my forearms. I tried to quell it but failed.

"Can you shoot one more arrow?"

"Yes." I took one from his bag, nocked it, and anchored my aim.

"Follow through this time. Like you did when you flung it with your bare hand."

I swallowed a deep breath and fixed my target, which had been an ambitious—or perhaps stupid—choice. Only one of my arrows had reached it. The cold air slid down my throat, luffed my lungs, and eased the muscle spasms. As my breath puffed out like a white cloud, the arrow whizzed off the bow string, slicing noiselessly through the air.

It reached its target.

8
THE EXPERIMENT

"I did it," I whispered, afraid that if I said it any louder, the arrow would slide out of the bale and fall, and that would cancel my accomplishment.

If Kajika were a normal man, a simple archery teacher, he might have beamed at my achievement. Since the hunter was neither normal nor simple, there was no proud smile, no happy yelp, but shadows had shifted out of his eyes. "Commit the feeling of that last shot to memory."

I nodded so enthusiastically, my ponytail danced.

He grabbed his bag and walked a straight line to the bale, collecting arrows along the way. I covered the rest of the barn, snatching the missiles that had gone astray.

When we'd picked them all up, Kajika asked if I had energy for one more exercise. I said yes. Adrenaline and pride masked my soreness. I'd probably pay for it later.

"We will develop your reflexes now."

I wanted to say good luck with that, but Kajika had vanished. He reappeared behind me. By the time I turned, he'd blurred into another part of the barn. I ran, spun, stopped, listened, but unlike the arrow I'd managed to plant in my target, not once did I manage to pre-empt the hunter.

AFTER KAJIKA DROPPED me off at home, I melted into a bath infused with lavender-scented soap that bubbled as thickly as whipped cream. I submerged every last part of my battered body. My hair fanned out around me, as weightless and pliant as the blooms of algae that floated atop Lake Michigan after a windstorm.

Air bubbles snaked out of my nostrils, tickled my lips, but still I remained under the foamy surface. I spread my fingers, rolled them, spread them again. The water coated them like warm oil. I thought about how fluidly Kajika had prowled around the barn, how he'd distracted my senses by displacing objects with his mind, shifting my attention to places he was not, confusing me over and over. Would my own mind ever be as sharp as his? Did I have to shed another layer of rationality, accept that my body could perform medically impossible feats?

That led me to wonder if I could die. Like really die, the same way humans died, or had I somehow become like Kajika and Ace? Only killable by faerie dust or a bloody rowan wood arrow through the heart?

I emptied my lungs until they shriveled like shrink-wrap. Keeping my mouth closed, I waited to feel something. Not death—I wasn't trying to drown. Especially not in a bathtub. I wanted to see if my mind would cloud and darken, if my pulse would slow to a sluggish crawl.

I didn't get to finish my experiment as hands closed around my arms and yanked me out so hard, my lips ripped open like two strips of Velcro. Instead of screaming, I heaved in so much air my throat felt as though it had caught fire.

9

THE ANGER

I coughed and spluttered.

"Did you leave your mind behind in that stupid barn?" Ace growled, eyes incandescent in the daylight slotting through the window of the guest bathroom.

I blinked at him several times. A string of questions lurched into my head and tangled on their way out. "How did you— Why are— Were you following—" I coughed again, then remembered I was naked, and my cough turned into a gulp.

My lower body was hidden beneath the dense bubbles, but not my breasts. Foam slid off my skin, revealing more of me than I'd ever showed Ace.

Not that he was looking at my breasts.

He was way too busy glowering at my face.

I tried to yank my arms out of his grasp, but he only gripped them harder. "I'm not suicidal, Ace."

"Could've fooled me," he muttered darkly.

"How did you even know I was at a barn?"

"You think I'd let you go off with an unpredictable hunter? What if he'd decided to kill you? Or lock you up? Or—"

"Kajika might be *your* enemy, but he isn't mine."

"Exactly."

"Exactly what?"

"He could've taken you hostage. Used you to get leverage on me."

"He doesn't think I matter that much to you. He thinks we're just friends."

Ace snorted.

"What?"

"Come on, Cat. Kajika might be unpredictable and slightly unhinged, but he's not stupid, and you might be fairly friendly—on good days—but you don't go around holding people's hands."

A lot of things pricked me about what he'd just said. "On good days? Am I insufferable the rest of the time?"

A smile teetered on the corner of Ace's mouth but vanished when his eyes finally wandered away from my face.

"So?" I asked. "Am I?"

"What?"

"Ace! Eyes up."

He blinked, pupils pulsing, and then he unlatched his hands from my arms. I sank back underneath with a hard splash that tossed water onto his cloud-colored shirt and narrow jeans. The water-dark spot dried almost instantly.

"How did you get into my house?"

"Your front door was unlocked."

I herded soap bubbles over my chest. "You braved the wind chime?"

He didn't smile. "Do you still have feelings for Kajika?"

"What? Where is this coming from?"

He leaned back against the sink and folded his arms in front of his chest. "I saw you with him at the barn. You looked . . . I don't know—" He clamped his mouth shut for a second. "You looked happy to be there with him."

"You mean, when he pushed me against the rope fence and stripped off my clothes?"

Ace's jaw reddened so fast I half-expected to see smoke curl away from his skin. "He did what?"

I leveled my gaze on his. "You weren't there the whole time, then."

"You . . . you did something with him?"

The fact that Ace had jumped to that conclusion irked me. "Of course not." I rested my head back and closed my eyes. "Nice to see how much you trust me, though."

Silence.

I opened my eyes to see if Ace had left. He hadn't. He stood over the bathtub.

"It's *him* I don't trust," he said.

"I feel like we've already had this conversation. More than once. I have no romantic feelings for Kajika, but I don't hate him. That might not be what you want to hear, but it's the truth. Another truth. I don't hold his hand—not even on good days. I don't flirt with him, or any other guy for that matter. And I don't lead him on. That would be cruel. I might not be the most empathetic person in the world, but I don't like hurting people."

"You hurt me." For a hundred-and-twenty-year-old man, Ace suddenly seemed very young.

"You hurt me too."

His jaw set. "You mean because I'm getting married? I don't have a choice, Cat. I'm stuck with Angelina." He crouched next to the tub and raked his hand through his dark gold locks. "*You* . . . you had a choice, and you picked him."

I raised a hand and touched his jaw. Water trickled down his neck, but steamed off him with a hiss. How was he, of all people, so insecure? "To teach me to fight. That's all I picked him for, Ace." Sensing how glum this conversation had made him . . . had made me, I asked, "What would happen if you got inside the tub with me? Would your fire steam all the water out of the bath?"

He shut his eyes for a second. When he reopened them, they were searing. "Is that an invitation?"

I grew flustered. "I was just curious if there would be any water left."

"And here I thought you were scheming to see me naked, but I should've known it was a science experiment."

I popped a bubble with my forefinger. "You know me."

"I'm not sure I do." His gaze slid over my brow, my lashes, my nose, my mouth, my neck and lower still. "Sometimes, I'm not sure I do know anything about you, Cat."

My breath nocked against my vocal cords. "Come inside the bath with me." I took in the uneven height of his dark eyebrows, the blueness of his irises, the soft shape of his mouth.

A long beat passed. "Then I'll be all wet."

"You'll dry." I studied the rainbow gleam of a soap bubble.

In silence, he unlaced his shoes, unbuttoned his shirt. Concentration marred his features. I doubted he was concentrating on the mechanics of shoe laces and buttons. I bit my lip. Had I really just propositioned Ace to take a bath with me?

I blushed at my audacity.

I'd never done that before.

Ever.

He said he didn't know me, but did I know my own self?

He stood over me, jeans still on but bare chested, sculpted and golden, carved out of muscle.

I'd trailed my hands over his chest, down his back, but I'd never seen him without a shirt.

Wordlessly, he slid one foot inside the bath.

I raised an eyebrow. "Your jeans are still on."

The water hissed and warmed, but didn't simmer. Yet its temperature definitely increased.

"I know." He braced a knee on either side of my thighs, then lowered more of his glorious body inside.

"Why?"

He gripped the sides of the claw-footed tub. "Because I don't want our first time to happen after a fight."

I didn't want that either . . .

The water rose higher, heated up more.

"Am I about to be boiled?"

His strained expression turned amused. "The water won't get any hotter. But I can run some cold water if it'll appease you."

"Don't. I like my water hot." I coasted my hands up his arms that were hard and sinewy. I wondered if he worked out. There was so much I didn't know about him too. I told him this.

"Ask me whatever you want."

I raked my fingernails over his shoulders, down the sides of his torso. "Do you have a house on Earth?"

"No."

"Not even on Beaver Island?" The Woods supposedly lived there, in a luxurious, secluded compound.

"The houses on Beaver Island are just for show."

"But you have a house in Neverra?"

"Not a house per se. I live at the top of a *calimbor*. They are—"

"—skytrees. Borgo told me about them." I caressed his abdominal muscles that contracted and shuddered underneath my touch. "Do you have running water in Neverra?"

"Yes."

"Do you have a bathtub?"

"The size of a small pool."

"Do you have windows?" I ran my hands back down his arms. His skin pebbled.

"Yes." His voice had gone hoarse. He caught my hands and immobilized them. "I take it back."

"What do you take back?"

"I don't want to answer questions right now. You only get to ask me questions when you're clothed."

"Is my nakedness distracting?" If I hadn't been supremely nervous, I probably would've winked, but I was no *femme fatale*. I wasn't a virgin either, but I had such meager experience, which wasn't something I wanted Ace to deduce.

His features twitched as though he were fighting some internal battle with himself. I wasn't sure what the stakes were. I doubted he was nervous. He had trust issues, but he was neither introverted nor innocent.

Some part of him must have won, because his features evened out. He released my hands, grabbed the edges of the tub, and curved toward me. Slowly, delicately, he touched his lips to mine. His kiss felt like a question.

I threaded my hands through his hair and lifted myself to kiss him back, pressing my naked chest against his hot skin. He growled into my mouth.

When he dragged his lips off mine, he whispered, "Come to Neverra with me."

"I can't go there."

Could I even pass through a portal? I *was* part huntress. Hunters weren't allowed into Neverra. Perhaps they were allowed into the *Hareni* with their fellow Unseelie, but if I ended up there, then I'd only see Ace on the Night of Mist, which happened once a month—once a very long month. Days on Neverra weren't equal to Earth days. And the Great Spirit only knew how friendly the Unseelie were . . . "Faeries would kill me if I went."

"Only I can kill you."

"Technically."

"I'd keep you safe, Cat."

"How? By locking me up inside your *calimbor*?"

His lips thinned. He obviously hadn't thought through the logistics of bringing a huntress—part huntress—into enemy territory.

"Besides, I can't leave my father, Ace."

As though speaking his name had summoned him, I heard a door bang shut, followed by my name.

The bathroom door was thankfully not open, but it was unlocked. "I'm taking a bath, Dad," I yelled back. "Be out in a sec!" To Ace, I said, "You need to go."

His face had taken that grave quality again, the one that told me he was adrift in his thoughts. Chest rising slowly, evenly—unlike mine—he lifted himself out of the bath, wet denim clinging to his long legs.

"Can you throw me the towel on the rack?" I whispered.

Immobile, pensive, he dripped water onto the tiled floor.

"Ace?"

His gaze jerked to mine.

"Towel?" I pointed to the rack.

He grabbed it, unfolded it, and held it out. I climbed out of the tub. He folded it around me without peeking.

"What if I found a way?" he said.

"Found a way to do what?"

"To get you a portal stamp. So you could travel from Neverra to Earth whenever you wanted? Would you consider coming with me?"

My heart quickened. Slowly, I turned to face him. "Your people would punish you. Remember what they did to Cruz? To Borgo? You're the prince—"

"Gregor doesn't have the political pull to have me locked up, and my father wouldn't dare, because if he tried, I'd spread the news that Angelina isn't carrying my child. Having an affair is one thing. Impregnating a faerie other than your spouse? Not only is that frowned upon but the child is always expelled from the mother's womb."

My stomach lurched. "They make women have abortions?"

Ace nodded gravely.

"That's barbaric." Almost as bad as the punishment they'd inflicted on Borgo when they found out he'd slept with a huntress. Thankfully, they'd stopped punishing people with castration. "What happens to the babies who *are* born?"

"They are expelled from Neverra."

"So they die?"

"If they aren't pure fae, they have a chance at survival."

A chance? I wanted to yell at Ace that his people were cruel, but he wasn't at fault. His father, though . . . his father *could* change things. "What if the woman was raped?" I would drop the subject after this.

"Doesn't matter how the child was made." Ace delicately cupped my face, his touch feather-light. "When I inherit the throne, I will change that."

But until then, many would perish. Trying to eject the gory images from my mind, I asked, "If I went to Neverra with you, how would you explain my presence?"

"You'd be my concubine."

The term stunned me. And the idea bothered me. "I don't want to be your concubine."

He tossed his hands in the air. "I have nothing else to offer!"

I recoiled from the sharpness of his voice. "Let me be your Earthly girlfriend. I'm okay with that."

And I was. *For now.*

"Maybe I'm not," he said.

"You'd rather be my friend?"

His lethal look shut me up. "I need to think."

My heart held still. "About what?"

I never got my answer. He opened the window, levitated, and lurched out like one of my arrows. Instead of arching downward though, he shot up into the wide blue sky.

10

THE GLASS FLOWER

I ran hard and fast, covering miles of trail. My lungs burned and my thighs cramped, but I kept pushing myself until my mind no longer hummed with Ace's absence. Since our bath, he hadn't given any sign of life. I'd texted him. Called him. Made my heart beat faster. And still he hadn't returned.

Cruz had come, though. Twice he'd stopped by to check on me. Twice I'd asked him where Ace was, and he'd said Ace had sent him because he was busy. "Wedding preparations," he'd explained.

"Wedding preparations?" I'd asked, trying not to sound like a jealous girlfriend.

"Did you forget he's getting married to Angelina?"

"I didn't forget, but I didn't think the *prince* had to involve himself in the preparations."

"In Neverra, we have a lot of festivities leading up to our weddings. Bride and groom must be seen together." He'd squinted one eye. "Last night was the *duobosi*."

"The what?"

"The coupling ceremony."

A chill had zinged up my spine.

"The groom has to penetrate his bride in front of a small audience. You cannot imagine the fortune people spend to watch. Especially a royal *duobosi*." Cruz had studied my face. "Usually it's to gauge the quality of the man's seed, but since Angelina's already pregnant—" He'd tilted his head to the side. "I should probably let Ace explain all of this. I feel like it's causing you pain, and I'd rather not cause you any."

My throat had clenched so tight I could barely swallow. I'd never been jealous of anything or anyone. Why did I care now? Was it because I didn't know Angelina and secretly believed Ace was downplaying the importance she had in his life, or was it because being the *other woman* perturbed me?

"I need to get back to Neverra." His florescent green eyes had lingered on mine. As he'd turned to leave, he'd paused. "Are you okay, Cat?"

I'd said yes, but I hadn't been okay.

I *still* wasn't okay. I was a fool to believe there was nothing physical between Ace and Angelina. He might not care for her, but he had obligations, and those obligations sickened me.

After Cruz left, I went running. So that my brand flared long and hard. So that it reminded Ace of his connection to me. Reminded him of me.

He didn't come.

The following day, I laced up my sneakers and went for another run.

I ran faster and harder than the previous day. My feet didn't hover off the ground, and the world didn't blur past me, yet my speed seemed to have increased.

Was I slowly turning into a huntress?

Water whipped my face. *Rain?* Minutes before, the sky had been cloudless. Like silver barbs, the raindrops needled the exposed patches of skin on my body—my shins, my forearms, my forehead, my cheeks.

I swerved past pine trees and burgeoning bushes, snaked around the cauliflower-shaped pond and the little house I used to dream my family owned. I didn't stop until I reached the picnic area where I'd met with Borgo last.

Digging my fingers into a stitch in my side, I walked over to the spot where he'd exploded into ashes. A flower swayed in the gusty weather. It resembled a sunflower with its thick stem and mud-brown center, but its petals were violet and translucent, as delicate as the Murano glass vase my parents had purchased during their honeymoon.

I touched the flower. The petals shivered as though equipped with a pulse. I plucked one and laid it in my palm. It curled on itself like a caterpillar, and then it fractured like glass and turned to dust. Instead of leaving a residue on my wet hand, the dust vanished into thin air.

Would a human—a normal one—notice the petal's transformation like I had? Would they see the new petal already growing out, replacing the vanished one?

I stepped away from the flower whose head seemed to pivot toward me like a true sunflower, as though Borgo was somewhere in there.

"What should I do?" I asked the flower, all the while thinking I should probably not speak to flowers.

I squeezed the bridge of my nose and closed my eyes. It was a wonder it had taken me that long to completely lose it. That was probably why I suddenly cared about things I'd *never* cared about before. My world had finally spun off its axis.

MY HAIR and exercise clothes were soaked by the time I made it back to my house. My insides also felt cold and slushy.

I desperately wanted to call Cass. Talk it all over with her. I trudged past the hearse, hopped up the porch steps, and opened our unlocked door. The wind chime clinked feverishly over my head. I closed the door, kicked off my sneakers that weighed a ton-and-a-half from caked-on mud, and then peeled off my sodden socks.

"Dad, I'm home!"

There was no answer.

As I made my way to the kitchen for a glass of water, my bare feet left damp imprints on the wooden floor.

"Da—" The last letter evaporated from my throat.

My socks slid from my fingers and landed with a wet slosh at my feet.

I thought my heart had beat frantically while I was running, but it was nothing compared to the way it slammed against the walls of my chest at that moment.

11

THE KNIFE

*M*y father was gagged and cuffed to a chair, his light eyes wild with fear. I thought I heard my name on his lips, but his words were garbled by the scarf Stella had twisted into a rope and tied around his face.

An abrasive smile screwed up Stella's expression. Even though she'd grown up with Mom and Aylen, she no longer cared about my family. She no longer cared for her own family. The only person she cared about was herself. Maybe she cared for Gregor too.

I curled my fingers into fists. My nails dug into my palm.

"I waited to see if my dust would finish you off like it was supposed to, but here you stand." Her copper hair fell in rusty waves over her blood-red blazer. "Sadly, my patience didn't pay off."

Dad's head snapped toward Stella, then pivoted toward me. If he'd looked apprehensive and confused when I arrived, he was positively livid now. He writhed on the chair and the legs scraped against the tiles. Stella placed both her palms on his shoulders and pinned him in place.

"Get your hands off of him!" I screeched.

She leered at me. "Give it back, and I'll release him."

"Release him first."

She snorted. "Now, Cat, don't be unreasonable. I asked first."

"You're a sociopath. You don't give a fuck about people."

"I give a fuck about people. Those who matter, that is. And you are not one of them."

Dad's eyes glistened like his sweat-slickened forehead. I could take a lot, but tears from my father? That was my breaking point. "You should not have involved my father." My hand burned, yet Ace didn't show. I gritted my teeth. My voice hissed out of me, "Get . . . the hell . . . out of my house."

"Or what?" She glanced at my glowing hand. "Ace Wood isn't coming, Catori. Don't you think I thought this all out before returning to Rowan?"

She was toying with me.

Someone would show up.

Someone always showed up.

"Lily needed him. And you know how he is about his sister—she always comes first. Their relationship is a little incestuous if you ask me."

"I didn't ask you."

She smiled, her teeth a blast of white against her tanned skin. "Now, I've got things to do, so can we get a move on?" She lifted her hands off my father's shoulders and walked over to the knife block.

I dashed toward my father, but she was faster. She had one arm around his neck and the other bent toward his throat, the knife point pressing against the freshly-shaven skin of his throat. "Take one more step, and I thrust this knife into his throat instead of into yours."

I froze inches from him. If I extended my arm, I could touch his knee, but if I touched him, Stella would kill him. So I kept my arms locked at my sides.

Dad was still making sounds, but they no longer sounded like words. They sounded like sobs. Fury lapped against my body, spilled into my veins, expanded inside my bones, cold and hot and hard. My heart banged against my ribcage and yet my ribs didn't shatter . . . my breath didn't shudder. I was still and calm.

I had never.

Ever.

Been calmer.

The world swam out of focus. Only Stella's face remained sharp.

Her eyes flashed to mine.

Blackness stained the edge of my vision, darkened the room.

Thunder cracked outside the window. Lightning streaked the sky. Raindrops parted the purple sky and pelted the glass like mallets striking bass drums.

Water gushed nearby. Had the storm cracked the window? I didn't turn to look. I didn't want to let Stella out of my sight.

Something blasted against her cheek, smacked her head sideways. She shrieked. Her slender arms released my father and came up to shield her face from what had assaulted her.

Water.

But it wasn't coming from outside. It was coming from inside the kitchen.

Our steel faucet had rocketed off its base, and water spewed like a geyser. Instead of shooting upward, it arched toward Stella. Steam hissed where it hit her fire-warm skin and flowed off her in misty puffs.

Her shrieks faded to choking gasps. The rope of water speared her mouth. She clamped her lips and stared at me in horror.

Unlike the first time I'd moved water with my mind, I wasn't surprised. I welcomed the liquid release of my anger and steered it to fight the battle my limbs were too inept to wage.

I let my huntress move through me, inhabit all of me, no longer caring if she annihilated my useless faerie side.

My father's alarmed gaze reddened and widened, and his face paled. He sputtered as droplets showered his sweater and his jeans.

I closed the distance between us. Stella was still fighting against the hard jet, which trailed her when she ducked. The knife dangled from her fingers, the sharp tip blinking white and gray.

My throat pulsed as hard as my heart. Stella's dust pounded against my skin as though desirous to reunite with her. Well, I wouldn't release it; I would lock it away from this mad woman.

Instead of untying my father, I yanked his gag down, then shoved his chair against the furthest wall with strength I didn't even know I possessed. He had his back to me now, which was better. Safer. I didn't want him to see what I was about to do to Stella.

I yielded to the huntress, to the fluid thrumming inside my bones. Pulled it out of me. Pushed it toward Stella. She scrambled backward, skating over the slick floor. Her high heels skidded, and she fell backward, catching herself on the island. The knife flew out of her hands. I dove for it, but she rammed her body into mine, striking my cheek with the palm of her hand so hard, my neck cracked.

I saw stars.

But then I saw her.

She grabbed the knife.

The faucet still leaked, but the water no longer stretched to Stella. It simply dribbled over the sink's edge.

She thrust her stringy red hair back and stalked toward me. The knife gleamed in her unsteady, fisted hands. "You've become a huntress." She circled me.

I didn't move.

From the corner of my eye, I noticed my father struggling against the plastic zip ties Stella had used to hook his wrists to the rungs of the chair. If he didn't stop fidgeting, the hard plastic would bite into his skin, tear it.

He would bleed.

I ground my molars. I had fists. I had knees. I had feet. Granted they were bare, but I could still do damage. I threw myself at Stella, but she whooshed away. Her feet no longer touched the floor. I leaped for her, and again she escaped.

Her face contorted with a brusque smile that stained her brown eyes a foul shade of black.

I was done amusing her.

Her gaze flicked to my father.

I lunged for him, but she reached him first. She spun his chair into my shins. I tripped and landed hard on my backside. The back of my head hit a corner of the island, and red-hot pain exploded in my skull. I bit back a whimper and struggled back to my feet.

"You want to play hard to get? Fine. Let's play." With a flick of her wrist, she drew the knife across my father's throat.

"No!" I screamed.

His sliced skin puckered and reddened, and then blood oozed.

Poured out of him.

"NO!" She could take everything from me, but not my father. The scream felt as though it were shredding my throat.

A strange gurgling sound erupted from my father's mouth. Or was it coming from the cut? His spooked eyes flashed to mine, then rolled back into his head. I grabbed a kitchen towel and shoved it against the deep slice, but the blood saturated the towel in seconds, dripped over my knuckles, and streamed down my wet forearms in crimson rivulets.

Stella didn't stop me.

She didn't move.

Her mouth rounded in a soundless gasp.

"What have you done?" My nostrils flared with manic breaths. "What have you done?"

Her dust scorched me like burning embers. Keeping the pressure on my father's throat, I rubbed my neck, but then Dad gurgled, and both my hands returned to his wound.

Something smelled acrid, like fire and metal. I swallowed and realized the stench also coated my palate. Had Stella slashed my neck?

I jerked a hand back to my throat. The skin was smooth, deadened. Her captive dust no longer writhed underneath the slick pads of my fingertips.

She'd taken it back.

Stella's irises whitened, and then her face veined and grayed. Her body rigidified like concrete.

"Catori." Someone called my name.

I looked at Dad, but his lips were limp.

My name was called again. The voice was deep and familiar.

Cruz.

Someone had finally come, but they'd come too late.

I stared at my father. I felt empty, devastated, weak, helpless. Broken. I was broken.

"Dad, come on. Don't leave me," I sobbed. "Don't you *dare* leave me."

His skin was sallow. I pressed my blood-stained hand against his chest, feeling for a pulse.

I couldn't find any.

I craned my neck back to look at Stella. She still hadn't moved. The amber color of her hair had morphed into a storm-gray. The lustrous curls drooped, and then they fell away from her scalp like sand.

Skin flaked off her jaw. Her fingers turned to stumps and then her wrists sloughed off.

Like concrete blasted by dynamite, Stella burst into a cloud of dust.

She was dead.

She was dead, but so was my father.

12

THE BARGAIN

I pressed the kitchen towel harder against my father's throat, as though stopping the flow of blood could make his heart beat again. I wasn't a doctor yet, but I wasn't an idiot either. Keeping blood inside a body with no heartbeat wouldn't magically jumpstart a heart.

Magically . . .

"Cruz! Bring him back to me. Bring him back."

"I can't promise his spirit is close enough—"

"Stop talking and bring him back!" Tears ran into my mouth.

He crouched beside me. "If I manage, you'll owe me."

"If you manage, I'll be glad to owe you." My neck and chest throbbed. "Just, please . . . please bring him back." My voice was barely above a whisper.

He moved my hands off my father's wound, placed his own on the ebbing red flow, and murmured Faeli words. I didn't understand any of them. I didn't even try. As long as they worked, as long as they brought my father back.

I grabbed the knife that had fallen out of Stella's desiccated fingers and sliced the plastic zip ties off my father's wrists. Like dead weights, his hands thumped against the seat of his chair. I twined my fingers through his. Pulled his hand to my chest. To my frantic heart.

I willed his limp fingers to curl around mine.

They didn't.

Cruz's prayer became more insistent. The litany of his words more rushed. They vibrated inside the kitchen, overlapping with the slosh of water and the rolls of receding thunder.

The faerie's fingers sparkled with gold flames that quenched the blood. Slowly, the edges of the wound glowed and smoothed, rising to meet each other like a zipper. Cruz ran the pads of his fingers along the wound, and it mended, the skin weaving back together.

He'd repaired Gwenelda's wound in the same way. And after he'd restored her, she'd sputtered back to life. Could I start hoping the same thing would happen to my father or did I need to wait longer?

Eyes sealed shut, fingers roving over the hemmed throat, Cruz kept whispering words. I prayed my father's spirit heard.

I clutched my dad's hand as hard as he used to clutch mine when I was a little girl and we'd wander through the mall on Black Friday. When I complained he was hurting me, he would confess how afraid he was to lose me in the crowd.

Today, I was the one who feared losing him. "Daddy," I whimpered softly. "I won't let go. But don't let go either."

Cruz had grown quiet.

So quiet.

Crushingly quiet.

His green eyes settled over me.

I wanted to pummel him with my fists.

And I did. With my free hand, I hit him.

"Don't you dare give up. Don't you—"

He caught my wrist.

Held it.

Then I heard a gasp. A cough.

I spun my head back toward my father, barely daring to believe the noise was coming from him.

But it was.

His lips trembled.

His fingers writhed.

Cruz released my wrist.

I sprang to my feet and wrapped my arms so tightly around my father's neck, I thought I might choke him.

He was alive.
He'd come back to me.

13

FAVORS

"Cat?" My father's voice was so faint it barely ruffled my stringy hair. "What—" He coughed. And then he gagged.

I pressed away from him, fearing my hug was too fierce.

Dad rubbed his throat. "What the hell happened? Where's Stella? Cruz?" He peered at the faerie. "Why are you here?"

"Stella's gone, Dad."

"Gone where?" Dad asked.

I could feel Cruz's gaze on me as though he too was eager to know where she had gone. But he'd seen her explode into ash, so he knew where she'd gone. I realized he was looking at my neck.

I touched it.

I expected the dust to have vanished—like its owner—but it was still there, still ardently throbbing.

"What do you have on your neck?" Dad asked. "You got a tattoo?"

Why wasn't Ace's dust cloaking it? Had he finally retrieved it? Out of all the times I'd asked him to do it, he'd chosen now? "Where's Ace?" I asked Cruz, disregarding my father's appalled stare.

"Lily got into some trouble."

"And *you* couldn't take care of it?" I hissed.

"What possessed you to do that to your neck? If your mom were here—"

"Good thing she's not." I winced, instantly regretting saying that.

Dad blinked.

I was horrified I'd just lashed out at him.

Dad got to his feet. He marched to the overflowing sink. "Our kitchen is flooded. Where did the faucet go?"

I swallowed hard, tears clinging to my lashes, weighing them down. I sobbed. After everything, I thought I deserved to sob.

Dad came back toward me and gathered me into his arms. "Honey, I didn't mean to make you cry. I just thought that maybe . . . that maybe you could've gotten a tattoo some place more discreet is all."

That just made me cry harder.

He stroked my back. "Oh, sweetie. I'm sorry I yelled."

He held me tighter, and I melted into him.

"What was up with Stella? She was acting crazy. She clocked me, then tied me to a chair. Said you had something of hers. What did you take from her?"

The lump in my throat was too jagged to let words through. Not that I wanted to explain to my father what had happened. How could I explain it to him?

Dad pressed me away. "We need to call Jimmy. He needs to bring her in. She needs to answer for what she did. Where's my phone?" He patted his jeans. When his fingers came away from the dark denim, he held them out before him. "Where did this blood come from?" His eyes surfed to me again and traveled over my face, down my arms that were streaked with his blood. "Cat, did you cut yourself?" Dad searched the rest of the kitchen, found the balled, soiled kitchen towel and the fallen knife. "What the hell happened in here?"

I closed my eyes and wept, because weeping beat explaining what happened. I didn't even know where to start.

"Why is there mud on our floor?" he asked.

Because dust turned to mud when it was wet.

"Stella's gone, Dad."

"I can see that, but where the hell did she go?"

I looked at Cruz then, willing him to explain. I wasn't sure I had the strength to do it myself. Dad would think I was crazy. He'd have me committed.

"Mr. Price, it's a rather long and tedious story."

"You better start telling it soon then, son," Dad volleyed back.

He sloshed through the water covering the kitchen floor and

yanked open the cabinet door. He dropped to his knees and rifled underneath for the valves. The water finally stopped.

The kitchen sponge bobbed like a rubber duck around his ankles. Dad seized it and flung it onto the kitchen island, then knotted his arms in front of him.

"Like I said, one of you better start talking."

I looked for Stella's ashes, but they'd been swept away in the current of my anger. The glimmering flecks were everywhere and had turned the clear water murky.

"Cruz, can you burn this all away?" I gestured to the gray sludge. "I don't want a plant growing out of the grout."

"Seriously, Cat, a plant? You're worried a plant's going to sprout between the tiles?" Dad looked at me incredulously.

"And call Kajika," I told Cruz.

Was I striking bargain after bargain? How much was I going to owe him after today? I pushed that thought away. Now wasn't the time to think about *gajoïs*.

My dad was alive and well.

Cruz reached for his phone. He took the call into the living room, speaking quietly into the receiver.

"What happened this afternoon, Catori?"

My father never used my full name. *Never.*

"What was this talk of dust? Why did Stella want to kill you? Why did she want to kill me?" He rubbed his throat as though he felt the darned wound, but could he? Was it like a phantom wound?

"Dad, remember Ley's letter? Do you remember what it spoke about?"

His gaze shuffled over my face.

"The letter she wrote to her sister? The one about *pahans* and a *baseetogan?*"

I nodded.

"I don't understand."

"Well, Stella was part *pahan*. Part faerie," I added, in case he couldn't remember the meaning of the Gottwa word.

"Faerie? *Faerie!*" A vein popped feverishly at his temple. "Faerie?"

I nodded again. "And so am I . . ." I murmured. "So was Mom."

"*You . . .? Nova . . .?*" Like windshield wipers, his lids swept up and down. Unlike windshield wipers, they did nothing to clear his mounting incredulity. "Faeries?"

"Yes."

"Like Tinkerbell?"

I smiled. I remembered that had been my reference the first time I was told about faeries. "A little like her."

"You can fly?"

"No. I mean, *I* can't. But faeries can."

Dad wrinkled his nose and then he squeezed the sides of his face. "Are you on something? Are you taking drugs? Is that why you got a tattoo?"

I flinched. "No."

He tossed his hands up in the air. "You are not making *any* sense."

Cruz had returned. And he wasn't alone. Kajika stood next to him, chest heaving with rapid breaths, black hair slick with rain.

I turned to them, swallowing hard. "Kajika, I need you to wipe his mind."

"Wipe whose mind?" Dad asked.

The hunter's gaze ground into mine, and then it swept over the flooded kitchen. "Have *you* tried already, Catori?"

"No." Perhaps I should have, but I didn't feel like messing with my father's mind. Already, I'd lassoed a foreign force and wielded it without understanding what I was doing.

And then there was the dust.

I'd tasted it, smelled it. It had leaked from my skin and asphyxiated its owner. I had no idea how I'd done that.

"Erase everything from the moment he got out of his car."

"Are you talking about me?" Dad yelled, pushing away from the island. He gripped my shoulders and shook me. It wasn't gentle, but I didn't hold it against him. He was angry and confused. He had every right to be.

I placed my hands over his. "I wish you could keep all the things I told you. I so wish you could know everything that I know, but it will ruin your life. I don't want to ruin your life."

Dad stopped shaking me. He just stared down at me. His mouth opened, but he made no sound.

"Look at Kajika, Dad."

He stared at the hunter.

"You will change your clothes and then return to your car," Kajika started, his voice smooth and steady. "You will drive back to Bee's Place, where you will have dinner. When you come home tonight, you will have no memory of what transpired in your house. You will not recollect your discussion with your daughter. You will not remember seeing Stella Sakar."

Dad was as rigid as a totem pole, his eyes blank slates like Stella's had been in the last moments of her life. I shuddered at the memory.

Kajika's eyes gleamed like cut topaz to cement his *influence*.

I held my breath.

Without blinking, without looking at me, Dad walked past me, crossed the living room, and exited the house.

Once I heard the hearse's engine rumble, I dared breathe again.

Kajika stared at the water rippling around my ankles and then he stared at the tattoo of dust wreathing my neck. "Cruz said you killed the *pahan* . . ."

I nodded.

"Then why does your body still hold her dust?"

"I don't know," I whispered, wiping my chilled cheeks. "I don't know."

Cruz crouched and laid his palms against the liquid surface. Slowly, steam rose, and the level of water dropped and dropped until there wasn't a puddle left. The flames hissed and sputtered as they burned away the moisture.

Kajika watched him work.

"Maybe it'll go away tonight," I said as Cruz stood up.

"The dust disappears the moment the *pahan* disappears. If Stella has died, then you should not still possess her dust."

Cruz folded his arms, his leather jacket creaking. "I have a theory. Since Catori used the dust to *kill* Stella, perhaps the dust belongs to her now."

"You manipulated the fae's dust?" Kajika asked.

"I . . . I . . ." *Had I?* Or had Cruz used *his* dust?

"She did," Cruz replied. "I saw it rise out of her."

Astonishment spangled the hunter's face. "You can control *gassen*?"

I rubbed the synthetic hem of my sports top between my fingers. Could I?

"Did you steep this kitchen in water?" Kajika asked.

"Yes."

"You can manipulate *gassen and* water?" It didn't sound like a question. It was something else. Something dangerous and strange.

Amazement?

I pressed three fingers to my lips to calm my nerves. I couldn't think of this now. "Is she all gone, Cruz?" I checked the tiles that sparkled as though they'd been scoured and mopped with Clorox.

"Your kitchen is clean."

I loosed a sigh, let my fingers drop. "Thank you. Both of you, thank you. I know I owe you, Cruz." The faerie flicked his eyes to his black boots, as though he was embarrassed. I remembered owing Ace once. He'd asked me for my pillow. Once I'd handed it over, I no longer owed him anything. Perhaps Cruz could also ask for something trivial. "But I owe you too, Kajika."

"You do not owe me anything. Hunters do not strike bargains. We are not faeries." His words were as prickly as the thorns on the rose liana that had grown from Holly's ashes. "But I would like us to train tomorrow. I want to work on your mind's power, Catori. You must learn to harness it."

"I don't know, Kajika."

The hunter stepped close and laid his palms on my shoulders. "Power without control is as useless as a rifle without a bullet."

I still itched to tell him *no*, that I needed to recover from today, but because I felt like I owed him, I accepted.

He lifted his hands. "I must go home, but I will return tomorrow."

After he left, I bit the inside of my cheek.

"Cozying up to the hunter again?" Cruz asked, studying me.

"No. Not that it's any of your business."

Cruz's lips flattened. "Do you need anything else, or may I go check on my fiancée?"

"How many *gajoïs* do I owe you?"

He'd started to turn, but stopped. "Just one."

"What can I give you?"

"*Give me?*"

"To call us even."

His dark eyebrows slanted over his nose.

"Prove to me you're no longer a prick by claiming something now."

He folded his arms, squared his shoulders. "How much do you care for Ace?"

I frowned. "What does that matter to you?"

"How much?"

My stomach contracted. Cramped. He was claiming his *gajoï*. I placed a protective hand over my abdomen, as though a hand could shield me from the pain. It couldn't. "More than I should," I whispered in a hoarse voice.

The fist crushing my insides slackened, then let go.

Cruz walked to the window and opened it.

Before he dove into the thick, humid air, I asked, "What did Lily do?"

He pivoted back toward me. "Excuse me?"

"Why is she in trouble?"

"Don't you remember? She stole a book."

A millisecond later, I registered what he was talking about. "Gregor found out?"

"Took him five days, but he found out."

"Five days. It's been wee—" I cut myself off, remembering that time didn't flow the same.

"'Til the next time, Catori."

I wanted to say, *tell Ace to come and see me*, but that sounded needy and desperate, and I didn't want to be either. Besides, I shouldn't need to remind my boyfriend to visit me.

So I stayed silent as I watched Cruz's ascent into the pink-streaked sky.

The storm had passed. Stella was gone. The mess was fixed. My father was alive. I no longer owed a faerie a favor.

So why didn't I feel serene?

14

THE BROKEN ONES

I took a long shower. You'd think I would've had enough of being wet for a day, even a week, but deep inside, in the most unreachable trenches of my soul, I felt filthy.

I'd killed a woman. And not just any woman. Someone I had known forever. Someone I had once respected immensely.

How was I supposed to tell Faith her mother was gone? Sure, they weren't close, but did that mean Faith wouldn't care that her mother no longer existed? I slammed my palm against the shower wall. How would I tell Cass she'd lost her aunt, Etta she'd lost her sister, and Jimmy . . .? Didn't they deserve to know that yet another member of their small family had left them forever? I flexed my fingers and dug my nails into the tiles.

I wouldn't tell anyone. It would go on top of the pile of secrets that was so high I could barely see past it anymore.

I washed my hair a second time, frothing up the shampoo and massaging my scalp until it tingled, and then I scrubbed my skin with a loofah, working harder on my neck than any place on my body. Maybe if I scoured the spot long enough, it would tear and release Stella's dust.

I dropped the loofah.

I got out of the shower and wrapped a towel around myself, and then I reached into the mug that held my makeup and razor.

I grabbed the razor and drew the blade up to my throat. My hand shook, but I desperately needed to get rid of the dust. Choosing the furthest place from my artery, I scored my skin.

I didn't feel anything at first. But then the wound burned, and blood trickled down. I flinched and my pulse quickened. The razor clattered into the sink. I didn't dare pinch my lids shut. I wanted to see the dust seep out. I wanted to see it leave my body. Willed it to find its way. The only thing that came out of me was more blood. It dribbled down my clean skin, over my collarbone, between my breasts.

I gritted my teeth. "Get out." I tried squeezing the dust out, but that increased my bleeding. "Get out!"

My hand glowed and burned with Ace's mark. I hit my mirror with my fist. It didn't crack. But something slick rushed through me, flowed underneath my skin. I stared down at my hands, flipping them over and over. My skin seemed to sparkle faintly.

I must really be losing it.

Water dripped from my shower head.

I looked back down at my hands. Looked back at the shower.

I closed my eyes and breathed.

In and out.

In and out.

Whatever moved underneath my skin stilled.

I opened my eyes as my bathroom door flew open.

I spun around. If it was my father, he would freak.

"What the fuck are you doing to yourself?" With one step, Ace was next to me. His hands were on me, his fingers roaming over my skin to find the source of blood.

"Careful!" I stepped out of his reach. "My blood could kill you."

My blood *could* kill him, but only if it came in contact with his heart. That wasn't the reason I stepped away from him. I stepped away because I was mad.

Incredibly mad.

I hadn't even realized *how* mad until he'd burst in.

He scowled at me; I scowled right back.

"Cat, why did you fucking cut your neck?"

"I'm trying to get Stella's dust out of my body."

"She doesn't deserve it back."

I gave a dark laugh. "You didn't hear the news?"

"What news?"

"I killed her today. In my kitchen. Suffocated her with her own dust. *Cool*, huh?"

His dazed expression told me he did not find this cool.

"Is it still there?"

He snapped out of his trance. "Is what still there?"

"Stella's dust? Is it still there? I want it out of my body."

His gaze skimmed my throat. "It's still there."

"How the hell do I get it out?"

"I didn't understand why I got my dust back, but now I think I do." His eyes were slightly unfocused. "You have your own now."

"I don't want my own dust!"

"If you used it to kill her, then maybe you can use it to create illusions."

"I don't want to create illusions! Ace, you're not hearing me. I want it out of me! OUT!"

His eyes gleamed like a clear, midnight sky. "Maybe you're becoming a faerie . . ."

I shook my head. "Impossible. I can control water." My shoulder blades dug into one another as I pulled the towel tighter around me, not because it was slipping, but because my world was falling to pieces, and I needed to feel something solid. "At least, I assume I can. I blew the faucet apart. I just made water leak out of my showerhead. Faeries have fire, not water. So no, Ace, I'm no faerie. If anything, I'm a huntress with faerie abilities."

"Or a faerie with hunter capacity."

"Or I'm just a freak." Annoyance dripped from my voice like water dripped from my hair. "That's another possibility."

Ace closed in on me. "You're not a freak, Cat." His fingers lifted to my self-inflicted wound. "You're not."

I recoiled. "Don't touch me."

"I won't die." A small smile tugged at his lips.

"That's not why."

His hand plummeted to his thigh. "Did I do something to make you mad?"

"It's rather what you didn't do. What you didn't say."

He folded his arms. "Explain."

"I shouldn't have to."

"Oh yes you should."

"My brand flared more than once, and you never came."

He expelled a grating breath. "I'm sorry, but it's been a real shit storm up in Neverra."

"Did the spectators at your *duobosi* get rowdy?"

"What?" His voice sliced the humid air of the bathroom like a scalpel.

This time, I was the one who folded my arms.

"Angelina's pregnant, so our *duobosi* was canceled. Who the fuck told you about it anyway?"

"Who do you think?"

He growled and scrubbed a broad hand over his face. "Don't believe anything Cruz tells you anymore. He's a liar. The worst kind."

"But I thought you two—" Ace glared so hard at me that I asked, "Why did you send him then?"

"I didn't, Cat. He must've seen my hand glow," he said darkly. "He backstabbed Lily, Cat. Told Gregor she stole the book. And now . . . now . . ." Darkness knotted over his face, shadowed his eyes. "Now Gregor turned off her portal stamp."

"So she can't travel out of Neverra?"

"Yes. Until they decide what her true punishment will be. Because they *will* punish her. Our father told Gregor to judge her like he would any traitor."

Shock, worry trampled my irritation. "Oh . . ."

"So I'm fucking sorry I didn't come. I'm fucking sorry you had to deal with Stella alone. I'm fucking sorry Cruz planted ludicrous images inside your brain." He breathed heavily, frantically.

"My father died today," I told him softly, not because I wanted to make him feel guilty, but because I wanted him to know why I'd killed someone. "Stella killed him. That's why I killed her."

His rage flatlined. "Shit, Cat." This time, when he approached me, I didn't shy away.

"Cruz managed to call him back, and Kajika erased his memory of it, but yeah, he died. Right in front of me." I shook my head from side to side gently, trying to dislodge the image of the knife slicing his skin. It didn't go away. It probably would never go away. I closed my eyes, but that only made the memory more vivid. I lifted my eyelids. "So I'm sorry I lashed out, but I'm really upset right now." Tears stumbled out of my eyes and rolled down my cheeks.

Ace swiped his thumb over my face and cradled my jaw. "Fuck, Cat, I'm so sorry. So fucking sorry." He slid his hands around my neck and crushed me against him. His fingers threaded through my hair, stroked the nape of my neck. Suddenly they stilled. "Tell me you didn't strike a bargain with Cruz."

I tilted my face toward his. "I didn't have a choice, Ace. My father . . . he was gone."

His lips flattened.

"But don't worry. He already claimed his *gajoï*. I *made* him claim it. I'm not naïve anymore."

My comment didn't seem to appease Ace, whose mouth was still a flat line. "What did he ask for?"

I swallowed, gazed away from his face. His shirt collar was soaked in my blood. "I bled all over you."

"What did he ask for?"

"We need to get the blood out."

"Cat—"

"I don't want to tell you."

"We're way past you not telling me." Ace wrapped his fingers around my upper arms and held me at arm's length. "What did he ask for?"

"Ace . . ."

"Tell me."

"Ow. You're hurting me."

His fingers uncurled so abruptly I almost lost my balance.

As I rubbed my upper arms, a chilling thought crept into my core. I attempted to reason with myself that my imagination was running wild. But the more I twisted it over and over, the more I examined it, the more terrible sense it made. "He asked me how much I cared for you," I finally whispered.

Deep grooves formed between Ace's eyebrows. "That's what he wanted from you?"

I gazed into his troubled eyes.

"What did you tell him?"

An abrupt decision solidified in my mind. I despised the mere thought of it, but if Cruz had turned evil, what choice did I have? "The truth."

"Which is?"

"Which is something I don't want to share."

"Why not?"

Like a bow string, my heart quivered. "Because it'll hurt your feelings."

Ace's expression bruised.

A minute slid by in silence.

"I want to stop this. Stop us. It's been fun, Ace, but I don't want to be a *concubine*. I don't want to be that girl who waits by the phone—by her *brand*—for her boyfriend to show up. I don't want to come second to your sister." Ace's lips parted as wide as his eyes, but I continued speaking so he couldn't. "We aren't suited for each other, Ace."

His breaths pulsed against the tip of my nose. Hot. Rapid. And then his face contorted. "What are you talking about?"

"I'm talking about how wrong we are. I know I've said it before, but I've had time—*days*—to think, and I don't want to get in any deeper with you."

Ace flinched and stepped back. The way he looked at me minced my heart into tiny pieces, but I couldn't back down.

"If my brand lights up, don't come. And don't send anyone else. I can take care of myself." I glanced at my toes, at the plum-purple polish I'd applied a week before when everything was still bright and lovely, when my father hadn't died yet, when I hadn't killed someone, when Cruz hadn't asked me how much I cared for Ace.

He shuffled back toward me, his suede loafers settling an inch from my toenails. Ace's hands were engulfed in flames.

Was he going to set me on fire?

I jerked back, hit the glass shower partition. Ace brought his hand up. I twisted my head and flattened my cheek against the still foggy glass. He raised his hand to my throat. I sucked in a breath, bracing myself for his searing touch. Blue fire danced over his skin. Over mine. My skin crackled. Sparked. I expected his fire to climb over my chin, travel down my collarbone, but it remained localized.

"Are you removing Stella's dust?"

"I can't manipulate another faerie's dust."

"Then what are you doing?"

"I'm hemming your flesh," he answered.

"Why?"

He squinted in concentration. The acrid, animal scent of burning skin prickled my nose. When he brought his hand down, he asked, "Did Cruz ask you to break up with me?"

"What?" My stomach hardened. I placed a palm against it, as though a palm could placate the sudden ache.

"I fixed you; you owe me. Did Cruz tell you to break up with me? Was that his *gajoï*? Is that why you're pushing me away?"

Grief swelled in my throat, but my eyes stayed dry.

His hands gripped mine, squeezed them. "Tell me!"

"He didn't ask me to break up with you." The confession raced up my sore throat.

Ace's usually golden skin turned silvery-white. He released my hands so fiercely my wrists knocked into the glass behind me, and then he backed away fast.

My heartbeats merged into one solid vibration.

He studied my face one last time, then grimaced. His disgust and spent hope pierced a red-hot path straight through my heart.

He turned.

Left.

Fled.

Hate. That was what he would feel for me from now on.

But this hate . . . it would keep him safe.

Cruz had double-crossed Lily and lied to me about Ace sending him. Perhaps I was being paranoid, but if Cruz spent his favor on a question about my feelings toward Ace, I could only imagine what he would do with my answer.

15

FAITH'S FATHER

I practiced with Kajika the next day, but neither my head nor my heart were in it. All of my being was fixated on the ache inside of me.

During my sleepless night, my heart had swollen like a bruise.

"Catori, you are not even trying," Kajika said.

He was right. I wasn't. I ran the thick hem of my hoodie between my numb fingers.

"Let me take you home."

"I don't want to go home." Home reminded me of Stella and Ace.

"Where do you want to go?"

I shrugged. "I don't know."

"Are you feeling guilty about having killed the faerie?"

"A little. I've never killed anyone before. And don't tell me it gets easier, because I don't want to kill again."

"You might not have a choice if the Great Spirit is turning you into a huntress."

"*Everyone* has a choice. We're human. We make our own choices."

Kajika narrowed his eyes. "Some choices are fated."

"Oh, don't give me that! There's no such thing as fate."

Like Kajika, Mom had believed in fate. She also believed fate could be altered if you willed something hard enough. As a kid, I'd felt her conviction was an oxymoron. If you believed in a puppet master, how could you also believe a puppet could move its own strings? Maybe my metaphor was awry. Maybe Mom hadn't imagined humans as puppets, but as actors with a script and a director.

Ugh . . . Why was I thinking about freaking puppets? "Can you drop me off at Cass's house? She lives on Downing—"

"I know where she lives." Kajika crouched to gather the equipment we'd used.

"How?"

"I know where all faeries reside."

"Cass isn't— I mean, she is, but she doesn't even know what she is."

"I am aware of this, Catori, but I am nonetheless cautious. You should be also. Especially now that you . . ." He let his voice drag off, but I heard the implied words. *Now that I've killed a member of her family.*

I tugged on my ponytail, made it so tight I thought my hair might pop out of its follicles.

"Will you confess to her?"

"No. I have so few friends." Truthfully, Cass was the only friend I had left. "I can't lose her."

He nodded gravely. "So you will pretend it did not happen?"

"Exactly."

"Will Faith not wonder?"

"She'll assume her mother never came back from one of her trips. Stella was always gone anyway." My gaze zipped to his. "You won't say anything, will you?"

He unrolled his long, muscular body. "It is none of my business, Catori." He heaved the duffel bag over his shoulder.

As we walked out of the barn, I bit down on my lip. "You don't trust Cruz, do you?"

"Why do you ask?"

"Because if you do, you need to stop. He's evil."

Kajika frowned. "*Evil?*" He spoke the word almost as though it were foreign to him, but if anyone knew evil, it was a hunter who'd lived through the Dark Day.

"Remember the book that faeries stole from me?"

"The one that was afterward stolen from them?"

I nodded. With a fingertip, I traced the W on my hand, but touching it felt like running a blade over my heart, so I jerked my hand away. "It wasn't stolen from them, Kajika. Lily traded it for the spell that transferred my brand to Ace."

A breeze flipped the nascent leaves on the trees and ruffled the blades of grass.

"When Gregor realized it was gone, Cruz pointed his finger at Lily, and now she's in trouble. He backstabbed his fiancé, Kajika. I don't know much about faerie relationships or politics, but that seems pretty cruel and wrong. So promise me not to trust him."

He gave a curt nod. "I will be especially wary from now on."

We climbed into the rusty truck. For most of the drive, my thoughts wandered back to Ace. My eyes burned with tears that finally spilled over.

Kajika glanced at me but didn't ask any questions. Maybe he already knew—he seemed to know everything that concerned faeries—or maybe he didn't want to know. Good, because I didn't want to discuss my heartache with him. Not because I thought he didn't know much about it. He and my father were the two leading experts on the subject, both having lost their other halves, but I didn't want to discuss Ace with Kajika.

I wanted to discuss Ace with Cass, though. But I needed to be careful about what I told her in case Cruz paid her a visit. Cruz couldn't know I'd broken up with Ace to protect him. Cruz needed to believe I didn't care about Ace.

We drove in silence the rest of the way. When we passed Holly's property, I recalled the conversation I'd had with my father a couple weeks back. Apparently, Holly had bequeathed her property to me. Dad had asked if I would expel *all those vagrants*—Kajika's clan had become so numerous, they'd set up tents. It did look like a music festival campsite now. Even though I'd told Dad I would think about it, I hadn't thought about it. I'd been too busy thinking about a bunch of other things.

But now that I did, I decided that as long as Kajika was around, I wouldn't evict his clan.

Soon, we passed Blake's rectangular house. A light was on in the living room. My heart squeezed as tight as a fist.

Kajika cocked his head toward the house too. I watched him watch the house as we slid past it.

"Is Blake's consciousness still very present in your head?"

The car jounced over a pothole. Winter had been cruel to Rowan, pockmarking our town's asphalt roads with treacherous cracks and shallow craters.

"He has become dimmer, but sometimes, when I get close to things he loved, one of his memories will strike me."

I studied Kajika's profile. I wondered if by *things* he meant people too. Did Blake's passion for me still torture the hunter? I didn't dare ask, because if it did, I wouldn't know what to say or how to deal with it. It wasn't my fault but filled me with guilt nonetheless.

We drove by several more houses, some circled by white picket fences yellowed by winter, some by patchy hedges in dire need of a trim, before pulling up in front of Cass's two-story house.

I hopped out of the car and shut the door. "Thank you," I said through the open passenger window.

"I promised I would teach you—"

"I'm not thanking you for that. I'm thanking you for not pushing me to tell you what's wrong."

He didn't respond.

"You're a good friend."

His mouth pressed tightly together. "The one thing I never wanted to be."

I stiffened.

After a long beat, he sighed. "Would you like to train this weekend?"

I nodded, then backed away from the car.

Once he made a U-turn and left, I walked up to Cass's front door. My finger was about to touch the doorbell when the front door opened.

Cassidy screeched, then clapped her hand over her heart. "You scared the bejesus out of me, Cat."

"And I didn't even say BOO." I smiled. "Where are you off to?"

"Faith called to ask if I could give her a hand at the bakery this afternoon. She has an ultrasound. Still can't believe she's going to be a mama." Cass scanned the street, eyes darting left and right behind her bangs. "I shouldn't say this, but I can't picture her being very good at it." She bit her lip, wrinkled her nose. "I really shouldn't have said that. That was pretty nasty."

"You're just saying what everyone's thinking. Do we know who the father is?"

"She hasn't told me, but she and I aren't close." She took her car keys out of her bag.

"Want company?"

"You're not busy?"

"Nope."

"Where's lover boy?"

I shrugged. "I wouldn't know."

"Why wouldn't you—"

I made a sad little sound and pressed my knuckles against my wobbly lips.

"Did you guys break up?"

I nodded.

Her arms went around me and tucked me in tight. "Aw, sweetie."

A dam broke inside my heart. I cried for Ace, but also for my dad and Stella. I wanted to tell Cass everything. Because I couldn't, I cried harder. I was such a mess.

"Come on, let's get you a cupcake." She unwound her arms, grabbed my hand, and dragged me over to her bubblegum-pink car.

"I don't want a cupcake," I mumbled. Cupcakes reminded me of Stella and Ace.

She settled behind her steering wheel and pulled her seatbelt across her chest. "What about a slice of pound cake?"

"I'm not hungry."

"You don't need to be hungry to eat cake. Plus you look like you just worked out"—she nodded toward my attire—"so you need to replenish your energy." Her eyes snagged on my neck, around which I'd tied a thin scarf. She hooked her finger into it and tugged it down. Her eyes grew as wide as snow globes. "You got a tattoo?"

I swallowed, about to tell her it was a temporary tat, but it wasn't like it was going to go away.

I'd tried.

I'd failed.

"Yeah. Bad idea."

"Are you joking? It's hot! But I *am* a little pissed you didn't tell me about it. I would so have gone with you. I've been dying to get a tattoo on my hip." She pulled my scarf further down, then made me twist my neck this way and that to get a full picture.

She squinted, which made me wonder if she could see the dust move. Part of me wanted her to; another part of me didn't. "It's gorge. Where'd you get it done?"

Automatically I told her, "The tattoo place in Ruddington." Technically, I did get a tattoo there—the word *human* on my hand.

She pulled the car out of the driveway. "What made you get it on your neck?"

"Gottwa tradition. Women would get tattoos around their necks after their first kill." *What in the world prompted me to add that last part? Was it a way to confess without confessing?*

Cass jammed her foot into the brake pedal. My body lurched forward. "You killed someone?"

I blinked at her, blanched. "What?"

She pointed at my neck. "You just said women got them—"

"I just meant it was Gottwa tradition. It set the strongest females apart."

"So it's to show everyone you're badass now?"

My lips twitched with a despondent smile. "Exactly."

"Your mom would've been proud of you. Upholding Gottwa traditions and everything."

My dear mother. Would she have been proud? Nah. "She would've flipped out."

Cass tipped an eyebrow up. "What did your dad think?"

"He hasn't seen it yet." Kajika had wiped his mind, so he'd forgotten about it. "He'll probably hate it."

"Whatevs. It's *your* neck. *Your* choice. It's not like you're thirteen anymore. Speaking of being thirteen, I decided to do a bonfire on the beach for my birthday. Did you ask A— *Crap.* I'm sorry. You probably don't want him there."

I squashed my lips tight and nodded. It's not that I didn't want him there, but I was quite certain he wouldn't want to be there.

"I invited Lara and Josh. Did you hear they're engaged? How insane is that? I also asked Robbie. He said he'd come and bring some of his Cornell buddies and . . ." She continued listing our high school friends, then started on her summer camp friends. When we parked in front of the beachside bakery, she was still filling me in on the gossip. "Oh, and Mara's also expecting! She's due this summer, just like Faith. But she's married to the baby-daddy."

"So basically, the whole state of Michigan is attending your birthday party?"

Cass grinned. "Basically." She whipped her bag from the backseat and twisted the key out of the ignition.

Astra's was busy. Faith snaked around the bakery, carrying a tray topped with mugs and plated cakes. Her cheeks were flushed and shiny with sweat. The second she saw Cass, she exhaled, but then her blue gaze narrowed on me.

I trailed Cass behind the white marble countertop and through the swinging door. A moment later, Faith erupted into the pantry. "What's she doing here?"

"Hello to you too, Faith," I said.

Cass pulled her denim jacket off and hung it on a peg in the wall. "She came to hang out—"

"It's a real job, Cass, not a playdate," Faith snapped.

Cass rolled her eyes. "Chill, Faith. I know what a job is."

"If you have an extra apron, I'll help out."

"I don't have money to pay you both."

I jammed my hands into the pockets of my hoodie. "You don't have to pay me."

"You'd do it for free?" Faith's dark amber eyebrows almost collided on her pale forehead. "Why?"

"Because I live at home and don't need the money."

"Right." She folded her arms over her stomach that now ballooned out. "Your new boyfriend must pay for everything now."

I decided not to let her tone get to me, even though Faith was quite the pro when it came to getting under my skin. "You know me. I'm all about handouts."

Faith jerked back, her glossy reddish-brown hair frolicking around her shoulders. It took her a moment to recover from the shock of my admission. The worst part was she actually believed me. "Okay, but lose the hoodie and the scarf. You look like a tweaker."

I was about to lash back, but decided to let my throat do the talking.

So I unrolled my scarf and unzipped my hoodie. Faith's eyes bugged out. "What the fuck is on your neck?"

Your mother's stupid dust. Obviously, I didn't say that. "Something's on my neck?" I palmed the spot she was looking at, then approached the mirror hung next to the door.

Cass laughed. "She got inked. I think it's pretty awesome."

Faith handed Cass a purple apron, then tossed one to me. "Wait till her skin sags."

My lips quirked into a smile. Faith was one brutally honest girl, but these days, I seriously favored honesty over backstabbing.

"Keep the scarf, Cat. I don't want the customers fleeing because they think you're a Ruddington biker hoe."

I snorted.

"That's cold, cuz," Cass said, tying her dark hair up into a ponytail.

"Well it's true. Who gets a freakishly enormous filigree tattoo on their neck?"

"Could've been worse. Could've been on my face."

She grimaced as though a shot of tequila had gone down her airway.

"'Scuse me!" came a voice.

"On it," Cass said, swinging through the door to serve the customer.

I tied the purple apron with the gold comet and star logo around my waist, then looped the scarf back around my neck. "Congrats. By the way." I gestured to her belly.

She blushed, and the freckles dusting her nose darkened. "Don't bother trying to be nice. I know you don't like me."

I was taken aback. "I honestly meant it. We might not be good friends—friends at all—but that doesn't mean my feelings extend to the innocent life inside your stomach."

Faith pushed her hair back. "Aren't you a doctor-in-training?"

I frowned. Was she going to ask me to deliver her baby? "I am but—"

"Let me share a little something with you that I learned five months ago. Babies don't grow in stomachs. They grow in uteruses."

I almost laughed. Actually, that was a lie. I laughed. Doubled-over. And it wasn't even that funny.

Faith's resting bitch face contorted with a brisk smile that stayed as she unknotted her apron and grabbed her coat and handbag. Before leaving, she said, "You can keep the tips for yourself."

That may have seemed like a small thing, but for Faith, letting me keep anything of value was an extreme concession. Like Mr. Hamilton, she wasn't generous, even though, unlike Mr. Hamilton, she was raised with money.

Her daddy had been a wealthy man. Maybe because he was a faerie. All faeries seemed well-off. As I joined Cass in the bustling bakery, I wondered about Faith's father. I wondered if he was still alive. I wondered if he lived in Neverra.

When customers trickled out and it became relatively quiet, I asked Cass about him. "What was his name?"

"Peter."

"Do you have a picture?"

"There's one in the employee bathroom."

"In the bathroom?"

"Yeah." She aligned the remaining cupcakes. "Behind the toilet paper rolls."

"Seriously? That's where she keeps his picture?"

"Well, he did break Stella's heart."

Would Ace shove my picture in his bathroom cabinet? Did he even have a picture of me? Knowing him, if he did, he'd probably burn it. The next time I went to the bathroom, I checked the closed cupboard, and sure enough, slotted behind the black rubber plunger, was the portrait of a man with a tanned, oval face covered in stubble, a nose as thin as a bread knife, spiky brown hair, and hazel eyes. Somewhat handsome, but severe looking.

I snapped a picture of him. Faeries had a file on me. Only normal to start a file on them, gain a bit of leverage. Especially now that I'd burned my bridges with the only faerie who'd liked me.

Watch out, world, Catori Price is finally getting smarter.

Or my sanity was fraying at the edges. That was a real possibility too.

16

THE TABLOID

*H*elping out at Astra's Bakery turned into a part-time gig. Not because Faith thought I was a particularly gifted waitress, but because her doctor had put her on bed rest, and I was available.

Fueled by pent-up energy and rising guilt, I worked more hours than I was paid, baking up a storm in the adjoining kitchen. My confections weren't half as pretty as Astra's used to be, but since I borrowed her recipes, they turned out equally tasty.

Weekends were craziest, but Faith, who kept grumbling that her mother was totally irresponsible, hired a second waitress. Once I'd gotten the hang of the register and dealing with customers, working at the bakery became a pleasant break in my days. Another plus: it got me out of the house where Dad and Milly talked cadavers and wakes. Luckily, the dead weren't dear friends or extended family. Sadly, business had picked up. Two funeral houses had closed down in the neighboring towns, which funneled work into Rowan.

On my days off, I would meet Kajika at the barn to train. The weather warmed and the days lengthened, so I took to running every day. Sometimes I would wake up before dawn and hit the forest; sometimes I would run after work, up and down the sunset-streaked beach. My body grew stronger. Sinewy muscles rounded and curved beneath my skin that took on a copper hue. The only part of me not developing was my mind. However hard Kajika made me work on it, I couldn't access whatever part of my brain manipulated water. A gift I'd never coveted became a source of great frustration.

On the upside, it comforted me that I hadn't flipped and become a huntress. I wasn't sure what I was anymore. Worse, I wasn't sure what I wanted to be. I'd come to terms with the fact that I was different, not completely human. The tattoo wreathing my neck reaffirmed this on a daily basis.

I'd stopped wearing scarves when a heatwave coursed over Michigan, toasting the long strip of white sandy beach and heating the top of the lake. My tattoo had caused quite a stir in our small town. For a couple days, that's all anyone talked about, but then high school prom happened, and streamers and corsages replaced talk of my inked neck.

Did I mention that no faerie visited? None. Zero. Zilch. Perhaps they were flitting around other parts of America. Or maybe they were sunning themselves in Europe. Didn't everyone go to Europe in the spring?

"Want another slice?" I asked Faith, who was flipping through a tabloid in one corner of the bakery.

Without looking up, she said, "Do I look like I need another slice?"

"You're pregnant, Faith. Not fat."

She squinted suspiciously up at me, then flipped the magazine closed and laid her hands on top of the cover, lacing her fingers together. "Why are you still here?"

I bit my tongue to block a sour comeback. I didn't want to lose this job. Working, along with my grueling workouts and nightly Netflix marathons with my father, were the only things keeping me from thinking about Ace and how much I missed him. "Sorry." I slid her empty plate on my tray and turned.

"Catori." Faith's voice was so sharp it had me spinning around. "I asked you a question."

"And I'm answering proactively."

"I didn't mean right now. I meant, why are you still working here? Why aren't you interning in a hospital?"

Oh.

I must've stood gaping a long time, because Faith rolled her eyes. "I might be a bitch, but I'm not *that* bitchy."

I pressed my lips closed.

"Am I?"

Instead of answering, I said, "I'm only in my second year of college. No hospital would give me an internship."

Faith stroked her expanding belly like bearded men stroked their facial hair. After long seconds, she paused, but kept her palm on her swollen abdomen. "The doctor said I could come off bed rest and start working again."

My stomach filled with ice. I wanted to say, *I need this job. Don't fire me. I'll work for free.* But all of that sounded pitiful and desperate, so I nibbled on the inside of my cheek instead.

"So . . ." she continued.

My heart banged. My brand burned. "So you don't want me here anymore?"

Even though Faith's gaze was leveled on my hand, it seemed elsewhere. "So if you want to do something else, Catori, you can do something else."

"I'm happy to stay on."

One of her eyebrows jerked up. "Really?"

I nodded.

"Well, I guess . . . until Mom comes back, I could use you."

My stomach clenched as though a faerie were claiming a bargain. But there was no faerie and no bargain, just guilt. Heaps of it.

"Sounds fair." I took the rag off my platter, scrubbed at a coffee stain on the long communal table, then repositioned the little pots filled with lavender and teal succulents. "Do you miss her?"

"Missing someone who doesn't care about you is a waste of energy." She rubbed her stomach again. "I know everyone thinks I'll suck as a mom, but I plan on being there for my little girl."

"You're having a girl?"

She nodded, a dreaminess entering her expression, softening the never-bending line of her mouth. In all the years I'd known Faith, this was the first time I didn't regret saving her from choking on a piece of meat back in junior high. Maybe Faith had a good side. Maybe—

"In case you didn't hear . . ." She pushed the magazine toward me and tipped her chin toward it. "It's a boy."

On the cover of the tabloid was a picture of Ace and Angelina.

I dropped the platter.

The rag hit the floor wetly. Faith's plate cracked. Chocolate crumbs rained down over my white sneakers. The bakery turned very quiet, yet my ears buzzed.

I crouched, grabbed the platter, and tossed the ceramic shards onto it. My heart thumped louder as I remembered Ace helping me clean up the broken shards of my mother's mug.

Hands shaking, I gathered the cake crumbs with the rag, then stood back up.

Faith studied my trembling hands. "You should read the article."

"No thank you," I whispered.

Before I could walk away, she added, "Sometimes it's better to be alone than in bad company."

I kept my face blank as I sped away, toward the swinging door and into the employee bathroom, where I splashed freezing water against my face. It numbed my eyes, but unfortunately didn't manage to numb my throbbing heart.

I closed up late that evening. No one was waiting for me at home, and I had no plans for the rest of the night. Dad had gone fishing with the sheriff, and Cass was celebrating her mother's birthday.

As I swept the floor, I thought about what to get Cass for her birthday, which was three days away. Cass loved everything, but I wanted to get her something meaningful instead of a gift certificate at Dillard's. Even though I was sure she'd be plenty happy with that.

I hadn't turned off the radio, and it was playing some sappy love song that made me want to slit my wrist. I gritted my teeth and willed the DJ to play something else . . . anything else.

The broom slipped out of my hands when I spotted the magazine Faith had tauntingly left behind. I marched over to it and seized it, ready to shove it into the trash, but once I stood over the garbage, I couldn't release it anymore.

So I returned to one of the long tables, took a seat on the bench tucked underneath, and read the article, staring at each picture, committing each detail to memory. It wasn't so much Ace I was studying, but his fiancée. She was perfect. Large tawny eyes, thick lashes, straight, glossy brown hair. Her skin was flawless and golden. Her body thin. Where Faith was very obviously pregnant, Angelina's stomach was tight and tiny. Maybe faerie babies didn't grow the same way as normal babies. Then again, Faith was having a faerie baby, too.

What bothered me most about the article was the happy picture the reporter painted of the young couple.

The worst part was that they *did* seem happy.

Like the dishrag I'd washed and wrung out, my heart twisted and squeezed. My eyes remained dry, though.

Finally, once I'd read the article enough times, once I'd flagellated myself long enough with the pictures of the blessed couple, I rolled up the tabloid and stood. I was about to walk it to the garbage when the door of Astra's jangled.

I spun around. "We're clo—" The last syllable froze in my throat. And then the magazine slid out of my fingers and flopped onto the floor like a dead fish.

17

NEW ROOMMATE

I wasn't sure how long I stood there in silence, staring at Lily and Ace, but the sun, which had begun dipping below the horizon when I'd started tidying up the bakery, was gone now.

Another song came on the radio. Peppy. Rhythmic. It wasn't in English. Or maybe it was.

Ace had cut his hair. Buzzed it short. It made him look older, tougher. "Cat."

My heart skipped at the sound of his voice. "Ace."

My brand burned. His palm glowed. He curled his fingers into a tight fist as though to block the sight of the light.

I nodded to his sister. "Lily."

"Is this a bad time?" he said, at the same time I said, "Didn't think you guys were ever coming back."

I breathed in through my nose, out through my mouth. Supposedly that sort of breathing was calming—or so Mom had told me. I didn't feel any calmer. I did feel more lightheaded, though.

"Lily needs a place to stay." Ace's words were like sharp needles. They pricked my lungs and freed the heady air filling me.

"The palace ran out of rooms to let?"

Neither sibling smiled. Not that I was trying to be funny. I was in too much shock for humor.

"She severed her engagement."

Silence bleached the air and effaced the music.

Lily twisted a lock of blonde hair around her finger. Over and over. The movement was hypnotic.

"What do you mean . . . *severed her engagement?*" Did he mean what I thought he meant? That—

Ace tipped his head to the side. "She called off her wedding."

I gasped. It was soft. Barely audible. I clapped my hand over my mouth.

Lily's large gray eyes set on mine, rimmed red but dry.

"*Wow.*" I spoke against my hand that smelled of confectioner's sugar and clammy incredulity.

Lily dipped her head down, tucking her chin into her slim neck.

Ace squared his shoulders that seemed to have gotten broader. "Could she live with you?"

"With me?" I squeaked.

Lily glanced up, worry—or embarrassment—creasing her brow.

"Look, I know we seem like we have lots of earthly connections"—he tipped his head to the magazine at my feet, and my cheeks flamed—"but I would trust none of them with my sister."

"You'd trust me?"

"I know, right? Pretty pitiful, considering."

I felt the jab of his words and the answering bitterness underneath my ribs. "How long will she be staying?"

Ace's blue eyes darkened like rushing storm clouds. He barely parted his lips as he said, "Until her fire burns out. Six months. Maybe more. Maybe less. Depends how long she survives out here." His voice was so low it scattered goosebumps over my exposed arms. "We'll pay you of course—"

"Shut up," I growled, angry he'd think I required payment. "Of course she can stay with us."

A long beat passed.

Lily raised her face. She signed something to her brother.

"I know you don't particularly want to see me, Cat, but I want to visit. *Often.* Will that be a problem?" There was a challenge in his gaze.

"No." I swallowed hard. It would simply kill me to see him every day . . . "I'm not often home these days anyway."

"New job?" He gestured to the bakery.

I nodded.

"Working off your guilt?"

I folded my arms. "Something like that."

Lily signed something to him. He signed something back. And then his arms went around her and squeezed her so hard she seemed to vanish inside his body.

I picked up the broom and scooped up the crumbs with the pail, then grabbed my jacket and switched off the music and the lights. When I reemerged through the swing door, only Lily remained, looking as empty as the large, noiseless, dusky room.

18

CHANGES

I led Lily into the ground-floor bedroom then asked if she needed anything, but she shook her head. Seeing her empty hands, I went upstairs and gathered a pair of leggings, a T-shirt, a new toothbrush, and toothpaste, then knuckled her closed door. When she opened it, I handed her everything. She signed what I imagined meant *thank you*. Maybe it meant *I need to go shopping*. Or perhaps: *go away*.

After she vanished back inside her bedroom, I did laundry, then dragged a chair underneath the wind chime and unhooked it, depositing it in a large Ziploc, which I stashed inside a cupboard.

And then, still rattled by the evening, I watched mind-numbing TV on the couch until Dad arrived, keeping the volume extra low, so I didn't disturb my new house guest. Several times, I stared at her door. I wanted to knock, ask her why she'd done it, but deep down I knew her reason: she'd seen the true face of her fiancé and had decided dying was better than marrying him.

A while later, Dad walked in, jaw ruddy from boating, eyes bright from beer. "Hey, sweetie." He dropped a kiss on my cheek, then sat beside me and kicked off his shoes.

"Caught lots of fish?"

"Tons. We should go out on the lake this weekend."

"Sure." I used to go fishing with Blake all the time. I sighed at the memory. "Dad, we need to talk." I sat up, muted the TV, then swung my legs over the edge of the couch and angled my torso toward my father.

His reddish tan vanished. "Are you pregnant?"

I blinked, surprised that this would be his first thought. "No. Course not. I'm not even seeing anyone."

"You're with Kajika a lot."

Dad still thought Kajika was a distant cousin of mine, which made his comment even more bothersome. "Kajika and I are friends. Besides, do you seriously see me having a fling with a cousin? *Yuck.*"

His eyes skimmed my tattoo, which he'd blamed on Kajika. "Yeah. I don't know why I said that." He draped an arm over the back of the couch. "So what do we need to talk about?"

"We have a new house guest."

"We do?" He pushed away from the backrest and peered at the closed guestroom door. "Is Aylen visiting again?"

I smiled. Dad loved Aylen like a sister . . . like an annoying little sister. "No. Not Aylen. Lily Wood."

"Lily Wood?"

"Yeah."

"Lily Wood's moved in with us?"

"Yeah."

A beat. A blink.

"She had a falling out with her parents."

Dad's eyes crinkled with a pensive frown. "Will Cruz be joining her?"

"No. Cruz will not be joining her. They broke up."

"Oh." He scraped his hands down the sides of his face as though trying to wake himself up.

"I told her she could stay as long as she needed. I hope it's okay."

"Of course it's okay." He squeezed my knee. "I like Lily. She's a sweet kid. Plus, it'll be nice to have another person in the house."

"Am I not enough for you anymore?" I teased him. "Are you bored out of your mind?"

Dad's mouth quirked into a smile. "I dare anyone to say living with you is boring."

I grinned.

"You cannot get bored of someone who makes you want to tear your hair out."

"What? Me?" I teased.

"That tattoo . . ." He shook his head, but at least he wasn't scowling anymore.

The first week I'd lost the scarf, he couldn't look at me without glowering at my neck as though it had wronged him.

"You can't get bored of someone who feeds you too much good food. Who fills the fridge with your favorite beer. All my clothes are getting tight, by the way."

"Good."

Dad smiled. "You can't get bored of someone who takes such good care of you. How do you even have time to do all you do, what with your new job—which everyone is telling me you're amazing at."

I rolled my eyes. "I'm not that great—"

"George's wife raved about your strawberry jam cupcakes. All night."

I linked my hands together, rubbing my knuckles. I wasn't a fan of compliments. I didn't know how to deal with them. I was the same way about presents—awkward. "Just following Astra's recipes," I said softly.

"Are you leaving me?"

"What?"

"Is that why Lily's coming to live with *us?*" He air-quoted the word *us.* "Because you don't trust me to be on my own?"

"No, Dad. Lily's coming to live with us because she really does need a place to stay. I'm not going anywhere."

"You're allowed to, you know." His gaze was on his bare feet, on his long narrow toes that were paler than the rest of his skin. Like me, he'd tanned. Unlike me, he tanned red; I tanned brown like my mother. "Cat, living with my baby girl is a dream come true, but it's *my* dream. Not yours. You need to go back to your life. Conquer that world you've been so adamant about conquering ever since your granddaddy taught you the definition of the verb at the ripe old age of four and a half."

Funny the things Dad remembered and I didn't. I leaned against him. "Daddy, I'm *happy* to be here with you. Truly, I am."

"I'm just saying . . . I'm okay now."

"I'm glad you're okay, but I'm still not going anywhere."

He stroked my shoulder. "I noticed you took the wind chime down again."

"The noise bothers Lily. But I didn't throw it out this time."

A long beat passed. "I'm sort of happy you took it down."

"Really?" I pressed away from the big, solid man who'd unfalteringly loved me for the last nineteen years.

"Yeah. Even though I'm not trying to erase your mom, I am trying to heal, and that thing tore me up each time I heard it chime."

"I thought you wanted it there."

"I didn't like that you'd thrown it out, but"—he swallowed—"I'm glad for the silence."

For a long while, we both stayed quiet. Then Dad said, "Did you watch the new *Bloodlane* episode without me?"

"No."

"Want to watch it?"

I nodded, unmuted the television, and burrowed against my father. But then I looked at the closed door and sprang toward it. Knocked. A couple seconds later, Lily peeked out, dressed in the leggings and T-shirt I'd lent her. They were baggy on her.

When she saw my father, her eyes widened.

A warm smile curved his lips as he signed something.

She smiled. Signed something back.

"Want to come and watch TV with us?" he asked, using his voice instead of his hands.

Lily was probably used to fancy dinners and glamorous parties— watching TV with us on a worn couch was probably not her thing.

Surprisingly, though, she trailed me into the living room and sat rigidly on one end of the couch.

Dad glanced at me. I bit my lip. I didn't think telling her to get comfortable would make her comfortable, so I didn't say anything. Before the episode started, Dad filled her in on the plot of the show. She listened with such rapt fascination you'd think Dad was explaining the mechanics of black holes. When I pressed play, she leaned a little further back into the couch.

I glanced at her screen-lit profile. Never in my wildest dreams would I have imagined I would be living with Lily Wood, and I'd had some pretty wild dreams. Most of them about her brother and the hunters buried in our backyard.

Another hunter had starred in my dreams a couple nights ago. A squat man discussing the terms of Jacobiah's accords with Negongwa.

The voice of the man I inhabited was loud, his words cutting, his legs short, hairy, and ropy with muscle.

Fog and the strong, spicy scent of male had assaulted my senses, making their disagreement hard to concentrate on. When I'd woken up, only a single word came back to me: *nockwad*. The rest had remained as fuzzy as the air inside the sweat lodge.

I'd looked up *nockwad* in Ley's dictionary.

Nockwad meant mist.

Mist reminded me of the Night of Mist—the one night in a Neverra month the Unseelie could come out of their underground home and revel with their Seelie brothers and sisters.

I sighed and burrowed deeper into the fluffy cushions behind me, dragging my legs up against me. I swear I was certifiable—believing spirits could really visit my mind.

I felt Lily glance at me. If she could see inside my mind, she'd probably hit the road. I looked at her and offered her a smile. She spun her head away and blinked at the TV.

Ace trusted me, which still rattled my mind, but not Lily. And I understood. I'd kissed her ex-fiancé, broken up with her brother, cozied up to Kajika. How dire had her options been for her brother to suggest living with me?

19

THE CASTES

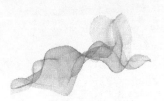

The following morning, I was supposed to train with Kajika. I wasn't quite sure if it would be kind to leave Lily alone on her first morning, but I didn't call to cancel. He needed to know that Lily was living with me. He needed to warn the other hunters to stay away. Not that any had dared come up to my house since they'd attacked me with rowan wood arrows.

When the pickup rumbled into the graveyard at nine o'clock, I hooked my thumbs through my jeans' belt loops and ambled down my porch. Kajika frowned when he noticed I wasn't wearing exercise clothes, but then his frown turned into a nod of approval.

"Good thinking, Catori. You will not always be in elastic clothes." I must've jerked in surprise, because his eyebrows slanted. "Was learning to fight in stiff clothes not your intention?"

If his eyes hadn't set to a place over my shoulder, I might've teased him about his *stiff* clothes comment.

Dad had gone to have breakfast with Bee, and Milly hadn't shown up yet to determine the cause of death of the newest cadaver in our basement, so that left Lily. She stood in the open doorway, her thin hand clutching the side of the door like her balance depended on it.

I turned back toward Kajika to explain.

His gaze slammed into mine with the force of a punch. "What is Lily Wood doing here?"

I rested my forearms on the truck. "Lily Wood is living with me."

"What?"

"She called off her engagement to Cruz."

"I do not understand the connection."

"Breaking that sort of bond gets you kicked out of Neverra," I said in a low voice. I didn't think Lily needed, or *wanted,* to relive the horror of her decision.

He glanced behind me again, but Lily had retreated into the shadows of the house. "For how long?"

"For as long as she has left," I whispered.

He frowned. "I do not understand."

So I explained it to him. And then I told him to warn his new clan that she was off-limits.

"Are you certain she has not been sent to spy on you?"

I recoiled, lowered my arms. "That's—" I was about to say ludicrous, but was it? A chill oozed through me as wetly as a creeping slug.

"You did not even consider the possibility? Faeries love to trick people. Especially hunters. It is their specialty."

"Hunters are so hung up on that tiny trait of our personality."

In slow motion, I rotated toward the voice.

Ace stood on the porch steps, hand on the balustrade, buzzed hair glinting gold in the white sun. His gaze skidded over me, then skidded off.

"Is he *also* living with you, Catori?" Kajika asked.

My neck pivoted back toward the hunter so fast it cracked. "No!" I said, but my stupid face flushed.

"I just came to drop off some clothes for my sister. Can't have her running around naked. Don't want her to be mistaken for a hunter."

Kajika's lips pressed so tight his upper lip vanished into his lower one. "Was that meant as criticism, *pahan?*"

"Nope. Just an observation."

Testosterone zinged through the air as loud as the birds chirping in the leafy rowan trees.

"Ace, do you swear Lily's not here to spy on me?"

His face shuttered up. And then he snorted. "I knew you disliked me, but now, at least, I know how much."

I bit my lip to stop it from wobbling, then disguised the sting of his words with annoyance. "Just answer the question, Ace."

"Would you even believe my answer?"

"Yes. I would believe your answer."

"You should not believe anything faeries—"

I flung my hand up to shush Kajika.

"Lily is not here to spy on you."

For a long minute, we stared at each other. I was pretty certain it was the most loaded stare in the history of humankind.

"What about you?" I finally asked.

"You think getting her to live here is my way to spy on you?" His upper lip curled in disgust. "Cat, I've moved on."

I sucked in air. That's not how I'd meant it. But now that I knew . . .

Crap . . . it hurt.

While I still pined for him, he'd replaced me. I wondered if he'd even waited a day to choose someone else. And I didn't mean a Neverrian day, I meant an Earth day.

"If you've got some place to go with your boyfriend"—he gestured to the car—"I'll stay with Lily."

"Kajika is not my boyfriend," I bit out, "but we do have somewhere to be." I hopped into the cab and slammed the door shut. "Drive," I hissed when Kajika still hadn't put the car in gear.

We didn't talk about Ace or Lily the entire way to the barn. We didn't talk period. I sulked while Kajika remained steeped in that pensive silence of his.

That morning, I was a tigress.

I fought harder than I'd ever fought, ran quicker than I'd ever run, and sent arrows flying straight into the heart of my targets with such velocity that if those targets had been faeries, they'd all have died.

ACE WASN'T there when I got home, but Lily was. She was reading one of my grandmother's books on Gottwa history.

"Brushing up on your enemy's history?" I asked drily.

She blinked at me and closed the book. And then she took her phone out of her silk vest pocket, typed, and angled the screen toward me.

It read, *You are not my enemy.*

I raked my hand through my hair, matted with sweat from my strenuous workout. "Is Ace still here?"

She shook her head. Then added to the message on her phone, *I promise I am not spying on you. Living with you wasn't my first choice.*

"But someone turned you down?"

She bit her lip. Typed again. *My first choice was death, but Ace wouldn't kill me. And you can't kill yourself with your own dust.*

My heart knocked into my ribcage, which made my brand flare. It wasn't the first time today—it had been lit up like a Christmas tree all morning.

He's still hopeful he can get me back inside Neverra.

"Is there a way?"

She shook her head gently. If Lily had been anyone else, if *I* had been anyone else, I would've hugged her, but she was Lily and I was me —both of us guarded and reserved.

I did sit on the arm of the couch, though, curling one leg beneath me.

Lily typed again. I read over her shoulder. *I met Milly. She seems nice.*

"She is."

She didn't recognize me.

"Why would she recognize you? You haven't been back to Rowan— *Oh.* You mean because you're famous?"

Lily shrugged.

"You're that famous, huh?"

She nodded, then pulled up a search page and typed in her name. Articles flooded the screen. The first one was titled "No Double Wedding for the Wood Children."

My eyes widened. "It's in the news?"

She didn't answer. Not that my question required an answer.

"You think reporters will come to Rowan?"

They might. She raised her large silver eyes to me before returning her gaze to her screen. *If you want me to leave, I—*

I laid my hand on her bony shoulder and shook my head. "If anyone tries to approach, I'll kick their asses back to wherever they came from. I'm strong now." I flexed my arm, which was toned and possessed a slight bulge.

Is that what you do with Kajika?

"Yes. I make him teach me to fight. We meet twice a week."

What has he taught you?

I hesitated to tell her.

Sensing my hesitation, she wrote: *You don't have to tell me anything. You don't even have to talk with me if you don't want to.*

"I don't mind talking with you, Lily. I'm sort of surprised *you* want to talk with me. What with what happened between me and your brother."

That's between him and you.

I nibbled on the inside of my cheek. "Kajika is training me to use a bow and arrow—very 1800s of him. He insists it teaches me accuracy and develops muscle strength."

Lily wrinkled her nose. Her grandfather had lost his life to that weapon centuries ago.

"He's also coaching me on my running. I don't run as fast as he does, but I run fast. Like Olympic-medal fast."

If faeries and hunters ever made peace, and medical school was no longer an option, I could make a career as a professional runner. It was far from what I dreamed for myself, but it would pay nicely.

"He's also trying to help me tap into"—I pressed a fingertip against my forehead so as not to say the word out loud. I didn't think Milly could hear anything, but better safe than sorry—"but that's a bust."

You mean, move things with your mind?

"I managed twice, three times. Well, four if you count the storm, which may have been me or may have been mother nature . . ."

You made a storm?

"I'm not sure, but I seem to be able to control"—I dropped my voice to a mere whisper—"water."

Aren't you a hunter?

I shrugged. "Why? Can't hunters manipulate water?"

Lily shook her head.

"I thought they could move anything with their minds." To hell with keeping my voice low.

Not water.

What did Lily mean?

The blonde faerie tapped the Gottwa history book on her lap. *Only Daneelies can move water.*

"*Daneelies?*"

A long time ago, there was a third caste of faeries. I must've looked deeply confused because Lily added to her message: *The Seelie: us. The Unseelie: the Forma. And then the Daneelies. They were the smallest caste. Instead of fire, they had water mixed with blood in their veins. They were the ones who created the mist on my grandfather's orders. Once he no longer had use for them, he got rid of them.*

"*Got rid?* You mean banished them here?"

Lily stared at me gravely. *I mean massacred them.*

My saliva thickened, soured.

Although I never met my grandfather, he was considered the most ruthless Neverrian leader.

More than ever, I believed that if one positive thing came out of the Dark Day, it was Maximus Wood's death.

"And you think I could be a Daneelie?" I asked in a quiet voice.

I have no idea, but if you can move water, then maybe. If you are though, then you can't tell anyone, because Daneelies are everyone's enemies. The forma detest them for imprisoning them and the Seelies fear them because Daneelie magic can undo the mist.

"Do the hunters hate them too?"

The caste became extinct around the time hunters were born, so hunters never encountered Daneelie. At least that's what I thought. The extinction part. Her gray eyes skimmed my face. *The fact that you're here makes me think otherwise.*

I linked my hands together.

But I could be wrong.

But she could also be right.

*To answer your earlier question, if hunters encountered a Daneelie today, they would probably hate them. Daneelies, like Seelies, had dust. Hunters hunt everyone with dust. I think your people—*she erased the last two words and replaced them with: *the hunters called them Mishipeshu.*

I'd heard that word before. I racked my brain to locate the memory. Had my grandfather told me stories about them? The knowledge of where I'd heard it spilled like an injection into my veins, cold and slow-moving. "I read about them in the book you—" I was about to say *stole*, but substituted it for the word, "lost. They were shapeshifting faeries who lived underwater."

She pushed her hair behind her ear. ***They didn't really shapeshift, but their skin coated in scales under water.*** A diamond the size of her lobe twinkled in the ray of light slanting through the window. ***Can you breathe underwater?***

"I never tried." Goosebumps prickled my forearms. "Oh my God, you think I could?"

She shrugged a shoulder. ***Daneelies could, so maybe.***

"This is all so insane." I rose from the couch and paced the living room. Without pausing, I asked, "Why would Holly tell me I had a choice between hunter or faerie if I was something else entirely? Plus, her twin sister, she drowned, so I don't see how— Unless she didn't drown? You think Chatwa faked her death?" I stopped pacing.

Lily crooked her finger at me, and I approached.

Ace saw a picture of them in your room. They didn't look alike apparently. Are you sure they WERE twins? Maybe they weren't related.

Blood must have pooled into my heart, because my chest felt hot and close to bursting.

Lily whisked back the glimmering curtain of hair that had settled around her face as she typed: I'm serious though, if I am right about this, you have to keep it a secret.

"Ace knows. I mean he knows I moved water."

He didn't tell me. Maybe he didn't connect the dots. Does anyone else know?

I nodded, and my head felt like it weighed more than the rowan wood caskets of my ancestors. "Kajika knows," I admitted softly, "but he believes it's a hunter power. Besides, I really do descend from the Gottwas, so maybe it is."

Lily added a line of text: ***If it's only Ace and Kajika, then you should . . .***

"Cruz knows. I think."

Lily craned her neck to look into my face. Her pupils expanded, ate up her irises. In slow motion, she lowered her somber gaze. Her fingers hovered over her digital keyboard as though unable to write the thought pulsing through her mind.

She didn't have to write it, though, because I knew exactly what she was thinking.

If Cruz knew, then I was in serious trouble. "He's going to kill me."

After a very long beat, Lily typed: *Or he's going to use you.*

I wasn't sure which was worse.

2 0

REVELATIONS

Over dinner the following night, I asked Dad if Ley and Chatwa were *really* related.

"I don't understand your question, Cat."

Dad had taken Lily and me to the Japanese restaurant in Ruddington where Dad and I ate the night I'd learned about Forest Print—the printing house in Detroit Holly/Ley had used to print her book.

"Holly told your mother they were. I don't see why she'd lie."

I saw quite a few reasons why she'd lie. To protect her sister from other faeries. Because she didn't know the truth herself. To protect me.

"This somehow feels like *déjà vu*, huh?" Dad stared out the window at the inky spread of water.

"What feels like that?"

"Discussing Chatwa here. Last time we came, we talked about her too." He studied the menu. "You girls know what you want to eat?"

We both nodded.

He signaled for a waitress. "I suppose you could exhume her body and test her DNA if you're *that* curious."

Considering Holly had turned into a flower, that was impossible. Flora DNA would probably not match human DNA.

"Or you could test her nephew. That would be less messy than digging her up."

Lily tipped her head to the side, so Dad explained, "Kajika was her great nephew."

Although Lily righted her head, her frown didn't dissipate.

I gave her a look that I hoped translated into *I'll explain later*, then lowered my gaze to my wooden chopsticks. I separated them, the wood splintering unevenly. When I realigned them, though, they joined seamlessly.

"Or you could get a DNA sample from a hairbrush if those gypsies didn't toss all her things away."

I jerked my gaze up because that *could* work. Unless faerie DNA disintegrated like their owners.

"They're real busy tonight." Dad still had his arm lifted but no waitress was coming our way. "I'll go tell them we're ready." He walked over to the sushi bar.

"Does DNA turn into ash?"

Lily typed: *No clue. BTW, Kajika is your cousin?*

"No. He's from another tribe." Dad was making his way back over, so I added quickly, "But Dad thinks he's related to my mother's family."

Dad dropped back into his chair. "So what did you girls do today?"

"I worked out, and Lily read."

"You like reading? I love reading."

"No, Dad, you love the *idea* of reading."

"I have lots of books—"

"That you never read."

"Sadly, that's true. But I want to read more. It was my New Year's resolution."

"It's your New Year's resolution every year."

Dad grinned. "Does Cat drive you crazy, Lily? 'Cause she drives me a little insane."

"Hey!" I tapped my father's hand with one of my chopsticks.

"Honey, I meant that in the best possible way."

"Puh-lease." I rolled my eyes. "There is no good way to mean that."

Dad chuckled. Lily smiled. I did too, because it was a nice change from discussing my motley gene pool.

"Are you both going to Cass's birthday party tomorrow?"

Lily looked at me.

"Yeah. We're both going. I mean, if you want to go, Lily. There's going to be a lot of people. Cass invited everyone on her contact list, and she has *a lot* of contacts."

"You should go. I'm sure you'll meet nice kids."

I doubted Lily wanted to meet any nice kids.

The waitress came over to take our order then. After Lily pointed to her selection, and Dad and I ordered, he asked, "If your brother ever wants to join us for dinner, he's always welcome. I know he and Cat are good friends."

Unfortunately, I was sipping my iced seltzer water when he said this, and some of it shot up my nose, which was horrible.

Lily signed something to my dad.

"Don't thank me. I like Ace. He's a sweet and responsible kid. Unlike Kajika."

I was still coughing. "Dad, Kajika and I aren't in a relationship. Really. Really. Really. We aren't. I swear on—" I was about to say Mom. Instead, I said, "On my own life."

Lily observed me in that incisive way of hers, as though she were peeling away the layers until she could see the hidden core.

"That boy's troubled. And trouble."

"Dad," I hissed.

He raised both hands in the air. "That's my two cents."

"Can you please cut him some slack? He was married, and his wife died. Out of everyone, you should understand how that feels."

I hadn't meant for it to come out as brutally as it did.

Dad blanched. "What?"

"And then he lost his family in a"—I looked at the ice cubes floating in my glass—"in a fire."

"What?" Dad's voice was a mere whisper.

"He's had a tough life, which has made him tough. But he's not a bad person."

Dad knocked over his beer. "Oh! *Oh* . . ." It trickled onto his jeans. "Oh Great Spirit . . . that's . . . that's . . . I'm . . ." He flung his paper napkin on the fizzy yellow puddle to sop up the liquid.

I covered his shaking hand with my own. "You didn't know."

"But— Oh, Cat, why didn't you tell me?"

"What would it have changed?"

"I wouldn't have had so many negative thoughts about him for one. *Ugh.* Poor kid. Is that why he fights for a living?"

I nodded. "But, Dad, he doesn't like pity, so don't ever mention any of the things I told you, okay? Actually, pretend you don't know anything."

Dad's cheeks were still pretty pale. "Did *you* know, Lily?"

She nodded.

Dad scraped a hand over his face. "I feel like a jerk."

"You're not." I squeezed his other hand.

"If he ever needs to talk about his loss, I'll listen. Will you tell him?"

"He doesn't like talking about Ishtu."

"*Ishtu?*" Dad asked. "Was she also of Native origin?"

"Yeah."

"Your mom wanted to name you that—"

I knocked my knee into the table. "What? She did?"

"Uh-huh. Apparently, you had an ancestor called like that. It means sweet in Gottwa. Was Kajika's wife Gottwa?"

"Yes," I said, my throat as hot as the air pulsing from the vent next to me.

"I didn't think there were many Gottwas still living."

Even though I always wondered why my parents had chosen a Hopi name for me, I was incredibly glad it had won over the Gottwa possibility.

"What happened to her?" Dad asked, as the waitress deposited a bowl of edamame on our table.

I glanced at Lily. "She was killed in a freak accident."

Dad gasped. "Great Spirit, what a life!" He shook his head. "I'm not sure I'm hungry anymore."

He still ate the edamame and his entire platter of sushi, but he was uncharacteristically quiet during the entire meal. Even though I felt bad for burdening my father with this knowledge, I was glad he finally knew, if only to stop being so critical of the hunter.

BIRTHDAY PARTY

"*A*re you sure you want to go?" I stood in the doorway of Lily's bedroom, watching her tie the laces on her white sneakers embedded with sparkly stars. The shoes looked new, like everything Lily wore.

She stood up and signed something, but remembered I had no knowledge of sign language, so she seized her phone off her made-up bed—maybe I was prejudiced, but for royalty, I found Lily quite tidy—and wrote: *If you don't want me to go, I'll stay here.*

"It's not that. I'm just worried you won't have much fun. Human parties are . . ." I attempted to fit the correct words: loud, messy, reek of beer.

I like human parties.

"Okay then, let's go."

Lily picked up a large white box tied with a black ribbon.

"You got her a present?"

She shrugged. *It's not much. Just clothes.*

"Which is Cass's favorite thing."

I'd crafted a lariat with beveled amethysts—apparently, they were the stones for protection—and three feathers from the tin Mom and I had filled over the years. I was never a woo-woo sort of a girl. Mom and Aylen were the ones who believed in the magical capacity of minerals. But since I'd discovered that opal contained magic—it made things and people invisible to faeries—I was willing to risk ridicule.

Maybe amethysts were just pretty purple stones. In that case, Cass would have a pretty purple necklace.

"You might want to grab a jacket, it gets cold at night."

Lily smiled at me. *My fire hasn't burned out yet.*

Guilt amassed in my throat, formed a large lump. "I'm sorry, Lily, I—"

She waved her hand as though it wasn't a big deal, but it *was* a big deal, because Lily's life was a blazing wick that was burning down.

"So you're *never* cold?" I asked, as we walked out to my silver Honda.

She shook her head and climbed into the passenger seat.

I started the car, and a loud Kygo song blasted out of the stereo. I lowered the volume and drove out of the cemetery.

"Are there lots of parties in Neverra?"

Lily nodded, then tipped her phone toward me. *Almost every night. Fae LOVE reveling.*

"Are they fancy?"

She bobbed her head. *Caligosupra parties are, but not caligosubi parties. Those are more human-like. And way more fun.*

I presumed *caligosupra*—faeries who lived above the mist—were wealthier than those who lived below the mist—*caligosubi.*

"Do you miss your home?"

She relaxed her head against the head rest and looked out her window. After a while, she nodded.

When I'd left Rowan to go to college, I hadn't missed home much, but comparing leaving my small town for a big city in the same country to being expelled from your *only* home was ludicrous. Lily hadn't left out of boredom; she'd been kicked out . . . locked out.

"Kajika's coming," I told Lily.

She glanced at me. In the obscurity, her eyes glinted like a cat's. "Hopefully alone, but maybe Cass extended the invitation to his new friends."

She twirled a lock of hair around her index finger, and the ring she wore cast tinsel over the dashboard.

"If you want to go home early, just tell me and—"

She placed a hand on my arm, then moved it off and typed. Her white screen filled with quick words: ***Don't worry about me. I know I look eighteen, but I'm ninety, Catori.***

Right. "Sorry."

She shook her head, and a half smile crept over one side of her mouth. It resembled her brother's smile so much that my heart compressed. ***You're much nicer than you seem.***

"Thanks?"

She laughed, which loosened the tension that had coiled around my limbs the night Lily had appeared on our doorstep. Not that I thought having her live with us would be the worst possible thing, but I *had* expected it to be strange.

And it hadn't. Which was the strange part.

A couple minutes before we reached the beach, the throbbing music overpowered my car's low stereo. The frenzied rhythm pumped against the tree trunks nearest the beach and echoed over the smooth lake, along with peppy chatter and raucous laughter.

I parked behind a long line of cars, grabbed the velvet jewelry pouch, and waited for Lily before making my way onto the beach. We walked toward the blazing bonfire surrounded by swaying, scantily-clad girls and shorts-and-baseball-cap-clad boys. So she could place the people she was about to meet, I told Lily some stories about my high school days, stories I'd pushed into dusty recesses of my mind. One of them was about Blake. I had to stop midway through, because a ball of grief as thick as a cork jammed up my throat.

Lily brushed my arm. I didn't dare look at her until I was certain I'd reined back the tears. This was Cass's big night. I needed to be happy tonight—at least pretend to be happy. I realized I hadn't been happy for a long time.

"Cass will have more exciting stories," I finally croaked. "She was popular."

As though she heard her name on my lips, Cass sprinted toward us, tossing herself and her drink over me. Most of her beer landed on the sand, but some sprinkled my cut-offs and legs. I suspected it would be the first of many drinks spilled over me tonight.

"Happy birthday, sweetie." I pressed the pouch into her hands.

She opened it instantly, tipping the contents over on her palm. "Oh . . . my . . . freaking . . . God. I LOVE it!" She wrapped it around her neck, then hugged me again. The stones glimmered against her bare throat, and the feathers quivered in the placid wind.

Lily handed her the big white box, and Cass tore it open. Her eyes snapped open so wide, they seemed to eat up all her face. Or at least what could be seen of her face behind her long bangs.

"You didn't!" she gasped as she held out a pair of fire-engine red leather pants and a black lace top. She tackled Lily, giving her a hug that would've knocked her over if she hadn't been a nimble faerie. As Cass raved about her new clothes, I scanned the beach for familiar faces. Found many. Two held my attention.

Kajika had come, but not alone. Alice was with him. Where she looked at ease, he looked like a weed in a flowerbed.

Once Cass had departed to greet more guests, I nodded toward him and asked Lily, "Want to stay here or—"

Lily shook her head and tagged along. I circled the driftwood arranged around the blazing flames. I touched Kajika's arm, then said, "Hey."

His eyes went straight to Lily. Alice's too. Where Kajika's stare didn't bother me, Alice's did. I couldn't explain what it was about her, but the huntress made my skin crawl. Perhaps because she was unpredictable and new and vindictive. Kajika never did anything fast.

Except moving.

He moved fast, but he thought and acted on his thoughts slowly.

"She brought a faerie?" Alice wound a hand around Kajika's forearm.

He shrugged her hand off. "Lily Wood comes in peace, Alice."

Alice glared at Lily; Lily glared right back.

Alice pressed up on her tiptoes to reach Kajika's ear, and still she didn't reach it. "She's a faer—"

"I know what she is." His voice was rough and deep, and as fierce as a whiplash.

"We're making exceptions now?" she asked disdainfully.

"Lily is not here to cause us harm."

Alice's eyes darted to mine. She must not have liked what she saw in them, because she looked away, eyes so thin they were mere slits. "I need a drink. This party reeks of adolescent hormones."

When she walked over toward one of the coolers spilling over with ice and beer bottles, I asked Kajika, "Did you find anything?"

Still staring at Lily, he pulled a Ziploc from his jeans' back pocket. "A comb. It had a hair. I do not know if it is hers, though."

I studied the ivory comb.

"For all it is worth, Catori, I never believed Ley to be a part of your family, even though Gwenelda insisted she was."

I bit my lip. "I guess I'll know in a couple weeks."

"If you want to leave now," I told Kajika with a smile, "you can. You look like you're about to have an aneurism."

"Aneurism?"

"Like your head's about to explode," I explained.

He folded his arms that were ridged with muscle. "I am fine."

I smirked. "You look really uncomfortable."

The hunter kept staring around him, unsmiling. Yeah, this was torture for him. Alice returned with two bottles. When she offered one to him, he raised his hand. Told her he did not drink. She shrugged. Chugged one bottle, cast it into the lake with a throw that was too powerful to be human, then started on the next.

I caught a couple people staring at the huntress's toss, discussing it in loud whispers.

"Tone it down, Alice," Kajika growled.

She rolled her eyes and downed the second beer which she tossed a couple feet away. "Better?"

"You should not dull your senses with alcohol."

"Yeah, yeah," she muttered. "It barely gives me a buzz anymore."

"Hey, Cat!" Cass waved me over. "Robbie and Mara made it!"

"I see that." I smiled in their direction. "I should go say hi. Lily, want to come?"

She nodded eagerly.

When I reached them, Robbie enfolded me in a bone-crushing hug. "If it isn't my favorite feline."

"Shut up," I said, but smiled.

Robbie had been Blake's best friend, but we hadn't hung out much as kids because he was always studying, which won him a free ride at an Ivy League.

He extended his hand toward Lily. "I heard we had a celebrity in our midst. Pleasure to meet you."

Lily shook his freckled hand.

Two guys I didn't know pushed their way over to us at the mention of celebrity. "I told you it was Lily Wood," one of them told the other. And then he tried to put his arm around her shoulder. I shoved him so hard, he toppled over. Jaw as red as Cass's new leather pants, he shot back up to his feet. "She your lesbian lover or what?"

"I don't share with my sister. That would be wrong on so many levels."

I snapped my neck toward Ace, who stood so close to the bonfire, it seemed like the flames were seeping out of his skin. He strolled over to us and draped an arm around my shoulders, and even though I needed to push that arm off, remind him that I wasn't his, I let him hold me long enough to prove his point.

As soon as the sleaze-ball retreated with his slimy friend, I ducked out from under Ace's arm.

"Who were those assholes?" Ace asked.

"Guys I met at a club," Cass mumbled. "Probably shouldn't have invited them."

"You okay, Cat?" Ace's gaze roamed over me.

"They hit on your sister, not on me."

His blue gaze danced in the flames.

My heart pitched. "Did Cass invite you or did you invite yourself?" I made sure my voice was as dry as sand.

A muscle leaped in Ace's jaw. "People usually have to pay a fortune for me to make an appearance at their party, but tonight I stopped by for free." He smiled, and it was so frosty, it flicked all the warmth from my body. "Don't get your thong in a twist, Cat. I'm not staying. I just came to check up on Little Sis, and then I'll *flit* back away." He flapped his hands at his side.

When I'd first met Ace, he'd been arrogant and standoffish, but never hateful. The way he looked at me now . . . it was so filled with hate that I backed up. I would've run away had I not spotted shimmering flecks in the distance. Kajika and Alice were already prowling toward them. I took off after the hunters, not to join their ranks, but to hold them back.

"Kajika!" I called out to catch his attention.

The hunter stopped. Turned. Waited. "What are *golwinim* doing here?"

"I have no fucking clue," Ace growled back. He stood right behind me.

"You didn't come with them?" I asked.

"Do I look like I need bodyguards?" There was a serrated edge to his tone that sliced right into me.

Lily put a hand on her brother's arm as two of the fireflies morphed into men with gleaming gold eyes. Their skin, like Ace and Lily's, glowed in the moonlight. But it was the only part of their body that blazed since their black-clad bodies melted into the darkness of the beach.

"Silas?" Ace said.

"Ace." The golwinim I imagined was Silas inclined his head toward Ace. "The hunters hold one of ours. We came to request his immediate release."

"The *pahan* is lying," Kajika shot back.

"Unlike your people, I don't lie, *ventor*," the second guard growled.

Kajika lunged for him, but the guard, whose feet weren't anchored to the ground, shot away.

"Kajika, don't," I yelled. "Not here." I looked back at the bonfire and the human bodies around it. We were much farther than I'd originally thought, but still too close.

"They insult me, Catori. I do not lie."

I touched his back. "I believe you."

"Who do the hunters have?" Ace's eyes dipped to the spot of skin I'd touched.

"Pietro," Silas answered.

Ace's gaze jerked up to the guard's, face paling. "The hunters took him?"

"We followed his trail until we could no longer follow it. They have him in the house, but there is too much iron to step inside."

"I was just in my house. We hold no faerie inside," Kajika volleyed back, temper flaring.

"We do." The disembodied voice belonged to Alice. "I mean we did. He's no longer there."

Kajika's shoulder blades strained so precipitously they seemed about to snap off. "You took a *golwinim* prisoner?"

"He's the fae who killed Tom."

"Why was I not informed of this apprehension?"

"Because you're too soft on faeries."

Kajika's fingers curled into fists. "That is untrue."

"Then why are you always hanging out with *her*?" Alice's gaze set on me. "She's part faerie, isn't she?"

I felt Lily look at me then, but I didn't dare let the huntress out of my sight.

"You are all fools! Our people do not punish *pahans* by kidnapping them," Kajika hissed, and Alice took a step back. "We strip them of their *gassen*. Lead me to him, Alice."

Silas said, "I will follow."

"No you won't," Alice snarled. "Besides, we're not releasing him, so fuck off."

"Your hunter died of his own fault. He attacked Pietro with arrows. Wounded him." It was Silas who answered.

More *golwinim* took human shape and crowded around us.

"Even though I was not aware of the capture, the *golwinim* was spying on the cemetery," Kajika explained. "Many times, I caught him circling Catori's house."

"What?" I gasped. "Why didn't you tell me?"

"He was following orders," Silas answered. "He had no intent to harm her."

"Whose orders?" I asked.

The guard's golden gaze surfed straight toward Ace's face.

I spun around. "You had someone spy on me?"

Ace folded his arms.

"Since when?" I repeated, advancing toward him. I was about to punch his chest, not hard, but hard enough to drive in the message that I did not appreciate being spied on.

Ace gripped my wrists and held them away from his body. "Calm down."

"Calm down?" I tried to swing my fists, but his fingers were a vice. "Let go!"

"Or what?"

Anger welled behind my breastbone and flooded my body.

"You're going to spear me with one of your little rowan wood arrows?" Steam hissed between Ace's clenched fingers, curling into the night.

Kajika must've assumed it was smoke, that Ace was setting me on fire, because he moved toward us with the ferocity of a wild animal. Instead of loosening his hold on me, Ace spun me around and pinned his arms around my torso, before shooting upward, too high for Kajika to reach, but low enough that we could still hear the hunter's growl and see the slender wooden stick aimed toward Ace. Kajika had no bow, but I didn't doubt he could launch it powerfully enough to reach Ace.

"No!" I cried out.

Kajika loosed the arrow. Ace soared sideways. The arrow whispered past us, then plummeted into the dark lake beneath our hovering feet. The next moment, the guards pounced on Kajika.

"It's not what you think." Ace's breath was hot against the nape of my neck.

"Tell them not to hurt him!" I yelled.

"Why can't you care as much about me as you do about Kajika?"

"Ace, call them off before they kill him, or I swear I'll—"

Ace flipped me over. "You swear what? That you'll kill me?"

I glared at him, my hair flogging my face and his like a whip. "I will never forgive you if they hurt him. *Never.*"

Ace's pupils throbbed wildly, fiercely. The next second, he dove toward the beach. I shut my eyes, sure that we were about to crash, but the impact was soft. Ace released me inches off the ground. When I pressed up, my cheeks, palms, and knees were coated in sand. My feet slipped as I raced toward Kajika, who sat, arms scraped and leaking blood. The guards were gone. Only Lily, Alice, and Ace remained.

Rage roared inside my ears, as loud as a crashing wave. "What did they do to you?" I yelled, collapsing onto my knees and taking the hunter's arm.

Seconds later, screams erupted down the beach from us. My pulse pounded as I looked toward Cass's party, certain the *golwinim* had attacked *them*, but it wasn't the *golwinim* who'd attacked.

It was me.

THE CONNECTION

A wave hit the bonfire so hard the flames fizzled out. Gray smoke rose from the pile of wet sticks. The lake recalled its foamy waters, preparing another powerful roll.

People screeched, but they also laughed. Some began whipping off their sodden T-shirts and wringing them out. This time, when the wave struck them, they body-checked the cold water with eager squeals. The lake pulled away again, bloated again, spilled again. I wanted to yell at them to get out of the water, but couldn't get my mouth to work.

A hand touched my shoulder. *Lily.* She stared down at me, lips pressed together, head shaking. She squeezed my cold skin.

Keeping my gaze affixed to hers, I inhaled, exhaled, concentrating on evening my labored breaths, flattening my thunderous pulse. Slowly . . . slowly, the lake calmed. Soon its moon-lacquered surface barely rippled.

"What the hell was that freak storm?" Alice's squinty eyes were on the lake.

No one answered her, but I could feel the weight of Ace's stare. Kajika was in too much pain to look at me. He probably hadn't even realized what was happening around him.

"Show me your arm," I said.

But he kept it away. "It is healing."

The blood had stopped oozing. The same way I'd healed back in

Ruddington when the faerie had singed my hand, Kajika's skin knitted back together. Soon the faerie guards' slashes were mere pale lines. And then they were gone. And yet Kajika kept nursing his arm.

"Does it hurt?" I asked, trying to displace his fingers.

His feral eyes glowed almost red in the darkness, but his glare wasn't directed at me.

It was directed at Lily.

She backed away.

As I stood on legs that felt like cotton candy, Kajika growled, "For my protection?"

Ace came to stand between the hunter and his sister. "What happened?"

"She marked me, that is what happened!" Kajika released his wrist, which glowed with a W.

Lily curled her pale fingers to stanch the glow radiating from her palm.

"Stop saying it is for my protection! You *pahans* do nothing for others. Everything you do, you do it for yourselves."

I frowned. "No one's saying it's for your protection."

"Lily—" Kajika started but stopped speaking.

My gaze swung between the faerie and the hunter. Was Lily signing to him? Did Kajika understand sign language?

Lily's hands were firmly planted by her thighs.

Silent words shivered in the black air, accompanied by heavy stares.

"What the hell's going on? And more importantly, where are your little fireflies?" Alice asked.

"I sent them home," Ace said.

"I hope you told them not to show their rotten faces around Rowan again," Alice spat. "If they care to keep their rotten faces, that is."

"Give me Pietro, and I will tell them to keep their distance."

Alice shook her head, her boy-short hair fluttering around her face.

"Take me to him, then." Ace's stance was so rigid he resembled a marble statue.

"I do not answer to *pahans*."

"Kajika, tell your little huntress friend to release my man, or skies help me, I will tell the *lucionaga* it's open season on hunters."

Kajika didn't even seem to be listening. He kept staring at Lily, whose eyes had grown as wide as the moon.

My forehead grooved as he rose, as he took a step toward the faerie who cowered behind her brother.

"Don't you dare touch my sister," Ace growled.

"Remove your mark." Kajika squeezed his palms over his ears. "Remove your mark before I go crazy!"

"It can't be removed, Kajika." I looked at Ace. "I tried."

Ace held my gaze a second, but then looked away, jaw set in an inflexible line.

Kajika pressed his eyes shut so hard his entire face rumpled. "What have you done to me?"

Fear was stamped all over Lily's face.

"Stop it, Kajika. Stop yelling at her," I said.

"You do not understand what she has done!"

"Yes, I do. I'm marked too." I showed him my hand in case he'd forgotten. The brand wasn't flaring, though—for once.

"It is not the same." He backed away, but stopped suddenly. "Or is it?"

I frowned, not understanding his question.

Like rubber bands, his eyes snapped to Lily's, before shutting again. He made a sound like an animal in pain and then took off running down the beach. When I turned back toward Lily, she was shakily signing something to her brother.

Alice started to turn in the direction Kajika had fled.

"Take me to Pietro," Ace told her.

"He's in the abandoned lodge next to the cemetery. Go find him yourself," she snarled. "You can pick him up from there. Sorry, *pluck* him up. I'd heard you turned into flowers when you died, but I had to see it to believe it."

"What?" Ace's voice vibrated inside my bones. "You killed him?"

Alice fixed him with her snake eyes and then she started running, but Ace flew toward her and flung his shimmering dust into her face. She froze. Her body contracted, fell, and shuddered like a cockroach. And then she retched. She rose to her knees and threw up again. She began to scuttle away, but fell face first in the pool of vomit that was sinking into the sand.

I spun around. "Ace, stop. Stop or this feud will never end." I raised my palms to his face and pressed them against his hot, bristly skin to force him to look at me.

When he did, his eyes were slick with bloodlust. "If anything happens to my sister, another hunter dies. Perhaps this time it will be you." He ripped his face out of my cold, cold hands and shot up into the sky.

My eyes swam. I pressed the heels of my palms into them as I dropped onto the beach. A hand skimmed my knee. I opened my sore eyes. Lily was kneeling beside me, holding her phone out.

Would you like me to burn away her body?

"She's really dead?" I croaked.

Lily nodded.

I swallowed back the *no* pulsing against my palate. How could I explain Alice's death to my father? To Kajika? What revenge would the hunters wage on faeries—on Ace—if they discovered that he'd gassed her?

So I nodded, and Lily rose to her feet and walked to the crumpled body. Blue flames flickered over her skin and then lurched toward Alice, laminating her body in flames that ate at her clothes and then at her form until there was no more body, only ashes on the sand. Pale ashes that would not transform into a commemorative plant. Pale ashes that would be swept into the lake. That would sink to the bottom like silt.

I shivered, frozen by the horror of what I'd just witnessed, frozen by Ace's cruel retribution and pitiless warning. I shook harder.

Lily returned to me. Crouched before me. Raised her phone. *He would never kill you, Cat.*

Laughter and earsplitting music whirled around us. Those noises sounded so wrong.

Cat, he won't. Pietro was one of his closest friends.

All the more reason to kill me. Pietro died because of me. I prayed I was wrong, but I'd tasted venom on Ace's breath.

Let's go home.

Home. She considered my house *home.* The thought buffeted my thrashing emotions. "I won't let anyone hurt you, Lily." And not because I didn't want to die—which I didn't—but because what happened tonight was in no way her fault.

If anything, she'd saved Kajika by marking him.

Even if it had incensed him.

I let her hold my arm as we walked back toward Cass's party. I was glad for the support. As we made our way toward the crowd, I realized I hadn't asked Lily to save Alice. Maybe she could've called her soul back. Did that make me complicit in her murder? My gut rolled like the waves earlier and nausea crashed up my throat and into my mouth. I spun away from Lily and emptied my sour stomach. Tears pricked my eyes like needles.

Throat on fire, I swallowed.

Lily rubbed my arm, which brought on more tears, because my mother did the same thing when I was sick.

I scrubbed my hands against my swollen eyes. "Why was Kajika so angry with you?"

She glanced at me, bit her lip, then looked toward the calm surf dappled with demented partygoers. The water would freeze their drunken asses if they weren't careful.

Lily's phone appeared in front of my eyes, too bright in the darkness. I squinted to read her words, but then my squint turned into a wide-eyed stare.

"There you are! I was looking for you two everywhere!" Cass yipped, trotting toward us. "Did you see those waves? They were in-fucking-sane!" Her clothes were matted to her body, the feathers of the lariat glued to her speedily-rising chest, her bangs stringy. "I'm going back in. Come with me!"

"In a sec, Cass," I said, my voice shaking.

"Are you all right? You look like you've seen a ghost."

"No, no ghost," I whispered.

Lily's fingers tightened around my arm.

"But yeah, I don't feel too well. I think I got food poisoning."

Cass wrinkled her nose. "Aw. That sucks."

I nodded. "I'm going to head home. Happy birthday, sweetie." I freed my arm from Lily's grasp to hug my friend. "Be careful in the water."

Cass rolled her eyes.

As Lily and I watched her run back to the calm surf, I said, "Maybe it's because the mark is so fresh."

Lily gnawed on her lip.

"Did you know that could happen?"

Her gaze still cemented to the swimmers, she shook her head.

I scanned the beach for Kajika, but the hunter was long gone. "Do you think he can still hear you?"

She hoisted her shoulders.

No wonder Kajika was pissed. The bond had opened a direct line of communication between his mind and Lily's. "Can you hear *him*?"

She shook her head.

"Wow. That's going to be weird. *Wow*."

Lily winced.

"Maybe it'll stop tomorrow."

23

SIGN LANGUAGE

*K*ajika showed up at the crack of dawn the following morning. Dad wasn't awake yet and neither was Lily. I was only up because I started work at that time.

He got out of the pickup, slamming the door so hard the car shook. "I need to see her."

The checkered navy curtains of Lily's room were closed. "She's not awake."

He stared at the unmoving curtains. "She is."

"You can hear her?" I asked, partly astonished and partly worried.

"Do you think I am lying?"

"No." I pulled my denim jacket closed and started toward my car, but stopped in front of Kajika. "Look, she didn't know this could happen."

"I cannot have a faerie inside my brain, Catori. I will go insane. Already I have Blake's memories, now Lily's voice!"

"Calm down."

"How can I calm down? My head"—he tugged at his hair so hard I thought he would pull it out—"my head no longer feels like my own!"

I placed both my palms on his shoulders to calm him down and to hold him back. I feared he would barge into my house and strangle Lily. "Can you hear her when you're far away?"

"No."

"Then just stay away."

"Can she hear *my* thoughts?" His gaze was as wild and unfocused as his manners.

"No."

"Are you certain?"

"She said she couldn't, and I believe her."

He snorted, backing up so that my hands fell away. "You still trust faeries after they spy on you."

"Lily had no idea."

"Uh-huh."

"Kajika, even if Lily knew, she's not the one who asked him to spy on me, okay? That was all Ace. And trust me, I'm mad. Really mad, but I'm also exhausted right now, and I don't want to think about last night. Not right now anyway. Now you should go, because I need to go."

"I want to talk with her."

"Come back tonight."

"Now."

"Kajika—"

He stalked past me toward her window and knuckled the glass so hard I expected it to shatter. The curtain fluttered, and then Lily appeared, a ghostly apparition against the darkness of her room. Seconds ticked by in wary silence, seconds during which the hunter and faerie watched each other. I advanced toward Kajika, laid a hand on his forearm.

He shoved my hand off, then moved away at that lighting speed of his, lips curled into a snarl, palms sandwiched around his skull.

I stalked after him. "Wait."

He lunged into his truck.

I held on to his door so he couldn't slam it shut. "What was that? What just happened?"

"Let go, Catori."

"I won't let go until you tell me what she said."

"She said . . . she said. It does not even matter what she said. What matters is that she can speak inside me!"

"Maybe she can learn to control it."

He rubbed at the brand that flared on his wrist, rubbed it as though trying to erase it.

"Promise me you won't hurt her while I'm at work."

"I do not make promises I cannot keep."

My pulse thrummed underneath my skin that suddenly felt icy. "If anything happens to her, Ace said he would kill me."

Kajika snorted. "The faerie would never harm you."

"He killed Alice last night."

"He did what?" Kajika's gaze slammed back against my house, against Lily's curtains that were luckily closed. I didn't want her to be at the receiving end of that look.

"I tried to stop him."

"Sure you did. You did not even like Alice."

My fingers tightened around the cool metal doorframe. "Just because I disliked her doesn't mean I wanted her dead. You know me better than that!" My words, or perhaps my delivery, made the hunter's scowl falter. "Kajika, you kill Lily, Ace kills me. And then it becomes an all-out war, and innocents will get hurt in the crossfire. Is that what you want?"

A vein pulsed in the hunter's temple. "I would never have killed Lily," he muttered, staring daggers at his wrist.

"So I can go to work and not fear she'll be gone when I come back?"

Kajika raised his eyes back to mine. They were tinged red from lack of sleep. "She protected me last night."

I startled. "You believe her now?"

"I know how faerie brands work. It does not mean that I appreciate being branded or that *she* will not kill me if she desires me gone."

"I would never let her, Kajika. Besides, she is dying. So your brand, it'll fade."

Unlike mine.

I released his door and curled my fingers into a fist. My nails bit into the soft flesh of my palm.

"Did Alice attack Ace?" Kajika asked after a long beat. He sounded tired, drained.

He sounded like I felt. "She taunted him. From what Lily tells me, Pietro was one of Ace's closest friends, and from what I've gathered, Ace doesn't have many friends."

Motes of pollen glimmered in the pink dawn. It reminded me of *gassen*, or what I could see of it. Apparently, it was fluid, but not to hunters. Hunters saw through dust.

"Where is Alice's body?"

I swallowed, and my throat felt coated in thorns. "I asked Lily to burn it."

"You did what?" He slapped his steering wheel. "We do not burn our dead!"

The tips of my ears flamed. "Kajika, I was alone with Lily last night. I couldn't exactly drag a dead body down the beach. Not in front of the town. Imagine how many minds you would've had to wipe this morning."

"I would rather wipe hundreds of minds than have one of my people turn into ash like a fucking faerie."

I flinched. "I'm sorry." A breeze kicked up my hair. I ripped my hand through my loose strands, dragged them off my face, and coiled them beneath my collar so they would stay put. "I didn't do it to offend you." Tears pricked my tired eyes. "It was a shit night. A really shit night. So forgive me for Alice." I closed my eyes. Inhaled deeply.

For long seconds, silence entrenched us. I waited to hear the car door slam shut, the motor rumble. When neither happened, I cracked my lids open.

Kajika's bronzed skin was mottled with livid red splotches. "I must inform the others. And I need to speak to Gwenelda."

Annoyance lifted off his skin and turned the air acridly pungent. He was vexed he'd been left out of his clan's dealings, which I could understand. I wondered about Gwenelda's reasons for going behind his back. Had she stopped trusting Kajika because he was friends with me?

He shut his car door, and I jumped.

"Are you angry with me?" I asked.

Head bent over his steering wheel, he said, "I am angry with the world right now. I am angry with myself for not realizing what my people were doing. I am angry with Lily for marking me. With Ace for killing one of our own"—he looked up at me—"for threatening one of our own."

Relief coursed through my veins as powerfully as the wave had rolled over the beach last night. I suddenly wanted to tell Kajika about it, ask him about the *Mishipeshu*, pillage his mind for any fact he could have gleaned about this supposedly extinct caste.

"Are we training tomorrow?"

I blinked at him. "You'll still train me?"

"Yes."

I smiled, and my heart lightened a little. "Nine o'clock?"

He nodded, turned the key in the ignition, then drove away, tires spraying gravel on the emerald grass.

A breeze brushed through the rowan wood trees and lifted particles of dry dirt that plinked against the headstones of my ancestors. I never approached the rowan wood circle, never dared walk over it for fear of one of my ancestors sticking their hand out and seizing my ankle. It was a stupid fear, of course. To awaken, they had to be unburied and a spell had to be read. And there was no way in hell I would plant a shovel in that part of our background. Not that I would shovel any other place in our backyard. I might've been born to parents for whom death wasn't creepy, but to me, death was chilling.

Our front door swept open, jolting me out of my macabre thoughts. Lily was dressed in skinny jeans, a silky white shirt, and her starry sneakers. I cocked an eyebrow. She held her arms out in front of her, then with both forefingers extended, she bent her arms, and pointed at herself, then at me, and finally at my car.

"You want a ride?" I asked.

She joggled her head. Not a nod, but also not a no.

"Kajika promised not to hurt you."

She flipped her hand palm-side down toward her chest and drew a circle. I wasn't sure what that meant. She walked toward me, typing at the same time. When she arrived next to me, she propped her phone in front of me. On it was written, *please.*

I flattened my hand and made a circle. "This means *please?*"

She smiled and nodded, her golden rope of hair swinging around her slender neck. ***And this means come.*** She repeated her earlier sign.

"How do you sign *yes?*"

She made a fist and flicked her wrist twice.

I mimicked her, which earned me another smile.

As we walked to the Honda, she showed me how to sign the word car. Learning something that had nothing to do with faeries and hunters kicked some of the dread out of my bones. As I manned the bakery, Lily taught me more words. By the end of the day, I could make a couple sentences.

I was so proud, I displayed my new talent over dinner. Dad beamed, then insisted on being taught more phrases. We spent the rest of the meal attempting to make sentences and laughing when those sentences went awry.

Although I didn't want to go to bed that night, the second my head hit the pillow, I fell into a deep, dreamless sleep.

No.

That was false.

I did dream.

I dreamed of Ace.

I dreamed he'd asked me to marry him.

I woke up before giving him an answer.

24

DEVIL INCARNATE

*W*hile I worked on improving my aim, movement caught my attention. I turned my bow and arrow toward the spot that had shifted, finding it was a person and not a wild bird.

I lowered my bow. "Lily?"

She combed her fingers through her hair that had snarled from her flight. In seconds, the strands were separated and rested smoothly against her flushed cheeks.

Kajika stepped in front of me. "What are you doing here, little *pahan?*"

With her fingers inverted, she pressed her palms together, then slid her hands slowly out. I didn't know that sign, so was thankful when Kajika said, "Peace?" He spit out the word. "I do not care if you come in peace. You should not be here at all."

"Kajika, it's okay. We have nothing to hide."

His shoulders tightened. "You will stay quiet?" He made a noise that sounded so savage, Lily stepped back, tripping on an old beer can. She fell, eyes wide in surprise.

I shot out from behind Kajika and extended my hand. Once she latched onto it, I hoisted her up. The back of her white shorts was stained brown.

I'm not sure why I laughed—it was incredibly childish—but I couldn't help it. Lily's cheeks flamed as she took in her mud-spattered shorts.

"I'm sorry." I pressed my forearm against my mouth to throttle my out-of-control giggling.

Blue flames engulfed Lily's right hand.

Kajika, who must've thought Lily was about to lash out at me for making fun of her, rammed into me and hauled me back. The corners of Lily's lips turned down as she loosed the fire on the stain. In seconds the brown was all gone, but not her frown.

"That is what you *say*," Kajika hissed.

"What does she say?" I shoved him off me.

"That she was not going to burn you."

I twirled and glared at Kajika. "Of course she wasn't going to set me on fire!"

"You are mad at me?"

"You think the worst of people."

His jaw set.

"But thank you," I conceded. "For having my back. You okay, Lily?"

"Are we going to have a tea party, or are we going to work on improving your skills?"

"Did you just make a joke, Kajika?" I grinned.

The hunter scowled at me, and then he scowled at Lily. I'm not sure what she said through their bond to earn her a scowl, but considering she smiled, it must've been something that pricked Kajika's ego.

"Catori, get in position."

Still smiling, I flicked two fingers against my forehead. "Yes, sir."

"Her target is that tree." Kajika pointed it out to Lily.

For the past half hour, I'd been squinting at the squat, flowery tree that looked, from where we stood, no bigger than a pink-haired troll figurine. It was ridiculously far and out of my reach. I nocked an arrow, closed one eye, then raised my bow. I let it fly in the right direction, but it fell far, *far* from its mark. I didn't have the strength to power that shot.

"It is not impossible," Kajika grumbled.

"Well it's not easy."

"I was not talking to you, Catori."

"Oh." I glanced at Lily who had her arms crossed over her chest.

"Catori, give me your bow."

I handed him my bow.

"The *pahan* doubts my skills."

"Kajika's really good, Lily."

She fixed her gaze on Kajika's hands that fit a feathered arrow against the bow string. He pulled his right arm back, sinews and tendons shifting underneath his sun-browned skin. He closed one eye, raised his hands. His chest lifted slowly, fell even slower. I held my breath.

He released the arrow. It ripped through the blue air, a sharp white blur that shrank until it was barely visible. A white dot on brown bark.

"Told you," I whispered to Lily. I hadn't doubted he would hit the tree, but that didn't lessen my awe.

Kajika pressed the bow back into my hands, a bead of sweat trickling down the side of his smug face.

Suddenly, he looked up at Lily, the smugness gone. "Yes, it was static, but we do not train on moving targets." A beat passed during which Kajika's brow, in turn, creased and smoothed. "Are you volunteering?"

Lily's eyes didn't leave the hunter's face.

"I have a few store-bought ones made of bamboo."

I gasped as I made sense of their one-sided conversation. "Absolutely not! We are not shooting at Lily."

"Bamboo will not poison her."

"But iron will."

"The tips are not made of iron. And they are blunt."

"Still," I said, heart knocking around my ribcage. "I'm not shooting at Lily, and you're not either!"

Lily placed her hand on my arms and tipped her face down.

"She is telling you that faeries move fast and that if you train on unmoving targets, all of it will be for nothing. You will not stand a chance."

"But—"

"Why would you help us, Lily?" Kajika asked. "What do you get from this?"

Her face colored. She dropped her gaze to a patch of yellowed grass.

"Why must Catori improve fast?" Kajika cocked an eyebrow. "Danny? Who is Danny?"

Lily soared toward the tree Kajika had hit.

"I can still hear you," he said, but it was so low that *she* wouldn't hear him. "*Daneelie*. Who is this *Daneelie* person, Catori?"

Cold sweat stuck my T-shirt to my suddenly rigid spine. "Maybe . . . me."

His frown deepened.

I spun my mother's ruby ring around my finger. "The Gottwas called them *Mishipeshu*."

"*Mishipeshu*?" His amber eyes widened. "*Mishipeshu*?" He stared at me as though I'd somehow morphed into a scaly monster.

"*Part*. I'm still part hunter. I might be. Lily doesn't know for sure. Besides, you hate Seelies, so shouldn't that make you happy?"

"I do not know what to make of this. I have never encountered a *Mishipeshu*, but I have heard stories. Stories that would give you nightmares."

I shivered.

"Can you shapeshift?"

"They don't really shape—"

"Can you?"

"No."

"What about breathing underwater?"

"I haven't tried."

"*Oh, Gejaiwe*," he murmured.

If only imploring the Great Spirit could answer our questions, but the Gottwas' Great Spirit was an Unseelie stuck in the dormant body of Negongwa, not an actual divinity that could solve problems. Of course, Kajika didn't know this. He believed hunters had been created to kill faeries. He didn't know hunters were made from a caste of imprisoned, bodiless faeries. That conversation needed to happen soon.

Lily was back. She signed the word *sorry* to me. I signed back, *it's okay*.

"I'm actually relieved he knows. Now he can tell me everything he's learned about *Mishipeshu*."

He was still observing me through narrowed eyes.

"I'm still me, Kajika."

"*Mishipeshu* were pure evil, because their magic was tremendous and dangerous, and their use of it cruel."

Great. So now I was part devil, part useless hunter, and part frightened human. And possibly part faerie. I hadn't gotten Ley's DNA results back.

"I realize that, Lily. I realize Catori is not malevolent, but power changes people. And most often, not for the better."

"I'm not going to turn into some monster, you guys." I repeated, "I'm not," because Kajika didn't seem convinced.

"I understand."

"What do you understand?" I asked, annoyed not to be a part of their silent conversation.

"I understand why you need to improve quickly. If you can manipulate the mist like Lily thinks . . . if Cruz and Ace know . . ." He let his voice trail off, but his unspoken words chilled me down to my very core.

25

DROWNING

*K*ajika's stories spun on a loop inside my mind, weaving themselves into vivid images. I'd slept fitfully, and not because of dream marriage proposals this time. My nightmares had pulled me out of bed long before my alarm would ring.

I pulled on running gear and left my house under a pearl-gray sky. Night lifted as I ran through the forest, past the cabin where Ace's friend had been killed and a new emerald-green vine coiled through a broken windowpane, past the cauliflower-lake. I erupted from the entrails of the forest onto the beach just as the sun peeked over the horizon. Sweat cooling, I stood unmoving on the white sand, watching the orange ball of fire rise over the lake, tinting the water blue.

I studied the water with apprehension and curiosity. I needed to know. This would either confirm I was indeed losing it or it would confirm I was part Daneelie.

After making sure the beach was deserted, I tugged off my T-shirt, rolled down my running shorts, kicked off my sneakers and socks. In my running bra and black underwear, I approached the cool surf. My toes sank in the wet sand as I walked farther. Green algae stroked my ankles and bare legs as I went deeper.

A violent shiver rocketed through me as I plunged in. Like millions of tiny needles, the water prickled my skin. I broke the surface and trod water until a minute amount of warmth trickled into my icy limbs.

I closed my eyes and inhaled deeply. And then I let my body sink. The air snuck out of my nose in a stream of tiny bubbles. I sank deeper as my lungs emptied. When they ached, I parted my lips. A jet of freezing water flooded my mouth. I gagged as it slid inside my throat. I clamped my lips shut, and even though I was dying to return to the surface, I powered through my desperate craving for oxygen. I opened my mouth again. Again, water shot down my throat, which clenched and contracted. It was no longer frigid but hot and thick, like boiled sap.

I needed to get out. With my prickling fingertips, I touched my arms and squinted through the water at my legs. No scales had formed. Lily had been wrong. Or if she'd been right, I had too little Daneelie blood for it to affect me.

Something splashed next to me. I jolted backward, pushing against the water to tread out of the way of whatever feathery beast had decided to dive in.

Lungs on fire, I kicked to break the surface just as two arms scooped me up and rocketed me up and out. Cold air slapped my wet skin. The arms released me over the beach.

I GASPED as my body collided onto the sand. And then I choked on the burning strip of oxygen that shot down my throat. I lurched onto my hands and knees and gagged as lake water spilled out of me. My body spasmed, and it felt like a boat was crushing my organs. Another spasm. Water laced with bile shot out of my mouth. How long had I been under? Two, three minutes?

When the coughing stopped, I sat back on my heels, whipped my hair out of my eyes, and turned to thank the person for coming to my rescue even though I hadn't needed rescuing.

Piercing eyes stared down at me. Angry. Narrowed. And blue.

So blue.

"What the hell were you attempting?" Ace's voice sounded far away, even though his body was close, inches from mine.

"Why . . . you . . . here?" My teeth chattered.

"I'm here because your fucking brand went haywire. Were you trying to drown?"

I locked my gaze on the foaming wavelets licking the shore. My experiment had failed. I couldn't breathe underwater. The texture of my skin hadn't altered. Since I didn't want to tell him I'd attempted to breathe underwater, I asked, "Why did you . . . have me spied on?"

"Pietro wasn't spying on you. He was looking out for Lily."

"You swear?"

"Were you trying to drown?"

"Pietro wasn't there fo—"

"Were you trying to drown?" he yelled.

"What does it . . . matter to you?"

He shuffled backward, palming his hair. "It doesn't matter. Your life *doesn't* matter to me. *You* don't matter to me! The same way I don't matter to you."

I wanted to tell him that he still mattered to me, but I couldn't admit that.

His body vibrated with fury. It rose off him like the tendrils of steam from his clothes. His jeans were almost dry, just like his white button-down shirt.

"You were right." I spoke slowly, evenly. "I tried to kill myself."

He tensed. If someone were to sketch his body at that moment, they would only need to draw angles and straight lines.

"Because I'd rather die by my own hand . . . than at yours."

His eyes shone so bright in the cool morning they looked like glow-sticks.

"So next time . . . please don't come . . . don't save me."

"Next time?" He gasped, then shook his head wildly. "Fine. *Fine.* Kill yourself! Giving up is so human."

"Why are you angry . . . if you don't care?"

"Because, Catori, it's fucking selfish of you, that's why! My sister would give anything to live, and you would give anything to die. Do you realize how fucked up your logic is?" he bellowed. "Do you?"

Ah. He wasn't angry because he cared about my life, he was mad because he cared about his sister's life.

Returning my gaze to the vast body of water beyond me, I said, "Go away, Ace. Just go away. I can't take your disdain right now."

He didn't go away.

My eyes stung. I closed them, then whispered, *"Vade."*

When I opened my eyes several minutes later, he'd heeded the Faeli word he'd taught me a long time ago.

He'd left.

26

THE SWIM

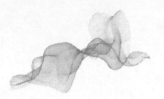

"*I* can't breathe underwater," I told Lily in a low voice, when she dropped by Astra's later that morning. "And my skin stayed . . . normal." I placed a mug of steaming, spicy tea in front of her. Chai, her favorite. "I tried this morning."

She wrapped her hands around the warm porcelain and peered into the milky brown liquid. After a second, she picked up her phone and typed, *Maybe it's a skill your body needs to learn.*

Making sure no customer was trying to get my attention, I dropped on the bench opposite her. "How am I supposed to pick up a skill without someone to teach me?"

Kajika might find out something useful.

"Or maybe you're wrong. Maybe I'm not that at all." I plopped my elbows on the table and cradled my achy forehead in my hands. Between not sleeping enough and my altercation with Ace, I felt like roadkill. I looked like it too. After getting home, I attempted to camouflage my under-eye circles with concealer, but however much I smeared on, the purple tint of my skin remained.

Lily touched the back of one of my hands. Pointed to her phone. *We'll figure this out.*

I nodded just as the door chimed. Faith waddled in, stomach first. I stood up lightning-fast. I didn't want her to think I was slacking. "Hey."

She stopped next to me and frowned at Lily. "I heard you two are living together now. Is that true?"

I nodded.

Faith made a face as though she'd sucked on something sour. "Why? Don't you have a way nicer house on Beaver Island, Lily?"

"She's not talking to her parents," I explained, hoping this was okay to share.

"Because they took Cruz's side after you cheated on him with Alessandro Bloom?" Faith asked.

Lily nodded, then sighed, while I blinked at her.

"Was it to get back at him for playing tonsil-hockey with your new roommate?" Faith tipped her head toward me.

Lily typed. *No. Alessandro was just irresistible.*

"He is real hot. Anyway, gotta drop off this bag. This pregnancy is killing my back, and my ankles have become kankles. *Ugh.* Three more months to go . . ."

Once she left, I hissed, "You cheated on Cruz with an actor?"

Lily rolled her eyes. *Of course not, but that's what the papers are saying. Better that story than the real one.*

I must've still looked aghast because Lily grinned and added to her message, *I have a type, and that type is dark-haired and handsome. I would never go for a blond guy. You can have all the blonds, Cat.*

I didn't want *all the blonds.* I wanted one blond, and that blond no longer wanted me.

Faith swung back into the room, so I left Lily to her reading and went to see if there was anything Faith needed me to do. Nothing beat menial jobs to rid my mind of thoughts of Ace.

THAT NIGHT, Kajika stopped by as Lily and I were getting dinner ready. Dad was hosting a wake at someone's house, but would be home soon.

I poured the hunter a glass of water and set it on the kitchen island. He drank deeply, then leaned against the kitchen island and folded his arms.

"Gwenelda remembered a story about *Mishipeshu.* Apparently their scales were made of metal, like an armor. Unlike armor, though, the scales were an aphrodisiac, so often times, faeries harvested them and ground them into a fine powder they would ingest or sell for profit."

"You mean, they plucked off their own scales?" I wondered if it equated waxing or peeling off skin. And then I shuddered at that contemplation.

"Sometimes. But more often"—Kajika eyed Lily—"other faeries would remove the scales against the *Mishipeshu*'s will."

Horrified, I stared at Lily. "Is that true?"

She shrugged. Did she think it was no big deal or had she shrugged because she didn't know the answer?

"She has heard of it," Kajika said. A beat passed. "It is the rarest commodity on the Neverrian marketplace nowadays, apparently."

Lily narrowed her eyes at Kajika.

The hunter slanted his dark eyebrows right back. "Catori should know, especially if she truly is part *Mishipeshu*."

"Maybe I'm not." I stirred the tomato soup on the stovetop, a recipe Blake had taught me a long time ago. "This morning, I went for a swim in the lake and tried breathing underwater. All I got was a lungful of water. And my skin didn't change." The creamy, tangy aroma propelled me back to a time and place when life was simpler. When skin didn't morph, corpses didn't rise from graves, and fire didn't run in people's veins.

"No!" Kajika's harshly spoken word brought me back to the here and now.

I set the wooden spoon down and turned. "No, what?"

The hunter's eyes were leveled on Lily like a double-barreled shotgun. "Nothing."

"Oh, come on!"

Lily grabbed her phone and started typing, but Kajika whisked it out of her hands. Instead of going after him, she walked toward the drawer where we kept the takeout menus. She took one out, uncapped a pen, and touched the tip to the paper, but Kajika ripped it from her.

Lily folded her arms and glowered at him.

"I imagine you will tell her after I leave, but it is a dire idea. Not to mention dangerous. What happens if she cannot come back, or if others notice her? Have you considered that?"

Small grooves splintered Lily's glare, swayed her certainty.

"Are you kidding me? One of you better tell me what's going on or I'll—"

"Knowing how reckless you can be, it is better you do not know. For your safety—"

I folded my arms in front of me. "I'm not reckless."

Lily pursed her lips.

My experiment slotted back to the forefront of my mind. "Not *that* reckless. Please tell me."

Neither spoke.

Lily's eyes dipped to the kitchen tiles.

"I'll find out sooner or later. I'd rather sooner than later."

"Fine. Lily would have told you anyway." Kajika let out a gravelly sigh and gave Lily back her phone. "She believes that you have to visit Neverra for your powers to manifest. Apparently *bazash* who are born in the human world do not have fire in their veins until they visit the *baseetogan.*"

My arms untied and plummeted against my sides like limp ropes. "You guys seriously think I'd risk going into the *baseetogan* to activate powers that could potentially enslave me or get me killed? I might be reckless, but I'm not on crack. I would never *willingly* leave my world and my father to become a faerie mermaid. Especially not after all the stories I've heard about the place. I mean, I have freaking faerie dust stored in my neck."

"Faerie dust you can use," Kajika said.

"It's still a hunter marking," I said, at the same time as Kajika said, "You did not tell Lily?"

He cocked an eyebrow at me.

"No I haven't told her. I was trying to forget about it," I mumbled.

"She killed Stella Sakar with it," he said point-blank.

A gust of air escaped through Lily's parted glossy lips.

"It happened once. For all I know, it was a total fluke and will never happen again. I don't even know how I did it." I pressed both my palms against my face and heaved a frustrated sigh. "All these weird things are happening to me, and I have no control over them. Sometimes I want to scream."

Thin fingers wrapped around my wrist and pried my hands away from my face. Lily stared up at me, her expression gentle.

"She says she can help you control it," Kajika said, shoulders squared tightly.

"I'd rather you help me remove it," I told her.

Her face scrunched up in disappointment.

"She says it is a great gift," Kajika said.

"It might seem like a gift, but to me it's a constant reminder of the life I took."

"That is because it is the first life you took, Catori. You always remember the first life you take." Kajika rubbed his hands as though he were washing away invisible blood . . . or dust.

"Even more reason to get rid of it. Is there a way, Lily? Please tell me there's a way."

She released my wrists, then turned to Kajika.

"She says that if the faerie dies, her dust should have vanished. There is no precedent for why you were able to use it, or why it is still inscribed on your skin if it belongs to you."

"So basically, she's saying there's no way to get rid of it?"

"She is saying that if there is a way, she does not know it."

"*Ugh.*"

"You should take her up on her offer, Catori. Learning to use it will be another weapon in your arsenal."

I was not interested in collecting weapons or waging war. I was not interested in killing more people. I wanted to study. Become a doctor. Save lives.

Why was the world adamantly giving me tools to take lives instead?

27

REVENGE

*I*n the end, I decided to take Lily up on her offer to learn to control Stella's dust—*my* dust. Originally, I hadn't wanted to learn, but then Kajika said, *what if you inadvertently killed someone you love with it?* That was motivation enough to learn to wield the undesired power safely.

So the following day after work, I drove to the barn with Lily. It seemed like a remote enough place to manipulate poisonous dust.

"How about a gasmask? Would that keep the dust out?" She wasn't worried about teaching me, but *I* was worried for her.

She shook her head.

"Or a bandana?"

She grinned and rolled her eyes, then signed that it would be okay. I wasn't convinced. Not in the least.

"How about you stay in the car and text me directions?"

She signed, ***stop***.

But I didn't. I came up with tons more ideas that sounded way more brilliant in my head than spoken aloud.

Once we arrived in front of the barn, the sky had darkened so much I almost missed the rusty pickup truck parked on the side of the building. "Did Kajika know we were coming?"

She shook her head. ***I didn't tell him***, she typed, just as her phone died. She grimaced, then dropped it in the cup holder with a sigh.

We parked next to the barn that glowed and colored the uneven land yellow. The door creaked as I pulled it open.

Kajika was training on the punching bag in the corner, an Eminem rap song blasting from a portable speaker. He was so focused, he didn't notice us at first, but it didn't take him long to sense he wasn't alone. The second he picked up our scents, his head snapped in our direction.

Sweat dripped down the sides of his concentrated face, down his ropy arms, down his carved pecs. Even though hunters didn't glow, he was so slick and flushed he looked lit from within.

"Hey," I said. "We didn't mean to interrupt."

Kajika trod toward us, unwrapping his gloves as he moved, but froze midway, one glove off, one glove on. His gaze zeroed in on Lily. So of course, I stared at her too. Spots of color stained her face.

I stared back at Kajika, frowning. His Adam's apple jostled in his glistening throat as he focused his attention on his hands. He pulled off his second glove, then, in a voice that was as tense as the line of his shoulders, he said, "I was just leaving."

"You don't have to go."

"I need to get home. Gwenelda has just returned."

"Returned from where?"

"A trip."

His vagueness didn't sit well with me. Gwenelda wasn't the type to take a vacation, so where had she gone?

Kajika crouched to retrieve his little speaker that was still spewing music. Once he powered it off, the barn became stiflingly quiet.

The stubborn set of my mouth or the hands I planted on my hips must've alerted him that I wouldn't let him leave without a better explanation.

As he flung everything inside his duffel bag and rose, he said, "She is still trying to locate other Gottwa descendants."

"Did she find any?"

"I will discover this tonight."

As he walked past us, Lily kept her gaze averted—not only averted but her eyes were closed—while Kajika's were wide open and unabashedly taking in the faerie.

What had she thought through their bond that made her so uncomfortable and him so shocked? The second the truck rumbled off, I asked her.

She bent her elbows, pressed the tips of her index fingers to the tips of her thumbs and shook her hands laterally and symmetrically. The sign for **nothing.**

I snorted. *Nothing, my foot.*

She crooked her finger at me, then signed the word **phone**. After entering my passcode, I passed her my phone. I thought she would type out an explanation, but I was wrong. She wrote step-by-step instructions of what I needed to do to pull the dust from inside of me.

But my dust lurked in a different place than hers.

I told her this. She simply bobbed her head and wrote **try**. So I tried doing exactly what she'd written—squeeze my hands tight until they prickled with the nervous tension of the magic desirous to be released —but besides embedding crescents into my palms, nothing happened.

She made fists, then opened her fingers and turned her palms face-side up. Gold specks flickered in the air over her palms. I stepped back. It was involuntary—I trusted Lily—but my body remembered the acrid taste as it had slid down my airways and swelled the lining of my throat. Lily balled her fingers, and the twinkling motes snuck back under her skin.

As soon as the air stopped shimmering, I gulped in a hungry lungful.

Lily slid my phone out of her denim shorts' back pocket, typed in my passcode, which she'd apparently learned by heart, and wrote, **You don't have to hold your breath.**

A thought slithered into me at her words. "The one time I used it"— Stella's gray face swam in front of my eyes—"I tasted it. I don't think it came from my fingers, Lily. I think it came from my throat. Is that possible? Could it leak out through the tattoo?"

With you, anything is possible. Do you remember how you coaxed it out?

"You mean, besides feeling homicidal?" I carved my hand through my loose hair.

I'd tried to erase the memory of that day from my mind, but it lurked just beneath the surface, its strings shivering in my peripheral vision. If I so much as plucked one of the strings, the entire confrontation unfolded, beat by awful beat. I closed my eyes and tugged on the string inside my mind, unspooled the memory. I shivered and shuddered as it played again in vivid detail. Like a kids' coloring picture, it filled with new spots of color.

"It pulsed furiously, as though it wanted to get out. As though it had a mind of its own or was a separate entity."

Lily listened, face cocked to the side.

"When I touched my neck, the skin was deadened. That's how I knew it had left my body, but I thought it had left because Stella had somehow taken it back. I didn't realize the dust had *escaped* to kill her."

Chewing on her bottom lip, she typed, *The only reason we bring it out through our hands is to better control it. Technically it could come from any place on our bodies . . . But our dust is spread thin in our veins, whereas yours is localized in one place. What happens when you touch the tattoo?*

"The dust pulses harder." I touched the tip of my index finger against one spot on my tattoo to show her—if there was even anything to see.

Lily stepped in closer, eyes going from narrow to wide in seconds. *It rushes to your finger. I mean the other lines stay visible, but it's like a volcano in that one spot.*

"Don't stand so close, Lily."

She shushed me with a flick of her hand. *Put your entire palm over your tattoo and tell me what you feel.*

It felt as though I'd lowered my hand inside an ant farm, as though thousands of tiny furry legs were traipsing over my palm. I told Lily this.

Pull your hand away really slowly.

I stepped back—even though Lily was fearless, I was cautious—and yanked my hand off.

Lips pinched, she shook her head. *What part of really slowly did you not understand? Try it again. SLOWLY.*

I placed my palm against my throat and waited for my hand to feel engulfed by ants again. When my skin tingled, I pulled my hand away excruciatingly slowly, millimeter by millimeter. The tingling continued but the sensation changed. It was almost as though some magnetic field had formed between my throat and my hand, like my skin had been covered in cobwebs and those cobwebs were stretching as I pulled.

I peeked down, and sure enough, glittering filaments strained between my palm and my throat. My heart sped up at the sight. Amazed and shocked, I tugged my hand off, and the invisible threads tore. "Did you see that?"

Lily nodded, a smile brightening her face, which was too close to me again.

"What the hell are you doing, Lily?" The gruff, intrusive voice made both Lily and me spin.

Ace stood mere feet away, a deep scowl ingrained in his features.

Lily relaxed and signed something to her brother. I picked up no words in the rapid-fire series Lily executed, but I imagined she was telling him she was teaching me to use dust.

Ace signed back to her, his scowl deepening so fast it would leave permanent grooves in his forehead if he wasn't careful. One sign, a fist knocking against his temple, was familiar to me: *stupid*.

I folded my arms against my chest tightly. "Don't call her stupid."

That caught Ace's undivided attention. He glared. "She teaching you sign language too? *Wow.* And here I thought my sister was the smart one."

Lily's breaths hitched, and then her hands zipped through the air to form more words.

Ace barely glanced at the frenzied movements of her hands. "I found a better arrangement for you. A penthouse in New York. I secured it and stocked it. Let's go."

My heart whacked my ribs, and my brand flared. I wanted to say, *don't take her away* and *Lily's safe here*, but was she? In a town overrun by hunters? With one hunter who could read her thoughts? Keeping her here would be all shades of selfish.

Ace's palm glowed so brightly, it turned into a beacon of light. He curled his fingers into the tightest fist known to mankind. "A fucking hunter can get into your head, Lily. It's not safe for you here."

Lily signed something.

"I know I'm the one who brought you here, but I don't know what I was thinking." Anger flowed off him in fierce gusts.

"Is it really for her safety that you want to take her away?"

Ace closed the distance between us so fast his heated breaths hit the tip of my nose. "You're flighty and irresponsible. With poisonous blood and an unhealthy fixation on learning to use your hunter skills. Since I've dropped her off, you've put her in danger more than once. First you bring her *here*"—he spit on the floor—"with a hunter, and not just any hunter, but your little fuck buddy."

I jerked away from him, dust pulsing so hard against the skin of my neck I clamped my mouth shut and gritted my teeth to keep it in. Not that it would lurch up my throat. At least I'd figured out it didn't work that way. "He's not my *fuck buddy*," I hissed.

"Whatever. You and him, you're not good for her. You're using her, milking her for information on how to destroy faeries. Don't think I haven't attended your little *training* sessions." He air-quoted the word training.

That set me off. I poked him with my finger. "If you *watched* them, then you'd know your sister came of her own volition and volunteered to help. I didn't drag her here and make her teach me anything. Besides, I have no fucking interest in killing faeries." I was still poking him when what I really wanted to do was push him away. I shoved him hard, but his body didn't budge. I tried again but it was like trying to displace a brick wall.

He smirked. "All those hours of practice with Kajika and not much to show for it, huh?"

His sarcasm pissed me off. But it wasn't the only thing that pissed me off. My freaking weakness ticked me off. Ace caught my wrist and held it. I pulled, but couldn't break free of his hold.

"I take it back," I said.

His pupils widened, turning his eyes as dark as my own. "What part do you take back?" His voice was so husky it thickened my blood.

I raised my chin. "The part where I said I had no interest in killing faeries. There is one I could do without."

"Careful, little hunter."

"Of what?"

He yanked on my wrist, almost dislodging my shoulder. I staggered forward, slamming into his hard chest. He dropped his mouth to my ear. "Of me. Of what I could do to you."

My imagination got carried away, and not with scenes of torture.

The panoramas in my mind were of a much different nature. Inches of bare skin. Warm fingers and tongues. Sweat beading down a sculpted torso. Hardening nipples. Mine. His. A hand sliding down. A sapphire ring glinting on slender fingers.

Was that supposed to be my hand? I didn't own a sapphire ring.

Cold air filled my mouth and throat like a gulp of wintry lake, stinging my lungs. I felt disoriented, confused, as though I'd stepped out of my body and was watching a stranger. A stranger who was fantasizing about a deadly faerie.

Like an elastic, I snapped out of my trance. "How dare you, Ace?" I yelled. "Using *captis* on me!"

Although his features tightened, his fingers did the exact opposite. I slipped my wrist out of his hold and nursed it against my rapidly rising chest.

"Was that even me in your twisted scenario, 'cause I don't have a sapphire ring!"

He frowned.

"What game are you playing? Break the little hunter's self-esteem, then break her freewill? You might think I'm weak and pliable, but I could hurt you if I chose." Tears pricked my eyelids. "I could *really* hurt you, Ace Wood." The outline of his body feathered. "I just choose not to."

He stayed still.

So very still.

The dust in my neck still pulsed, but its rhythm had turned sluggish, as though it felt the immediate threat to its owner was gone. I looked for Lily, but she was no longer there. I wondered when she'd left. Before or after her brother had toyed with my emotions?

"You are such a child, Ace." I knew the man in him would hate that comment. Sure enough, he flinched. "Picking on me because I ended things between us. Your sister is a million times more mature than you. You don't see her vengefully plotting Cruz's destruction, even though what *he* did to her is unforgivable."

Ace stared at me, his eyes a blur of blue through my tears.

"I pushed you away for your own good," I murmured. "How is that unforgivable?"

After a terribly long beat, he said, *"My own good?* How about you let me decide what's good for me, Cat?"

And then he stalked out of the barn.

Once the heavy door banged shut, I yelled from frustration. And then I strode over to the punching bag in the corner and smashed my fists into the hard leather until my knuckles cracked and bled.

THE FOREST

*W*hen I arrived home that night, knuckles as raw as my mood, I half-expected Lily to be gone, but she was having tea with my father in the living room, laughing at a story he was recounting.

Dad jumped to his feet at the sight of me, his gaze zipping down to the dried blood coating my hands. "Honey, are you all right?"

Lily peered at my hands over the rim of her tea mug, a frown pleating her brow. Did she think it was her brother's blood?

Silly me.

Faeries had fire, not blood. I might've laughed maniacally if I hadn't felt so drained.

Dad must've thought I was in shock, because he led me over to the couch and made me sit next to Lily. She set her mug down.

"I'll get some antiseptic and Band-Aids." He climbed the stairs two at a time.

I wanted to tell him it was okay, but decided to let him baby me, if only to get a little privacy to find out if Lily was leaving. Before I could ask, she tapped on my phone's lit screen.

"*You* had my phone?" I'd spent way too long scouring the barn for it.

She clicked her nail against the screen to get my attention. *Right.* Her message. **You didn't make up?**

I looked up so fast, my neck creaked. "You thought we'd make up?"

She nodded.

I sandwiched my lips. "That's not going to happen, Lily."

Why not?

"I thought you were staying out of the Ace-and-Cat-drama?" From the tapering of her eyes, I guessed that answer didn't please her, so I added, "Ace is too childish for me." I added a sigh to my explanation so that she believed it.

Lily blinked and leaned away from me, as though my comment had physically pained her. I tugged a hand through my hair, which was still damp from my strenuous punching session.

"I found the antiseptic, but where are the Band-Aids?" Dad asked, rushing down the squeaky stairs.

"Kitchen drawer," I said.

Drawers clanked and banged as he searched for the right one. I could've given him clearer directions, but it bought me a few more seconds. "You're not leaving, are you?"

Still looking at me through those pained gray eyes of hers, she shook her head, but it was so faint, it was barely a shudder.

Exhaling a frustrated breath, she seized my phone again and typed a message just as Dad reappeared from the kitchen with everything he needed to patch me up. If only he could patch me up on the inside too, slap a Band-Aid or two on my heart. As he worked on one of my hands, Lily lifted the phone in front of my face.

My cheeks flushed bright as I read it, and brighter when Dad's eyes darted toward the screen. I grabbed the phone from Lily's hand and powered it off before he could read any more. If he caught any words, he didn't mention them.

Lily rose and walked to her bedroom, shutting the door behind her.

"So who did you punch?" Dad asked after a long stretch of silence.

"What?"

He nodded toward my puckered knuckles.

"A punching bag."

"Is there anything left of it?"

A small smile flitted over my trembling lips. "Believe it or not, it looks better than me."

After Dad tended to my broken skin, he looked up at me. "What made you assault a punching bag?"

I sighed. "I was angry. At a boy." Not only was my answer truthful, but it would put a stop to the discussion. Dad enjoyed discussing boys as much as I enjoyed funeral shop-talk.

Surprisingly, he asked, "Kajika?"

I shook my head. "No. But, Dad, you really don't have to worry."

"My little girl injures herself over some boy, and you don't think I'm going to worry?"

As he squashed the unused Band-Aids back inside the little carton, I stood up and kissed his forehead. "I promise, Dad, you have nothing to worry about. By tomorrow, I'll be over him."

He let out an unconvinced grunt, but he didn't say anything else or go after me when I went to my bedroom.

I closed my door softly, then slid down the painted wood and turned my phone on to reread Lily's message.

My brother might act like a child sometimes, but he is the kindest, most loving and protective person in your world AND in mine. And he loves you. Yeah. LOVES you. You'll never find a better man, Cat. Never. You are an IDIOT. That's all I'll say. After this, we'll never speak about it again, because if we do, I'll get really really angry with you and call you an idiot AGAIN!

The tiny black curves making up her words fragmented and aligned at wrong angles, blurred and blotted. I blinked. They cleared up and realigned, their curves again smooth and unbroken. But then new tears formed in my strained eyes and the message distorted again.

Ugh. I tossed my phone on my bed and wept for my sorry-ass self a while longer. *Maybe I am an idiot, Lily, but I'm an idiot who's trying to keep your brother safe.*

THE FOLLOWING MORNING, after a restless, dreamless night, I pulled myself out of bed and went running before dawn broke over Rowan. I ran hard and fast, my brand burning so hard it felt like the fiery W was leaking into my blood.

Ace didn't show up. Not that I was expecting him to. He no longer came when my brand flared.

Instead of taking my usual route toward the beach, I headed in the opposite direction, down winding trails I hadn't taken in years. Woodchips crunched under the soles of my sneakers, leaves on low branches fluttered as I blew past them, birds chirped in the tall pines, insects buzzed beside my head. None of those insects glowed unnaturally.

After half an hour, I turned back and walked to catch my breath. Just as I was about to pick up the pace, so I wouldn't be late to work, a body dropped from the sky.

A glowing and very familiar body.

It landed inches from me.

"Hi, Catori."

I froze, then scanned the woods for other faeries, but the rest of the forest was calm.

Too calm.

Dreadfully calm.

THE PROPOSAL

*C*ruz stood before me, eyes blazing green in his tanned face. He smiled, a chilling, too-bright smile. I scrambled backward, stumbling over a thick branch. I grabbed hold of a trunk to steady myself.

Slowly, I reached into my pocket for the tiny rowan wood arrow Kajika had given me. I never left the house without it anymore.

Cruz punched the middle of my arm, making the stick fly out of my grasp. He picked it up, and smoke curled from his skin. He flung the poisonous wood wide into the brambles, and I cursed myself for having whipped it out so clumsily.

My dust pulsed against my throat. I raised my hand to it, touched it.

"Hands down, Catori. I didn't come here to hurt you."

Heart zinging, I let my arms drop. The W burned harder, a stinging reminder of the bond I'd broken because of the boy standing in front of me.

"Why'd you do it, Cruz? Why'd you tell Gregor that Lily took the book? I thought you loved her . . ."

"She was guilty. You know it. Why would I take the fall for something I never wanted in the first place?"

"You never wanted what?"

"To sever our bond. I liked being linked to you. I liked you. I thought it was mutual until you met the prince and forgot all about the pauper."

I backed up, and my back hit the tree. This was crazy-talk. Cruz was crazy. My fingers scrabbled against the rough bark behind me. It wasn't rowan wood, but if I could break off a large enough piece, I could hit Cruz with it and stun him long enough to raise my hand and try to coax my dust out. Was I really contemplating asphyxiating Cruz?

"Ace and I are no longer together in case you haven't heard. We weren't right for each other."

"Oh, I heard. That's why I'm here."

"I'm not looking for a replacement, and if I were, it would certainly not be a traitor or a faerie. I'm done with faeries."

Cruz smiled again, that sleazy smile of his that made his eyes glow artificially. "But faeries aren't done with you, Catori."

My breaths hurtled up my throat, pumping my chest out and in.

"Guess what?" His leather jacket crackled smoothly over his white V-neck as he approached me.

I gulped. "What?" I slid my nails under a piece of coarse bark, wheedling it until I could slip the tips of my fingers underneath.

"You still owe me two *gajoïs*."

My fingers froze. "You said we were square."

He grinned, then lifted three fingers and bent them as he ticked off. "Saving your dad. Cleaning up your kitchen. Calling Kajika to the rescue."

My hand skidded down the uneven trunk. My entire body vibrated with equal parts anger and dread. They swarmed me so fast my vision darkened. I blinked, hoping my mind wasn't about to shut off.

Cruz looked toward the sky, then toward me. "Neat party trick."

The clear sky was now tiled with woolly gray clouds. *Shit.* "Hunter powers are fascinating."

He cocked his head to the side. "Hunters can control the weather?"

I swallowed. My throat felt parched and bloated. "We can control lots of things."

"Show me."

"I hear there's a fabulous circus in Detroit. If you're that desperate for entertainment, I suggest getting yourself a ticket."

He chuckled. "The only performance I'm interested in is yours."

"Are you claiming your *gajoï*? If so, I'll oblige."

He cleansed his face of amusement. "No."

"Well, then, there'll be no display of supernatural powers this morning." My fingers crawled back up the trunk.

He leveled his gaze on mine. "You will ask me to marry you."

I froze. "I most certainly will *not*." As though Cruz had wrenched his fist inside my abdomen, my gut clenched. I brought both my hands to my stomach. The pain intensified so fast and so hard, black dots danced on the edge of my vision.

"You will."

"No," I croaked. My stomach contracted so violently, I bent over and threw up. I'd skipped dinner and hadn't had breakfast yet, so the only thing that came out was acrid bile.

Maybe I could beat the pain. Maybe it would go away if I waited long enough. My stomach spasmed, and again I heaved. Cold perspiration coated my forehead, ran down my jaw. Goosebumps rose over my collarbone and neck.

My neck.

I lifted a hand to where the dust pulsed like an infection, but Cruz caught my wrist. He knew. *He freaking knows how it works!* How? Had he also spied on my training session with Lily? Had Lily told him? The thought of them having a conversation was ludicrous.

Clasping both my hands now, he crouched in front of me. A nerve ticked in his jaw. "It won't stop until you ask me."

"Why?" I whispered. "Why are you doing this?"

"Because I want to and I can."

I desperately wanted to kick him, but pain scrambled my brain and impaired all connections to my limbs. A crippling ache gripped my gut. I screamed. Screamed for someone to come. Anyone. Ace's name was on my lips, but I didn't utter it. Not in front of this insane faerie.

I thought about Lily as sweat poured down my collarbone. To think she'd been engaged to this asshole. I swiped my tongue over my lip, dug my teeth into my lower lip.

The idea slammed into my harried brain with such force, it jerked my body. Lily's punishment for breaking her engagement was fatal because her body wasn't made to live outside Neverra.

Mine was.

Besides, his bargain involved marriage, not a move to Neverra.

When a new wave of pain pounded into my center, I hissed, "Fine! Will you marry me, Cruz?" Like shrapnel, the words blew away the crushing force.

"It will be my honor, Catori Price." Cruz let go of my wrists and rose to his feet.

I slapped him. Instead of incensing him, my reaction made him smile. In that moment, I detested him more than I'd ever detested anyone.

"Let's get the second *gajoï* out of the way. What else do you want from me?"

He swiped his finger down the bridge of my nose as though I were his pet. I snarled, which just increased his smile. "Oh, dear Catori, what would be the fun in playing all my aces in one sitting?"

"Something's seriously wrong with you, Cruz," I muttered, my breathing choppy, my words even choppier. "Why? Why do you want me to marry you? Is this some sick fantasy of yours? Is it to punish Lily?"

He loomed over me, eyes shadowed by the black curls of hair falling over his forehead. "It's to punish *you*, Catori."

"Me?"

"You rejected me, and then you made me look like a deranged, needy man. Oh. And then you dated my closest friend, my brother. Cruel behavior has consequences."

"What a great wife that'll make me."

"My thoughts exactly."

"I was being sarcastic."

"Perhaps I was too." He hooked a finger underneath my chin, raised my head so that our gazes locked. "I should get our love nest ready."

I shoved his fingers off my chin. "I might be marrying you, but I'm not moving to Neverra with you."

"Yes, you are. That's the only place faeries can be officially joined."

"Should've included that in your—" My stomach clenched, which made my teeth clench in turn.

He grinned. "It was implied. Glad your body knows the rules."

Ugh!

"I'll pick you up at dawn."

"Fuck you."

"You don't need to pack anything."

Tears blended into the sweat tracking down my face.

"You'll be ready, right? I won't need to chase you down?"

"Do I have a choice?" I muttered.

He shook his head. "Don't look so angry. You'll *love* Neverra."

Even though accepting shattered me, I spoke the words before the pain made me black out. The Great Spirit only knew what Cruz would do to me if I were unconscious. "I'll be ready."

As quickly as an anesthesia, numbness replaced pain.

"I'll probably get killed as soon as I step through the portal," I said bitterly. "You forget I'm part hunter."

"I forget nothing."

I frowned, rubbing soothing circles over my abdomen even though it was no longer cramping.

"I also haven't forgotten that only Ace can kill you, but I doubt he'll bother."

The clouds mottled the sky overhead. "He might kill *you* once he knows you forced me into this."

He smirked. "Catori, don't you think I've had time to plan this all out? I'm a hundred steps ahead of you. You won't be informing him that this is a bargain. You'll be telling him this was a choice. *Your* choice."

"Why would I ever do that?"

"Because I have something you want."

My brand flared, burning bright in the gray cover of trees and clouds. Had he kidnapped my father?

"You care about Lily."

My head jerked back in surprise. Where was he going with this?

"I can get her back into Neverra."

My eyes widened, but squinted almost as fast. "You're bluffing."

"I don't bluff. But, hey, if you don't want to save your new little friend, then by all means, tell Ace."

I could feel the storm in the sky, humid and sticky like a second skin.

I was engaged to a monster.

"I'm not the girl you fooled a long time ago."

"Oh, I know that. I know exactly what you are."

I sucked in a breath. Did he know Lily's suspicions about my nature? I blinked as frustration fractured my eyesight into a thousand dull pieces. "I hate you." I whispered the words, but he heard them, because his jaw flexed.

"The best marriages aren't built on love."

"The best marriages aren't built on hate either," I hissed.

"Arranged marriages—"

"Stop trying to justify yourself! You are spiteful, and by God, if I didn't care for Lily, I would kill you on the spot, but I'd rather save her life than end yours. Lucky you, huh?" I gave a dark, brittle laugh.

His face became an impassive mask as his feet levitated. "I'm going home to announce our imminent union."

I leveled a gaze that would have killed him if dust could shoot out of my eyeballs. "When will you tell me how to save her?"

"On our wedding day."

"Which is when?"

"During the next Night of Mist. In eighteen Neverrian days."

I did the math at lightning speed. Eighteen Neverrian days equaled ninety Earth days. *Three months.* "Will you let me come back here at all?"

"If you behave, perhaps."

"And you swear that in three months, you'll tell me how to get Lily back inside Neverra?"

"On my mother's life."

"You don't give a shit about your mother."

"I've changed my mind about her."

I snorted. "Why doesn't that surprise me?"

"If I were you, I wouldn't waste what precious hours you have left here spiting me. I'd go home and spend it with your father. After all, you won't be seeing much of him soon."

His reminder was a nail gun aimed at my heart, and his eerie smile the finger on the trigger, embedding spike after spike in my shuddering organ.

"You might want to tell your father you're taking a little trip."

How far could I get before Cruz returned to fetch me? I could board a plane and fly to South America or Canada. And then what? Live on the run? The second my brand flared, Ace would locate me. He might not drag me back if he knew what Cruz wanted from me, but for him to know, I would have to tell him about the bargain. As though my stomach had heard my internal musing, it cramped.

Reneging on my bargain wouldn't save Lily's life. Besides, running would still separate me from my father and probably shred my stomach.

Eighteen days.

I could survive eighteen days in Neverra. I pushed away the reminder that those eighteen days would last much longer than normal days.

"Oh, and inform your father that where you're going, cell phone reception will be spotty. Don't worry though, every couple days, I'll go through a portal to send him a reassuring text message from your phone. Or you can tell him we're eloping." His eyes twinkled at the suggestion.

I would most definitely not tell my father I was going to get married to Cruz Vega. But would he find out? "Will it be in the papers?"

"If you want it to be."

"You're giving me a choice?"

"I'm not all bad, Catori."

Yes, you are. You are a hundred percent evil, Cruz. I didn't voice my thoughts, but I made sure my scowl conveyed my opinion. "It stays out of the papers."

"Noted."

"And once we're married? Once I've fulfilled my end of the bargain, will I be allowed to get a divorce—or whatever the hell it's called in Neverra—and move back here?"

Cruz frowned. For all his careful planning, his grooved forehead and narrowed eyes told me he hadn't considered what would happen after the wedding. "I suppose you'll be free to do what you wish, but once you break a marriage bond, you will be locked out of Neverra forever."

"Not forever if you have a way back in."

A ray of sunlight broke through the clouds and struck his face.

"Not that I'd care. I have no desire to live in Neverra."

"Enjoy your last day on Earth, Catori," he said, before soaring heavenward. If only a plane could knock him out of the sky. It wouldn't kill him, but maybe it would hurt.

THE LIE

"*A*ren't you supposed to be at Astra's?"

Dad and Lily were sitting at the kitchen table, sharing breakfast. My stomach twisted as I stared at the golden triangles of toasts on their plates, at their juice-filled glasses, at the knob of chilled butter set out between them.

"I need to talk to you, Dad."

My father's face went a little yellow. "Is it about that boy?"

I lowered myself into one of the wooden chairs, keeping my spine and shoulders taut. Not that I could've loosened them if I'd tried. I was wound up so tight, it was a wonder I'd been able to make it home without collapsing and sobbing over my miserable fate. "It's not about a boy. It's about . . . *me*."

The morning light that filtered through Grandma Woni's crocheted curtains turned Lily's eyes silver.

I rested my elbows on the wooden tabletop and cradled my forehead with my hands. "I don't know how to say this without it hurting you."

The air stilled around me, thickened, became stifling.

"I'm going on a trip." I swallowed. "For three months. I . . ." I looked up at my dad. "I applied to a Young Doctors Without Borders program back in January. But with Mom's death, I forgot all about it. I received word today that they'd found me a spot with one of their teams." The lie was spilling out of me with such ease, it made me sick. "I can't turn this opportunity down. It's too good to turn down."

"You almost gave me a heart attack." He smiled gently. "That's wonderful news. I'm so proud of you, honey."

I could feel Lily's dubious gaze on me. Unlike my father, she wasn't falling for the lie I'd concocted during the long walk home through the woods.

"Where are they sending you?"

"Africa."

"Where in Africa?"

"Rwanda."

"Wow, that's far away."

"Yeah." Tears tracked down my cheeks.

Dad brushed them away. "Honey, if you don't want to go—"

"I don't want to leave you." I threw myself in his arms and wept against his flannel shirt.

He stroked my hair. "I can come visit."

No he couldn't, and that thought crushed me even more.

Chair legs scraped. And then footsteps sounded on the creaking planks of the living room. Lily had left. Was it to give me time alone with my dad, or did she know I was lying and couldn't bear the sound of me talking?

"When do you leave?" he asked.

"Tomorrow."

"Tomorrow? But don't you need a plane ticket and a visa and immunizations?"

"I'm up to date on all my shots, and the organization already got me a ticket and a visa."

Dad's big hand worked its way through my knotted hair. "Oh," was all he said for a long while. Then, "I can go to the embassy and see if I can get a visa quickly."

"Dad, as much as I want you to come with me, I don't want to have to say goodbye to you twice." I inhaled deeply, then pressed away from him.

His hand tumbled against his lap.

"Besides, I'll be working nonstop. So it would just be a waste of money to come for a visit. Maybe in a month—" My voice cracked.

"Maybe in a month I can come back for a visit. Maybe." A cork-sized lump obstructed my throat. "I hope you're not angry with me."

"Course not, honey, although next time, I'd appreciate more than a twenty-four notice to get used to the idea of my baby leaving home."

There would never, ever be a next time. "I promise."

He swiped my tears away and smiled. And that smile undid me completely.

Shoulders quivering, I burrowed back against him. "I love you, Daddy. I love you more than anyone in the world."

"Right back at you, kiddo." His voice snagged on each one of his words.

He held me a while longer, rocked me a while longer. When I'd calmed down—in other words, become completely numb—Dad told me he needed to go talk to Milly about taking over the appointment he had that afternoon so he could spend the entire day with me. "You want to go boating? I can ask George if he could lend me his fishing boat."

"Sure." I would go crazy if I stayed cooped up inside my house all day. Plus, Dad loved being on the water. I was up for anything that made my father happy.

"Why don't you get the packing out of the way, and then we'll head out?"

"Yeah. I'll go do that." I dug the heels of my palms inside my eyes, then rose, and climbed up the stairs to my room.

"By the way, a letter arrived for you this morning. I left it on your desk."

I climbed the stairs faster, then walked over to my desk and picked up the thin white envelope. I recognized the logo right away. It was the DNA testing facility I'd sent Ley's and my hair to. I'd paid extra to speed up the process.

Although my heart felt like a piece of coal, charred and desiccated, it vibrated as I ripped the envelope open with my finger and pulled the single sheet of paper out.

CAGES AND DOORS

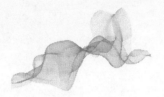

I wasn't related to Ley.

Ley had not been Chatwa's twin sister.

Or maybe she had been, and it was me who wasn't related to Chatwa. But I looked so much like her, there wasn't much doubt in my mind that I was her flesh and blood.

I spun, about to sprint downstairs to inform Lily, but froze. She was standing in my doorway, one hand planted on a slender hip, the other holding out her phone. *What the hell was that?*

Since I didn't want to talk about *that*, I yanked her into my bedroom, flung my door shut, and waved the paper in front of her face.

She read it over quickly, then her gaze jumped to mine, lips forming a perfect O. She typed quickly on her phone: *I was right!*

"You were."

She stared at the paper some more, but then her eyes lifted back to mine and she pointed to the floor, opening both her palms and turning them toward the ceiling.

I bit down on my lower lip. How I wished the DNA test could have distracted her until the next morning. I sighed. She would find out sooner or later, but I'd rather she found out once I was gone.

You're seriously leaving for Africa?

I nodded.

That's crazy. But sort of cool, I suppose.

I folded and refolded the paper as though it were some elaborate origami.

By the way, I meant to ask you why you had a picture of Gregor on your phone.

"A picture of— On my phone?"

She crooked her finger at me. I handed her my cell phone—which showed three missed calls from Faith. I'd messaged her during my trek back to the house that I couldn't work at Astra's anymore, but obviously, my messages hadn't been enough of an explanation for her.

Lily entered my password, then clicked on my photo app and brought up the picture I'd taken of Faith's father.

I blinked at the picture, then at Lily. "*That's* Gregor?"

She nodded.

When I'd confronted Stella in the hospital, she'd said Gregor wasn't Faith's father. She'd lied! It wasn't as surprising as it was shocking. Why had she lied?

Lily tipped her head to the side, then touched the back of my hand to get my attention.

"He's Faith's father," I explained.

Her already large eyes grew wider.

"Yeah . . ."

I went back to wondering why Stella had lied to me, and something Ace had told me returned to me. "Is Gregor married?"

Lily nodded.

"Was he married to Stella Sakar?"

Lily shook her head.

Stella had claimed she'd kept Faith in the dark about Neverra because Astra demanded it, and perhaps Astra had cautioned her daughter to keep Neverra a secret, but perhaps Stella had kept Faith away because she knew the law: her bastard daughter would die.

Stella lost some of the monstrosity she'd accumulated in my eyes during her last days in this world. She *had* cared for her daughter. At least enough to want to keep her alive.

Unless . . . "How long has Gregor been married?"

For almost as long as my parents.

He'd been married when he'd had an affair with Stella. Which confirmed her chest had harbored an actual heart.

I closed my eyes, breathed in deeply. Guilt and shame consumed me. But then I remembered she'd killed my father, and that thought drove away the guilt and shame.

A knock made my lids jolt upward. I was about to say come in when I realized the banging was coming from my window and not my door. I spun around.

Ace was floating in front of the glass, a wolfish grin plastered on his face and a bouquet of gold roses clutched in his hands. A wire of tension wrapped around my throat. He tapped the glass again, and even though my body felt weighted down, I jumped.

Lily walked over to the window and opened it.

Ace drifted inside my bedroom, landing soundlessly on my carpet. There was something off about his grin. Something that tightened the wire and turned its edges barbed.

"I hear congratulations are in order." His voice was off, too. High-pitched and merry.

I flinched.

He tossed the flowers onto my bed. Instantly they turned to sparkling dust. Oh God, had they grown from the ashes of a dead faerie? The unearthly particles blinked into oblivion.

A deep groove settled between Lily's narrowed eyebrows.

"Catori hasn't told you her incredible news?" His eyes blazed an icy blue.

I lowered my gaze to my black socks, apprehension simmering underneath my skin.

"She's getting married!"

Lily turned to me so fast, her hair fanned out. And then her hands moved.

"In Africa?" Ace frowned. "No, no. She's getting married in Neverra."

Lily's hands froze. I didn't dare look at her face. I steepled my fingertips against my temples and closed my eyes.

"She asked Cruz to marry him. Isn't that so fucking romantic?"

Lily raised a hand to her gaping mouth.

Silence. The worst possible kind, the type that was so thick it caked everything in a room and soiled the air.

"Did you always have feelings for the traitor—meaning while we were together—or did they develop when you found out he was *available?"*

I didn't answer, but I did raise my face. Lily's hand slowly fell off her mouth. She shook her head, and I could tell she was screaming at me inside her skull, screaming how stupid I was, how reckless. Finally, she signed something I didn't understand.

Ace frowned, then scowled. "How can you not care?"

Lily gesticulated her hands.

"He was the love of your life, Lily!"

She moved her hands again, and the fury that had iced his eyes when he'd dropped into my room returned with a vengeance. Shards of it lifted off him and sliced through the air, chilling my already clammy skin.

Ace exhaled roughly. "This is why he walked all over you, Lily. Why he screwed everything that moved. Because you are too soft. No man could ever take you seriously."

Lily's cheeks reddened as though her brother had slapped her.

"Get out of my room, Ace," I said, my voice returning, steady, strong. Hurting me was one thing, but hurting Lily . . . that was unnecessary.

Ace speared me with a thorny look, and then he leaped through the window and shot into the sky.

I slammed my window shut, then turned toward Lily whose entire upper body was shaking, from her head to her torso to her hands. She clutched her phone and typed. *You don't actually like Cruz, do you?*

"Of course not."

But you asked him to marry you? I can't decide if you're stupid or stupid.

I bit down hard on my lip.

Why did you do it?

Because I don't have a freaking choice. As the thought skimmed my mind, my traitorous stomach cramped. "You said that if I went to Neverra, my powers would manifest."

Her jaw clenched, and then her fingers flew over the touchscreen. As she typed, I thought, *Well, this isn't so bad. She could've thought you'd done it to hurt her.* I could live with being considered stupid.

You didn't have to freaking marry a faerie to get there! You could've asked my brother to take you. I have friends there. I could've asked them to take you! Do you realize what you've done? Do you get the insanity of your plan? Do you even have a plan? She paused and looked up, first at me then at the ceiling, and then she stared back down at the phone. *We have to tell Ace why you're going. He'll help you.*

I swallowed. "That would make him my accomplice. I don't want to put him in danger."

Now you're being noble?

I rubbed my brand. "Only he can kill me, right? You said he wouldn't kill me."

Death is far from the worst thing that can happen to you in Neverra. Do you know that they have torture cages? Insects that can eat your gray matter? Carnivorous flowers that can poison you?

I swallowed.

You have no clue what world you just decided to go gallivanting in, do you?

I pushed back the locks of hair that had escaped my ponytail. "Tell me about it then."

Cupolas look like gilded birdcages. They're the faerie version of a prison cell. They float around Neverra for all to see. Once the gate is sealed, the cage draws the prisoner's nightmares and fears to the surface and plays them out so vividly the prisoner becomes crazed. I've seen some people tear off their own skin, so convinced were they that faerie fire was burning it. One even bit off his tongue, mistaking it for dust. Most don't make it an hour in those cages.

"I'll be careful not to end up in one, then."

She dropped onto my bed and stared up at me. *Don't go. It's not worth it.*

Would she be telling me this if she knew I was going so I could save her life?

Her face became animated with an idea. I sat beside her and read the words popping onto my screen over her shoulder. *Once your powers come in, break your engagement.*

"That's the plan," I lied.

Lily's breathing seemed to ease. *Better come into them quickly, because I'm not sure how long Gregor and Lyoh will leave you alone.*

"I'll try. And, Lily? Thank you."

She frowned.

"For not hating me."

I might not hate you, but I still think you're massively stupid.

I nudged her with my shoulder, and she smiled. And then she took my hand and squeezed it in her blisteringly warm one. With her other hand, she typed, *Kajika's going to go insane.*

"Just make sure he doesn't kill too many faeries while I'm gone."

That'd mean spending time with him.

"Would that really be so bad?"

Lily's cheeks flushed pink as she extracted her hand from mine.

"That's why he was shocked yesterday, wasn't it? Because you had some indecent thoughts about him?"

She shook her head, but toyed self-consciously with the hem of my comforter. It had taken me a little time to figure out what had happened at the barn, but I had. Normally, I wouldn't even have talked to Lily about it, but now that I was leaving, I wanted to encourage this attraction. If anyone could keep Lily safe, it would be Kajika.

"He's a good person."

She made a face.

"But doesn't he smell bad to you?"

Sometimes.

"Only sometimes?"

Opal camouflages his scent.

"Really?"

Yes, really. Can we not talk about him right now?

"Okay."

So we discussed Neverra instead. She listed the names of the people I could trust: Veroli and Dawson. Warned me about poisonous plants and made me swear not to pet the wild dogs or I would open a tele-pathic link with them, and I did *not* want to be inside their heads.

After an hour, Dad came to get me for our boat ride. He invited Lily to come with us, but she told him she wanted to stay home and read. I doubted she would read. I smiled gratefully at her for letting me have my father to myself for a couple hours.

After the boat ride—which felt like a frozen moment of splendor in my crazy life—I stopped by Astra's and explained about my trip to Africa. After a lot of glowering, Faith wished me a *bon voyage*, then told me not to expect my job back when I returned.

I smiled. "Send me a picture of your baby once she comes."

Faith didn't look at me, but nodded. Although her face had widened from the pregnancy and her eyes were blue instead of brown, her resemblance to her mother was so strong it made me shiver.

"Thank you for trusting me with the bakery."

She flapped her hand before giving me her back. In the glass of the swing door, I caught her wiping a tear. I wondered if those tears were for me or if they stemmed from the frustration of having to man her mother's business on her own again. I pretended not to see them as I left.

I stopped by Bee's next. For the first time in a very long time, Bee was in the room, gray hair wrapped in a neat bun. She smiled at me, but there was something sad in her smile. I suspected that every time she looked at me, she saw her grandson and remembered how he'd ended his life because I hadn't loved him like he'd loved me.

Still, she smiled and hugged me, and I hugged her back, wishing I could take some of her pain away. Perhaps not seeing my face would help her heal. When she went to attend to a customer, I sat on a barstool in front of Cass, who was sporting the amethyst necklace I'd given her for her birthday.

Tears bloomed in her eyes when I told her I was leaving for three months.

"But your birthday. I had everything planned." She walked around the shiny wooden bar and pinned me down with a long hug that almost made me topple off my barstool. "Bee, can I take off early? It's Catori's last night."

"Go, hun," Bee said. "And, Catori, be safe."

"I will." At least, I would try my best. I kissed her papery cheek and left with Cass to drive around in her little pink car. We listened to music, pulled into a drive-through and ordered junk food and extra-large sodas, then drove, talking about everything and nothing.

"I'm coming back," I promised Cass when she dropped me off.

"But then it'll be September, and you'll be going back to college and —" Her voice broke with a sob as giant as her compostable soda cup.

I hugged her tight and thanked her for being the most incredible friend in the world, and then I made her promise to hang out with Lily from time to time. After nodding, she drove away in her eyesore of a car.

Inside, Dad and Lily had prepared a feast. I hadn't been hungry when Cass bought me a burger, and I still wasn't hungry, but I ate the meal they'd prepared. My poor, distended stomach grumbled plaintively.

I didn't try to sleep that night. Instead, I stayed up all night watching TV with Lily. Although Dad tried to stay awake, he snored after the second hour of TV. I woke him gently and helped him up to his bedroom.

"Wake me when you need me to drive you to the airport." He yawned. "Love you to the moon and . . ." His last word tangled with his pillow.

"I love you even further than that." Tears coursed down my cheeks as I closed his door.

I tiptoed back down, feeling the creak of each step inside of me, storing it inside of me—the sound of home. I never thought I'd get emotional over a staircase.

I waited for dawn like a prisoner awaits his executioner. When pale light crept over the windowsill and tinted the living room, my heartbeat grew more frantic.

Better come up with an excuse why it didn't work out in Africa, she'd written on a sheet of paper.

I frowned at Lily.

For when you break your engagement.

A knock sounded on the door.

Lily's eyes moved to the door. She took both my hands in hers and squeezed them hard. And then she released me and wrote: ***Can you tell Veroli not to worry?***

"I will, if I meet her."

Oh you'll meet her. She flicked her palm so that it hovered in front of her, then bent her middle finger and touched her chin, mouthing two tiny words: ***Good luck.***

I would need more than luck to get out of Neverra. I would need a damn miracle. "Tell Kajika . . . tell Kajika not to hate me too much."

Lily smirked softly, then she shuffled into her bedroom and closed her door so I could open mine.

LOCKER NUMBER FOUR

*C*ruz studied my face, took in the under-eye circles I hadn't even tried to camouflage. I suspected it would be the first in a long series of sleepless nights.

He extended his arms. "Climb on."

I glared at his proffered hands.

"We need to get to the boathouse."

Right . . . One of the portals to get to Neverra was in locker number four. The little metal box transformed, for the right people, into a gateway to the faerie isle.

"I'll drive there."

"And leave your car parked at the beach for three months?"

"No. You'll drive it back, then fly back over."

He squinted one eye, not liking my suggestion, but I didn't care if he didn't like it. He tried to touch me, but I jumped back. "You touch me, Cruz, and I'll cut off your hand."

His jaw tensed. "I'm going to have to touch you to get you through the portal."

"Until then, you keep your hands to yourself."

I skittered down to my car and started the engine. I drove slowly past Holly's field. In the distance, I spotted several hunters walking the perimeter. They might not have been running wild around Rowan, but they were there, ever-present. I thought I spotted Kajika but was too far away to be certain.

I wondered how he would react to my departure. Would he think me stupid or courageous? My mind emptied of thoughts after that.

The air was nippy, and the smell of the Michigan spring was green and wet.

When I parked by the boathouse, Cruz was already there. I squeezed my steering wheel then heaved myself out of the car and dropped the keys in his open palm.

As he drove away, I slid off my sneakers, rolled up the hem of my stretchy jeans, and walked to the lapping waves, reveling in the feel of the fine grains of sand beneath the soles of my feet, between my toes. Bees buzzed over the white trilliums tucked between the shifting hemlock dunes, and goldeneye ducks swooped overhead, cawing before landing with great fanfare on the sapphire waters.

"What happened to you, Chatwa?" I whispered to the lake.

As though the lake were trying to answer my question, it splashed my jeans all the way to my knees. I shivered, but didn't step back. Too soon, I'd be ripped from my home.

When I sensed a presence behind me, I closed my eyes, sent a silent farewell to my world, and turned. Cruz nodded to the boathouse.

I walked back up the dunes, grabbed my shoes, and entered in front of him. I sat on a bench, dusted the sand off my feet, and put my shoes back on. Cruz headed to locker number four and eased it open.

"How does it work? Are you going to shrink me?"

He smiled and offered his hand, and this time, I had no choice. "Toss out those arrows in your pocket."

How had he known?

Swallowing hard, I dug into the pocket of my windbreaker and extricated the white rowan sticks.

"All of them."

I fished the two remaining ones out, leaving my pocket terribly empty.

Cruz placed his free hand against the back of the locker. The circle slashed with irregular lines flared on his wrist.

I simply had time to think, *the key to the portal*, when my body was sucked up as though through a giant straw and funneled through an opening that wasn't supposed to accommodate a human body and yet stretched widely, viscously around me like a warm mouth.

PART II
NEVERRA

33

FIRST SIGHT

I didn't close my eyes as I went through the portal, not that
there was much to see, but there was much to feel. It was like
penetrating jelly that didn't stick, dark jelly that absorbed all the light. I
half-expected to hear a slurping noise, but there was no noise.

Just impossibly thick silence.

When my head broke the gummy surface, noise didn't return. My
shoulders pierced the top of the portal, and the hush grew deeper. The
jelly slid off my chest, my waist, my thighs, my legs, and finally freed
my feet, before hardening beneath my soles.

Only my pounding heart and rapid-fire breaths shattered the
endless silence surrounding me. I looked down and gulped. I was
standing on a fisheye lens no thicker than the blade of a knife that
magnified the inside of the boathouse.

Slowly, I lifted my chin and stared around me. A breeze blew
strands of black hair around my face. It smelled like snow and metal
and mud, yet there was no snow, no metal, no mud. At least none that I
could see.

I pressed my hair behind my ears.

Thick-trunked trees circled around me like silent sentinels, roots so
far below and crowns so far above me that it was impossible to tell
their size. Vines as large as tunnels spiraled around the great trunks. I
squinted when movement caught my attention. Dark dots scuttled up

and down the vines like shield bugs, except they weren't insects, they were people. And they were looking at me. Staring.

Thousands of them.

I backed up, and my foot hit air. I flailed, gasped, but Cruz caught me and tugged me back on the manhole-sized portal.

"You know how to make an entrance," he said.

I clamped my mouth shut so tightly, my teeth bit down on my tongue. I tasted blood. Blood and fear and weakness. My ribcage ached. My muscles trembled as I faced the bewildering immensity surrounding me.

Birds glided around my mirrored lily pad.

Not birds.

People.

People were flying.

Hundreds of them!

Circling Cruz and me like buzzards scenting a carcass.

I shuddered again. Cruz's hand tightened around mine. Was he scared I would leap to my death instead of facing my new life? If that was his conclusion, then he didn't know me well. I might've been a lot of things—trusting, stubborn, dithering—but not suicidal.

I looked at the faeries sailing lazily through the air, trying to spot a familiar face. Not a single one struck a chord within me. Was Ace among them?

I inhaled a sharp breath that went down like an icicle as one faerie rose before me and reached out. The searing fingertips skimming my arm made me jolt backward. My back hit Cruz's hard chest.

"Tell them not to touch me!"

"They're curious. Most of them have never left Neverra. Never met a hunter."

I crouched and scraped at the surface of the portal that was no longer gelatinous, but hard as glass. "Take me back," I said urgently. I kept digging. One of my nails caught on the edge and ripped. "Take me back!"

"There's no going back. Not for a while."

He reached around my waist and yanked. His arm, like a claw, hauled me off the only piece of solid ground and dangled me like a field mouse over a void that seemed to stretch forever. Instead of flying me downward, Cruz flew upward, into a band of clouds so thick I felt them around me, a cloying ocean of spider webs. The silken threads clung to the exposed skin of my neck and face and hands, wrapped around my ankles.

With my hands, I brushed them off. I quivered as more encased me. Swiped my palms over my cheeks faster, wishing I'd worn a face mask and a helmet.

"The mist will vanish once the sun warms your skin."

The mist.

This was the infamous mist! Which meant . . . which meant the Woods' castle was close. We broke through the cottony layer of mist, and there it stood, rising behind a carved pink marble arch that could accommodate the passage of a hundred people holding hands.

Beyond the arch sprawled a courtyard of buffed white stone that glimmered like rock salt. Massive pillars, made of the same polished stone, held up a vibrant hanging courtyard as vast as the cherry fields surrounding Holly's house. Turrets covered in moss spiraled to points on which rested pink-veined spheres that looked like solid chunks of rose quartz. The few doors I could see gleamed gold, and windows sparkled like cut diamonds. Twin waterfalls coursed down the castle's white stone walls and filled two shallow basins at the center of the overhanging garden. The water gleamed silver and lavender in the brilliant sun.

Lavender. Because the sky was purple. Not blue.

Faeries twirled around us. They didn't try to poke or prod me, but they flew so close I could feel their fiery breaths on my forehead. Goosebumps coated my body like the mist had earlier.

We landed on the stone terrace. Roots from the overhanging garden poked out of the dirt that magically hovered over our heads. Lianas with glittery flowers swung like a beaded curtain from the ceiling of packed soil.

"Linus asked to meet you before the ceremony tonight."

I flung my gaze to Cruz's face. "Linus?" I choked.

"Linus Wood. Ace's father."

"I know who he is." I shivered as dread hardened my shoulder blades. Around us, other faeries had landed.

I startled when I recognized two of them. They were Lily's friends, the ones I'd seen back at Astra's the day Stella tried to feed me a mallow-spiked cupcake.

One had dyed pink hair, and the other a glossy brown mane that hit her exposed hipbone. All the faeries wore clothes, but the fabric was gauzy and pearlescent, revealing curves and bulges. Thankfully, they weren't transparent in the places that mattered.

Cruz was still holding on to me. Part of me wanted to pluck his fingers off my arm; another part was thankful for his touch. Until that part remembered it was his fault I was in this strange land in the first place. He tugged on me, and although I followed, I shrugged him off. Close, but no longer touching, we walked through the crowd that parted around us.

I stared around me as we passed a set of colossal golden doors and entered a large hall with a distant, vaulted ceiling. It was lined with those diamond-cut windowpanes which refracted light over the white stone floor.

Ahead of me loomed a raised dais. And from that dais rose a tree with translucent amber leaves. A seat was carved in its trunk. A man with thick, strawberry-blond hair topped with a gold wreath sat in it.

The infamous Linus Wood.

There was something of Ace in that face. The chalcedony-blue eyes, the golden skin, and the chiseled square jaw. But where Ace's handsomeness blazed off him, this man's beauty was as cold and hard as the floor beneath my feet.

As I approached, his calculating gaze swept over me, from sneakers to snarled hair. Next to him stood two women. One of them was his wife—I recalled her name from the article I'd read on Ace and Angelina: Addison—a former actress and model with shoulder-length blonde hair, unmoving shiny red lips, and large gray eyes that seemed vacant. The other one was Ace's fiancée, Angelina, an oval-faced, dark-haired beauty with cleavage that rose alluringly out of a silver bra. Her long fingers, fitted with more rings than most people owned, stroked her bare, rounded midriff incessantly. She stood as close to Linus as his wife did, perhaps closer, her upper lip hiked into a small, repulsed smile over her very white and straight teeth.

"We finally meet, Catori Price." The boom of Linus's voice made me jolt and grab onto Cruz.

When I realized I was clinging—*again*—to the faerie who'd ruined my life, I let go and put some space between us. He might've been the lesser of two evils, but he was still evil.

Linus glanced at his wife. "She's pretty, isn't she, Addi?"

Sluggishly, Addison's face tipped down toward her husband, and even more slowly, she nodded, but her eyes were unfocused. In college, I'd been around a lot of stoners, and that's how Addison Wood struck me, as a woman hopped up on some drug that decelerated her body's responses.

Linus grinned wolfishly at me. "I hear you will be joining our family."

I didn't answer. What was there to answer?

"We are very excited to meet a real-life hunter."

"Half-hunter," Cruz corrected Linus.

Linus flapped his hand as though that wasn't important. "Where is my son? Ace!" His voice reverberated in the enormous throne room. Hushed whispers swarmed around me. "Ace?" he bellowed again, but was met with silence.

"Would you like us to fetch him, *Massin?*" a golden-eyed guard asked.

Linus flapped his hand again. "As long as he's here tonight, there's no need. After all, he knows the girl." His gaze swept over me again.

My shoulders locked tight, and a bead of sweat traveled down my spine. A burst of churning air blew against my clammy cheeks, whipped my hair in a frenzy. I looked up and almost ducked when I saw the smooth underside of a black leathery wing brushing the air over my head.

There was a dragon.

A real-life dragon.

I stared around me, half-expecting to see people fall to their knees and scream, but people barely even blinked at it.

My heart held so still I thought it would shatter if someone flicked it.

The black-scaled dragon landed softly on the stone floor and tucked its fibrous wings alongside its body. The large body shimmered, and then its edges blurred and shrank into a lithe, human body.

A woman clad entirely in skin-tight black leather replaced the dragon. Her cropped hair was as black as Cruz's, her eyes as green as his. Which made sense. The—what had Borgo called her?—*draca* was Lyoh Vega, Cruz's mother.

The woman who'd killed my lookalike Ishtu eons ago.

Her eyes narrowed as she studied me. Did she see Ishtu? She approached us, touched two fingers to her son's forehead. He bent his head.

"Blessed be the skies that brought you safely home, my son," she told him, before lifting her fingers off his forehead. Her hand traveled toward my head.

I jerked backward. My heart stammered and spun, and my brand flared to life.

Lyoh's eyes traveled to my hand. "I thought the girl was bonded to you?"

"Why in Neverra would you think such a thing, mother?"

"Patila saw a V."

The name conjured an image of the ebony-skinned faerie I'd met in Ruddington, the one who'd seared my fingertips.

"There have always been two Vs, mother. Ace beat me to her."

Why was he lying?

Lyoh studied her son, then her gaze traveled over my face again. She lifted her middle and index fingers again, and although I shied away, the tips met my forehead. "May truth line your heart, Catori."

A little shock of electricity zapped through me.

"Yes, I am quite terrifying. But only to those who seek to wrong our world."

I jumped as I realized she'd just read my thoughts.

"Do we have your blessing, mother?"

A smile tugged on one side of her mouth, and my throat went very dry. My tongue darted out and moistened my lips.

"You are a lucky girl, Catori. Our kind does not usually mix with undesirables. But since you are also part Seelie"—gasps rose from the assembly—"I cannot outright refuse a union between you and my son."

Dread drained the blood from my face, suctioned it out of my extremities. I shivered.

As though feeling the terrible chill racking my body, Cruz sidled in closer to me. "Let's not overwhelm my fiancée in her first hour among us. Linus, may we be excused? Catori and I have much to discuss before the ceremony tonight."

Linus leered, then fluttered his fingers, his wreath winking in the faelight. "Of course. Of course. Enjoy your *discussions*." Laughter rang through the assembly. "See you at sundown, Cruz . . . Catori." He kissed his index and middle finger and held them out to me, then rose, and trailed by Angelina and Addison, disappeared behind his tree-throne.

"Mother." Cruz inclined his head toward his mother, whose eyes had arced back down to my hand, to the faint white lines of the W.

She backed away from us. Cruz took my limp arm, spun me around, and tugged me back through the throngs of people. When we arrived at the edge of the stone terrace, he scooped me up and dove off, then darted like one of my arrows toward the copse of giant trees.

I clung to his neck, fear knocking into me each time he winged around a trunk. We went so high, I expected my ears to pop, but they didn't. Maybe, like the sky's color, the air pressure was different in Neverra. At least the air held oxygen like the air back home.

Home.

It already felt so far away.

Three stories from the crown of a tree, our flight slowed. One last swoop, and we landed on a small wooden porch with no railing. Clearly, faeries had no fear of falling. I didn't let go of Cruz until he'd walked far enough from the edge of the landing pad. When he set me down, my legs threatened to give, feeling more like gummy worms than solid muscle. I reached out for the wall of rough bark in which was carved a door. He pressed his fingertips against the wood and pushed it. The door swung heavily.

Wordlessly, he led me inside the dark hollow that brightened as he stepped inside. There were no lamps, yet the vast space was bright. The wall opposite us was one large panorama of sky and sun and floating palace.

I approached the window, and my eyes that had managed to stay dry slickened with tears.

Trapped.

I was trapped.

Like a baby bird that didn't know how to use its wings. Unlike the baby bird, if no faerie magic coursed through my veins, I would never learn to fly.

I thought of the bird I'd healed at Holly's when I was small. I remembered how her hand had closed around mine as I'd held it, how a smile had creased her face when I'd opened my palm and the broken bird had writhed, alive again. Had I done that? Or had Holly?

What the hell was I? And how the hell would I find out trapped within a tree trunk?

"You should rest, Catori."

I squeezed my eyes shut to press back the tears before he could see them. "Can your mother read minds?"

"Only when she touches you."

"Good thing I wasn't thinking of my changing brand when she did."

He didn't respond.

"Why did you lie to her?"

"That is none of your concern." His green eyes settled on the mist floating below the palace.

Arms folded, I turned toward him. "I'll be your fiancée soon. Am I not allowed to know your secrets?"

"Someone will come to dress you an hour before the ceremony."

"I thought you and your mother were close now."

"Which leaves you many hours to relax." He extended his hand. "Give me your phone, so I can text your father that you arrived in *Rwanda* safely."

I stared wide-eyed at him. "It's barely been one hour."

"Not on Earth."

I dug my phone from my windbreaker. The screen was scrambled, the pixels blinking strangely. Ace hadn't lied. Phones really didn't work here.

I handed it over.

When Cruz started toward the door, I asked, "You're leaving me alone?"

He twisted around. "Would you rather I stay?"

"No."

A groove appeared between his eyebrows. "Then I will see you tonight."

When the door of the apartment swung shut behind him, my body gave an involuntary shudder. I stared at the space around me, a vast canopy bed made up of crisp white sheets, bookcases filled with leather-bound books. I picked one at random and read the title: *Plantae*. I flipped through it. There were pages and pages of text, but none of it was in English—*Faeli*, I supposed. The blocks of text were interspersed with etchings of strange plants. Some of them resembled familiar plants with long stalks and wide leaves, but some were unlike anything I had ever seen, made of feathers or dotted with star-shaped berries. I flipped through the rest of the book, then replaced it and wandered through the rest of the apartment. I discovered a bathroom made of wood and rough gray stone.

I turned one of the knobs in the shower. Water hissed through hidden pipes before finally spurting out. I reached out with my palm, but yanked it away almost immediately. It was freezing.

I searched for another knob, but there wasn't another one, and then I remembered: made of fire. Why would faeries need warm water?

I exited the bathroom and wandered through the living room that consisted of four large armchairs centered around a circular fireplace —hazardous inside a tree. Then again, humans built wooden houses with working fireplaces.

I returned to the window. The farthest I could see was where the mist licked the bark of the skytrees. *Calimbors*. The word Borgo had taught me hit my brain like a smooth rock skidding over a pond. My mind rippled with more memories, then associated those memories with the facts I'd gleaned from Lily and Ace.

In my perch, I felt like a rock climber dangling on the side of a cliff. My purchase on my new world seemed tenuous at best, but at least Lily, Borgo, and Ace had given me tools to use.

After a long while, I turned away from the window, shrugged out of my windbreaker, kicked off my sneakers, and climbed onto the bed. I didn't think I could sleep. Not in a strange bed with adrenaline spiking my blood.

What if Cruz returned?

What if faeries crept up to the window to peek inside?

What if . . .

I yawned.

34

PURPLE

I woke up with a start, my senses on high alert. Even though I was still curled on Cruz's bed, with my head turned toward the empty window, a presence stirred in the apartment. Water hissed, followed by a low humming that was too feminine to be Cruz.

The wooden floorboards creaked underneath soft footsteps.

The humming grew more insistent, and I realized the song was familiar. It was the title melody from *Titanic*—Mom's favorite song.

Without moving, I listened.

I wondered if this woman had traveled to Earth and watched the movie. I closed my eyes. Her rendition was slower, but still completely on tune. Mom had worked to the soundtrack of the movie for days on end, until she discovered another movie soundtrack and switched it up. But *Titanic* was a staple that returned, whereas most of the other soundtracks never did.

The humming stopped so suddenly, my lids flipped up.

"You're awake." A short woman with round, flushed cheeks stood in the doorway of the bathroom. The first thing that struck me was that she didn't dress like faeries. She wore a stiff green kimono paired with matching wide-leg pants and beige fabric slip-ons. "I'm Veroli."

My head spun as I sat up. I placed my palm against it as I stared at Veroli, one of the people Lily told me I could trust.

"Slowly. Get up slowly. You've been sleeping all day."

Sure enough, outside, the purple sky had deepened to an ultraviolet shot through with glimmering trails of light. They were the only source of light in the otherwise moonless sky.

"*Lustriums.*" Veroli tipped her round chin to the glittery streamers. "They're clusters of stars. I don't think you have them where you come from."

My eyebrows slanted over my forehead. So she hadn't come to Earth. But she knew Celine Dion, which must mean faeries had access to earthly entertainment.

"I drew you a bath."

I didn't want to take an ice bath.

She let out a little laugh. "Don't you worry, I heated up the water."

I wanted to ask how, but instead, I blurted out, "Are you a faerie?"

She smiled again. "I am a *calidum*. Half faerie, half human. I have just enough fire to turn water warm, but not enough to fly. I can hover a couple inches off the ground though." She demonstrated this by gliding over to the bed. "Lily said you were pretty, but I didn't expect you to be *this* pretty. It's the cheekbones. They're so high."

I brushed off her compliment, not because it wasn't sweet, but because it surprised me. "Why are you being so nice to me?" I asked cautiously.

Yes, Lily said I could trust Veroli, but if she liked Lily, then she couldn't possibly like Cruz. Not after what happened. And me, the girl who caused the rift . . . How could she even bear to look at me, much less be friendly?

"Why shouldn't I be nice to you? Are you a bad person?"

"No. Maybe. Sometimes. I don't know." I tipped my head to the side. "What about Cruz? Do you hate him for what he did to Lily?"

Her forehead rumpled and little lines burst around her eyes. "You can't hate your own children."

"Cruz is your— I thought Lyoh—"

"Lyoh is his true mother, but I raised him, so I consider him mine."

"Oh."

Her mouth curved with a smile. "I also raised Lily and Ace. And my own son, Dawson."

Lily had mentioned I could trust Dawson too. "You were their nanny?"

"I like second mother better, but yes . . . nanny." She landed back on the floor with a *whoompf*. "How's my Lily adapting?"

I lowered my legs over the side of the bed, but before standing, I dug my fingers into the soft gray sheets. "She told me to tell you not to worry."

"Of course she did. And of course, I will. I really hate faerie rules. Most of them are so darn antiquated!" A tear crept out of her eye. She sniffed and knuckled it away. "I really need to get you ready now." Her voice was a mere whisper. She rubbed her palms together until they sparked with shallow flames. "Let me reheat the water. It gets cold pretty fast all the way up here."

I stood and followed her into the bathroom. When she turned, she craned her neck. "You're so tall."

I cringed.

"Are all hunters as tall as you are?"

"No," I mumbled, swallowing back a lump of shame. How I hated to be reminded how unfeminine . . . how undainty I looked.

"You're just one of the lucky ones, then?"

"Lucky?"

"Height is an evolutionary trait in Neverra. Most faerie women are not especially tall."

I frowned.

She unabashedly studied me from head to toe. "Is the water temperature to your liking?"

I dipped my hand inside. "It's perfect. Thank you."

"Clothes off then."

I waited for her to leave.

She didn't. "Come on, deary."

"I can bathe my own self."

"Nonsense. It's part of my job."

"You don't have—"

"Right. Ace mentioned humans were prudish. Well, you don't need to be a prude around me."

"I—"

She clapped.

Sensing this was a lost battle, I cast away my human primness and unzipped my jeans, then pulled off my tank top. Humming the *Titanic* tune again, Veroli busied herself with lining up pots that seemed carved out of turquoise. I quickly unclipped my bra, dropped my panties, and slipped into the warm bath.

Veroli gathered my clothes and put them into a fabric bag, then returned toward me. Keeping my arms tied around my chest, I asked, "You've seen *Titanic?*"

She stopped humming and went as white as Cruz's comforter. "No."

Her reaction told me she had, but for some reason needed to lie about it. Were human movies forbidden here?

"What is *Titanic?*" Her eyes darted to the side even though there was nothing to see on the side.

"A movie. The song you're humming was the lead song on the soundtrack."

Fingers trembling, she scooped something out of a turquoise pot. It looked like soap but it could've been frog saliva for all I knew. "You don't say."

"It was my mother's favorite movie. Favorite song too."

"She doesn't like it anymore?"

My heart rattled. "She died. A couple months ago."

Veroli clapped her mouth. "Oh, deary. Cruz told me, but I forgot. Oh, I'm so sorry."

"It's okay." I pulled my knees into my chest.

In silence, Veroli worked whatever she had in the palm of her hand into my hair, and then she scooped water out with a shiny gray shell and poured it over my head. Warm water that smelled like lavender and musk ran down my face. She applied something else to my hair, then used a comb to help it penetrate. "No wonder my boys have been fighting over you."

I sucked in some air.

"You're so exotic-looking." When I stayed silent, she asked, "So how did Cruz win your heart?"

"He didn't."

Her hands stilled on my hair, and silence stretched between us.

After a long while, her voice broke the stillness. "Then why did you ask him to marry you?"

I wished she would start humming again, if only to replace the misery ballooning in my chest. "Since when do faeries marry for love?"

Slowly, she tugged the comb through my hair. "I thought humans married for love."

"But I'm not human, am I?" My voice was a biting whisper. This woman didn't deserve that tone. I sighed so deeply, it made the surface of the water quiver. "I'm sorry. For snapping at you. It's not your fault." My voice broke. "None of this is your fault."

Veroli's plump hand cupped my cheek and pulled my face up toward hers. "You don't owe me an explanation. I'm sure you have your reasons for marrying Cruz. I know what he did to Lily was . . . unexpected, but I don't think he was trying to hurt her. I think there is more than meets the eye . . . and I suppose I hoped you would know something I didn't. None of my children are talking to me. Well, not about the important stuff. And they're not talking to each other either, and I'm worried because I love each one equally and irrevocably." Her warm, calloused thumb slid over my cheek, before releasing my face. "Or maybe Dawson is right, and my heart is filtering out the truth."

I didn't dare say anything after that, because truth was, I didn't know what to say. Veroli rinsed my hair and then ran a soft sponge over my shoulders with that same musky-smelling soap. Aylen would love the smell. The thought of my aunt made me tuck my knees closer. I should've called her before leaving. Should've asked how she was doing. Should've told Kajika to send one of his hunters to check up on her. *No.* I didn't trust any of his hunters. I didn't even trust Gwenelda. Only him. I should've asked *him* to go check on her.

I inhaled the sweet perfume. "My aunt makes soaps. She'd love this one."

"She might not love it as much if she knew how it was made." I felt a smile in her words.

Eyes wide, I looked up. "How—"

"Beetle shells."

"B-bug shells?"

"Once dried, the shells are crushed and—" Veroli must've sensed my disgust because she said, "I should probably have told you it came from a flower."

I shook my head. "I appreciate the honesty." The problem was that now, I didn't feel clean. Who would after bathing in desiccated insects?

Veroli asked me about my aunt, which got me speaking of home.

Her eyes glazed over in wonder as I told her about Rowan, about my father, about the beach and the lake. Soon I was towel-dried and made-up, and she'd weaved my hair into an elaborate braid laced with gold chains.

"Now for the dress."

She went into the bedroom and returned minutes later with a swath of purple draped over her forearms. "Brides get engaged in purple, then marry in red."

"Did you make this dress?"

"I don't have that talent, deary. This was made in the palace by the queen's seamstress." She pinched the shoulders and let the fabric unspool. It scintillated as it settled over the wooden floor, gleaming purple and silver. Stones that resembled small diamonds glittered at the neckline and hem.

I touched one. "Are these . . . diamonds?"

"Yes."

"Real ones?"

Veroli nodded. "*Caligosupra* don't wear fake ones."

I'd never possessed a diamond before, much less an entire dress dripping in them. Veroli slid it over my head and tightened the violet ribbons woven in the back until the top was so snug I could barely breathe. Thankfully the skirt was fluid and floated around my legs.

"Mother?" yelled an unfamiliar voice.

"She's almost ready, Dawson." Veroli tugged on the ribbon one last time, then walked around me and took me in. When she smiled, I flushed.

My bare feet gleamed with red nail polish. "What about shoes?"

"Seelies don't wear shoes."

"You wear shoes."

"I'm a *calidum*, not a Seelie."

I wanted to tell her that I wasn't a Seelie either, but she latched on to my waist and spun me so I could see my reflection in the mirror behind me.

I blinked at the girl staring back.

It wasn't me.

But it was.

"Thank the skies you are getting engaged tonight." When I frowned, she added, "Unbound women can be claimed by any man and"—she dropped her voice to a loud whisper—"another archaic rule is that women must submit to men's desires if those men are superior to them on the social ladder."

I gasped, appalled. "You're kidding?"

"Sadly not, deary. I tell you, so much needs to be changed here. Dawson, she's ready."

No footsteps warned me of the arrival of another person. The newcomer's bare feet didn't rest on the ground. They hovered several inches above it. The boy was blond with a sprinkling of freckles that turned red when his wide blue eyes set on me.

Dawson ran a hand through his wild hair, his eyes darting everywhere but at me. "I'll be your *taxi* tonight."

"My taxi?"

Veroli laughed behind me. I spun toward her to understand. Once she got herself under control, she said, "Dawson's flying you over to the palace."

"Oh." I'd assumed Cruz would be back for me.

"Don't worry. I have a good track record. I only drop twenty percent of my customers."

My eyes widened and my mouth rounded in a gasp.

"Dawson!" his mother said.

He rubbed the back of his neck. "Sorry. That was probably not funny. I'm nervous. I've never seen a girl like you. Wow." His face glowed as red as a stop sign. "I have no filter. Sorry." A sheepish grin lit up his face. "I promise I won't drop you."

In spite of all the sucky feelings and panic coursing through me, I smiled. "I'd appreciate not being dropped."

"I'm sorry, my boy is a talker. Takes after his father." Veroli yelped with laughter.

"Sheesh, Mom, Catori will think we're wacky."

"Humor has never hurt anyone."

She was right. Humor was a balm, not a weapon. "Thank you, Veroli."

"It was an honor to be at your service, deary. Now you better get going, or you'll be late." She began to rearrange the messy bathroom.

"You're coming, aren't you?"

"Me? No. *Calidums* aren't allowed to attend royal ceremonies."

"I'd like you to come."

She smiled at me, then touched two fingers to the word *human* tattooed on the top of my hand, over the faint white W. "I have so much to do." She pulled back her fingers. "You must go now. I don't want to get in trouble for not delivering the future bride on time. May the skies bless you, dear Catori." She closed her eyes and curtsied.

Which made me flush. When I hadn't moved for a long time, Dawson spoke my name.

It made me jump. How many times had I startled today?

He gestured for me to follow him. Not wanting to get either mother or son in trouble, I trailed him through the dimly-lit apartment, but stopped next to the roaring fireplace. Squeezing my hands into fists, I watched the flames dance.

Six months ago, I'd been celebrating the holidays with my family around another fire, discussing plans for my future. None of those plans had included moving to another world and participating in a sham wedding. All of them had included realistic human dreams: acing classes, landing a summer internship in a hospital or a clinic, maybe meeting a nice boy. None of those plans had included getting married.

Married.

Shit.

Black dots ate away at my peripheral vision. I lowered myself into one of the chairs, tucked my head between my knees, and breathed.

A warm hand touched my shoulder. I flinched. The hand lifted.

"Catori?"

Filling my lungs with what felt like my last breath, I looked up into the boy's concerned face.

"Nervous?" he asked.

My gaze slid back to the fire. All of this was a strange dream, but like with all dreams, I would wake up.

I would get out of here.

Eighteen days.

Almost seventeen.

I stood up, my eyesight clearing. Clear.

"Your tattoo's neat by the way," Dawson said.

I touched my neck. Even though it pulsed, the dust had become part of me, like a second heart, so I tended to forget it was there. As I drew my hand away, the dust stuck to my fingertip, glowing like a golden ribbon.

Dawson backed away, stumbling into the chair next to him. "Y-you have *wita*?" he stammered, while I lifted my fingers in front of my face.

The ribbon seemed almost solid. Never had it looked like anything other than particles. Had I lost my *sight*? Had coming to Neverra somehow annihilated my hunter gift?

My name was spoken, but it sounded like it was coming from a great distance.

Was I actually part Seelie somehow? Maybe Ley wasn't related to me, but maybe I was still related to a faerie. Maybe I wasn't Daneelie after all. Or was I all three? Could a human be all three? Four, if you took human into account.

Human . . .

Was I even still a human?

"Catori!"

This time, I snapped out of my daze. My hand jerked down to my hip. The ribbon tore off my fingers and nipped my neck, the dust returning to its home underneath my skin.

Veroli stood next to her son, the top of her head barely reaching his shoulder. They both gaped at me, the flames from the fire flickering in their wary eyes.

"I told you she was more Seelie than Unseelie," Dawson whispered loudly.

Veroli glared at him, then turned her slanted gaze to me. "She doesn't have fire in her veins. Maybe a *calidum*?"

I swallowed, not really knowing what they wanted to hear. Would it reassure them if I confirmed I was part Seelie? I lowered my eyes to my immobile hands, to the glossy, blood-red polish Veroli had brushed on my nails to match my mother's ring. "I don't know what I am."

Silence entrenched all three of us.

Veroli huffed after a very long moment. "What you are is late. Very late. Dawson, take the girl now before they send a *lucionaga* to fetch her. They are not the most gentle specimen in Neverra."

I shivered at the thought of a lethal faerie guard coming for me.

Veroli's gaze trailed me all the way to the platform outside the apartment door.

"So I have to admit something." Dawson raked his hand through his tousled hair. "I've never carried anyone before."

I stayed close to the trunk. I didn't think some magnetic force would drag me down into the black void, but having something to hold onto was reassuring. "Never?" I croaked.

"I mean, I've carried girlfriends . . . Okay no." He scratched his ear. "I haven't."

I wasn't sure whether to be amused or terrified.

"Ace was supposed to come, but he told Cruz he couldn't make it, so Cruz asked me."

My heart lurched. Ace was supposed to bring me. What sort of twisted scheme had Cruz thought up? Resentment supplanted shock. "I'm sure you'll make a great . . . taxi."

Dawson smiled and stopped rubbing his earlobe. "So how, um . . . should I . . .? How do you want to be carried? Piggyback?"

I laughed, but pressed a fist to my mouth when he grimaced. "Sorry," I breathed.

He scrunched up his mouth. "Help me out. How should I carry you?"

I laughed again as an image of me riding on a faerie boy's back cropped up in my mind.

"Don't pick on Dawson," a gruff voice rising from the darkness said.

My laughter withered like a rose in autumn.

I searched the darkness for the owner of the voice. Found him hovering inches from the platform. His face didn't glow here. Or maybe I couldn't see its glow, yet another confirmation that I'd lost my sight.

"Oh hey, Ace," Dawson said, as Ace landed on the platform.

His dark gaze swept over me. Not once. Not twice. But many . . . *many* times. Goosebumps unfurled over every inch of my body.

"I've got it," he said. "I've got her."

How I wished he really had . . . *me*.

Ace patted the boy's shoulder. "Go and get yourself a good spot. The palace is jam-packed."

"You sure?"

"Yes. *Vade!*" Ace said.

After Dawson dove off the platform, neither Ace nor I spoke for excruciatingly long seconds.

Finally Ace extended both his arms. "Shall we?"

"Why did you come?"

He paused, evaluating my question. "Because it was either see you walk down an aisle or never see you walk at all. I don't trust Cruz, but I also don't trust Dawson to fly you over, Pietro's dead, and my other friend among the *lucionaga* was busy, so I have no one else to delegate your safety to." His arms were still extended. "Consider helping you survive your first day in Neverra my engagement gift."

Hesitantly, I made my way toward him, but stopped a hair's breadth away from his fingertips. "Are you still very angry with me?"

"Disappointed. Confused." His arms arced down. "When I talked about bringing you to Neverra, you looked like it was the worst idea in the world. Now, I think you just didn't want to come here with me."

My pulse throbbed at my temples. *Wrong. Wrong. Wrong.*

"But I also don't think you like Cruz, so I'm not really sure why you're here." His blue gaze dug deep into mine. So deep I thought he would see right through me. I lowered my eyes, terrified he would, and Cruz wouldn't uphold his end of the deal. "Is it to make me jealous? Because if it is—"

I raised my gaze back to his, pitched an eyebrow up. *Finish the sentence, Ace.*

"If it is, then you succeeded."

My heart fluttered softly.

A frown touched his lips. "But if that was your plan, Catori, then I feel incredibly relieved, because I don't like girls who play games and pit one boy against another. You call me childish, but trying to make someone jealous is immature and cruel. I don't need a person like that in my life."

Misery hit me dead center, spreading like a toxin through the rest of my body.

"Anyway"—he rubbed the back of his neck—"I don't want things to be strange between us now that you're here to stay. I'd like to think we could possibly be civil. I don't expect or want friendship, but I already have a long list of people I dislike, and I'd rather not have to add one more name. Can we move past our . . . *past?*"

My lungs felt compressed by the overwhelming loss brought on by Ace's analysis. I'd lost so much because of Cruz.

So damn much.

My hatred for him grew into something solid that hardened inside my heart and my throat, and blackened all my thoughts. "I don't intend to hurt you again, Ace."

A smile as limp as the arms he extended again wobbled over his lips. "Cruz will send someone else to fetch you if we don't leave now."

I walked into his arms on legs that didn't feel attached to my body. One arm slid underneath my knees, the other underneath my back. Although he didn't cradle me against his chest, he held me steadily.

The purpling evening flogged my dry, cold cheeks as Ace soared soundlessly around the massive trunks of the *calimbors*. At some point, I raised my eyes and watched him watch everything but my face. "Was . . . Pietro . . . only there for Lily?"

His Adam's apple jostled in his stubbly throat. "He was looking out for the two of you."

I touched the edge of his jaw. "Why did you lie about it?"

His jaw flexed as though he was about to answer, but he didn't. At least not for a long moment. "So what did you think of my father? Charming man, huh?"

"He's"—I searched for the right word—"intimidating."

Ace grunted. "He's far worse than that." His blue eyes burned a path over my face.

Before I could ask what he meant, our bodies dipped, and then he was unhooking his arms from underneath me. My bare feet met cool, buffed stone.

"Was traffic bad?" The gravelly voice snaked out of the shadows. Then green eyes alighted on me.

Ace glowered at Cruz, lowered his eyes to my face, scraped a finger across my jaw, and then walked into the cavernous mouth of the palace.

THE FIRST CEREMONY

"*D*id you tell him anything?" Cruz asked, after Ace had disappeared inside the palace.

Animated with voices and flickering lights, the palace looked more inviting than it had this morning, yet I longed to go anywhere but inside.

"And lose the ability to bring Lily home?" I shook my head. "I am way more desperate than I am dumb."

Cruz's eyes glowed like twin lanterns against his shadowy features as he scrutinized my face for longer than necessary. In the end, he said drily, "Hold my arm."

"You don't want me any more than I want you, so why the hell are we doing this?"

"Arm," he repeated.

Now that *really* made me want to hold him.

"I've already explained my reasons to you, Catori."

"Revenge? I think that's done and out of the way."

"It's just beginning." There was something ominous about his tone, something unsettling about the glassy look on his face.

What else did he have in store for me? For Ace? Was marrying me really a fuck you to his closest friends, almost siblings? Or was it somehow part of a bigger plan?

He blinked, and it wiped the brooding glint in his eyes. "As for you, you're doing this for Lily. My arm, Catori. Now."

When I still didn't place my fingers around the sleeve of his purple tunic, which looked designed for a maharajah, Cruz plucked my fist from my side, lifted it, and crushed it against his arm.

He jerked me forward. I almost tripped on the hem of my dress. Lifting the soft material with my free hand, I adjusted my strides to match his hurried ones.

Flames hovered over a crowd that put a Super Bowl stadium to shame. I yanked my gaze from Cruz to the sea of faces surrounding me. Even though shadows dappled the bejeweled mass of bodies, the faeries' eyes shone as bright as the gems hooked into their ears, looped around their throats, and woven into their hair.

The floating flames shifted and assembled over Cruz and me. They wreathed our heads as we walked down the aisle, approaching the throne tree on which Linus sat with his gilded, leafy crown, bracketed by his wife and Lyoh Vega. All three wore black, but it seemed almost different shades. Addison's dress was sheer and glittery, Lyoh's tight and glossy, and Linus's tunic resembled Cruz's, strict but cut from a swath of satin.

Ace and Angelina stood on one side of the raised dais, bodies parallel but not touching. If anything, they leaned away from each other, and his arms were crossed. I'd expected Ace to have downplayed his dislike of his future bride, but his body language confirmed everything he'd told me.

Although I didn't want to look away from him, I remembered people were staring at me. Which meant they would follow my line of sight. What would cross their minds if they saw me staring at their prince on the day of my engagement?

The other side of the dais was occupied by a single body. A man of average size and average build with hawk-like features, light eyes, and autumn-colored hair. When he caught me looking, I lowered my gaze to the purple fabric that swirled around my ankles.

Cruz's hand was a manacle. I felt like a prisoner being led to her execution. In a way, I was a prisoner and this was an execution—the slaughter of my freedom.

Lost in thought, I didn't realize Cruz stopped walking until he jerked me backward. I stumbled. Looked up. First at Cruz and then at the spot before us where tendrils of black smoke were knitting together to form an object.

My eyelashes hit the arch of my eyebrows when the smoke stopped shifting and revealed a gleaming black cauldron.

Silence filled the room and buzzed in my eardrums, and then that silence was replaced by a chant. Every faerie was chanting. My frenzied mind attempted to make sense of their song, but my grasp of Faeli was too poor. Confused and more agitated than when I'd stepped into the palace, I inched backward. Cruz tightened his hold on me.

The contents of the cauldron began to glow as tendrils of glittery green smoke bubbled over its thick, dark lip.

The chanting stopped so suddenly that my ears rang from the deafening silence. Without explaining, without asking, Cruz dragged my hand toward the faerie vessel. I tucked my fingers into my palm so hard little crescents of self-inflicted pain bloomed on my skin.

"Place your hand inside," he murmured.

I turned wide, terror-filled eyes on him. Was he crazy? Whatever it contained was bubbling, boiling. Maybe he was impervious to heat but I wasn't.

"Now." Jaw clenched, he added, "Please."

As though a *please* would sway me.

It didn't.

It absolutely didn't.

The cauldron's contents cast moving shadows across his face. Without further ado, Cruz yanked on my hand and plunged it inside.

I hissed even though it didn't burn, and then I wrenched my arm back, but my hand had fused to whatever was inside. I felt my pulse everywhere, in my ears, my throat, my jaw, the spot between my eyes.

Cruz sank his hand inside beside mine.

Scintillating strands of magic rose and snaked around both our forearms, sizzling where they made contact with skin. Like when I'd pressed my hand over a lightbulb as a child to examine the map of veins irrigating my body, my skin turned translucent. Instead of opaque and red, the blood in my veins shimmered as the strange light inside the cauldron traveled up my arm and into my shoulder blade, and spread into my chest.

The same was happening to Cruz. Even through his tunic, the path of magic was visible.

A new sonorous chant eddied from the crowd. My veins prickled, and I hissed out a breath. When the slow burn of the W lit up my other hand, I sought Ace out. He had his arms folded stiffly in front of him, and the most intent expression marred his handsome features.

The chanting stopped, the threads of magic scampered back inside the cauldron like vines, and then the whole thing puffed into oblivion.

Blinking wildly, I dragged my hand into my chest and massaged my palm. It didn't hurt, but felt funny, like anesthetized skin.

A clap, as loud as a shotgun, resounded in the grand hall. And then more clapping ensued, filling the space with a thunderous din. The applause made my stomach knot and roll.

"You could've warned me about the process," I muttered.

Cruz took my arm as ungently as the last time. "It's done."

I shook my head. What had happened to make him so bitter? Was it Borgo's death?

He spun me around. "We must open the festivities."

As he tugged me back through the rows of ogling, joyous faeries, I asked, "What was inside the cauldron?"

"All the bonds ever established in Neverra." His mouth was set with a rigid smile. I wondered if anyone could mistake it for a true one.

"How do you break a bond?"

Cruz glanced at me. "You call on the Cauldron and place your hand inside. It'll exact a price for removing your promise."

"Leaving Neverra."

He nodded.

I thought of Lily, of how terrifying the decision must've been for her. "What is expected of us now?"

"Tonight?"

"Tonight, and in the next seventeen days."

"Tonight, we revel. Then in a week or so, there will be the *duobosi*—"

"I'm not sleeping with you!" I hissed. Not in front of an audience and not in the privacy of an apartment. "And don't you dare use your third bargain to make me," I added in a low, threatening voice.

Cruz had the audacity to smirk. "We'll discuss it when the time comes."

Revulsion crawled through my veins. I wouldn't do it. Couldn't do it. Could I? How far would I be willing to debase myself to save a friend's life? Then again, if he used his last *gajoï*, I wouldn't have a choice. At that moment, my hatred for him deepened again.

"There'll be a couple other parties to celebrate us," he continued.

When we emerged on the *lustrium*-lit terrace, Cruz wrapped his hands around my waist. Air swished beneath my feet as he flew me up and deposited me on the overhanging terrace, next to one of the silvery basins. He released me but stayed close to my side, eyes riveted on the twinkling spheres bobbing on the basin's strange surface.

The waterfalls behind me didn't roar like waterfalls on Earth. On closer inspection, it wasn't water that poured down the side of the palace, but a denser, almost liquid mist.

Faeries began streaming onto the mossy terrace, and the fire that had festooned the grand hall now settled in the trees. Although their trunks were similar to the *calimbors*, their crowns were made of violet, cotton-candy-like swirls.

"Mallow trees," a voice explained.

I snapped my attention away from the fluffy leaves and met a pair of hazel eyes.

I had a picture of those eyes and that face on my phone.

THE ENVOY

"*S*tella hasn't been able to retrieve her dust, I see."

Gregor Farrow—Faith's father and Neverra's *wariff*—didn't know his mistress was dead. I side-eyed Cruz. What game was he playing? Keeping some secrets from Gregor, yet feeding him others?

Lyoh Vega brushed past Gregor to join us.

"I hope you do not plan on capturing any more faerie dust, Catori," Lyoh said.

"I didn't come to police your world." My voice didn't rattle even though every last organ in my body trembled from the proximity of so much power.

She began lifting her hands to my forehead, but I stepped back.

"If you have nothing to hide, then you will let me read your thoughts."

"Why don't you read your son's thoughts?" I answered. "He'll show you my intentions for coming to Neverra were noble." I wanted to expose Cruz, expose his true intentions, since he wouldn't share them with me. But as soon as I said this, I thought about Lily and how it might work against me.

"My son's mind is the only mind I cannot access. Didn't he share this with you?"

I blinked up at Cruz, whose expression was so rigid his face seemed made of plaster instead of skin.

"One thing I have learned from you, mother, is the importance of secrecy and the unnecessity of sharing information that doesn't concern another person. I strongly believed, and still do for that matter, that my imperviousness to your skill didn't concern my future bride."

Lyoh's eyebrows dipped as she observed her son. It seemed as though she couldn't decide what to make of his reasoning.

From the corner of my eye, I spied Ace speaking with his mother. He towered over the small blonde, whose hand was settled on her son's forearm. Serpent-like diamond rings gleamed on each one of her fingers.

After a while, she lowered her hand and her glossy red lips fell, and then her shiny gaze slid over Cruz, over me. She crushed one hand to her chest, wrinkling the funeral-black fabric of her dress, and backed away from her son before taking flight. She soared a story high where two hovering faeries pushed open another set of golden doors to let her in. Once inside, they closed the doors and remained stationed next to them like gargoyles.

When I looked back, Ace was gone.

"Can I have a word with you, Catori?" Gregor asked.

Although wary, I nodded. He tipped his head to a path shaded by a trellis covered in glittery rose lianas, and knotted his hands behind his back. I stared at the roses that reminded me of Holly. Were these flowers born of faerie ashes too?

"So you're the *wariff*, huh?"

"Until I die."

"What does a *wariff* do?"

"Everything your president does. I'm the commander of the army, and I enforce punishments. I'm the guy you don't want to mess with. And don't believe for a second that being the *draca*'s daughter-in-law will spare you from punishment if you commit an infraction. Only the royal family gets free passes. From time to time."

"Lily didn't get a free pass."

Gregor flicked his eyes over me. "She stole a dangerous book and handed it over to our enemies."

"A blank book is hardly dangerous."

Gregor stopped walking and pivoted to face me. He was a little shorter than I was but didn't try to compensate by adding inches of air beneath his bare feet. He did puff out his chest like a frigatebird, though. "You see, this is the part I don't believe. Stella told me you tried to have it reprinted, and that your aunt read passages out to her. So unless your aunt has a knack for improvisational theater, there were words inside the book. Words that *you* read. And I'd like to know what they were to understand what *your* people are planning to do to *mine*."

"My people are humans. Not bodiless faeries."

"I should perhaps involve the *draca* in this little conversation."

"I'd rather we don't. However lovely she is." I gave him a saccharine smile. "Allow Lily to come home, and I'll tell you if I saw anything in the book."

He grunted. "Lily is a traitor. Even if she hadn't broken her engagement, I would've found a way to banish her. We don't allow traitors in our midst."

"Well then, I can't help."

He squeezed one of his eyes shut a little. "Stella said you were—"

"How wonderful. You met our dear *wariff*." Ace wrapped an arm around my shoulder. If Gregor weren't standing in front of me, if thousands of faeries weren't swanning around us, I might've rested my head against his shoulder and let out a little sigh.

"What did Stella say about me?" I asked, her dust roiling in my throat.

"Yes, what did charming Stella Sakar have to say about the *draca*'s future daughter-in-law?" Fire and spice lifted off Ace's skin and scented the air. Like a nicotine addict, I pulled in long drags of him.

Gregor narrowed his eyes. "She said Catori was a wonderful girl, and one of her daughter's closest friends."

I snorted, before casting my own barb. "*Her* daughter?"

Gregor frowned. "*Isn't* Faith her daughter?"

Did he not know, or was he playing dumb? When had he left Rowan?

"To tell you the truth," Gregor continued, "I'm surprised she didn't make it to your engagement. Hopefully she'll make it to the *duobosi*, though."

Ace's arms tightened around my back, his fingers digging into the flesh of my arm. Unlike Cruz's unyielding grip, I didn't mind Ace's hold. It felt possessive, protective. I supposed he wouldn't wish a public mating ceremony on his worst enemy.

"Tickets are already selling out, I hear," Gregor said.

I flinched. Ace slid his hand off my arm, but kept it on my body as though afraid I might keel over from dread if he didn't hold me up. He splayed his hand on my lower back, just underneath the ribbon Veroli had tied firmly.

"You know, Ace, I take it back. Cruz and you were terrific diplomatic envoys. Especially Cruz. Not only does he return with a huntress, but he's apparently got Gwenelda in his pocket."

"Gwenelda would never trust him," I said.

"With all the excitement, you two probably haven't had much time to talk about much else than your undying love for each other." Gregor smiled, his teeth a slash of cruel white. Faith had that same wide, blinding smile, except on her, it was attractive. On him, it was borderline grotesque. "Now that you can no longer interfere, she will awaken the hunters."

My fingers rolled into fists. "She will *not*."

Ace had become one solid block of man next to me. His breathing had turned shallow, and pulsed from his barely parted lips. He looked over at Cruz, deep in conversation with Linus Wood. "Excuse me," he murmured. He pulled his hand away from me and walked toward his father and Cruz.

The spot he'd touched turned icy cold, and I shivered. Or perhaps it was the idea that Gwenelda was going to wake the hunters in my backyard that made me shiver.

So Cruz made me move to Neverra to get me out of the way.

Bastard.

I would kill Cruz if anything happened to my father.

"You seem agitated, Catori," Gregor said.

"And you seem calm. Aren't you concerned about waking the hunters?"

"We've waited two centuries for Negongwa to cancel his regulation on our dust. In a matter of days, we'll be able to return to Earth with a limitless amount of dust."

"But many more hunters will be waiting for you there. Don't you fear them?"

"You speak as though we're planning on letting them live after the regulation is canceled."

"You're going to kill them?" I hissed.

He leered at me. "If they get in our way . . ."

I glared hard at Gregor before heading toward Cruz. "I would like to leave."

He observed my furious expression with disconcerting calmness. "Linus, my fiancée is in a hurry to celebrate. Will you excuse us?"

I was certain my cheeks were as crimson as Ace's were pale.

"I was so looking forward to getting to know you, my dear," Linus said, his voice as oily as his slicked-back, orangey hair. "Let me at least get you a glass of sparkling faerie wine." He clicked his fingers, and a faerie in a dress as green as the moss on the turrets extended a twinkling gold sphere toward Linus.

He plucked it from her, shooed her away, and squeezed the ball between his fingers. The glittery exterior popped, leaving behind a clear goblet filled with a deep amber liquid. Linus extended it to me, but I shook my head.

"Thank you, but I don't drink." Especially drinks that could be mallow-spiked. My stomach rumbled though, and I realized it had been hours since I'd eaten. Dozens of hours. But what could I eat in this world that wouldn't screw with my mind or poison me?

"You are missing out, my dear." Linus tipped the glass to his mouth and gulped down the contents before tossing the goblet in the air, where it burst like a soap bubble.

I stared at the empty spot for long seconds.

"Catori, tomorrow the *calidum* are celebrating Middle Month." Linus burped. *Twice*. "The marketplace will be decorated for the festivities, and everyone will be selling their best wares. I'd appreciate it if you would accompany me. Especially since Cruz will be leaving on a diplomatic mission first thing in the morning."

Diplomatic mission, my ass. I still couldn't believe he and Gwenelda could be working together, but their desires were aligned. Gwen wanted to awaken her tribe the same way the faeries did. But where Gwen wanted to be reunited with her family, faeries wanted their dust regulation annulled so they could swarm our Earth. They'd kill Negongwa and his people the second he lifted his ban.

"I'll send a *lucionaga* to pick you up at sunup," Linus said, even though I hadn't accepted his invitation. I'd hoped my lack of answer would be understood as a refusal.

"I can pick her up," Ace grumbled. "I'm going anyway."

One of Linus's thick, honey-red eyebrows lifted while my cheeks colored. Everything I'd done to protect Ace would be for nothing if he didn't stop acting so concerned about me.

"Doesn't a prince have better things to do than carry around someone else's fiancée?" I asked.

A smile squeezed onto Linus's tanned, barely lined face.

Ace stepped back, surprise and hurt warring over his features. "Right. What was I thinking being chivalrous?" His tone cut deeply. "Perhaps I should go with Cruz to control the awakening of the hunters."

I tried to move my gaze off from Ace's face, but the masochist in me couldn't look away.

"I would rather you keep an eye on my fiancée," Cruz said. "No one understands hunters the way you do."

Ace snorted.

I whipped my gaze toward Cruz. Was he trying to trap Ace, or did he honestly believe I was going to wage a one-woman attack on faeries to chastise him for awakening the hunters?

Actually . . . Could I threaten him in some way to make him stop? Lily had mentioned a place called the glades—one of the Daneelies' homes. "I'd love to see more of your kingdom, Mr. Wood. Do you think I could get a tour tomorrow after the Middle Month celebration?"

"*Massin* Wood." Linus wrinkled his nose. "Mr. Wood sounds so very human."

"Excuse my unfamiliarity with your language and customs."

"You are excused, my dear."

Cruz's hand snaked over the spot where Ace's hand had been minutes ago. Unlike Ace's hand, the warmth that leaked through his palm felt intrusive, scalding. "I think that's a wonderful initiative. Will you provide my fiancée with a tour, Ace?"

"I'm sure Catori will be more comfortable visiting Neverra with a *lucionaga*." Ace didn't look at me as he said this, but the horrified shiver coursing through my body ignited my brand, which ignited his palm.

He curled his fingers, then nodded. "I have another party to attend. Enjoy your evening, Catori. I hope Cruz will be gentler with you than he was with Lily."

I gasped while Linus laughed. Cruz, at least, had the decency not to react.

After taking his leave, Cruz airlifted me back to his apartment. As soon as the door closed, I yelled, "Is that why I'm here?"

His thick brows slanted underneath the black waves of hair strafing his forehead. "Is *what* why you're here?"

"So you could get me out of the way to wake the hunters?"

"No."

"Then why?"

"I've already explained my reasons why."

I folded my arms. "If those were your reasons, then I don't understand why you want Ace to spend the entire day with me tomorrow."

He tilted his face to the side.

"Are you trying to annoy him?"

He smirked. "I doubt forcing him to spend the day with you is an annoyance."

"He doesn't like me anymore, so yeah, it is."

"Doesn't he?"

My arms fell out of their tight knot and knocked against my sides. "I don't understand you!"

"Don't waste your time trying to."

I scraped my hands down my face and exhaled a violent breath.

"Spend your time trying to understand yourself, Catori."

What was that supposed to mean? "I understand myself just fine."

"Do you?"

I frowned.

"Veroli will be here in the morning to dress you." He started to turn. "Oh. And I had a meal delivered for you." He pointed to the fireplace where a silver platter had been deposited on the stones surrounding it. "There is no mallow in the food, or poison for that matter. Have a lovely night, Catori."

When he started toward the door, my heart banged against my ribcage. "Cruz, if you awaken the hunters using *anyone* I know, I will make your life hell."

A brazen smile stirred on his lips. "I'm betting on it."

He winked and then was gone, leaving me so frustrated I paced and prowled until the sky was deep violet and the fire had almost burned out. I added more logs, pinched a bite of food from the plate, and waited for my head to feel lighter. When nothing happened, I wolfed down the food. And then, thanks to a surplus of adrenaline, I went to the bookcase, selected a book, and forced myself to read it.

While I was stuck in this god-forsaken land, I would learn as much Faeli as I could.

37

AIR SHIPS

The air smelled spicy and rich. Mom must've made cinnamon rolls. She always added cinnamon to her baking, be it savory or sweet. My stomach growled, and its growl made me stir.

I squinted at my bright surroundings.

I wasn't home.

I wasn't even close to home. And my mother couldn't be baking, because my mother was no longer alive. The realizations drenched me like buckets of icy water.

I lay still for a moment, listening and looking. There was no noise, but someone had come because a heavy fur cover was tucked around me, and I hadn't put it there. The hearth no longer danced with flames, the bay window framed a pale periwinkle sky, and the platter with my dinner had been replaced with a silver bowl full of small golden puffs.

I stretched, then cracked my stiff neck. The fur slipped off my legs and pooled onto the floor, revealing the purple fabric of last night's dress. At least no one had taken it off me, which was reassuring. I tugged on the ends of the ribbon, and the bodice fell away from my constricted chest. How I'd managed to fall asleep in that straitjacket was beyond me. I worked on my hair next, removing all the pins that had surely left indents in my scalp. I shook out the braid and massaged my head, which felt hazy from too much sleep. Or maybe it was from all the Faeli books I'd attempted to decipher.

Cool air whooshed against my back. I spun toward the front door as Veroli bustled in. "Blessed morning, deary."

"Good morning." The answer was robotic because in no way was it a good morning if I was still here.

"I didn't want to wake you, but I was told to have you ready by midmorning."

She placed a bulging fabric bag on the floor and bent at the waist to retrieve scraps of sheer turquoise fabric. The outfit I was to wear.

I yawned. How long had I slept if nights were longer in Neverra? Twenty hours?

"I made you *cannelati*."

I frowned.

Veroli pointed to the silver bowl. "It's traditional *calidum* fare. We make it at Middle Month." She sighed happily. "Soon the sunlight will reach us."

I picked up one of the golden puffs and sniffed it before placing it on my tongue, where it melted into a delightful puddle of cinnamony sweetness. "What do you mean?" I filched another puff.

"The mist will soon be flush with the ground. For two days, we marsh-dwellers will get sunlight."

The puff fell from my fingers. "You only get two days of sunlight a month?"

"Yes. It's especially hard on the land-growers. They get in so much trouble if their produce isn't succulent enough, but most vegetables and fruit need sunlight, a small fact that seems to escape the *caligosupra*."

A piece of a long-ago conversation returned to me. Back at Bee's, Borgo had touched upon some of Neverra's politics. He'd said mist-dwellers paid marsh-dwellers with sunshine and mallow. I now understood why anyone would accept payment in the form of light.

Veroli bustled over to me, turquoise fabric streaming behind her. She removed the ribbon I'd untied, then helped me wriggle out of my dress. Still reeling from the fact that the lower castes had restricted access to sunlight, I didn't put up a fight about having someone else dress me. I let Veroli loop the new fabric around me and tie it snugly over my ribcage. She layered a bra made of leather over the fabric and tightened it until my breasts were sandwiched together.

I self-consciously tried to loosen the strip of brown leather binding my breasts. "Um. Do I have to wear that?"

"You could go without, but the fabric is transparent."

My cheeks smoldered. Definitely not an option then. "Why can't I wear clothes like yours?"

Veroli tutted. "Because you're a *caligosupra*. If you were to wear a green tunic, you might be mistaken for a worker *and* I'd lose my job." Her small fingers worked through my hair. "Cruz didn't sleep here last night?" She shook out my tresses that settled in crimped waves over my shoulders.

"He had to return to Rowan," I mumbled.

"I'm sure he'll be back soon."

Did she think I was sad he'd left me? Not wanting to remind her of my strong dislike for her "child," I asked, "Have you told anyone about what you saw last night?"

Silence.

Then, she said, "No."

Relief warmed my core.

"Catori, can all hunters manipulate *wita*?"

"No."

Veroli made me sit down, then proceeded to swipe her palms over my face. My skin warmed and tingled.

I snapped away from her. "What are you doing?"

"Removing your makeup to apply it fresh."

"You're burning it away?"

She nodded. "Quicker than water and oil."

It might've been quicker, but it had to be more dangerous. What if she singed off my eyebrows and lashes?

She rested her palm on my shoulder. "I'm not looking to hurt you."

"O-Okay."

She went back to getting my face ready, and I let her. That wasn't to say I wasn't concerned, but I forced myself to sit still. When she declared me ready, I rose from the armchair.

I inspected my legs swathed in the billowy turquoise fabric tied with wide strips of leather around my thighs and calves. "The celebration is on the ground, right?"

"Right."

"Don't I need shoes then?"

"*Caligosupra* feet never touch the ground."

"You forget I can't fly."

"I don't forget anything."

"Then—"

"Don't you worry, you will be carried through the marketplace."

"I don't want to be carried."

She gave me a strange, almost distressed look. "You won't have a choice."

I set my jaw and dropped that conversation. There was nothing Veroli could do about my way of transportation. "How long would it take me to walk down the spirals?"

"All the way down?"

I nodded.

"Half of an hour."

I blinked. "That's it?"

"That's it? Oh. You're thinking in human hours. I'm speaking in Neverrian hours."

Right . . .

Her short forehead furrowed. "Close to three human hours, I would think."

"Three hours?" I yelped.

She nodded. "Ace is working with some of our smarter brethren on building an *elevator*." She enunciated each letter in the word. "Is that how your people say it?"

I nodded. Ace had touched upon that once. It had seemed odd to me that a world full of magic would need such a human contraption, but now I understood. "Do you walk up here every morning?"

"Oh, skies, no. My cousin drops me off on his way to work."

"Your cousin?"

"He has a lot of faerie blood, so he landed the job of transporting those who can't fly up to their places of work. He doesn't deduct anything from my wages, though." She beamed. "Dawson's going to start training with him soon. He needs to get his license to wield *runas* first."

"*Runas?*"

"They're big baskets made of *volitor* fronds."

I'd read about *volitors* last night. They were like palm trees, but unlike palms, they floated. "Do *runas* float?"

"Yes."

"Has anyone ever thought of adding a motor to them to make them into air boats?"

Her brow creased further. "Boat?"

"You know, like the *Titanic*?"

Her gaze darted to my red fingernails. Then she cleared her throat and shook her head. "You should tell Ace. He'd like that idea."

I didn't think he'd like any of my ideas. Not after how rude I was to him last night.

A trumpet sounded, knocking Ace right out of my mind. I stumbled against the pile of books next to the armchair. They crashed onto the floor.

"Your ride has arrived."

I crouched and gathered the books with trembling hands. Veroli knelt beside me, laying a palm on my arm. "I'll take care of this."

Nodding, I stood back up.

"From the sound of it, it must be a royal *runa*. Only royal *runas* can make fanfare."

Royal? Did that mean Ace had come to get me?

38

MIDDLE MONTH

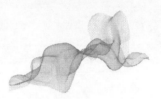

J took baby steps toward the door. When I drew it open, my breath tangled in my throat and made me sputter. It wasn't Ace, but Veroli had been right. It was a member of the royal family who'd come.

Angelina stood next to what looked like a gondola basket. "Morning to you, Catiri."

I ground my teeth so tight the enamel was sure to chip. "It's Catori."

She smiled brightly. "Oops."

When I hadn't moved from the doorway, she patted the basket that rested on the back of a flying male faerie.

"Linus asked me to fetch you."

I still didn't say anything.

"If we don't hurry, we'll miss the air joust tournament. I have bets on who's going to win, so I don't want to miss it." Her too-perfect smile was still intact. "Come along."

I unglued the soles of my bare feet from the wooden boards and walked toward the *runa*. Carefully, I climbed inside of it.

Angelina gracefully soared into the basket beside me.

"You're not flying?"

"Ace doesn't want me to overexert myself." She patted her protruding stomach.

I wanted to ask if it was actually Ace or Linus who'd asked her to take it easy, but it wasn't any of my business. Besides, I shouldn't care.

Our faerie hot air balloon took flight. I clutched the ochre edges of the basket, fingers whitening as we descended. *Calimbors* rose around us, and soon their crowns melded with the lilac sky. Green-clothed bodies stood on the spirals wrapped around the thick trunks, almost indistinguishable amidst the spots of moss mottling the bark.

Angelina waved at them like a Miss America contestant, her plastic smile in place. "It's a boy, you know." Her lips barely shifted as she spoke.

"What's a boy?"

"Why, my baby, of course." She gave a little laugh. "Don't you read human magazines?"

Right.

"Well it's a boy, which means I'm carrying a future monarch. I was thinking of calling him Kingston. What do you think?"

"I think it sounds Jamaican."

She lifted her chin up haughtily. "Well I like it. And Linus likes it."

"Does Ace like it?"

She fixed her wide orangey-brown eyes on mine. "He'll have to."

"Fathers don't get a say in Neverra?" I made sure my expression was curious and not taunting. I didn't need to make an enemy out of Angelina. It was surely wiser to make a friend of her.

Her smile morphed into a brighter one. "They do. When their wives allow them one."

"I thought women had to do everything men asked in Neverra."

"Women like you, yes, but not women like me. I'm a royal *caligo-supra*. Only Linus and Ace can ask things of me. They are my only superiors."

"So they could have a say in naming your child?"

"They have more important things to bother with than naming children."

The *runa* dove into the cottony mist, which wrapped around my bare skin like wet hair.

I rubbed my arms once we'd passed through it. "What about Addison Wood?"

Angelina squinted one of her eyes. "What about Addison Wood?"

"Isn't she higher on the food chain?"

"She is, but the only thing that interests her is chewing mallow, so she's out of it most days." Angelina brought her lips closer to my ear. "There's not much of a mind left in that head of hers. Mallow is extremely addictive, almost as addictive as Daneelie scales."

A chill swept over my skin, colder than the strands of mist that still clung there.

"But unlike mallow, Daneelie scales don't screw up your head in the long term." She waggled her eyebrows. "Have you ever tried them?"

I shook my head.

"I'll get you some today. An early wedding present."

"I'm— Thank you but I'm not interested."

She *tsked*. "That's because you've never tried them." She went back to waving at the curious bystanders crowding the spirals. Suddenly, smears of sapphire blue broke the surrounding gray-greenness. It took another couple seconds to realize that those smears were flags. They flapped over an enormous canopy woven from flowery vines and leaves.

The basket veered to the right so suddenly that Angelina snapped her neck up and bit out Faeli words that I suspected were as unpleasant as they sounded. Our faerie "driver" murmured excuses, his eyes cutting to the spot we'd dodged.

A gilded birdcage larger than our *runa* flitted in the air next to us. A body was sprawled inside. Gray hair curled around the prisoner's limp shoulders, fluttered in the nippy breeze like the leaves on the pergola below. "Is that a . . . a . . .?"

"A *cupola*? Yeah." Angelina pinched her lips. "It's in such poor taste to have it floating around so close to the marketplace during Middle Month, subjecting *caligosupra* to the spectacle. At least the prisoner is unconscious. Their screams can be really grating." She sighed deeply. "I bet it was Lyoh's idea. She's more beast than woman if you ask me. Sometimes I think she'll turn into a dragon permanently."

I scanned the dim sky for a black-winged creature. None appeared.

"She doesn't like me, but she doesn't like anyone, so I don't take it personally. She doesn't even care about her own son, although now that he shook off Lily, who between you and me, was *such* an ankle-grabber, he rose in her esteem. Don't get me wrong, Ace's sister was plenty nice, but so freaking desperate. Men aren't attracted to desperation. I tried to tell her, but she wasn't interested in my advice."

I would've smirked at that last part, had I not been so peeved by Angelina's use of the past tense. I didn't want to hear Lily spoken of as though she were already dead.

"Anyway, since he disposed of her," Angelina droned on, "even though she was his ticket into the royal family—the *draca* seems to appreciate her son more."

The ground rose beneath us fast.

Soon the tiny forms next to the leafy big top became bodies. The pinheads became upturned faces. I recognized Linus. He sat in a golden *runa* flanked by four golden-eyed guards. He smiled widely when he spotted us. And then he turned and spoke in Faeli to someone on the ground. It took me a minute to make out the body lurking in the shadows of the marketplace. Once I recognized it, I hardly noticed anything or anyone else.

Unlike his father who hovered several feet in the air, Ace had his feet firmly planted on the muddy, mossy ground.

Our "driver" lowered us further, then leveled off behind Linus. I'm not sure what inspired me to hop out of the *runa*—probably my desperation for firm ground—but I jumped out as soon as I deemed the ground close enough. A collective hiss echoed around me.

"Catiri?" Angelina yelped, shooting to the edge of the basket.

I shot my gaze up to her face. Her cheeks were pale and her plump mouth was parted wide. "What?"

"You're not supposed to wade on the marsh."

A chill went up my spine. Cold green muck sucked at my feet. Was it like quicksand? Would I vanish into the belly of Neverra? Maybe it would spit me right into the *Hareni* . . . Would that be so bad? "Why not?"

"Because it's dirty," she hissed.

Ace walked out of the shadows. "To better hunt faeries, hunters rolled themselves in mud. So I doubt she'll mind a little dirt."

More gasps.

I narrowed my eyes at Ace. Was he trying to get a rise out of me or out of his future wife?

"You could set a better example, son," Linus said.

"I would not want to rise higher than you, father."

A crushing silence enveloped the large crowd. Someone cleared their throat. That someone was Gregor. He dangled in midair next to the *lucionaga* shielding the king. "The jousters are ready to begin, *Massin.*"

Trumpets sounded around us, their sound building to a crescendo as two silver-cloaked men flew over my head, stopping just before Linus. They bowed deeply, then nodded to each other and flew dozens of yards away.

As the trumpet sound petered out, Ace said, "How was your night, Catiri?"

Keeping my gaze on the silver-cloaked faeries, I whispered, "Shut up."

Ace chuckled. The faeries squared off and angled their torsos parallel to the ground. Arms outstretched like Superman, they soared toward one another.

"So what are the rules of this game?"

"A fight to the death."

I spun toward Ace. "Death?"

His blue eyes were soft on my face. "The first to asphyxiate the other with dust can ascend over the mist and become a *caligosupra.*"

"They kill each other for status?"

"Most people would rather tread sky than mud."

Goosebumps coated my skin as the crowd cheered. I tipped my head back up as one of the faeries performed a backflip to get away from the other.

"I'd advise you not to watch, little hunter, but I wouldn't be so presumptuous as to think I knew what was best for you."

Reproach colored his tone. I folded my arms in front of my chest. The air was chilly under the mist, and although Ace was standing close to me, the fire burning beneath his skin barely warmed mine. His eyes traced the tiny bumps on my skin.

Shrieks followed by laughter rose from the crowd. I looked back at the jousting faeries. Grappling against each other, they twirled and whirled in the air. Suddenly they came apart again.

I was about to ask Ace how long it would last, but he was no longer next to me. I shivered at the iciness that enveloped my body in his absence. I'd been wrong. His fire *had* warmed my skin.

I concentrated on the fight overhead, wincing when one faerie plummeted from the sky and landed with a wet thud against the ground. For several minutes, the man didn't stir. I bit down on my lip as the other faerie shot straight for him, a spear clutched in his hand. Where he'd procured himself a weapon was beyond me. He tossed it at the fallen faerie. The fae rolled away, and the spear broke into a million glimmering pieces. The particles streamed back toward the faerie who'd wielded them and vanished inside his palm.

The spear was made of dust!

Something soft settled over my shoulders. White fur.

"Veroli should've dressed you better," Ace grumbled.

From the corner of my eye, I noticed Gregor watching us. I stepped away from Ace. "Thank you," I murmured, wrapping the heavy pelt tighter around me.

I looked back at the spectacle that enchanted the large audience. A small bird with a sharp beak shot out of the other faerie's palm.

"Is the bird made of *wita*?" I thought I knew the answer, but wanted confirmation. And maybe it was my way of telling Ace I saw more than shimmery particles.

Ace didn't respond right away. "You see a bird?"

"Don't you?"

"I've always been able to see the shape of *wita*. I didn't think you—" He stopped talking.

My throat felt dry. I swallowed, and my saliva wet the sides of my throat, but didn't soothe it.

"You can really see a bird?"

I nodded.

His dark eyebrows slanted over his nose, and then his gaze dropped to my exposed neck, and then lower, to the fur.

"I think Neverra did something to my sight," I finally managed to say.

"Maybe it's stifling your hunter side."

I chewed on my bottom lip. That didn't sound like a good thing. If anything, that made me more vulnerable.

Ace pushed my fur cape away and wrapped his fingers around my forearm, which made my brand burst to life. "You don't feel warmer." His palm glowed, yet he didn't seem to notice it. "Has anything else changed since you arrived?"

A great uproar had us both looking back at the fight. One of the faeries, the one with the backside covered in green muck, turned as gray as a storm cloud before breaking into thousands of glittery pieces. I winced, squeezed my eyes shut, and turned away. Laughter and clapping erupted around me. Then the trumpets sounded again.

Ace's hand, still wrapped around my arm, tightened. And then his long thumb stroked my skin. "It's over."

Tears pricked my throat. "I think I'm going to throw up." I lunged away from him just as a wave of nausea hit me dead center. I gritted my teeth and breathed slowly, forcing back the acrid bile. I managed the extraordinary feat of not throwing up. When I straightened up, Ace, who'd fisted my hair, let go, and my long locks settled against my cold, cold cheeks.

"And here I thought hunters took great pleasure in seeing faeries explode into ash." Linus's voice snaked over to me, edged in a mirth that made my stomach roil all over again.

My horror-stricken gaze struck his ruddy face.

He laughed. "Why don't you come and sit in my *runa* for the visit of the marketplace? You'll see better from up here."

Ace stiffened next to me.

"I don't want to seem ungrateful, *Massin*, but my human legs would prefer walking. Would it be all right if I remained below?"

"You are free to do what you like, but try not to brush against the *caligosubi*. They might rub off on you." His words elicited delight from his courtiers. "I suppose my son can fend them off. He's talented at keeping people away."

"I try my best, father." He sent his father a jagged smile.

Nonplussed by his son's retort, Linus clapped, and the faerie carrying his *runa* dashed into the enormous pergola that stretched two stories high. A procession of *runas* followed. Only Gregor hung back, hovering mere feet away from Ace and me. He observed us a moment, but then Linus called him, and the *wariff* dashed to the front of the convoy.

"You don't have to hang back," I told Ace.

"And risk you brushing against *caligosubi*? Skies forbid that should happen."

I smirked, but then I didn't. "After what I said yesterday, why are you even talking to me?"

Ace glanced at me, his gaze as warm and soft as the fur cloak around my shoulders. He dipped his face toward my ear. "Because you want me to be angry with you and leave you alone."

I whipped my gaze up to his.

His blue eyes gleamed in the darkness of the leafy canopy. "I still don't understand why you're so desperately trying to rile me up and push me away, but don't think for a minute I'm not working on finding out."

"Ace—" I started but stopped. If I told him to stop trying to figure it out, it would be a confession, and confessions had to wait until my marriage or I wouldn't be able to bring his sister home.

But what if he guessed? Would Cruz revoke his bargain? Perhaps he *was* twisted enough to do that.

"There's nothing to figure out." I stomped ahead of him, trying to put space between us.

He grabbed my arm through the fur and spun me around.

I shook him off. "Don't."

"Don't what?"

"Don't touch me."

"Once upon a time you couldn't get enough of my touch."

I swallowed hard, his palm glowing with my drumming heartbeats. "Don't flatter yourself."

A shadow crossed his face, but then was gone. "Why's your heart beating so fast then?"

"Because I'm afraid."

"Of me?"

Of how my body reacts to yours. Of how I feel around you. "Yes."

His nostrils flared. "I can work with fear. What I can't work with is indifference."

"Ace, I'm taken. Forget about me. Live your life."

"You're in no place to give me advice about my life."

I shut my eyes, opened them again.

"Besides, I just want to be your friend. Nothing more."

"Why do you even want to be my friend?"

"Because Lily told me to watch over you."

Lily . . .

Her name brought back thoughts of home. "Are the hunters . . . awake?"

Tendons showed through his taut neck as he turned his face away from mine. Around us, green-cloaked faeries stood expectantly behind long slabs of stone on which were arranged a hodgepodge of shiny and colorful wares.

"Ace?" I touched his hand to get his attention.

His eyes found mine again.

"Did Cruz and Gwenelda wake them?"

"Yes."

Time stopped. Noise vanished. The world around me became one great puddle of color. "Is my father . . . is he . . .?"

"Your father's unharmed. He won a cruise in the Caribbean a couple days after you left."

"He did?" I croaked.

Ace smiled.

"He must be in heaven. He loves boating so much."

"I know."

A tear slid down my cheek. "Did he really win a cruise or did you—"

"Does it matter?"

"It matters to me."

"Will I be in your good graces again if I said I'd bought him a ticket?"

"You were never in my bad graces."

His smile diminished. "Could've fooled me."

My bottom lip trembled, so I bit it.

Ace's hand arced toward my face but stopped midway. He curled his fingers and brought his fist back at his side. "And when your father returns to Rowan, he won't even realize anyone dug up his backyard. Kajika promised to return the site to its original aspect, and Lily is overseeing it."

My heart leaped with gratitude.

"We better start moving, or you'll sadden many excited *caligosubi*. Being able to show off their craftsmanship on Middle Month thrills them almost as much as when they get their two days of sunshine."

"That's plain barbarism."

"Don't say that too loud, Catiri, or you might incur my father's wrath."

"And if you keep calling me Catiri, you'll incur my wrath."

A smile broke over his face, chasing away the shadows that had roamed over it since the day I'd ended things between us. "Your wrath amuses me."

Even though my veins were devoid of fire, I felt warm and light. But then the noise of the marketplace crashed into me like water released from a dam. I remembered we weren't alone . . . that others, like Gregor, were watching, so I schooled my features into a blank, bland expression. "You never did take me seriously. Then again, you never take anything seriously. Life's just one great joke to you."

Ace's entire face pleated.

Unable to stand his disappointment, I lowered my eyes and traipsed ahead of him, making my own way into the shadowy, boisterous marketplace. Selfishly, I wanted him not to give up on me, not to leave, but he left.

And it hurt so damn much.

39

THE EARRINGS

Gregor took Ace's place at my side. Although his feet didn't touch the ground, he hovered beside me.

As I approached the first slab of stone on which were laid out twinkling jewels, I asked, "What sort of money do you use here? Beside sunshine and mallow."

Gregor peered down at me. "Copper coins."

"And how can I procure myself copper coins?"

Gregor whistled, and a *lucionaga* approached.

The golden-eyed man inclined his head. Silky strands of brown hair escaped the leather cord he'd used to tie back his shoulder-length hair. For some reason, he looked familiar. "*Wariff.*" I'd definitely heard him speak before.

"Cruz's bride desires a bag of coins. Get her one." When the *lucionaga* flew away, Gregor said, "Now that you and Cruz are engaged, you have access to his wealth, and from what Lyoh tells me, his father left him everything he owned. Which is a consequential amount."

A blush warmed my cheeks and nose. "I'd rather not use his money."

"Do you have copper coins of your own?"

"No."

"Mallow?"

I shook my head.

"And you can't fly, so if you want to purchase anything here, you don't have much of a choice."

"I don't really need anything," I whispered.

"*Caligosupra* rarely need anything."

"Is there really no other way to buy something?"

He cocked his head to the side. "Until you become pregnant with your husband's child, you can't offer your body for a price. So no, there is no way for you to make a *quick buck*, as they say in your world."

I recoiled, mouth twisting in disgust. Had he really suggested prostitution?

"Don't look so revolted. I know for a fact humans sell their bodies, too. I've bought my fair share."

The little hairs on the nape of my neck rose. "Just because some women are okay with that doesn't mean *I* am."

"I give you a couple years before you change your mind."

"Never."

Gregor smiled ruefully. "Would you like to bet on that? That's another way you can make money around here."

Someone touched my hand then, whisking my attention from Gregor's leering face. A small woman stood next to me, hunched over a gnarled branch she used as a walking stick. She pressed a pair of carved red earrings inside my hand.

I blinked as a *lucionaga* seized her shoulders and yanked her away. He growled words to her that made her cower behind the long slab of stone, then tossed her the walking stick that had tumbled from her hands. It struck her raised arm.

Still clutching the earrings, I stared at the brute, who was barking orders at the other sellers. He was probably telling them not to approach me.

"How much does she want for these?"

Eyes shiny with shock—or was it hope?—the old woman spoke up, but her Faeli words didn't register with me.

Gregor scoffed.

"How much did she ask for?"

"Ten copper coins. A full month's wage." He shook his head, a disdainful sneer curling his upper lip. "They're surely not worth more than a single mallow leaf."

"How much is a mallow leaf worth?"

He slid his hazel gaze to me. "If a copper coin is worth a hundred dollars, a mallow leaf is worth one."

The *lucionaga* with the ponytail had returned, brandishing a velvet pouch filled with coins. He handed it to me, and although I felt using Cruz's money was wrong, not helping the people around me was downright criminal.

I drew the pouch open and selected a coin. "Are they all worth the same thing?"

Gregor nodded.

They weren't round, but they were shiny and heavy. A W like the one that graced my hand was engraved on one side, a wreath on the other. I dug out two more coins.

"Don't." Gregor's voice was low, almost menacing.

"Don't what?"

"Overpay for a piece of glass. It sends the wrong impression."

"And what impression would that be?"

"That you are a dupe *and* a fool."

I smiled brazenly and walked over to the crippled woman. I placed the three coins in front of her. A hush fell over the merchants nearest the woman. Their wide eyes followed my hands as they speared the earrings through my lobes.

I found their heavy weight incredibly pleasing. Especially when I noticed all the wrinkled noses of the faeries perched in their *runas*.

"Perhaps I was wrong about you," Gregor said, hovering beside me as I walked deeper into the marketplace. "You probably won't sell your body; you'll end up giving it away for free."

Biting retorts flickered through my mind. I counted to three to settle my rising nerves. And then I counted to three again. By my third time counting, I said, "Good thing I'm part hunter, isn't it? Who in their right mind would want to bed their worst enemy?"

Besides Cruz . . .

Not that he wanted to bed me, though. I hoped.

"We destroyed our worst enemies long ago."

I frowned. It hadn't been the answer I was expecting.

"You are merely a mutt with an alluring face."

Classy. Not that I expected more from him. "If the Unseelie aren't your worst enemies, then who are?"

"You mean, who *were*?" The corners of Gregor's lips curled upward. There was so much of Faith in him. How did he not know she was his daughter? Had he truly never found out? "The Daneelies, but we wiped that species out years ago. Has Cruz blessed you with their scales yet? It would do your frigid body wonders."

The desire to slap him made me curl my toes into the cold wet earth. "Thank you for the unwanted advice." For the rest of the market visit, I neither spoke to Gregor nor bought anything else. I simply meandered through the aisles, barely noticing what the poor *calidum* were trying to sell me.

Somebody touched my shoulder, and I jumped.

I spun around and met a blushing, freckled face.

*D*awson's gaze vaulted between Gregor and me. "Did I come too early to pick you up?"

Not early enough . . . "Am I free to leave, Gregor?"

"Do you see *cupola* bars around you?"

"No."

"Then you are free." He whistled, and a *lucionaga*—the one with the ponytail—appeared at his side. "Silas, you will accompany Catori and Dawson on their trek through our land."

Silas . . . The *lucionaga* I'd met on the beach the night Alice was killed.

Linus's *runa* parked above me. "Leaving so soon, Catori?"

I had no idea how long I'd been there, but surely it had been a while. My feet were numb with cold and my ears buzzed from the noise.

Linus's fiery-blond hair fluttered in the soft breeze gusting through the marketplace, which was rife with the scent of musky bodies and wet greenery. "Will you join us for supper?"

If I could help it, I wouldn't see the royal family until the night of my nuptials, but did I have a choice? I tipped my face up. "If I'm not too drained from my day, *Massin*, I'll join you."

"Don't overexert yourself then, my dear. We haven't had much time to speak, and I have *oh* so many questions for you."

My heartbeats turned to ragged thuds. I gave him a tight nod, then asked, "Must your guard really accompany us?"

Linus glanced at Gregor, and something passed between them. Thumbing his smooth chin, Linus said, "Silas is strong and will keep you safe from the animals roaming our land. Plus, he's extremely discreet. You won't even notice he's there."

Silas's gold eyes gleamed suspiciously underneath the dusky canopy. *Yeah.* Sighing, I walked ahead of Dawson through the rows of vendors. I looked for the old woman on my way out and found her surrounded by other green-clad sellers. Through the huddled bodies, her eyes met mine, and her face creased with an almost toothless smile.

The others around her twirled to stare. I self-consciously twisted my hair in a rope over my shoulder, and kept twisting it until I was out of the marketplace. Although the light was muted by the heavy cloud of mist, stepping outside felt like stepping into the brightest sunshine. I filled my lungs with the air that tasted so pure and vibrant I couldn't lap it in fast enough.

"So"—Dawson pushed his unruly blond hair out of his baby blue eyes—"you want me to carry you?"

"Nope. But any chance I could get my shoes back?"

"Your shoes?"

"I had shoes when Cruz brought me to Neverra. They're at the apartment."

"Sure. I can do that." He zipped upward, cutting through the mist like a knife through butter, leaving me alone with a glowering Silas.

He folded his large arms over his overinflated chest. "Is it true that you asked Cruz to marry you?"

"Maybe."

His thick eyebrows slanted deeper over his honey-colored eyes. "Why?"

"It's none of your business."

He flew closer to me, his feet inches off the ground. Unlike *caligo-supra*, he wore black leather boots that matched his all-black outfit of pants and T-shirt. If it weren't for his metallic eyes, he could pass for a secret service agent. "We protect our kingdom, so it is my business to understand the intent of our visitors. Especially visitors with Unseelie blood."

"Don't get your boxers in a twist. I'm not here to murder your king."

"Are you here to murder anyone else?"

I smiled sweetly. "Depends how rude you plan on being to me."

A whoosh of air lifted the ends of my hair as a body thumped next to me. Dawson's freckles glowed like red pepper flakes as he dangled my sneakers in front of me. Never had I been so happy to see a pair of sneakers. I took them from him, sat on a twisted root as wide as a carved bench, and holding my fur cape closed with one hand, I wiped the soles of my feet with my palms until Dawson crouched in front of me.

"I have a better way to get rid of mud."

"Let me guess . . . fire?"

He grinned. Blue flames flickered over his palms and burned away the muck that had hardened to clay. The fire not only cleaned, but warmed.

Once Dawson was done, I slid my feet inside my shoes. "How do people survive without fire around here?"

"They rely heavily on sky-dwellers." He rose, but didn't take flight.

"Is it always this cold?"

"Not when the sun shines," Silas said.

So ninety-eight percent of the time it was cold, which wouldn't bother those with fire in their veins. Finding no point in raging against the injustice of it all, I asked, "How big is Neverra?"

"Big," Dawson said. "But not as big as Earth."

"How long would it take me to see it all?"

"Days. I had a friend who mapped it, so he walked, and it took him an entire week before he made it back to his starting point. If you flew, it would only take a day."

But I didn't fly. I could run fast, though. My thighs and calves zinged in anticipation. Would Dawson find it strange that I liked to run? Borgo had, back when we'd crossed paths in Manistee forest. Marsh-dwellers seemed so intent on surviving, exercise was surely the furthest preoccupation from their mind.

"So where do you want to go?" Dawson asked.

I stood up, grabbed one of my feet, stretched the back of my thighs, then repeated the movement on my other side. "Where's the *Hareni*?"

Suspicion fired across Silas's bronzed skin. "You are not to approach the *Hareni*."

"Why not? Isn't it one of the sights to see in Neverra?" I didn't think it wise to needle a burly faerie guard, but couldn't help it. I didn't like to be told what to do.

Dawson had gone very rigid next to me. "It's not a good idea, Catori."

"Why can't I see where my *relatives* live? It's not as though they have a way out of there, do they?"

Dawson shoved a hand through his shaggy hair, freckles so red they looked like frozen computer pixels.

"You're not going there on my watch," Silas said. "There are plenty of other places to see. Pick another."

It had been worth a try. "I miss the lake by my house. You have any bodies of water in Neverra?"

Dawson's hands finally came away from his body. "We have glades in the east. That's where the Daneelie used to live, but they're all dead, so it's safe now."

Anticipation scampered over my skin, lifting it in goosebumps. "Can we go there?" I did my best to hammer down my excitement. "Or is it a no-fly zone for people like me?"

Dawson cocked a brow at Silas, seeking his approval. The faerie guard grunted something in Faeli that made Dawson give me a thumbs up.

"It's pretty far, though. Want me to call for a *runa*?"

"I'll run."

"I don't know if—"

"*Ventors* run as fast as we fly." All of Silas was still, except for the tendons shifting in his broad neck.

"Really?" Dawson's eyes widened.

I nodded. "But in no way do I run as fast as you fly. I'm not a hunter."

"Yet you have *wita* underneath your skin," the guard said.

"Because my blood contains a lot of iron."

Although the guard's unsettlingly shiny gaze was taped to me, he spoke to Dawson. "She killed Borgo Lief with her blood."

I became as stiff as the tree trunk next to me. "I didn't kill him. He used my blood to commit suicide."

Silas snorted.

I was about to insist that he had, but instead, said, "You knew

Borgo, Silas?" The guard's name came out of my mouth like the smack of a fin against a boat deck.

"The castrated outcast? Yeah, I knew him."

I would've snarled at him if I'd been the type to snarl. I turned toward Dawson instead, unhooking my heavy earrings and tucking them safely inside a fold in my pants. "In which direction are we heading?"

Dawson gestured to the right.

"Lead the way."

I took off behind him into the *calimbor* forest, trampling the spongy earth, hopping over gnarled roots. The heady mix of adrenaline and cool air seeped into my muscles and uncoiled my lingering tension.

At some point, Silas morphed into a firefly. Although he kept close to me—too close for comfort—he was so puny, I could almost pretend he wasn't there, or at least pretend he was a real bug instead of a shifter.

We loped through the forest of giant trees for miles. Crossed paths with a pack of wild dogs with fur as white as the cape Dawson offered to carry after I'd peeled it off my heaving shoulders.

All around me, life bustled. Unlike the animals that were clean and colorful, the marsh-dwellers were cloaked in the same green as the mucky moss splattered against my turquoise outfit and wore their wariness like a mask.

Most *calidum* stopped to stare at the strange sight of me running alongside a lightning bug and a flying faerie. I didn't stop to stare back, but I did look around. At the base of almost each trunk, there were openings. Some had words carved above them; others bore a symbol.

"Where do they lead?" I asked Dawson.

He spun midair to see what I was pointing at. "They're inns or shops. *Calidum* inns and shops. Sometimes sky-dwellers visit them, but they have their own places to eat and shop near the top of the *calimbors*.

"Will you take me sometime?"

"I can't because I'm not allowed inside *caligosupra*—"

"I don't mean the ones on top, Dawson."

"You'd want to go to one of ours?"

"Will they allow me inside?"

"We don't refuse anyone."

"Then I'd like to go. Maybe on our way back?"

Dawson must've been momentarily stunned by my request, because it took him a moment to catch up with me. "Okay."

We ran in companionable silence for another long stretch of time. When the forest finally gave way to a new landscape, I slowed. Ahead of me, a clearing glimmered. Swaying green stems, as tall as wheat stalks, were topped with what looked like fresh jewels. In fact, they were petals. *Glassflowers.* That's what I'd nicknamed the flower Borgo had turned into. Last night, while perusing the book about native Neverrian plants, I'd learned its true name was *adamans.* The breeze combed through the translucent purple petals that tinkled like my mother's wind chime.

I approached the field, but a hand held me back.

"You can't walk through *adamans*, Catori." Shadows pinpricked Dawson's clear eyes.

"Why not?"

"Because a lot of animals roam there. Animals that would get mighty angry if they were trodden on."

"Like what?"

"Like venomous *diles* and slithering *mikos*. They've got quills as sharp as needles. Besides, Catori, if I let you walk through it, A—" He shut his mouth and his cheeks flooded with heat.

"A?"

"*A* person," he said, insisting so much on the preposition, I cocked an eyebrow. "Likely *many*, will turn me into a pile of dirt. Please let me or Silas carry you over it."

I scanned the shimmering immensity that no longer seemed as beautiful as it had a few moments ago. "You. I'll let you carry me."

Dawson swallowed so hard his Adam's apple jostled in his skinny throat. "Silas might be more—"

"You."

"Okay." He let out a wary sigh. "Okay," he said more strongly. "Want to get on my back?"

I didn't laugh like I had the first time he'd made that suggestion. I nodded, and when he crouched before me, I climbed onto his back, looped both my legs around his narrow torso, and locked my arms around his neck.

"Ready?"

"Yeah."

Dawson dropped my cape, then sprang high so dizzyingly fast, I let out a little squeal and crushed his throat.

"Sorry," he mumbled.

The field of *adamans* rushed beneath us, shining like a purple ocean. I squinted to make out the land bordering the meadow. In the north, blue cliffs rose from a vast stretch of sunset-colored earth—sand perhaps? And up ahead, glistening silver pools marbled the land, interspersed by giant lily pads and small trees with serrated branches that reminded me of aloe vera, if aloe vera were mustard-yellow. As we dove closer, I realized the lily pads were in fact giant iridescent flat shells and the trees weren't planted into any soil. They floated over the silvery water, their roots reaching downward like tentacles, with only their tips immersed.

Dawson slalomed around the trees before landing on one of the shells. It bobbed underneath our weight.

"Welcome to the glades."

"Are those *volitors*?" I pointed to the tree nearest us, my index finger coming dangerously close to Silas's fire-lit bug body. I yanked my hand back and kept it close to my side.

"Yes!" Dawson said.

The strange, serrated yellow branch curled onto itself, as though afraid of us.

"They're shy," Dawson added.

My eyebrow tipped up. "You mean, the trees?"

His forehead ridged as though it were an odd question.

I kneeled on the edge of the shell. Even though the light was muted, the water twinkled.

"Are there any fish or other deadly creatures I should be worried about encountering?"

"There's nothing left down there but copper."

"Copper?"

"Uh-huh. The bottom is solid metal. Plants don't grow on metal. At least, not in Neverra."

I peered into the transparent water.

"So, are you going to jump in?" Dawson asked.

I wanted to, but what if scales formed on my skin? Would Silas kill me on the spot? "I'm thinking about it."

"Want me to go first?"

Before I could answer, he launched off the shell and somersaulted into the water, splashing my hands in the process. I pulled them back from the edge of the shell. Heart hopping, I looked for the faerie guard and found him droning behind me.

"Come on!" Dawson yelled.

I twisted back toward the glade, casting a furtive glance toward my hands. The only thing that glowed on them was Ace's brand. The shell seesawed again. Since there was nothing to grip onto, I backed away from the edge and bumped into legs. I assumed they were Silas's, but when I tipped my face up, the eyes looking down at me weren't gold.

ELECTRIC

Recovering from the shock of seeing Cruz, I rose slowly. "You're back." I was trying to keep my voice steady, but raw fear made it waver.

"I am. And just in time to see you swim in our waters. How exciting."

I dipped my chin toward my neck that vibrated with my frenzied pulse. "Why would that be exciting?"

"Because the glades are special to us Seelies. They're the last conquered territory in the kingdom." Cruz stared beyond me at Dawson, who was treading water.

His face was so red it seemed as though he were being boiled alive. "Was it okay that I took her here?"

"More than okay." Cruz smiled at him, white teeth gleaming between his parted lips. "Silas!"

How he recognized the guard in his bug form was beyond me.

The firefly morphed back into his delightful, brooding self. "Yes?"

"You are relieved of your duty."

Silas nodded, then shifted back to his insect body and buzzed off.

"You too, Dawson."

A breath snagged in my throat. "I'd like him to stay."

Cruz cocked his head to the side. "And I'd like to spend time alone with my fiancée."

My skin broke into goosebumps that made sweat bead on my upper lip. I licked the sweat off, then swiped my tongue over my lips, which felt chapped and raw. If I begged for Dawson to stay, Cruz might hurt him . . . or worse, make me hurt him like he'd made me hurt Ace.

My stomach tightened as Dawson soared out of the water, steaming as droplets evaporated off his skin and clothes.

An awkward grin bent his lips. "Sure thing, boss."

Geez. Did he think I was excited to see Cruz?

Cruz wrapped a hand around my waist. "Thanks for showing her around. Oh, and, Dawson, I left something for you at your house."

Dawson's eyes went wide. "What is it?"

"A surprise." When Cruz smiled at him, his smile unsettled me because it seemed warm and genuine.

Dawson shoved his almost dry hair back so many times, I was surprised he had any left. "A good surprise or a—"

Cruz rolled his eyes. "Just go home already."

Their interaction was strange, so devoid of the venom and calculated stares Cruz cast on everyone else.

Dawson bobbed his head in giddy nods, then levitated off the shell. I curled my fingers into my palms to stop myself from reaching out to him. I didn't want him to leave me, but how could I show him how unsafe I felt in the care of a man he clearly admired?

Once Dawson was gone, Cruz focused his entire attention on me. "Let's swim."

"I don't want to."

"Then why are you here?"

"Because you made me come."

"I don't mean in Neverra."

I knew he'd meant the glades. "I wanted to visit your world. My first choice was seeing the *Hareni*, but Silas said I wasn't allowed there."

"Did he now? How rude."

"I can go?"

Cruz nodded, and a black curl fell into his eyes. "Of course. I believe it's important to know where you truly come from. And I'll take you there as soon as we're done swimming."

"I told you I didn't want to—"

His palm twinkled as dust rose from his skin.

I jolted backward. "Why are you bringing out your dust?"

The ribbons twirled and fused into a pocket knife. He seized my hand and sliced my palm. I staggered, not out of pain, but out of shock. Using my moment of confusion against me, he grabbed me and jumped, dunking both our bodies into the water. I gasped, but shut my mouth when the warm, metallic-tasting water snuck past my lips, past my teeth and into my throat.

I writhed, and his arms fell away from my body. I slammed my palms into his chest, then kicked until I broke the surface. My blood raced through my veins, raging with indignation.

How dare he!

The second he told me how to save Lily, I. Would. Kill. Him.

The water slapped my face, its glassy surface no longer smooth. Seething, I forded toward the flat shell that was rocking like a kayak. I tried to grab onto it and hoist myself up, but my fingers slid. Cursing, I threw my foot up, but it skidded off, and I toppled right back into the careening surf. I looked for other options, but the *volitors*, as though apprehensive of losing their delicate balance, had lifted higher, their roots dangling several feet over the surface, out of my reach.

My last option was the faerie who'd dunked me in. I twisted around, my wet hair slapping my cheek. Cruz didn't bob next to me. I flicked my gaze upward, imagining him flying overhead, enjoying the spectacle of my struggle. He wasn't there, either. I blinked as water sprayed my eyes. Had he abandoned me? Fear crashed against my eardrums and foamed inside my belly as a stronger wave washed over my head, shoving me down toward a dark form that drifted as sluggishly as a jellyfish.

But it wasn't a jellyfish.

It was a body.

Cruz's body.

I squinted even though my eyesight wasn't blurry. Like everything else in this place, water here wasn't like water back home. Sealing my lips to preserve my breath, I waited for his body to writhe, for his hands to move, for his fingers to spread. Nothing besides his hair moved. Like seaweed, it undulated around his expressionless face.

My lungs seized as I ran out of air. I kicked back upward. As soon as my head broke the surface, I gulped air. *Fuck. Fuck. Fuck.* I ducked my head back under, surveying Cruz's listless form. Was he dead, or pretending to find out if I would save him?

A bolt of electricity hit my spine, making me yelp and arch. Had I run into something? I spun, my mind awash with utter terror. Nothing was behind me. The taste of metal filled my mouth and coated my palate. I twisted back toward Cruz.

"Shit!" I said out loud, forgetting I was submerged. The word rang out through the water almost as clearly as if I were speaking into air. I yelled Cruz's name. That too echoed limpidly against the gleaming copper floor.

Fear jammed into my throat like a wad of gum. Fear, but also resolve. However much I wanted Cruz dead, I still needed him to tell me how to get Lily back inside Neverra.

I dove and cut through the water toward him. Hooking my arms underneath his, I hauled him up. The silver spray still whipped my face, but the water had calmed. I took off toward the shell that no longer bobbed frantically, swimming hard. Harder than I'd ever swum before in my entire life because Cruz's body felt as heavy as my car.

When I reached the shell, I gritted my teeth and heaved his dead weight over. His head knocked against the iridescent surface so roughly I expected his skull to have cracked.

"Help me out here, Cruz."

He didn't answer. Didn't help.

Panting, I put my shoulders underneath his torso, clutched his knees with my hands, and shoved him hard again, using the slickness of the shell in my favor. Calling on every last ounce of strength, I pushed and didn't stop until his entire body flopped onto our pale life raft.

My chest throbbed with confusion and my arms shook with exertion as I heaved myself out of the glade and crawled toward Cruz's motionless form. Water steamed off the faerie's body and hair, hissing as it puffed and dissipated in the brisk air.

I raked my stringy hair out of my eyes, then placed the heel of my hand on his chest, pressed my other hand on top, and began to pump. Water trickled down my neck, snaked around my collarbone, and fell against Cruz's unmoving jaw, sizzling like oil in a hot pan.

Could faeries really drown?

"Cruz?"

No answer.

"If this is a test, it's not funny."

Nothing.

"Oh, for fuck's sake . . ." I bent over his inert body and released two rescue breaths inside his mouth, then resumed the compressions.

Something fluttered underneath my fingertips. A heartbeat.

I shoved my hair out of my eyes again and was about to resume the compressions, when I caught sight of my skin. Blood roaring between my ears, I lifted my hands and flipped them in front of my face.

Cruz's body spasmed next to me.

Blanching, I shoved my hands underneath my thighs.

His eyes opened.

My heart careened around my chest.

He stared at my face.

I froze.

He smiled.

THE HALF-SISTER

*C*ruz's forehead creased as his body spasmed again. When he squeezed his eyes shut, I reached up and touched my face.

Did it look like my hands?

My cheek felt smooth, like peach fuzz, but my jaw . . . My jaw didn't feel like my skin. My jaw felt like the skin of a lizard I'd caught one summer.

Fear cinched my ribs and blackened the edge of my vision.

Fuck.

Had I signed my own death warrant by saving his life?

Fuck. Fuck. Fuck.

I rose and paced the small space, then eyed the glade and contemplated jumping in.

Lily was right.

I couldn't believe she was right.

I was going to die now.

Cruz was going to kill me.

My eyes swam with tears as I stared at the copper floor that gleamed beneath the glade. My watery grave.

A soft voice rose behind me. Cruz's. "Ley was right."

My attention jerked back toward him. He sat up, complexion wan but eyes incandescent. "What do you mean Ley was right?" The heat in my voice blazed over the shell's smooth surface, skidded over the glades, and hit the floating trees. Their yellow branches curled onto themselves like octopus tentacles.

He rubbed his chest. "She could've mentioned I'd get electrocuted in the process of awakening your gene."

My muscles went rigid. "I don't—I don't . . . understand . . . *Ley?*"

Cruz scanned the sky around us. Was someone coming? Oh Great Spirit, was this a setup to prove I was the enemy? Was his mother on her way to arrest me? Shove me into one of her chastening birdcages?

I craned my neck, and although my eyeballs ached, I searched every last piece of land and sky for another person's presence. There was no one.

We were alone.

"I know you found out Ley wasn't part of your family, Catori," Cruz said softly.

My neck cracked as it bent back toward him. "How?"

"Lily told me."

"Lily? You spoke with Lily? She spoke to you after what you—"

"*Shh . . .*"

My throat clenched.

His gaze roamed the sky again. I didn't have to follow his line of sight to know we were still alone. He looked back at me, or more precisely at my arms that were locked at my sides.

"I've never met a real-life Daneelie," he said, his voice low and a little breathy.

I jerked my gaze down to my fists. My skin still glimmered with tiny scales, but they weren't as pronounced as before. "Are you going to kill me?"

"Kill you?"

"Am I not your worst enemy?"

His lips quirked into a smile.

"Why are you grinning?"

"Oh, Catori . . ." He inhaled a long, deep breath, then patted the spot next to him. "We've got a lot to talk about. You should sit."

"I'm fine standing."

"Cat—"

"Did you hurt Lily to make her tell you about the DNA results?"

His dark eyebrows slanted, darkened his eyes. "I would never hurt Lily."

"Never hurt her? You had her thrown out of Neverra."

"It's not what you think . . ." His voice was a mere whisper.

"Not what I think?"

"Please, Cat. Calm down and sit beside me." His gaze slid over the back of my hand, that was lit up like the sky on the fourth of July. "If Ace comes, I won't be able to tell you the truth about what's happening."

"The truth?" My words were more echo than sound.

He nodded to the spot next to him. I didn't go to that spot. But I sat. And not because he'd asked me to, but because my knees were weak with confusion.

"Talk."

His complexion was no longer waxen, yet he still seemed drained.

"How did Ley know what I was, and why would she tell you?"

"Ley knew because Adette confided in her, and she told me because I was her last living relative."

"You?"

He nodded. "Ley was my father's half-sister."

Like drying blood over an open wound, his words coagulated inside my mind, finally stoppering my gushing mystification. "His half-sis . . .?" I couldn't even form the entire word. Ley was Jacobiah Vega's *sister*? She was Cruz's aunt?

"My grandfather had an affair with a mortal woman a long time ago."

"A hunter?"

He shook his head. "Not a hunter. Just a human woman. He couldn't bring her here or recognize his daughter because—"

"She would've been killed. I heard what they do to extramarital children. Yet, she must've come here if she knew Adette, since my ancestor died in 1875. Unless Holly—I mean Ley—unless she was going on two hundred." She'd been old, but surely not that old.

"She lived here a couple years at a time, but she always returned to Rowan." His teeth dug into his bottom lip.

"So Adette was a . . . she was like me?"

He freed his lip. "No."

My brow creased.

"Adette wasn't part Unseelie," he said. "You are."

"She was all Daneelie?" I murmured the last word.

He nodded.

"But she lived on Earth?"

He nodded again.

"How did she survive outside of Neverra?"

"Daneelies aren't made of fire like Seelies. They are made of blood and water. Why do you think Maximus wanted to exterminate them, Catori? They were the most resilient caste, the strongest one, and that scared him."

"If they were so resilient and strong, shouldn't they have survived?"

"They did." His gaze brushed over my collarbone. "You're here."

I shivered, stared down at my hands. My skin still glimmered but was smooth again. Well, as smooth as skin covered in goosebumps could be.

"I'm sorry about your hand, but I needed your blood to touch the water to provoke the change."

In the madness, I'd forgotten all about the cut on my palm. Not even a faint line remained to mark the spot Cruz had slashed. "That's how it works?"

"That's how humans with Seelie ancestry turn their blood to fire when they enter Neverra."

I closed my fingers, then spread them out and stretched them. Like the rest of my body, they felt stiff. "Am I also part Seelie?"

"No."

Disappointment thumped in my chest like a heavy rock tossed into a pond. The Great Spirit only knew why I was disappointed about that. Maybe because, in some dusky recess of my mind, I'd held on to the dream of flying. I pushed that crushed fantasy away. "How did Adette survive?"

"A *calidum* found her after the slaughter. She was tiny, still a baby. She took her, hid her, and then carried her through a portal by pretending she was her child. They settled on the shore of Lake Michigan."

"Was Adette the only survivor?"

Cruz screwed up his lips. "I haven't heard of others."

I raked my hand through my wet hair, shivering as the cold air glued the soaked fabric to my skin. Before I registered movement, Cruz had shuffled over to me. I flinched when he pressed the side of his body against mine.

"You're freezing."

I tried to inch away but he wound his fingers around my forearm to lock me against him. "Tell me about Lily," I whispered. "Tell me the truth about what happened."

"The less you know, the safer she'll be."

"Safer?" I sputtered. "She's going to die."

"She's not going to die. I would never let her die."

"She can come back here?"

"Not yet."

"*Ugh.* Cruz. Just give me a straight answer already. I'm tired and confused and—"

"My mother can take any information from your head, Catori. The less you know, the less she can find out. Already, she could learn you are a Daneelie."

The blood drained from my face, and although Cruz's fire was warming me, I trembled. "But all of this—Lily, you and me—this is part of some plan?"

He nodded.

"And waking up the hunters?"

"Part of the plan too."

"And not telling Ace?"

"Just trying to keep him out of danger."

"You might be keeping him out of danger, but you're also keeping him in a damn foul mood."

"If I tell him, he'll have to leave Neverra until our wedding day. I assumed you wanted him near."

I side-eyed him. "Why would I want him near?"

Cruz smirked. "You forget my first *gajoï* was the truth about your feelings."

"I could've changed my mind."

"You could've, but you didn't."

I sighed. "Is it that obvious?"

"To me, it is."

I nibbled on my bottom lip.

"I'm not going to hurt him, Catori."

As though he felt I didn't quite believe him, he curled an arm around me and squeezed my shoulders. I let him hold me. I even leaned my head against his shoulder.

"So if I told him marrying you was a *gajoï*, you'd still tell me how to get Lily back in?"

"The less he knows—"

"The better. I understand." I drew a slow breath. "I really hated you."

"I know."

"You think your mother will find out about me?"

"I hope not, but if she does, I have a plan."

"And what is it?"

"Getting you out of Neverra fast. If she follows you back to Rowan, the hunters will take her down."

I pressed away from him and looked up into his face. "Take her down?"

"Kill her."

"You'd let them?"

"I'd rather do it myself." A beat passed. One silent beat. "Try not to let that enter your mind when you're around her, or she might kill me first."

I sucked in a breath.

His thumb stroked the top of my arm. "In case anything happens to me, Lily knows the entirety of my plan."

"Lily's in on everything?"

"I had Gwenelda fill her in before her people woke the hunters."

I blinked at him. "Is Lily mad?"

"Mad? She's livid. Then again, she was livid when I took you to Neverra, so nothing really changed."

"Will you guys get rebonded? Is that how you'll get her back in?"

His pupils throbbed. "I'm bound to you."

"But I can break that bond now that my Daneelie gene is activated. I can return to Rowan. And then—"

His thumb stopped moving. "That's not how I'll get her back in."

"Then—"

"Stop, Cat. I've said too much already."

I gnawed on my bottom lip. In my opinion, he'd shown me the tip of an iceberg.

"But I'll tell you one last thing. I'll tell you the reason why I can't take you back to Rowan. I need you to undo what your ancestors did to Neverra."

"What they did?"

He tipped his forehead toward the thick mist veiling the purple sky.

"The mist? You want me to undo the mist?"

"I've always longed to see what Neverra would look like without it. My father told me it was quite spectacular."

I raised my eyes to the woolly ceiling over our heads. Could I somehow control it now? "Cruz, I don't think I can—I'm one person. And not a very strong one at that."

He leveled his gaze on mine. "Why do you think we gave the book to the Unseelies? Why do you think we woke the hunters? You might be the only one who can manipulate the mist, but you are not alone. We will all help as best we can."

My stomach churned and twisted.

"You are not alone," he repeated, giving my body a reassuring squeeze that did the exact opposite.

I wasn't reassured. I was worried that all of his careful, intricate planning would be for nothing. How could a girl like me—so weak, so human—how could she somehow change the course of a world that wasn't even hers?

THE PUNISHMENT

*T*hat night, Cruz went to dinner at the palace on his own. The excuse was that I'd made a fool of him by wasting his money in the marketplace, and his punishment was keeping me from any festivities until he deemed me repentant.

"Any chance I could be unrepentant until our wedding day?" I asked him two days later.

Yes, two entire days. I'd stayed locked up in his apartment with only Veroli as a visitor. She brought me food, clothes, and offered to give me baths that I kept turning down. I'd bathed once since my swim in the glades, thanks to Cruz warming the water in his bathroom. He'd left me alone to steep in the blisteringly cleansing bath, alone with my blistering thoughts. Although my skin had glimmered in the water, no scales had appeared. Desirous to grasp the mechanics of my nature, I'd spent the past two hundred hours poring over books from Cruz's library, deciphering the Faeli language with the help of Veroli.

I'd gleaned a few interesting tidbits.

Cruz dropped into the armchair opposite the one I was sitting in and raked his hands through his black curls.

"I managed to read an entire book today. I didn't get every word, but Veroli was helpful. Apparently water used to cover the *Hareni*. It's the water the Daneelies used to create—"

Cruz sighed.

"What?"

His eyes were closed.

Pulse skittering like a broken strand of pearls, I asked again, "What?"

"I had to do something today." His eyes flicked open, gleaming so bright they looked slickened by starlight. "Something"—even the flames in the hearth crackled louder than his voice—"awful."

My mind flashed to Ace. "What did you have to do?"

The answer didn't come from him.

The answer came from the window.

From the wails penetrating the glass.

I stood up. On wooden limbs, I approached the sound.

Harsh sunlight glared on the metal bars of the *cupola* floating just outside the apartment. Inside the cage kneeled an old woman. She clutched the gold bars, knobby fingers wrapped so tightly around them I half-expected her to wrench them open, but the bars would sooner wrench her open than allow her out.

She lifted her face toward me, toothless mouth agape, a black hole in her too-white face.

I raised a palm to my mouth to stifle my horror, then tore it off and spun toward Cruz. "You have to get her out!"

"I can't, Catori."

I stalked back toward him. "She doesn't deserve this! *I'm* the one who chose to pay her. I should be the one in there."

"You wouldn't survive in there."

"She won't either!"

He scrubbed his hands down the sides of his face. "In all battles, there are casualties."

"*Casualties?* Cruz, this is unfair! This woman has nothing to do with your fight. She doesn't deserve to be tortured! To die over a pair of earrings!"

Another devastating cry sounded outside. My brain crawled in shame inside my mind at the sound of the woman's misery. "Cruz . . . please . . . get her out."

"I can't. It'll show weakness. I need my mother to trust me."

For a long second, I stared at him and tried to figure out if he was telling the truth. Was he really only pretending to be a monster, or was he one?

"Don't look at me like that."

"Like what?"

"Like you don't know me. You know me."

"Do I?"

He smacked his palms against his thighs, and the sound made me jump. "Who raised me, Catori?"

I frowned.

"Borgo and Veroli. *They* raised me."

I pressed my lips together. I understood what he was trying to tell me. That if he resembled anyone, it wasn't his mother. Finally, I sighed. "I saved your life. In the glades, I saved your life."

"I wasn't dying. I was just stunned."

"Still, I got you out. Don't you owe me now?"

"I never asked for you to get me out. Besides, only Seelies can strike bargains."

"Ugh!"

"Catori, if I could unlock those gates, I would. But I can't. I can't. So please, stop looking at me like that. Cover your ears and sit. Ingrid's old. She won't last long."

"Ingrid . . ." I whispered her name.

I didn't cover my ears, and I didn't sit. I walked back to the window, palms pressed against the glass, gaze pressed against the *calidum* suffering because of me. I murmured her name. Over and over, as though saying it could somehow lend her strength to survive the *cupola*.

But she didn't survive the faerie prison.

Blood foamed out of the black void that was her mouth, pink and red. It dribbled down her chin, stained her green tunic, plopped down on the floor beneath her empty face.

Black leathery wings swooped next to the cage, and then green eyes with elongated pupils met mine. Tendrils of smoke puffed out of the *draca*'s wide nostrils, billowed up the sides of her long, scaly muzzle, rounded her pointed horns.

I sensed her delight, her feeling of triumph. I wondered if she sensed my hatred. I hoped she did. She chuffed and then flapped her wings and flew away.

Lucionaga in human form arrived shortly after her departure. Their gold eyes traveled over my tear-stained face. Unlike the *draca*, their faces remained impassive. If they'd enjoyed the *calidum*'s punishment, it didn't show. Their fingers wound around the gold bars of the cage. With little effort, they dragged it away.

"Will they bury Ingrid?"

"They will return her to her family." Cruz's voice came from over my shoulder.

I turned to find him standing beside me, his face as stony as the *lucionaga*'s.

"Take me to them."

His lips thinned. "I don't think that's a good idea."

"Would visiting them put them in harm's way?"

"No."

"Then take me to them. You can tell your mother it was part of the punishment, to make me witness the devastation my pettiness caused."

He was quiet like a wolf was quiet, rolling my plea over in his mind.

In the end, he agreed to take me.

WHEN NIGHT FELL, he flew me through the grove of *calimbors*, swooping past branches and bridges, then darting underneath the mist, and flying lower still. We finally landed in front of a small door three stories from the roots of the tree.

Cruz lifted his hand to rap on the door, but his fist froze inches from the wood. He frowned at me. I self-consciously rubbed at my cheeks. "What?"

His squint accentuated, but then he blinked. "Did Veroli put makeup on your skin?"

"Makeup?" This was about makeup? Had she applied any? I dug into my mind but drew a blank. "Probably. Why? Did it smudge?"

"You . . . glitter, that's all."

I guess that wasn't a bad thing. I swiped a finger across my cheek, then checked my fingertip. It did glitter a little.

Frowning, Cruz finally knocked. A latch clicked, and then a small, round face jutted out. The child's gaze grew wide as it landed on Cruz, then wider still when it landed on me.

"Could we come in?"

The child gulped as he raised his gaze back to Cruz. "My"—Cruz cleared his throat—"bride-to-be would like a word with your mother."

"*Quid est*, Ranka?" came a thin voice from within. And then the door opened wider, revealing a small woman with a mop of red hair. When she saw me, she froze. "Come to tyke anudder one of us away?" She had a strange accent, the accent of someone for whom English wasn't the mother tongue.

Cruz spoke to the woman in Faeli. She eyed him suspiciously, then eyed me suspiciously. Finally she let us in.

I stepped over the threshold, but Cruz didn't. Something in the dark apartment made him halt. "I'm needed at the palace." His voice was loud, borderline arrogant. "I hope this visit teaches you not to toy with people from our kingdom. I'd hate to have to kill more because I cannot keep my future wife under control."

I frowned at him.

If he noticed my confusion, he didn't stop his strange act. "I'll send Dawson to fetch you once you've repented enough. Now go and make amends for the life you cost this family." He levitated, then soared heavenward.

What was that all about? Was a *lucionaga* near? I looked for a lighting bug, but besides a few *calidums* walking around on the ground below, eyes darting my way, there was no movement.

Unsettled, I walked deeper into the abode, and the woman shut the door. The interior was so dark, it took my eyes a few seconds to adjust.

"Take the earrings off."

I jumped at the sound of the voice. And then I stepped back when a familiar face loomed over mine.

"Unless you came to rub the reason Ingrid died in their faces."

Ace was here.

Here in front of me.

I blinked at the deep scowl marring his face. And then, with trembling hands, I touched the dangling earrings. "I wore them in her honor."

"*Honor?* What honor? She's dead. Because of those fucking earrings, she's dead!" He ripped them out of my lobes and chucked them so hard on the floorboards, they fractured.

My ears burned in shame, just like my cheeks and my eyes. I touched my lobes, felt something wet. Had tears dripped into them? My fingers came back sticky, red. Ace had torn my skin.

My pulse rapped the walls of my chest, igniting my brand. His hand glowed too.

Deep grooves flourished between his eyes as he took in my bleeding ears.

A wet towel was placed into my hands. It was the red-haired woman. She had no reason to be kind to me, yet she was.

"Thank you," I whispered. I turned toward her, cleaning my lobes. "What is your name?"

"Sarsay."

"Who was Ingrid to you?"

"My mudder."

"I didn't come here to apologize, Sarsay."

"Course not," Ace muttered.

I ground my molars together, resisting the urge to spin around and tell Ace to shut up. "I came to promise you that I will avenge her death."

Ace snorted behind me. The quarters were so tight I could feel his hot breath on the nape of my neck. "Planning on killing your future husband?"

I turned and glared up at him.

"Don't make promises you can't keep," he added.

"I will seek retribution."

A long beat passed.

The little boy stepped under his mother's arms. I looked around the small room for others, but found none.

"Is it just the two of you?" I asked.

"My hoosbund died a long time ago."

"And guess how he died, Catori?"

I didn't dare ask. Plus, I knew Ace would tell me whether I wanted to hear it or not.

"In a *cupola* too. But he wasn't as lucky as Ingrid. His agony lasted days. Not minutes, days!"

His tone made me wince and squeeze my earlobes tighter. Sarsay's husband's death wasn't my fault, yet he made it sound as though, somehow, I was to blame for it.

"Know why he was killed?"

I shook my head.

"The harvest he delivered to the palace didn't please the *wariff*. Gregor was convinced it was measly because he'd sold off his crops to marsh-dwellers, instead of reserving them all for the sky-dwellers." A terrible smile curled Ace's lips. "Gregor was right."

The woman pulled her little boy harder against her side.

"Sarsay's husband *had* kept the best from the *caligosupra*, but not because he'd sold anything to the *calidum*. He'd distributed it for free."

"It's in de past noo."

Ace's Adam's apple jolted in his unshaven throat. Days-old stubble cloaked his hard jaw.

The little boy sniffled. I crouched before him, touched his arm that was wound tightly around his mother's waist. "Ranka?"

He turned wary, glassy eyes toward me.

"I'll try to make the world you'll grow up in better."

"Don't you think I've tried?" Ace asked darkly.

"Your father still rules, so if you tried, you gave up too soon."

His nostrils flared with a breath. "Will you kill my father too?"

"I'll try my best." I leveled a smile on his disbelieving face. "I must leave now. I do not want to arouse suspicion. Take care of your mommy, Ranka." I touched Sarsay's shoulder. She stared up at me, a mix of fear and incredulity flashing in her eyes. I gave her the soiled towel and thanked her for her kindness. And then I stepped back toward the door and let myself out.

Once the door shut, I sidled against the rough bark and shut my eyes. What had I done? Making such heroic promises to offset the family's misery was downright cruel if I couldn't fulfill them . . .

Could I really take down this kingdom, or would this kingdom take *me* down and make a fool of me and my promises?

THE TRUTH

*T*he door of Sarsay's apartment opened and slammed shut a moment later.

Ace rounded on me, pinning his palms to the bark on either side of my head. "What the hell, Catori?"

Like the captive dust in my neck, I squirmed.

"What are you up to?" His fuming whisper touched the tip of my nose.

"Can you call Dawson? I need to get ba—"

He snatched me around the waist, then dove off the three flights that separated the landing from the ground. My belly hardened and rose from the abrupt fall. After we landed, he clutched my arm and yanked me past gaping *calidums*, through the squeaking swing doors of a place that resembled a Wild West saloon with a wooden bar, cow-hide barstools, wooden tables, and strange, curled antlers that hung from nails over the bar. Scantily-clad women preened around tables full of men in green tunics. Everyone looked up when Ace dragged me inside. Conversations died and curved lips flattened.

He exchanged Faeli words with the owner, who tipped his head toward another set of doors. Fear slicked down my spine as Ace hauled me through them and into a corridor lined with more doors. When we reached the furthest one, he drew it open and shoved me inside.

I stumbled onto a low stack of hay.

He flung the door shut, then stalked toward me. Without an ounce of gentleness he rammed me until I was flat on my back and he was on top of me, his big hands pinning my wrists over my head. I tried to shake him off, but he simply tightened his grip.

"Start talking, Cat," he growled.

"Get off of me."

"What the hell are you up to?"

"I'm not telling you until you get off me," I muttered. "Besides I've already said too much."

"Too much?" He snorted. "You said nothing that made any sense up there. You haven't made any sense for weeks now."

I stared up into Ace's livid face. His proximity made my pulse skitter, but not out of fear. Definitely not out of fear. I licked my lips, trying to calm the heat whizzing through my body. Now wasn't the time to get hot and bothered over a faerie who'd surely rather kill me than kiss me. As though sensing my erratic nerves, he added distance between his body and mine, but didn't release me.

"I don't play games, but you do apparently. What game are you playing now, Cat?"

Cat.

Not Catori.

Not Kitty Cat either, though.

"You wouldn't believe me if I told you."

"Try me."

I licked my lips again, this time out of nervousness. "If I tell you, you'll need to leave Neverra and swear not to return until the Night of Mist."

His temper spiked. "I'm not going anywhere. Now talk!"

"Swear you'll go, or I won't say a word more than those you heard up in Sarsay's apartment."

His pupils throbbed. "Fine. I'll leave."

My heart gave an involuntary shudder. Neverra without him would feel more hostile than it already was, but it was a small price to pay to make sure he stayed safe. "Marrying Cruz was a *gajoï.*"

"I knew it," he muttered under his breath. "Did he make you break up with me too?"

I didn't answer. Indirectly he had, but the decision had been mine.

"I'm going to kill him."

"No you're not."

Ace shook his head. "He made you marry him after he tossed my sister on her ass, and you're *defending* him?"

"Keep your voice down."

He untangled his fingers from my wrists and started to push up, but I latched onto his shoulders to keep him close, so I didn't have to yell. "Your sister's in on it."

A nerve jumped in his jaw. He didn't say anything for so long I thought he didn't believe me. I could still hardly believe it myself. If I hadn't received Ley's test results, if I hadn't morphed into a strange water beast, I would've had trouble believing Cruz's story. But facts were facts, and feelings were feelings, and as much as I questioned the swiftness with which feelings could alter facts and facts could alter feelings, I trusted Cruz.

"What exactly is my sister *in on?*"

I lifted my head up so my mouth was a hair's breadth away from the shell of his ear. "Destroying the mist," I whispered. "Killing the *draca*, getting rid of the *wariff*, and toppling your father."

A tremor passed through him when the side of his knees touched the sides of my thighs. I laid my head back in the hay and looked up at him. His eyes were closed. I studied the long black lashes lining his lids, the chiseled jaw obscured by stubble, the thick eyebrows several shades darker than his hair.

His eyes opened. Settled over mine. He was tense against me. The brooding sort of tense that told me he was weighing my words, deciding whether he could trust them.

"Are you sleeping with him?"

"With Cruz?" I squeaked.

"No, with Gregor." He rolled his eyes. "Of course, with Cruz."

"No." I shook my head, and pieces of straw poked my scalp. "No."

"I saw you kiss him."

"I haven't kissed him since he brought Gwenelda back to life."

"I'm not talking about months ago. I'm talking about three days ago."

"I didn't kiss him three days ago."

"I saw you."

"You must've seen someone else."

He snorted and rose, then paced the small, dank, musty room. "You expect me to trust you when you lie to my face?"

I pressed myself up on my elbows, alarm rocketing up my spine. "I di—"

"Stop denying it. Stop lying!" He made a fist with one hand and pressed his other on top, crunching his knuckles until they cracked. "I saw you in the glades. I saw you kiss him."

I almost smiled. I definitely sighed. "What you saw was me giving Cruz rescue breaths."

He stopped pacing, glowered. "Rescue breaths?"

I bit my lip. "I thought he'd drowned and I was trying to save him."

"Faeries can't drown."

My ears burned, which reignited the ache in my lobe where the skin was torn. I touched one to see if it had stopped bleeding and winced at the contact. Ace followed my fingers' ascent, and then he loomed over me and shoved my fingers away. In seconds, blue flames engulfed his hand and knitted my torn skin. I gritted my teeth at the searing pain, sweat beading on my upper lip.

"You'll have to get new holes."

"Thank you."

"I caused you the pain in the first place, so don't thank me. When people hurt you, you don't thank them. You don't defend them." I could tell this wasn't just about my earlobes. This was about a whole lot of other things. "Tell me the truth now, Cat. The real truth." His tone was pure steel.

"Is this a *gajoï*?"

"A *gajoï*? No. You didn't ask me to fix you."

"The day I sliced open my throat, I didn't ask you to fix me, yet I owed you."

"You didn't."

"I felt it. In my stomach—"

"That was guilt."

"You said it was a *gajoï*."

"I lied. *Once*. I lied once. I was hurt. Shoot me. How many times have you lied to me, huh?"

I bit my lip.

"Now tell me the fucking truth."

"I really did think Cruz had drowned. He wasn't moving. He wasn't breathing. I had to fish him out of the glades."

Ace bent at the waist and slammed his palms on the straw on either side of my elbows. His mouth was inches from mine. "Faeries. Don't. Drown."

I flinched. "I know that now, but I didn't know it then."

"So what? Cruz pretended to have died so you'd kiss him?"

"No."

"Then what the fuck happened out there? Why were you giving a fucking faerie mouth-to-mouth?"

I raised my chin. Ace had a right to be angry about a lot of things, but that didn't mean he should act like a dick just because he didn't understand. "I performed CPR on him because I didn't know what was wrong. But if you'd actually let me finish talking, I would tell you the rest of the story."

"Finish talking."

"Well, that really makes me want to talk now."

He gripped my chin. "What happened?"

I pulled my chin out of his hand, but kept my face angled toward his. "I stunned him. I electrocuted him."

"With what?"

A hefty dose of sobriety chilled my core. When we'd met, he'd thought poorly of hunters. What if he detested Daneelies like his brethren? True, he'd accepted me knowing I was half-hunter, but that was when he'd thought me half-Seelie. Would he accept me if he knew my other half wasn't Seelie?

I sighed. I was tired of altering the truth. "I'm mixed, Ace, but my other half is not Seelie."

He regarded me cautiously.

"When my blood mixed with the glade, I sent a charge through the water."

His pupils devoured his irises. "You mean to say that you're . . . you're . . .?"

I nodded.

"Impossible."

"Do you hate me even more now?"

"Why would I hate you more?"

"Because of what I am."

"I never cared about *what* you were, Cat. The only thing I've ever cared about was *who* you were."

I chewed on my bottom lip. What and who I was were so intimately connected that I wasn't sure there was a way to pick one without picking both, like removing chocolate from a brownie.

"Show me."

"Right now?" Sweat salted my lips.

"Right now."

"And then you'll leave Neverra?"

"Yes."

He rose, then extended his hand, and I took it. Once standing, I removed my hand from his.

"Is there another way out of this place than through the bar area?"

"No."

"What will people think?"

Ace picked blades of straw out of my hair. "They'll think we slept together."

"Isn't that forbidden now that I'm engaged?"

"It's forbidden to seduce an engaged woman. It's not forbidden to sleep with a woman who willingly gives her body to you."

"You dragged me inside. No one will believe I willingly gave you my body."

Ace smirked. "Leave them with a good impression, then. Pretend you just had the ride of a lifetime." I must've blushed, because he added in a muted voice, "It's better they think we had wild sex than they wonder what we actually did in this room."

My pulse quickened underneath my skin, and I swallowed but it didn't help settle my nerves.

"Take my hand and stay close."

Hesitantly, I took his hand. Unlike when he brought me inside, his touch was delicate, as though my fingers were crafted from porcelain.

Or maybe he didn't crush my fingers because he thought them toxic.

45

THE PROOF

*T*he land around the glades was tranquil at night. Dark and glittery, rocked by the tinkling of *adamans* petals, the low gurgle of water, and the soft folding and unfolding of *volitor* branches as the trees bobbed over the coppery liquid body beneath them.

As Ace flew me over, he didn't speak. Didn't even look at me. Tension billowed within me, hardening my muscles but softening my bones. When he set me down and his arms came away from my body, my legs threatened to give out. Thankfully, they held. I locked my knees and inhaled calming breaths that did little to calm me.

Neither of us spoke for a long moment, both of us busy scanning the sky for an unwelcome presence. No firefly spangled the darkness, no *calidum* crouched in the tall stalks of *glassflowers*.

When he nodded, I crossed the embankment, the soft soles of the shoes Veroli had procured for me dampening in the dank moss.

Even though the dress I wore tonight had long sleeves, the fabric wasn't thick enough to ward off the chill of the Neverrian night.

I kneeled by the water and began tugging on the intricate bow Veroli had tied to keep the bodice of my dress closed. How I longed for zippers and spandex. Such trivial yearnings. I thought of Cass then. She'd probably love everything about Neverrian fashion . . . about Neverra.

A pang of nostalgia hit me dead center. Cruz said he'd been sending my father regular text messages, but it didn't make the distance, the absence of his voice any easier. My fingers trembled as they worked on the knot.

Ace crouched beside me and coaxed the ribbon out of my fingers. Goosebumps rose where his warm knuckles brushed my bare skin. "You don't have to jump in, Cat. Just dip your hand."

Of course.

Silly me.

I bit my bottom lip, keeping my unfocused gaze on the shimmery water lapping against the mossy ridge.

Ace retied the ribbon so slowly I wondered if it was the first time he'd tied a ribbon. After he was done, I pushed my billowy mint-green sleeve up over my elbow and inched my hand toward the glade. When my fingertips connected with the water, the surface swirled. I lowered my hand further until the water coated my wrist. Unlike the air, the water was tepid and silky, like warmed oil.

The gentle current brushed through my fingers. I breathed evenly, waiting for my skin to change. I wondered if the water would affect my entire body or only the immersed part.

What if no scales appeared at all?

Ace would deem me a liar then.

When a minute had passed and nothing happened, I contemplated slicing my finger. I'd begun retracting my hand when my skin prickled.

Prickled and shimmered.

Shimmered and crackled.

I kept it submerged until my hand looked foreign, until it looked like it belonged on another body, one that wasn't human.

Once it gleamed like the copper basin, I lifted it out.

Ace didn't speak. Neither did I.

Water dribbled off my fingers, trickled down my wrist, down my forearm, bringing forth a change wherever it made contact. Soon my exposed arm was striated with tiny copper scales.

"Believe me now?" I asked softly.

He blinked. Once, twice, three times. And then his expression changed, his features smoothed and creased in endless ripples as he stared from my hand to my face. Deep grooves flourished between his eyebrows.

Ace had looked at me in thousands of ways, but never before in apprehension. Yet that was the emotion rolling off him: dread, dread mixed with hesitation.

"What are you doing, Catori?" The new voice punctured the night like one of Kajika's arrows.

Ace shot to his feet while I rose slowly, drawing my sleeve back down.

"Hi, Cruz," I answered, without explaining what I was doing. I believed it quite obvious.

"I was right to worry when Dawson couldn't find you. You've had a pleasant night?" There was an edge to his question that made me frown. We'd discussed telling Ace. Cruz had warned me to be cautious with our secrets, but said that ultimately it was my choice. "May I suggest that the next time you feel like frolicking, choose a less popular bar. Word about my loose fiancée has already traveled to the palace."

"We didn't—" I was about to tell him that our stint in the saloon was not in the least bit amorous when Ace zipped toward Cruz and flung a fist into his nose.

Cruz's head jerked back. No blood spurted from his nostrils, but the cartilage looked nonetheless mashed. Considering the force of the blow, it probably was.

A chill crept over me as soft as the fur cape Ace had given me during Middle Month. What I wouldn't give to have it draped over my shoulders.

Ace swung his fist again. Punched Cruz hard, this time in the jaw. And then he pounced on him, and they fell to the ground, a blur of swinging arms and ragged grunts. He straddled Cruz and pummeled him over and over. Faeries didn't bleed and they didn't break, yet I felt like Cruz wouldn't survive Ace's beating.

"Asshole! I trusted you!"

I touched Ace's shoulder. He flinched.

"Stop," I asked him gently.

He whipped his fevered gaze to me. His mouth, his shoulders, his entire body quivered with rage. He shot me such a brutal look that I stepped back. "I should kill you, Cruz. For what you did to Cat . . . to Lily . . . to me."

Cruz watched his friend in charged silence. "Did you tell him *everything*?"

"Yes."

A small frown gusted over Cruz's ruined face. I tried not to wince at the sight of his torn skin, his shattered nose, his crooked jaw. He would heal quickly, I reminded myself. His bones would knit, his cartilage would mend, his skin would smooth out.

"There's still one thing I don't get, though." Ace's voice was as sharp as the scent of moss on the brisk night air. "How the fuck did you get Cat to keep it all a secret from me, huh? *How?*"

I pulled in a breath and locked it inside my lungs.

Cruz observed me through half-lidded eyes. "I bought her silence with a promise."

Ace stared at Cruz, into Cruz, through Cruz. "What promise?"

"I told her I could get Lily back inside Neverra."

"You can get her back in?" Ace's entire back straightened, as though each one of his vertebrae were clicking into place.

Cruz's swollen lids rose further, and he narrowed his gaze. "I lied, though. There's no way back inside."

I jerked.

Cruz's lips bent. Ace smacked away his smile with a hard jab. All the blood that should've poured out of Cruz's body felt like it was pouring out of mine. I shivered, just as a piece of moonless sky shifted over us. The air stirred and the scent of burnt logs frolicked over the *adamans* field, fluttering through my hair as great black wings brushed the cold air.

Both Ace and Cruz looked my way. My gaze dropped to the hand I had plunged into the glade. The skin still glimmered. Not as noticeably as earlier, but still different enough to arouse suspicion. Ace rocketed out of his crouch and yanked his shirt off. Before my next breath, he'd dropped it over my head. And then he rubbed my arms, pretending to warm me.

Terror pounded in my veins and ignited my brand. It burned bright on the palm that was still frictioning my frozen body.

The *draca* landed on its clawed paws, folded its rubbery wings against its immense body. Smoke sparkled around it as it morphed into its human form. Lyoh's body was barely distinguishable in the darkness, like a chameleon against a leaf. No, that wasn't true. Except for her face and bare hands, Lyoh Vega was darker than the darkness.

Over Ace's shoulder, I caught the gleam of her green eyes. They traveled over my face, down Ace's bare back, then toward her son who'd pushed himself up. Blue flames slicked his hands as they moved over his face, repairing his injuries.

"You found them," she said.

Ace spun, shielding me with his rigid body. "With all due respect, go back to your perch in the sky, Lyoh. This is none of your business."

His familiarity startled me. I doubted many people dared address the *draca* in such a manner. I doubted many survived if they did.

"You broke a law, Ace, and you also embarrassed my son, so it has *everything* to do with me. As *your draca* and as *his* mother."

He snorted. "Right. You care about him now."

The air changed, turned denser as though the mist were descending. I checked the sky to make sure it wasn't. Even though the plan was to destroy it, we had to wait for the Night of Mist. Cruz feared that destroying it before then would permanently lock the *Hareni*. Perhaps it would permanently destroy it, but why risk it?

If I could even take on the vaporous mess my ancestors had left behind. What if I only succeeded at poking a hole into it? What good would that do?

Ace's body quaked with anger. "Catori, can you please enlighten our *draca* and inform her that *you* propositioned *me*?"

I drew my gaze off the mist, leveling it on Cruz. I didn't want to stare at Lyoh. Even though Cruz had promised she needed to make contact with a body to draw its thoughts, I didn't want to risk her seeing what was going through my head.

"I thought cheating was the norm up here." My voice was incredibly steady. "Was I not allowed to sleep with Ace, *draca* Vega?"

"It was truly your idea, girl?"

"Yes."

She squeezed one of her eyes shut a little. "After a mute, a whore."

"Don't you dare talk about Catori or my sister that way!" Ace's arms flexed. Before he could move toward the *draca*, I slid my hands out of the tunic and wrapped them around his biceps. I felt his breath hitch, saw Cruz's eyes widen. I released Ace immediately and dragged my hands back underneath his shirt. Was my skin still scaled and shiny?

Silence rushed over us like the glades' limpid waters and submerged us.

"Maybe I should cast you out of Neverra until Catori and I are married," Cruz said, "so my bride-to-be isn't tempted to cheat on me again."

"How your reasoning pleases me, son." A cruel smile snaked over Lyoh's mouth. "Imagine all the quality time you'll get to spend with your darling sister before her fire burns out."

Ace snarled at her.

"Did you hear she's become taken with a hunter?" Lyoh continued. "Do you approve?"

Cruz's features stiffened.

"You must, considering you covet Catori. Unlike my son, who's marrying her for political gain, what exactly are *you* gaining from bedding a huntress?"

The tendons of Ace's neck shifted like mooring cords.

Lyoh approached him, hand suspended in the air, index and middle fingers extended. Fear catapulted through me. Without dwelling on how much trouble this would get me into, I planted the hand that hadn't touched the water on my neck, waiting for the dust to stick to my sweat-slickened fingers, and stepped in front of Ace.

Lyoh paused, fingers inches away from *my* forehead now. Cruz's eyes were so wide, white appeared around his irises. His lips parted, but no sound came out.

"Touch him and I kill you," I spat out.

One of Lyoh's eyebrows quirked up disbelievingly. "*You'll* kill *me*?" She laughed. "Correct me if I'm mistaken, but you're all out of rowan wood sticks and iron."

My lips parted in a smile to match her own as I slowly drew my fingers off my neck.

Her hand catapulted down to her side, and she stepped back, attention locked on the ribbons of dust fluttering off my palm.

"I hear *wita* is pretty lethal."

Someone gasped. Maybe they all gasped. How *I* wasn't gasping was beyond me.

"Imagine if I shape a blade, wet it with my blood, and pierce your black heart with it. I did it to Borgo. Don't think for a second I would hesitate to do it to you."

Lyoh spoke to Cruz in Faeli. I caught the words *wita* and Stella. She was probably asking if he knew I could manipulate the stolen dust.

He shook his head.

She turned back to me, features as sharp as broken glass. "I suppose my son failed to inform you that threatening the *draca* is punishable by law. What is the punishment again, Cruz? One night in a *cupola*, or is it longer?"

I kept my jaw locked to silence my chattering teeth. For some reason, I thought of Kajika and of Lily, and how they'd called me reckless.

I was. So. Damn. Reckless.

I imagined them rolling their eyes at me, and somehow that eased my hammering pulse.

Blake used to say my mouth would get me in trouble someday. How right he'd been.

Ace shoved me aside. "I forbid it."

"You are not the king. You are also not the *wariff*. You have no political jurisdiction whatsoever. Only they have the power to pardon her, but if you ask me, keeping her little party trick away from her fiancé, from all of us, will win her extra time in the *cupola*. How do they say in your world, Catori? *Two strikes and you're out?*"

"Three." Why was I answering her? Because I was obviously stupid. The dust still sparkled in my hand. I turned my gaze toward it, wondering how to get it from my hand into the *draca*'s mouth. How had I done it with Stella? Did I just toss it? Or did I have to shape it into something first?

Lyoh's finger swept over my brow. I pitched backward just as Ace cinched Lyoh's neck with his long fingers.

"How my father could think giving you additional powers was a good idea," Ace growled. "You are a tyrant, Lyoh."

"I am faithful to the kingdom. A trait you are desperately lacking. To think you might be our next sovereign." She freed her head from his grasp. "I hope your father lives a terribly long life and that yours will be terribly short." Her green eyes slid back over to me. "Interesting thoughts, Catori."

My mind scrambled to remember what I'd been thinking of when she'd touched me.

"So you didn't only confiscate her dust, but you gassed Gregor's little concubine. He's going to love that."

Fear plopped against my skin like raindrops and ran down the runnel of my spine. "It was an accident."

"I don't really care. If you ask me, Stella Sakar was a nuisance."

"She killed my father."

"Well, at least she had a purpose then."

A soft wind grew and blew my hair into my face. The water in the glades splashed the mossy embankment, sprayed my legs, splashed Ace's bare back.

Lyoh smiled thinly before smoke billowed around her, distorted her hourglass form, and bloated her limbs. "Have a most pleasant evening, children." Bones cracked as they realigned in her body, fibrous black skin stretched over her human one. And then she was in the air, her enormous wings sifting the darkness, carrying her upward through the mist.

When she was gone, Cruz snapped, "What the hell is wrong with you? Threatening my mother? And when were you going to tell me about being able to use your dust?"

Back in the forest the day he'd claimed his *gajoï*, he'd swiped my palm off my neck. "I assumed you knew."

Ace turned on me. "Don't ever defend me again! No one can touch me because of who I am. *You*, on the other hand, have no status here!"

My hand flopped so fast against my side that the dust returned to its fleshy tracks. My hair settled limply around my face as the wind died. "Your father hurt Lily, yet she was his daughter."

"Because Lily wasn't marrying his concubine!" Ace tossed his hands in the air. "My father could have you killed. Killed!" He grabbed onto my arms and shook me.

"Lay off her, Ace," Cruz growled.

I pressed my trembling lips together.

"She won't make it an hour in a *cupola*," Ace snapped.

"I'll find a way to keep her out of one. But you have to go. You have to leave Neverra."

"If you think I'm going anywhere now, then you're as delusional as your fucking mother."

Cruz's Adam's apple bobbed. "Fine. But stay away from Catori *and* Lyoh. And you"—he wagged his finger at me—"never return to the glades. Never touch the water."

"Was my hand still . . . still different?"

"No." Cruz's black curls fell into his eyes. "Why couldn't you have kept your mouth shut?"

I wasn't sure if he meant the secrets I'd told Ace or the threat I'd made to his mother. Probably both. For the first time in my life, I wished I were mute like Lily. It would save me a heap of trouble. But since I *could* talk, I asked, "Is it true what you said before she arrived?"

"About what?" he barked.

Ace frowned.

"About Lily," I murmured.

Her name dispelled some of the tightness around his eyes. "Maybe. Maybe not. Right now, I don't feel like sharing anything with either one of you."

"Maybe I won't help you then."

"Let's wait and see if you'll be alive long enough to even try." Cruz snatched my arm, tossed me over his shoulder like a burlap bag, and sprang off the ground.

As we soared upward, I kept my gaze locked on Ace's upturned one. He didn't follow us. He stayed planted to the ground like an *adamans* flower, eyes glittering as wildly as their swaying, chinking petals.

46

WRONG COLORS

*F*or an entire day that felt longer than all the other days I'd spent in Neverra, I paced Cruz's apartment. Veroli tried making conversation, asking me about home, but I couldn't get my mind to switch off what was being discussed in the palace.

The following morning, when still no news had reached me, I stepped out of the apartment. I wasn't planning on going far—anywhere for that matter. I just needed to get outside, breathe air that wasn't tainted with fire and ash. I sat on the platform outside the front door, propping the door open with a heavy book so that it wouldn't lock me out.

How could a place feel like a prison and a safe haven all at once?

I closed my eyes and rested my head back. The morning sun beat against my face, warming the anxieties that made every nerve in my body tick, but not melting them. Not even the gentle brush of leaves on the large branches jutting around me helped settle my mind. It did fill it with sounds other than the perpetually rewinding version of my confrontation with the *draca*.

My forehead tickled as something scampered over my skin. I opened my eyes and brushed it off. A little beetle with an iridescent shell plopped on the platform next to me. It didn't move. Had I killed it? Its legs twitched, and then the air burst with a musky, floral scent. I leaned over to have a closer look at the bug when it sprayed its perfume again. Right into my face. "Ah . . ." I yelped, digging my hands into my eyes that stung and watered.

It took several minutes for the sting to subside, and when it did, I looked for the tiny creature, but it had scuttled away. What a nifty little weapon it wielded inside its diminutive body, both lure and toxin.

As though to remind an assailant of its escape, its delectable scent lingered long after it had gone.

Something tinkled, and then a shy "Hey," sounded beside me. Belly parallel to the ground, Dawson rose, and then a large, yellow basket appeared beneath him. Cheeks flushed, Veroli beamed at me from within the *runa*.

I stood up, walked over to the basket, and stroked it as Veroli clambered out. "When did this happen?" I asked excitedly.

"Cruz gave it to me! And then I got my license yesterday."

"I'll get set up." As she walked past me, Veroli cast a disapproving look at my jeans—my good old human jeans—and her fingers tightened on the fabric bag that surely held today's gauzy, impractical outfit. Her repulsion amused me. She seemed to love everything Earthly *except* for its fashion.

I stroked the *volitor* leaves that had been braided to form a sturdy shell. "How many *volitors* are needed to make one basket?"

"A lot. But their branches grow back real fast."

"You mean, you don't kill the trees to get the branches?"

"Of course not. We'd have no more *volitors* if we did that. They don't reproduce very fast."

"Does it hurt them?" I felt certifiable asking if a tree ached from being pruned, but *volitors* seemed skittish, more fauna than flora.

"They hum real angrily when we chop off their branches, but I don't think it hurts them. They don't bleed or nothing."

"Absence of blood doesn't mean absence of pain."

He pursed his lips and glanced at his *runa*. "Now I feel bad."

I touched his shoulder. "I didn't mean to make you feel bad. Maybe they don't feel anything."

"What if they do?" He rubbed the back of his neck. "When faeries come at them, they curl up and try to float away."

"Maybe they just enjoy playing hard to get."

Dawson raised anxious eyes to me.

"If their branches grow back, it must not be that painful." That was to assuage Dawson's tangible guilt. Why did I have to rain on people's parades? "Can you become my official carrier from now on?"

His skin turned crimson. "I've only been doing this a day. Maybe you should wait 'til I get better at it."

I smiled. "I'm sure you're already terrific at it."

"I do got good reflexes." His blush began to recede, patches of white skin supplanting patches of red.

I smiled. "Is that a yes?"

"If Cruz says okay, then yeah, I'll be your personal carrier."

He would say okay, not that I needed his permission. "Question, how'd you get your name?"

"Mom gave it to me."

I rolled my eyes. "I assumed that much. What I meant was, is it . . . I don't know . . . common?"

"No. I'm the only Dawson in Neverra. I don't know how she came up with it exactly. She said it came to her in a dream. I was almost named Jack." He grinned, that sheepish grin of his. "You know any Dawsons back on Earth?"

"A guy I met during orientation week in college was called Dawson. There are lots of Jacks, though. More common."

"I'd really like to stay and chat, but I should probably check with the boss to see if he's got more fares for me."

I patted the *runa*. "Of course. Go."

After adjusting the leather harness hooked over his back, he waved and took off.

"Bye, Jack Dawson."

He chuckled.

I waited until he'd vanished from view before retreating into the apartment. *Jack Dawson*. Why did that sound familiar? It hit me the second I crossed the threshold. "You named your son after the hero in *Titanic*?"

Veroli's face turned as pale pink as the dress clutched in her fingers. She zipped toward the door and shut it fast.

"What? Is it an offense to speak of movies here?"

"Not if you're a *caligosupra*. They have access to movies and books;

caligosubi don't. Apparently human distractions risk putting mutinous ideas into our heads."

"Are you serious?"

She nodded briskly.

"That's stupid."

"Tell that to our *draca*." Her forehead ridged in sudden anguish. "Actually, don't! Don't tell her anything. Please. I don't want another person getting hurt because of me." Her chin quivered as though she were about to cry. In the end, she didn't.

I touched Veroli's shoulder. "Who did she hurt?"

She hung her head and shook it. "Ace."

"Ace?"

"A neighbor snitched on me, and then *lucionaga* stormed my house. When they found the battery-powered DVD-player in my apartment, they were going to lock me in a *cupola*, but Ace told them he'd supplied me with the movies and apparatus. He insisted he should be the one punished." She swiped a tear off her cheek.

My breaths stilled. "So he was locked in a *cupola*?"

"It was far worse than that."

What could be worse than a magical torture chamber?

She sniffled. "Linus locked him into a marriage. He had the Cauldron bind them that very night."

My fingers froze on Veroli's heaving shoulders.

"Now he's stuck marrying someone he hates because of me. I tried pleading with the *wariff* to lock me up in a *cupola* instead, but Ace told his father not to listen to me."

"I'm sure Ace wouldn't want you to feel guilty, Veroli."

She sobbed harder.

"Besides, if I've understood Neverrian politics, he would've eventually been locked into another marriage."

She blotted her eyes on the sleeves of her green tunic.

"And Angelina's not so bad."

She let out a small snort that told me she didn't approve of Ace's fiancée.

"Why don't you move to Earth, Veroli? You're a *calidum*. You could survive there—"

Her lids snapped over her eyes like windshield wipers. "And leave my children? They need me."

"It doesn't have to be forever."

"There is no other way of leaving Neverra for a *calidum*."

"You mean, if you leave, you can never come back?"

"If I were a *caligosupra*, it would be different." She shrugged her drooping shoulders. "But I could never be a *caligosupra*. Dawson might be someday. That would be a good day." She knuckled a tear out of her eye. "Now let's get you into something . . . nicer."

I smiled. "Jeans are nice."

She grimaced.

"Fine."

As I unrolled my jeans, the door flew open. I froze. Cruz walked over to me as though in a trance. His face looked almost as ghostly as when I'd fished him out of the glade.

My nerves fizzed as though thousands of tiny bubbles were pop-popping inside my extremities. "My punishment's been decided?"

"Punishment?" Veroli said.

Cruz's tension soured the air inside the apartment.

"Okay," I said, "now you're scaring me."

His face morphed before my eyes, his features shifting then realigning. "One hour inside a *cupola*."

Veroli clapped a palm over her mouth.

I swallowed. "That's not so bad. Here I was expecting death by *wita*."

He jolted out of his stupor. "Not so bad! Catori, an hour is five where you come from! Five hours of reliving each one of your worst nightmares."

"It'll be fine. I'll be fine." I hoped.

Cruz began pacing.

"Has no one survived an hour?"

He stopped and jutted his head up. "A few, but the only reason *they* survived was because they were pure Seelies. Because *cupola* magic is painful to pure Seelies, but not lethal."

"Isn't Catori mixed?" Veroli's face was a quilt of tiny lines, but her voice was hopeful.

Cruz turned his eyes on me. They were as bright as traffic lights.

Not the right mix. "Maybe it'll affect me differently because of my . . . heritage."

"You can't even resist *captis*, but you think you can resist a magical torture chamber?"

"Does it work the same?"

"Does what work the same?" His chest was still heaving with ragged breaths.

"*Captis* and *cupolas*?"

"Why?" he barked.

"Don't bite my head off. It was just a question."

He seized my shoulders. "Can you resist *captis*?"

"No. Maybe. I don't know."

Threads of heat leaked through his fingers and wrapped around my arms like the softest of silks. I shivered. The intensity of his gaze was jarring. I felt like I should lean away from him, but found myself leaning toward him. Waves of warmth spilled out of him and fogged the air between us.

As though he were a lit wick and I was a trail of gasoline, his fire ignited me, seeped through the tingling barrier of my skin, enflamed my organs, warmed places inside of me hands couldn't reach.

I trailed my fingertips over the soft fabric of his tunic, feeling every thread, every fiber, the weight of the black dye, the scent of musk and soap. I felt all these things with my fingers but also with my mind.

When my fingers reached the hem of his tunic, I blinked, momentarily confused as to why I was feeling fabric. I lifted my gaze back to the face looking down at me.

Black and green, not blond and blue.

My fingers dipped underneath the fabric, set on Cruz's hot, hard stomach.

Not the right colors.

I blinked.

Like a whip made of nails, reality struck, whacked the gooey texture of my blood, liquefied it. Heart thundering beneath my ribs, I yanked my hands away from Cruz.

Cold sweat slickened my upper lip. Tearing my gaze from the faerie's face, I licked it away, then scraped all salty traces of fear with my teeth.

For a long moment, the room was achingly quiet.

He'd used *captis* on me.

What I felt, what I did . . . it wasn't real. I still felt incredibly stupid.

Without meeting Cruz's eyes, I asked, "Did you stop, or did I?"

"You did," he spoke slowly.

I inhaled deeply. Relief strummed over my frayed nerves. How I wished *captis* didn't work on me. Fantasizing about undressing faeries was all sorts of embarrassing. "You swear it? *I* was the one to stop?"

For the first time since he'd stepped into the apartment, his frown was replaced with something else. Not a smile, just something else. He gathered my clammy hands in both of his and squeezed them. "I swear it."

"Will that help me in the *cupola*?"

"If you can remember how you did it."

I nibbled on my lower lip.

"How *did* you do it?" Veroli asked, forehead scrunched.

"His color was wrong."

"My color?" Cruz's eyebrows slanted while my cheeks smoldered. Maybe he understood, or maybe he sensed I didn't want to elaborate. Whatever it was, he let it go. "Cling to that once you're inside. Focus on finding colors that are awry and details that are amiss."

47

BLACKMAIL

*T*he palace's pink arch swam in front of my eyes, and beyond it, the white marble courtyard filled with bodies. Had they come to support me or watch? Excitement shivered through the courtiers, where smiles glittered as blindingly as attire and jewels.

A frisson went through me as Cruz flew me down. I would get no support from this crowd. This was purely entertainment for them.

What a cruel, cruel world.

Not unlike my own.

When my bare feet touched the polished stone, the *caligosupra* hushed. And then they split into two columns so I could make my way inside the palace, where Linus waited on his carved tree.

As we'd discussed, Cruz wrapped a hand around my upper arm and pulled me after him inside the palace as though I were a baleful child. I expected the crowd to trail us, but four green-clad faeries shut the heavy golden doors after us, locking the others out.

Framed by the *draca*, the *wariff*, and a row of hulking *lucionaga* in human form, Linus sat, regal with his back straight, his face stern, and his wreath glinting. What would Neverra be like if Ace sat at his father's place, if Cruz were the *wariff*, and Dawson or Lily the *draca*?

Would it turn wondrous overnight? Would *cupolas* and the caste system be abolished? Would peace reign supreme throughout the land? A small thrill ran through my veins as the dream of a place ruled by people with hearts solidified into a goal.

It was dangerous to harbor such thoughts in the presence of someone who could read minds, so I focused on the tiny plan I'd hatched as Veroli wrapped a band of powder-pink fabric around my body and secured it with a broach inlaid with a sea of tourmalines.

I'd been tempted to discuss it with Cruz, but in the end, I kept it to myself. I wanted him to look surprised; thus I needed him to *be* surprised.

While he'd briefed me about what to say and how to act so my sentence wasn't extended, Veroli had stayed quiet, her reddened eyes barely making contact with mine.

Cruz and I stopped several feet from the dais.

For a long moment, no one spoke.

Then Gregor stepped toward the edge of the platform. "Catori Price, you've been found guilty of wielding *wita* to nefarious ends. How do you plead?" His face was a collection of hard planes interspersed by the thinnest of wrinkles, the face of a man who didn't allow himself to feel. "I repeat . . . how do you plead?"

I cleared my throat. "Guilty."

Cruz didn't stiffen beside me. He didn't soften either. We'd been through this part a hundred times.

"Your *cupola* awaits, then, *ventor.*" Gregor smiled, which accentuated his narrow nose.

Linus sighed, and it resonated in the vast, empty throne room. "I was so looking forward to your wedding."

"But not anymore, *Massin?*" I asked.

Cruz's fingers stiffened around my arm. Speaking my mind wasn't part of the plan, but I wasn't sticking to the plan.

Linus's thick, pale lips parted.

"I'm hurt that you have such little faith in my tenacity, *Massin.*"

"Catori, dear"—the king shifted on his throne, readjusting his royal-blue tunic—"if you make it out unscathed, I will throw you the most lavish of parties."

I squeezed a smile onto my lips. "Your kindness knows no bounds."

Cruz made a small sound that was a cross between a cough, a growl, and a gasp.

A warning.

But I wasn't done. "*Massin*, before I am locked in a cage, there's a matter I would like to discuss with your *wariff*."

Interest sparked, Linus leaned forward.

Lyoh's black eyelashes fluttered over her emerald eyes. "If it concerns Stella Sakar—"

"It does not."

I sensed Cruz stare at me, surprise rolling off him in supple waves. *Good.*

His astonishment would reassure his mother that Cruz and I were not allies. Allies didn't keep secrets from each other.

Gregor cleared his throat. "This matter will wait until—"

"It cannot wait. From what I hear, *cupolas* scramble minds. I wouldn't want to forget what it is I needed to discuss with you. Besides, you wouldn't want me to forget it. It will only take five minutes. Five human minutes. What does that equate to here? A single minute? Can you not spare a minute to hear me out?"

Come on. Bite already.

I swept my high ponytail over one shoulder.

Linus flapped his hand. "Allow the girl her minute, *Wariff*."

Gregor nodded to Linus, then soared off the dais and landed inches from me.

I shrugged my arm out of Cruz's fingers and followed Gregor. A *lucionaga* detached himself from the wall of others protecting the king and tailed us around the dais, through a courtyard lined with slabs of mirror that gleamed like immense sequins. I noticed handles on many of the slabs—doors.

Gregor gestured toward one of the doors and pressed it open before a green-clad faerie could assist him. He shooed the young girl away and waited for me to step inside.

I paused on the landing. "Tell your guard to wait outside."

Gregor evaluated me, as though trying to guess my next move. "Bind her hands."

I frowned, but didn't protest when the *lucionaga* ripped a liana from a nearby column and wound it tightly around my wrists. In truth, I was a little flattered. Flattered that Gregor regarded me as dangerous. No one had ever considered me dangerous.

After the liana was knotted, I walked inside the room and Gregor closed the door behind us. Inside was all carved wood and shelves filled with glass jars holding various strange creatures, a jawbone with four rows of needle-sharp teeth, hairless rodents, snakes coated in sharp quills, black scorpions the size of my palm with globular eyes.

"The most dangerous creatures in Neverra." Gregor's voice was so close to my ear, the hairs on the nape of my neck lifted.

"You give them too much credit and yourself too little."

Silence. And then, laughter.

His, not mine.

I was serious.

Like metal coins tumbling down a slot machine, it clanked out of his stretched lips and grated against the glass jars. "Linus is right. You are rather delightful." There was something slippery about the way he spoke the compliment, like an eel slithering among rocks, scenting the water for its next prey. He circled around until he faced me, then ran one of his hands down my arm to my elbow. "Have you come to beg for my forgiveness or for my mercy?" His rancid breath scorched the tip of my nose.

"Neither."

Gregor crooked my chin up with his free hand. I jerked my face to the side and my chin glided off. His eyes locked on mine, then slid up and down my body in a way that made me want to shower in Clorox. "A *gajoï* then?"

"I've come to blackmail you."

His fingers fell away from my skin and he grinned, a wide, lurid grin so at odds with his severe features. "Blackmail?"

"I know about your daughter."

"My daughter?" The grin faded like ink under sunlight. "I don't have children."

"You do. Her name is Faith. She runs her grandmother's bakery back in Rowan and is due to have a daughter of her own in a few months."

"Faith is Stella's daughter. Not mine."

"Oh, she's yours all right. Right down to your inimitable charm."

Gregor's complexion ripened, reddened, hardened. "Implications like these can hurt innocents. It could get this girl killed."

"Doesn't matter to me." Thankfully Gregor wasn't graced with

Lyoh's power of stealing thoughts or he would've discerned that I did care. "But surely it matters to you?"

Please, let it matter to you.

"No." His tone was harsh, yet wavered. "Not in the least."

"I wonder if it'll matter to your wife."

Uncertainty churned in the hazel depths of his irises.

"I wrote her a letter and entrusted it to someone who will deliver it if my sentence isn't trimmed down."

His jaw tightened. "You're bluffing."

"Am I? Why don't you ask Lyoh Vega to check if I'm bluffing?"

Gregor gripped my jaw with one hand and squeezed. "I could kill you. Right now. I could kill you."

"But you won't, because then Ace would kill you in retribution. I'm his to kill, am I not? But let's say he spares your life. Linus would surely demote you. I'm an interesting, shiny new toy, am I not? A little dangerous even. Just the sort of toys you enjoy playing with."

In a voice so low I had to strain to hear it, he hissed, "Does anyone else know?"

"No." A lie. Lily knew. For the first time in forever, I was glad she wasn't in Neverra.

He freed me so forcefully I skittered backward, almost tripping on the thick rug. "I'll shave off fifteen minutes."

I cocked a brow. "That's not very generous."

"More will look suspicious."

"Halve my time, or I let Lyoh touch my forehead and find out what we discussed in here."

A rough breath puffed his cheeks. "Fine."

The liana seemed to tighten around my skin.

"But, Catori, if *anyone* finds out, I'll lock you an entire night in a *cupola*."

"Understood."

"I lessened your sentence because you serviced me."

"Of course." Bile rose in my throat. "Who wouldn't want to?"

"Careful, or as soon as you're married, I'll use *captis* to play with the court's shiny new toy."

I'd kill him first. "I wouldn't put it past you."

He leered at me, then thrust the door open and shoved me out.

48

NOT CINDERELLA

The second we stepped back inside the throne room, the second Gregor announced my reduced sentence, Cruz's face rippled with relief, until Lyoh enquired what could possibly have changed the *wariff*'s mind. Gregor insinuated we'd shared a most pleasant moment. Shock—or was it disgust?—sheeted off Cruz. The fact that he believed I would debase myself bothered me. Would Ace also think I touched Gregor in intimate ways?

Lyoh's raised voice interrupted my wretched musings. "Why the skies gave you a brain if you don't utilize it is beyond me!" The rest of her blistering diatribe was in Faeli.

Linus listened. Smiled. She fell silent then. Here she'd been looking for support, and instead received amusement. In a flourish of smoke, she transformed into her black-winged alter ego and flew straight for the doors that the green-clad faeries scrambled to open.

Linus chuckled, then descended from his perch to join us. His *lucionaga* converged around him, gold eyes shifting unabashedly between their *wariff* and myself.

"Gregor isn't one to cut anything in half," Linus said. "Well . . . besides marsh-dwellers from time to time."

I grimaced.

A sly grin curved a side of his thick mouth. "I take it you must be quite good. I can't wait to find out for myself." He winked at me and then, feet not touching the ground, he soared out of his throne room. Two *lucionaga* preceded him, two flanked him, and two trailed him.

Gregor waited for us to follow, as though not trusting the promise I'd made of keeping his little secret.

Cruz's jaw was so stiff, he reminded me of the wooden puppets Cass and I built back in high school. Cass. I wondered what she was doing. And then I wondered if my birthday had passed. How long had I been in Neverra?

"What day is it back on Earth?" I asked Cruz.

His somber eyes shifted toward me. "May 29th."

I lowered my gaze to the smooth, pale stone underneath my bare feet. In two Neverrian days—nine human days—I would turn twenty.

My sentence had been cut in half, but would I survive a half hour in a *cupola*? Would I manage to swim through the nightmares and come out unscathed, or would I drown in the *cupola*?

Would I get to be a year older?

Would I ever get to see my father again?

Would I ever get to tell Ace how much he meant to me?

Misery crawled up my backbone, weighing heavily on my spine.

I didn't look around me as we walked out onto the terrace, but I did raise my chin and look up.

Straight at the gleaming, golden cage that was propped open, awaiting me like a chariot awaited Cinderella. This carriage wouldn't carry me to a grand ball, though. Where I was going, only specters awaited. And although faeries swarmed around me, none of them were a magical godmother who'd whisk me to safety.

I kept my eyes open as I stepped inside. I would need them to see once my world went dark.

49

THE CAGE OF NIGHTMARES

*T*he cage floated smoothly away from the palace. Floated over the mist that had drifted lower, uncovering dozens of thin slices displaying images of Earth. I wrapped my fingers around the slender bars, wishing that one of the portals would display my father's face, but the only images that floated over the flat surfaces were of foreign faces and places.

I stared around me, wondering when the *cupola* would start drilling my mind. Perhaps there was a glitch with this one. Or perhaps I was already resisting its effect. I raised my gaze to the crowns of the *calimbors*.

On a platform at the top of the tallest tree stood a rigid figure. Bare forearms were folded in front of a chest cloaked in a shirt that wasn't Neverrian-made. As blue as the earthly sky. The face was set in the deepest of scowls. How I longed to brush the hard line of Ace's jaw, run my fingers down the tendons of his neck, smooth the furrow between his eyebrows.

Would he ever let me touch him again if he believed I'd touched Gregor?

My fingers tingled. And then the tingle spread to my arms. To my collarbone. To my neck. To my cheeks. To my scalp. The world grew dark and still.

Then bright again.

Then dark.

Bright.

Black.

White.

The white became yellow.

The yellow became a door.

An open door.

In the doorjamb stood a woman.

My mother.

I gaped at her. Ran to her. Tears streaming down my cheeks. Her chest was hard and cold. Her arms were slack. I hugged her, pressing my ear against her chest. Her chest was silent but warm. Warm and sticky. Sticky like syrup. Syrup ran down my earlobe and into my hair. I wiped, and my fingers came back red. I pressed away from my mother's chest. Found it soaked with blood. Blood that was running from a gash in her neck.

Gasping, rubbing, I scrambled backward. Her black eyes dripped with more blood. It plopped in rhythmic beats against our kitchen tiles. She raised her hand, beckoning me to come to her. A ring gleamed on one of her fingers, black as her eyes, black as her hair, black as her nails.

Rubies aren't black.

The black stones caught the light, absorbed it, refracted it.

I waited for them to turn red, but they stayed black.

My mother had never worn a black ring.

"Catori." The voice sent a shiver down my spine. Made me forget about the ring. "Baby." Like falling water mixed with smiles. The most wondrous voice. A voice that could soothe any ache. "I've missed you."

My heart fluttered.

"Take my hand, baby."

I arched my fingers to reach hers, but stopped at the sight of the ring.

Red isn't black.

Black isn't red.

"You're not . . ." Not my mother . . . not real.

Her face turned into my father's.

290 | OLIVIA WILDENSTEIN

He was gurgling as blood dripped from his neck.

I backed away. My hands slammed against something hard. Something that clinked.

I drew my gaze away from the man standing in front of the yellow door. Stared at the red band twinkling around my finger.

When I looked up, my father was no longer there.

I touched my ear. Blood stained my fingers. Pulse skipping, I spun, looked for the source of blood. I was alone. Alone and bleeding. I touched my ear again, ran my fingertips down my neck, found slender grooves and furrowed skin. It was my own blood.

Just my blood.

Not my mother's.

Not my father's.

"Cat!"

I whirled around. Found Ace where my mother had been. "It wasn't black," I whispered.

Two *lucionaga* yanked him back. He flung them off him.

"What wasn't black?"

Black.

Plop.

Black.

Plop.

"Talk to me, Cat! What wasn't black?"

"I . . ."

The popping turned to whooshing. Wind blew, wet and wild, howling through the branches of the tree, sliding through the cracks in the clapboard walls of our tiny house, ruffling the polar fleece blanket tucked around our bodies, rustling and rough.

The scent of rain, laundry detergent, and cooking oil filled me. A candle fizzled, then whooshed out. I held my breath but then let it whoosh out too.

An arm stirred in the dark darkness, settled around my shoulders, pulled me into a pointy shoulder. A scrawny arm. "Don't be scared."

I sucked in a breath and pressed away from the bony body. "Blake?"

"This house will keep us safe."

Safe.

"Want to play hangman?"

"Hangman?"

"Where you have to guess letters before I hang you."

"You'll hang me?"

"If you don't guess the word."

"We never play hangman."

"What do we usually play?"

"Tic-tac-toe."

"Want to play tic-tac-toe instead?"

"I can't see anything."

"Give me your palm."

I gave Blake my palm, felt a nail gently slide over my palm to form an X. "Where are the lines?"

"*You* have to draw the lines. You like drawing lines."

"Blake, are you really here?"

"Touch my face."

I swept a trembling palm over the right side of his face. Found an ear where none had been the last time I'd seen him. "You have both your ears again?"

I moved my hand over more of his face that I couldn't see because it was so dark.

His cheekbones were hard underneath the pads of my fingers. "Your face. It's healed."

Bang. An explosion rattled against me. I latched on to Blake, hid my face in the crook of his neck. When silence returned, I ran my fingers across his face to check if he was still there. The skin underneath my fingertips sank like a soufflé taken out too early, deflating over the cartilage of his face. His nose flattened. One eye gleamed, not the other.

The air turned denser, leather and fumes.

"What's happening?"

His arm tightened around me, no longer narrow and bony. The arm was strong and crushed me. Flattened me against a chest that was hard and cold.

"You were my first kiss," Blake said. "Be my last, Cat."

"Your last?"

The air thickened until there was no more oxygen, only the musty, rank odor of car exhaust.

"We have to get out of here," I coughed, clutched my throat. "Blake—"

A mouth landed on mine, pulled my lips in like a suction cup. I dug my hand against the chest, shook my head from side to side, but the lips wouldn't let mine go. I clawed, screeched, but the sound only slid from my throat to Blake's without breaking out. I gripped the sides of his face, pushed, pressed, pinched. Nothing. I latched on to his ears and yanked.

Ears.

Blake only had one. He'd lost the other during the war.

But I was holding two ears.

Two.

The mouth freed mine, and I gasped for air.

Air that wasn't stained by fumes.

The darkness receded, became purple and gold.

Blake was gone.

Faces crowded around me. Eyes. Hundreds of them watched me. I turned, head pounding, heart thundering. "How much"—I croaked—"longer?"

A collective intake of breaths sounded around me.

Did she just talk to us?

She must still be in a trance.

No.

Yes.

Impossible.

I approached the bars, wrapped my fingers around them, fixed my gaze on a child with a long, narrow face and lips so red they looked chapped. I remembered my father telling me that when attacked, yelling at a crowd for help was useless. You had to single out one person and appoint them to save you. *Concern them and they will become concerned,* he'd said.

I pointed to the young boy in the tunic as bright as his lips. "You in the red, how much longer?"

His eyes that already ate up most of his face widened.

The cage shook. I rocketed backward against the bars. My head slammed against metal. Stars exploded at the edge of my vision. Latching on to the bars to keep my body upright, I tipped my neck up.

Dark curls swooped over a smooth forehead, green eyes seared into my face, long fingers curled around the bars.

"Cruz . . ." Had he come to set me free? Was my time over?

His mouth moved, and I strained to hear his words, but if there were any, they were lost in the deluge of air that swooshed through the bars of the cage, loosening my ponytail.

He yanked hard, then released the cage, sent it hurtling upward. I hooked my feet around the bars and gritted my teeth as my stomach soared into my throat. Gasps, shouts, screams echoed around me. Dots of fire whizzed around Cruz like shooting stars.

Another body shot toward him, gripped him, punched him. Like in a flipbook, the action uncoiled in bursts of motion.

Random words pricked my buzzing mind: *Cupola*, defective, Seelie, blood, mist.

I closed my eyes until the cage leveled and stilled, until my loose black strands stopped flogging my cheeks and forehead. Was the lull the onset of a new nightmare? Pulse thudding, I cracked my lids, and a spot of red bloomed in my hair-streaked vision.

I was still in Neverra. I didn't dare let go of the bars for fear of toppling. It was the little boy with the cold-burnt lips. He pumped one open palm in the air twice.

Ten.

Ten, what?

Minutes?

Screams sounded. I twisted in the cage. Pressed my forehead against the bars. A shiny lasso wrapped around Ace's writhing body, pinched his throat, pinned his arms to his torso, jammed his legs together. An inhuman shriek rose from my lips as he thrashed and twisted.

Cruz leered at his captured prey, then lifted the hand that wasn't holding the golden lasso. Ribbons of dust squirmed on his palm, danced in his wild eyes. With a feral growl, he tossed the dust. Like dry sand, it sprang off his hand and hit Ace's face.

Ace went still.

"Cruz. NO!" I screamed. I pulled on the bars, trying to force them apart, but the metal held. "NO!"

Ace paled.

Grayed.

Shouts echoed against the *calimbors*, ricocheted against the *cupola*, rebounded against my ribs.

A tsunami of anger rolled through me, rocketed out of me.

Like a rock breaking, Ace crumbled.

50

LOSS, LOST

"NO!" The cry broke out of my mouth as Ace's light blue shirt flapped emptily, rose like a wind-blown plastic bag, then drifted.

Cruz grinned as his dangling lasso coiled into his palm like a *volitor* branch. And then he was hanging to the side of the cage, his fingers inches from mine.

Calm. The word slid off his lips and snaked around me like his lasso.

The fuck I would stay calm! I scrabbled to locate my own dust. My hand trembled so hard I had to squash it underneath my other hand. Nothing prickled underneath my palm.

The dust had to be there, though.

Had to be.

I pressed harder, mashed my air pipe to seize it, wheezed, but kept clutching, adding more pressure. My throat clenched, and my lungs shriveled.

Prickling erupted under my fingers.

I loosed them off my throat.

Shouts.

More gasps.

Figures darted away, whorled into a long, runny smear, like paint dripping over a canvas, like rain dripping over a windshield. Air filled my mouth, buoyed my lungs, filled me with unadulterated adrenaline.

"I trusted you and you killed him," I growled.

The green eyes stared unblinkingly at me. The mouth opened and closed like a fish's.

I flung my hand toward the face.

The eyes went wide.

The fingers fell away from the bars just as an arm snaked around my shoulders. "He deserved to die. Like Stella."

I looked up into my father's face. "Dad?"

Ace's empty shirt slapped the cage, as pristine and white as falling snow.

White.

Not blue.

A bone-chilling hush fell over my body as I slid the fabric through the bars of the cage and ran it between my fingers. "It's white. Daddy, it's white!"

I looked up, but my father was gone.

Something clanked behind me. I spun. Found Ace standing, as pale as the white shirt that had evaporated from my fingers. His lips were rigid, his gaze tight.

My hair spiraled around my face, slicing my view of him. I rushed toward him, brushed his face to make sure he was real. His hands settled on my elbows, held them gently. I stared into the jeweled blue depths of his eyes.

"You killed him."

"I— I—" Heat pooled behind my eyelids as his declaration twisted like a steel blade inside my chest. "No . . ."

"Cruz is gone because of you."

My heart cracked as tears dripped off my chin, dripped onto Ace's purple shirt.

Purple.

I pushed away from him.

"You're not real."

"I'm real."

"You're not."

I hit his chest until my arms ached and my knuckles smarted. And still I hit, but Ace didn't disappear. I dug the heels of my hands into my eyes and crumpled to the floor. Agony seeped into my heart, cleaved it open like the serrated wheel of a can opener tearing through metal.

"I thought he killed you," I wailed.

"The only killer here is you." Ace's answer destroyed me.

51

DARKNESS AND LIGHT

*C*lapping erupted around me.

I jerked my head off my knees and gaped at the sea of faces surrounding the *cupola*, at the blinding smiles and twinkling eyes. Velvet pouches filled with coins jingled as they changed hands. The clamor was so loud, I covered my ears.

Long legs walked toward me, kneeled. Arms gathered me. "It's over."

I stiffened at the sound of the voice, leaned away. For a long moment, I held my breath. Then I lowered my hands from my ears and touched the boy's jaw. Looped one of his curls between my fingers. He felt real, but did that mean he was? "I . . . I killed you."

Cruz smoothed back my hair. "Did you?"

My brow crinkled. "Is this another . . . another—"

He shook his head. "It's over. I promise."

"What a show you gave us! Making us all think you were choking yourself when you were really pulling out your dust. Spectacular!" Linus's cheery voice made me touch Cruz's shoulder.

If I had truly pulled out my dust and flung it at Cruz, how was he still here?

"I have a bet on who was the intended recipient of your dust, Catiri." A giddy Angelina stroked the velvet underside of a pouch. "Will you tell us?"

I ground my teeth and turned pleading eyes on Cruz.

Conversations erupted around us. Names of possible recipients were tossed around the crowd

"Silence!" The king clapped loudly. "Silence. Keep your enquiries for this evening. I promised the future Mrs. Vega a grand celebration, and what a grand celebration it will be. Now give her space so she may gather her wits."

Conversations swelled as the courtiers broke into smaller groups.

I burrowed my face against Cruz's shoulder, whispered, "I don't want a party. I want to go home."

He sighed, then scooped me up and airlifted me out of the cage. I let my lids slide shut as the air buffeted my face, as the fire underneath his skin crept under mine.

"The dust was for me, wasn't it?" His voice was soft.

Without lifting my head, I murmured, "It was."

"What did I do to deserve to die?"

"You killed Ace."

A beat. "Sound reason to end my life."

"Is he okay?"

"If by okay you mean out-of-his-mind furious, then yes, he's okay."

I smiled, but then I didn't.

Then I cried.

Hours passed. Entire days. Purple mornings slid into violet evenings. Suns became *lustriums* which became suns again. I slipped from sleep to a state of semi-wakefulness where I noticed I was enclosed in soft sheets instead of golden bars, and that someone sat in the corner, watching over me, rocking in a yellow chair.

The chair reminded me of the one my grandfather had built for my mother when she was pregnant with me—surely a figment my addled mind had created for comfort.

Sometimes, Ace sat in it. Sometimes, it was Cruz. Sometimes, it was Veroli.

Soup was administered into my dry throat. Water was dribbled through my parched lips. A musk-scented sponge was swept over me.

A comb was passed through my hair. All these ministrations were made with the utmost care and in the utmost silence.

I was alive, but barely.

"SHE'S GROWING WEAKER. We need to get her up. Get her food. We can't just let her sleep." Ace's voice was hushed.

"What do you suggest?" Cruz snapped. "We drag her out of bed and force her to ingest a ten-course meal?"

"If that's what it'll take, then yes."

My lids fluttered over my eyes as I listened to them fight. Fight over me. How could they still care about me? I'd killed one with imaginary dust and the other with lies.

Their argument grew more heated, but I didn't understand what they were saying as they had switched to Faeli.

"Don't fight," I murmured.

Silence. And then two sets of bare feet padded toward me.

Ace crouched in front of me. "Cat?"

I looked at him, at his crumpled brow and tight jaw. "You died," I whispered.

"Cruz told me."

"He killed you."

He tipped one of his eyebrows up and smiled. "Wouldn't put it past him."

Cruz didn't smile, though. He stood beside Ace, arms folded against his chest, rigid as a washboard.

"You're angry with me?" I asked Cruz.

"I'm angry." His pupils throbbed. "But not with you."

"Did the Night of Mist already pass?"

He shook his head. "It's in four days."

"*Four?* I've been asleep for . . ."

"Nine days."

I sat up so fast my head spun. I'd assumed three or perhaps four days had come and gone, not nine.

Ace clutched one of my hands. "Hey there, Sleeping Beauty. You got to take it easy."

As I looked into his face, I thought of the *cupola*, of how I'd watched him disintegrate, of how angry it had made me, of how viciously I'd punished Cruz for what he'd done.

As though sensing where my thoughts had gone, Ace let go of my hand and swiped a finger over my brow. "You're safe."

It wasn't my safety I was worried about. I was worried about his, Cruz's, Lily's, my father's . . .

My father!

I'd slept through an entire earthly month, so I'd missed my birthday. Knowing my father, he must've called me a thousand times. He always phoned me for my birthday. "Cruz?"

"Yes?"

"Have you been sending my father messages?"

"Lily has your phone, Cat. She's been covering for you."

I let myself fall back against the mattress. The pillow puffed around my face. "Okay. Good . . ." Although I wished I could scrape away my imprisonment, forget everything from that day, it was now a part of me, as much as Stella's dust. Another scar. "Ace, promise me that when you become king, you will destroy the *cupolas*."

His Adam's apple bobbed in his cleanly-shaven throat. "If I bec—"

I rolled back up and gripped his fingers. "*When*, not *if*."

His gaze didn't leave mine as he amended his answer. "*When* I become sovereign, it'll be my first order of business."

"I better get up then. I can't help take down a world lying down."

"Cat . . ." Ace started as I swung my legs over the edge of the bed. My knees knocked together. They looked so huge compared to the rest of my thighs.

"I think I'll take you up on that ten-course meal."

A smile snuck over Ace's lips. "How about we start with a bowl of pasta with . . . what was it again? Ketchup?"

Emotion rose inside of me. Although it had been months since we'd discussed favorite comfort foods, he remembered. I clasped my hands together in my scrawny lap. "I . . . I wanted to tell you both something." I stared between their expectant faces. "I didn't"—I dropped my voice— "I didn't touch Gregor." I wrinkled my nose. When neither said anything, I repeated, "I didn't."

Ace splayed a warm, soft palm on my knee. "I know."

"How did you get him to reduce your sentence then?" Suspicion limned Cruz's tone.

"I know one of his secrets."

Cruz's arms slid out of their tight knot while Ace asked, "You black-mailed him?"

I nodded.

Cruz's black eyebrows slanted. "A secret we aren't aware of?"

I nodded.

"Will you tell us?" Ace asked.

I recalled Gregor's warning and shook my head again.

"Must be one hell of a secret," Ace said.

"It is."

"I need to go to the palace," Cruz said. "Report that you're awake and that the marriage can take place."

As he walked toward the door, I asked, "When I was in the . . . in the . . . *cupola*"—the very word tasted bitter—"did you toss the cage?"

"I did."

A thin gasp escaped me. "Why?"

"Because it was sinking into the mist, which causes your skin to . . . *change*."

My lips drew further apart. "You mean, I get scales?"

"Not scales, but you get *glimmery*."

"Really?"

"I first noticed it when I took you to Sarsay's house."

"Oh."

"Yeah. Try to stay away from the mist for the next couple days, okay?"

I bobbed my head in a nod. "How was my party by the way?"

Cruz paused, hand on the doorknob. "What party?"

"The one to celebrate my survival."

Shadows glanced over his face. "It didn't happen."

"Must've disappointed quite a few people."

"They were much too busy gossiping about the other happenings to ponder your party." A slash of white illuminated his dark face.

I raised an eyebrow.

"Ace will fill you in." He opened the door. "I'll be back soon."

Once he was gone, I turned toward Ace, who was still crouched in

front of me, face leveled on mine. My heart thumped, spreading goosebumps and heat into places that had felt numb and cold since I'd
emerged from the cage.

We observed each other in silence for a long moment. Then, "I was
so scared," he said, at the same time I said, "You don't hate me?"

His lips quirked into a crooked smile. "No, and that's not for lack of
trying."

I returned his smile, then flicked his chest. He caught my hand.
Wound his fingers through mine. Pressed his forehead against mine.

I felt his breath on the tip of my nose, on my parted lips, on my
teeth. "I'm sorry for everything," I whispered.

He pushed a strand of hair off my face and tucked it behind my ear.
"You have nothing to be sorry for."

I squashed my lips together.

As though he felt I didn't believe him, he took a seat on the bed
next to me and dragged my weak body against his, then stroked my
shoulder that jutted out of the loose tunic someone had dressed
me in.

As his fingers moved, my gaze roamed over the room and settled on
the chair in the corner. "Is that— Did you—"

"I took it from your attic. Let me tell you, it wasn't easy getting it
through the portal." He smiled sheepishly. "Your father won't get angry,
will he?"

I blinked at him.

Just blinked.

"I thought it would make this place a bit . . . *homier.*"

Pulse strumming, I stared at the chair so at odds with the neutral,
natural palette of Cruz's interior, the same way I must look to Neverrians. "So . . . what happened while I was sleeping?"

"Actually it happened while you were awake."

I glanced away from my grandfather's daffodil-colored rocking
chair.

"The mist shifted when you were in the cage." The *lustrium* hanging
in the amethyst sky painted the side of his face silver. "Depressions
appeared in it. It thinned out in places."

"*While* I was in the cage?"

"While you were in the cage."

"Did I . . .?" I let my voice trail off, not daring to fully speak the question.

"You got terribly angry at some point. Cruz believes anger triggers some sort of connection with your Daneelie power."

A beat passed. "And everyone noticed?"

"Some noticed. Most were too entranced by your show." He bit down so hard on his lip, a wisp of smoke curled out. He licked the gash and it sealed up.

"Those who noticed, did they link it to me?"

"No. Ever since the book went missing, Gregor and Lyoh have been convinced the Unseelies are preparing an attack. They assumed it was their first move."

I pressed my cheek to his shoulder blade. "My wedding will be such a bloodbath."

His arm curled around me again, his hand splayed on my waist. "A smoke bath. Not many of us bleed."

Even though I knew he was trying to distract me with humor, I couldn't smile. "Don't come to the wedding. Go to Earth and wait there."

"And miss you exchanging vows with another man?"

"I'm serious, Ace."

His fingers hardened, creasing the fabric of my tunic. "If you were serious, then you wouldn't seriously ask me to stay away and hide. What sort of man do you think I am?"

"The type who deserves to rule all of this." I gestured toward the window. "But you can't do that as a house plant."

I felt him smile against my hair. "Come on . . . a plant? At the very least, I'll be a tree. I suspect a *calimbor*."

"*Calimbors* are . . . are dead faeries?"

He chuckled. "Humans are so gullible."

His laughter frayed the steely fabric that had enveloped me since my brutal punishment and began to unravel it, one thread after the other.

INVISIBLE INK

*T*he following night, Veroli was getting me ready for a party. *My party.*

While bathing me, she'd frowned a great many times at the subdued sparkle of my skin, which I passed it off as an effect of the Neverrian sun on hunter skin.

"You don't have to do this," Cruz insisted, peering over my shoulder at my reflection.

Veroli gathered my hair and twisted it, then pinned it in a simple knot, pulling out tendrils to frame my face, which she'd left almost makeup free. The only hints of color were a thin coat of mascara and scarlet lipstick.

"I'm proving a point by attending."

He folded his arms in front of his navy tunic. "And what point would that be?" he asked, as Veroli clasped a choker around my neck. Obsidians as black as my eyes winked in their silver settings.

The necklace almost entirely covered my tattoo. I wasn't sure I wanted it covered, but then I didn't intend to fight tonight. What I intended to do was prove I was alive and well. "That they can't break me."

His green eyes gleamed in the mirror. "It doesn't matter what they believe."

"You're right. It doesn't matter what *they* believe. What does matter

306 | OLIVIA WILDENSTEIN

is what the *calidum* believe. I want those who are afraid of Gregor and Lyoh and Linus to see that *I* am not."

Veroli's hands slid down to my shoulders and gave a short squeeze. "I could tell them."

I smiled at her. "Telling them is not the same as showing."

Cruz grumbled something underneath his breath, then, "Is she ready?"

Veroli nodded, but fussed with the tendrils of hair around my face, but nodded.

I rose from the chair she'd set in the bathroom and returned to the bedroom. Cruz walked up to his bookshelf and grabbed a book, flicked through its pages, tossed it aside, then picked another.

I cocked an eyebrow. "What are you looking for?"

"I wanted to show you something."

"Okay . . ."

He flipped through it. "Where did Ace put it?" he muttered, turning the book over and shaking it.

A folded sheet drifted out like a feather. He bent to pick it up, to smooth it out.

"Ace told me you saw words on this, but I know your *sight* has changed since you've been here." He held the paper out. "Do you still see something?"

I blinked at the sheet. "Was that the page from my book?"

He nodded. "So? Do you see anything?"

I touched the paper where the imprint's name had been, where the rendering of the rowan tree had been. "There's nothing."

"You're telling me the truth?"

I bristled. "Yes. I'm telling you the truth. Why would I lie?"

His eyes landed on something behind my shoulder. Veroli. Although she was picking up odds and ends, she seemed to do so extremely slowly. "Veroli, would you mind giving Catori and me some privacy?"

She stopped what she was doing. "I want to help. Let me help you."

"Help us with what?" Cruz refolded the paper his adoptive mother was ogling.

Veroli planted her hands on her squat hips. "With what you're planning."

"We're not planning anything besides our nuptials."

Veroli raised her weak chin. "Have you forgotten who raised you, Cruz? I *know* you. I *know* Ace. I know these nuptials"—she pointed between me and Cruz—"are part of something else . . . something bigger."

"You know *nothing*, Veroli."

Her cheeks became the color of rare beef.

"Cruz," I said reproachfully.

"What?" he snapped. His tone brooked no argument. "You asked me to marry you, and I said yes. We do not love each other. It's a political alliance, a peace treaty with the Unseelies."

Veroli shook her head frenetically. "You take me for a fool, Cruz. I'm no fool."

"Leave us." His voice was infinitesimally milder. "Please."

Still shaking her head, she grabbed her fabric bag and zipped for the front door, which she shut with a bang.

I turned on Cruz. "How can you speak to her that way?"

"Speaking to her any other way would lead her to believe she could help, and she can't. At least not without risking her life. Would you rather I risked her life?"

I pursed my lips. "Of course not."

"Then don't involve her. Don't involve Dawson. Don't involve anyone you're not ready to lose."

I thought of Ace then. How I'd involved him. I wasn't ready to lose him, and yet I'd put him in harm's way. "Why did you want to know about the ink?"

He folded the sheet and refolded it. "Because I've had no contact with the *forma* since the *Hareni* was sealed off, so I haven't been able to give them the paper. But if you can't read it, then they probably can't either. Which will make their travel through portals on the Night of Mist impossible. Although there's the possibility that even though it looks invisible, the ink is still there."

"Ace told you everything?"

He nodded.

I chewed on the inside of my cheek. "Is that the plan? To set them free outside Neverra?"

"They want bodies."

I wrinkled my nose. Even though I understood—well, sort of—how being insubstantial could be upsetting, taking over human bodies sounded creepy, like something out of the Exorcist. "Maximus escorted the Unseelie who ended up lodging itself in Negongwa's body through a portal, right?"

"Right."

"So why can't *you* escort them out one by one?"

"Because after that happened, Maximus changed the magic of the portals."

"Change the magic back then."

He snorted. "It's not so simple, Catori. As you might be aware, now that your knowledge of our history has increased, Maximus was cunning. He had the faerie who changed the magical algorithm killed."

"And what? No one can undo what he did? If you lose the key, change the lock."

"To change the lock, we'd need to figure out where the lock is. And what it looks like. It could be anywhere in Neverra and could look like anything . . . a leaf, a cup, a piece of straw."

"You're kidding."

"In case you've forgotten, faeries love their little games as much as they enjoy tricking people."

Oh, how I knew. "So how do you rid people of their portal stamps if you don't know where the lock is?"

"A portal stamp is like a light switch, not a key. They can be turned on and off."

"So all we need to do is turn Lily's stamp back on? Who do we have to convince? Gregor?"

"Lily's stamp wasn't turned off, Catori. It was altered, so the portals will repel Lily, with or without an escort."

"So how do we change it back?"

"It can only change back if the cause for its alteration expires."

"Meaning?"

He raked his hand through his hair. "Meaning, when I die, so do all the bonds—live or broken—associated with me."

A racket exploded in my chest, brassy, shrill. "That's— That cannot be the— Was *that* your solution?"

Cruz's face was a patchwork of strained planes that creased where they joined. "No. I'm hoping"—he flicked the folded sheet of paper still clutched in his hands—"I'm hoping this will get her through."

Silence drenched the apartment and stilled my pounding heart. He *hoped* a piece of paper could somehow counter Lily's tainted stamp. "What if it doesn't work?" My pragmatic side reared its head.

"Then I'll kill myself."

"For a mastermind, that's a lousy solution. Lousy."

He growled softly. "You have a better one?"

"I do actually. Let's destroy the Cauldron."

He snorted. "You can't destroy the Cauldron."

"Why not?"

A barbed smile tugged at Cruz's lips. "Where do you think Neverra rose from? The Cauldron is the birthplace of every single thing and being here. You destroy the Cauldron, you destroy Neverra."

I felt my eyebrows pull up toward my hairline. "Still, there must be another way . . ."

"Welcome to my crusade. I warn you, it's infuriating. Every road I explore leads to a new wall. You're the first crack I've found, and I've been on the lookout for cracks a long time."

"There were others before me. Why didn't you use Mewari or Chatwa or Iya or my mother? Or Aylen?" I should probably not have reminded Cruz about Aylen. Odds were, he hadn't forgotten about her, but still.

"My father entertained the idea of bringing a Daneelie into Neverra, but my mother murdered him before he could convince Adette and Mewari to return. After he died, no one considered expunging the mist. In school, we were taught it protected us from the evil *forma*. Why would we want to destroy a shield? But then I learned the truth, and his crusade for peace and justice became mine." He drew in a long breath. "Ley was the one who taught me the *forma* weren't our enemies. She was the one who told me about my father's intentions and about the book that would help hunters travel to Neverra. She believed that bringing them here would break the mist's hold on the *Hareni*. Sadly, it didn't work."

"What do you mean it didn't work? The pages didn't work?"

"The pages worked. Chatwa traveled through a portal but—"

I gasped. "Chatwa's here?" *She didn't drown!*

"She *was* here. Back in 1938. But her presence didn't break the mist. And before she could reach the glades and activate her *other* nature, she was executed. A hunter in Neverra? You can imagine how my mother reacted to that." Cruz's eyes seemed to glaze over at the recollection.

"She's dead?" I murmured, realizing that I'd held out hope that somehow, somewhere, she was still alive.

"It was a public execution. My mother charred your great-grand-mother's body with her dragon fire, then gassed her." His chest rose, as though a cresting wave of nausea were rising inside of him. "After that, our relationship with the *forma* became tenuous. And that's saying it nicely. On the Nights of Mist, Seelies were told to stay inside their homes and splash lemon juice or vinegar onto their doors. The palace was doused in vinegar. It reeked of it. Neverra reeked of it for ages." He grimaced. "Only recently have we been able to interact agreeably with them, and that's only because faeries stayed away from your family and their graveyard. Apparently the Unseelie locked in Negongwa's body can communicate with them and has been reporting to them."

I crinkled my brow. "You mean, I've been watched by a buried spirit my entire life?"

"For your protection. It's a good thing."

Good, but unsettling.

So *very* unsettling.

"Have you never had strange dreams that didn't feel like your own?"

I jerked a little.

"You have, haven't you?"

"Kajika told me Gottwa spirits could reach out to humans in the realm of dreams."

"He still doesn't know his Gottwa spirit is an Unseelie, does he?"

"I haven't told him."

"Hopefully, Negongwa has set him straight, now that he's awake."

A two-hundred-and-fifty-year old man had emerged from a casket filled with spelled rose petals, like a person emerged from a relaxing bath. How I hoped no one had been around to see. "He's really awake?"

"He's really awake."

I shivered a little.

If I ever managed to return to Rowan, what would my world look like?

53

LOVE POTION

*A*fter Cruz dropped me off at the party, he left with his mother and Gregor to discuss battle strategies. My future husband was still playing the part of Lyoh's lackey. And even though he'd shown me a little tenderness back in the cage when he'd carried my shattered body away, he was back to acting cold and superior.

The party tonight was held in the belly of the palace, in a vast chamber below the throne room. A landscaped medley of lavender and jade-colored succulents covered all four walls, while lianas dripping with roses as pale as cream and as large as water lilies ran across the ceiling, partitioning the sprawling room. Apricot-colored paper lanterns drifted between the clusters of voluble faeries, casting shallow pools of light over their sparkling jewels and gauzy, candy-colored outfits.

I stood in the darkened fringes of the room like a wallflower. Where had my earlier audacity come from? I no longer wanted to be here; I no longer wanted to prove anything to anyone; I wanted to withdraw to Cruz's apartment, sit in my yellow chair, and rock the next four days away.

"Can you take me home?" I asked Dawson, to whom Cruz had entrusted me upon arriving.

He was bobbing his head to the haunting song rising from a chorus of willowy, half-naked women. "You want to leave?"

I nodded, my nerves as jumbled as the tangle of lianas overhead.

"But you only just got here." He blew his long blond bangs out of his eyes. "Plus, it's in your honor."

"Catiri!" A grating voice rose from the crowd, followed by a delicate flapping hand. "Woo-hoo!"

Now that Angelina had spotted me—and had alerted half the room to my presence—there was no more escaping. *Crap.*

"Ace is so lucky," Dawson mumbled. "She's so beautiful."

Angelina carved a path through the throngs of people. As per her usual, she wore an outfit that bared her taut, curved midriff. "How incredible is this party?"

Trying to pretend everyone wasn't staring at me, I said, "It's . . . something," while Dawson blurted out, "It's almost as incredible as you are, Angelina."

The compliment burnished Angelina's already bright ego. She laughed. "You're sweet." She pinched Dawson's flaming cheek. "What's your name?"

Dawson straightened like a snap bracelet. "Dawson. My name's Dawson. I'm Veroli's son and a licensed *runa* driver. If you ever need a lift, you can call on me."

Angelina twittered some more, and then she coiled her arm through mine and tugged me into the crowd. "He's as cute as puppy, isn't he? I wish I could have a puppy, but animals from your home can't survive in ours. Shame, huh?"

I looked over my shoulder to make sure Dawson stayed with me. Even though his eyes were downturned, he followed close behind.

"There's someone who keeps pestering me about an audience with you. Apparently you met back on Earth?" Angelina's feet must not have been on the ground, because her head was level with mine. "She's really taxing, but I promised her a couple minutes of your time."

How kind of Angelina to manage my social calendar.

We stopped in front of a woman whose skin was so dark it seemed to have swallowed all the light in the room. Only her eyes were colorful, a web of amber-green that matched the rope of emeralds coiled around the black plait she wore as a crown. "Catori Price."

Her name hit my brain like debris from a twister. "Patila." Last time I'd seen her, she'd blistered three of my fingers with faerie fire. "Fancy meeting you here," I muttered, gaze darting around me for a friendly face . . . *Well,* friendlier.

"Could we speak in private?" I wasn't sure if she was asking me or Angelina.

"I . . . I . . ."

Angelina flipped her hair. "All right, but no more than five minutes. Catiri has many rounds to make. She is, after all, quite the star tonight. Surviving a *cupola.*" She winked at me as though surviving a *cupola* had been some silly game instead of a deadly punishment. "I'll go get us a drink." She let go of my arm and sank into the crowd.

Patila stared beyond me at Dawson. "Can you tell your friend to leave too?"

"I'd rather he stay."

"I won't hurt you."

I snorted.

"You still wear a faerie brand. Only that faerie can kill you."

"Some things are worse than death."

"Why would I hurt the guest of honor? I'd end up in a *cupola,* which, unlike you, I most probably would not emerge from."

My dust swirled in its tracks beneath my necklace, as though reminding me of its presence. *My dust.* When had I stopped thinking of it as Stella's? I turned to Dawson. "Give me a minute, okay? After a minute, join me."

He studied Patila's stern face before saying, "If you hurt her, Ace will kill you."

"I don't doubt it."

Patila led me back toward the dusky edges of the room, away from the crowd and the floating paper lanterns. "Everyone seems convinced Ace branded you, but I remember your brand. It was a V. Not a W."

Her intimation propelled a chill through me. "You must've missed one of the Vs."

"I don't miss anything." She moved her face closer to mine and dropped her voice. The heady scent of tuberose lifted off her smooth skin like smoke and snaked into my flaring nostrils. "When Cruz told the *draca* I must've misread your brand, she punished Marcus; said my lie made a fool of her."

"What is it you want?"

She smiled. "I want Gregor to turn Marcus's portal stamp back on."

Marcus. The name called up silver hair, a man as white as Patila was black.

"He's my husband."

"What makes you think Gregor would listen to me?"

"He listened to you once already." An oily smile curved her lips.

Like a spider watching a fly hurtle straight for a web, Patila sensed she'd entrapped me. She was wrong. She might've have stunned me midflight, but her web would tear like the mist in a few days.

"It will have to wait until after my wedding."

She nodded just as a faerie breached the thicket of bodies next to us, looming over everyone else, even though his feet were firmly planted on the buffed stone floor. The second Ace's eyes met mine, he moved toward me. "Patila." His voice was sharp.

"Ace."

"I hope you're not bothering Catori."

"We were just catching up." She grinned at him, then at me. "Weren't we?"

I returned her cutting smile. "Absolutely. It was such a pleasure seeing you again, Patila. Will you pass on my best wishes to Marcus?"

"I will. Have a pleasant evening."

After she'd retreated into the crowd, Ace bowed his head toward me. "What did she want?"

"She wants me to have a *talk* with Gregor about Marcus's portal stamp."

"The nerve." He studied the crowd as though looking for her.

"She says she remembers my brand. That it wasn't always a W."

"Good for her."

"I told her I'd talk to him after my wedding."

"There you are!" Angelina's high-pitched voice chafed against my already raw nerves. "Here." She pushed a gold goblet into my hand.

I sniffed it.

"Relax. There's no *mallow* inside," she cheeped. "I heard you weren't a fan. If you don't believe me, ask my darling fiancé to taste it. He'll tell you."

I bit my lip, considered asking Ace. Finally, I took a tiny sip. It tasted like sweet wine that had been left to steep too long in a metal receptacle. When the world didn't tilt or break out in strange hues, I took another sip, and then another. Soon I'd drained the goblet. As though it hadn't quenched my thirst, I licked my lips. They tingled deliciously. I licked them again. The taste, the feel of my tongue was almost debilitating.

Ace seized the goblet from my fingers. "What was in this?"

Angelina grinned. "My wedding gift to Catori. Well, to Cruz *and* Catori."

Anger fell off Ace in waves that pounded against me, inside of me. My thighs clenched as I felt his emotion *everywhere*. I must've moaned a little because his gaze snapped back to my face.

"You gave her Daneelie scales?" he yelled.

"Uh-huh. I bought a small packet at the market during Middle Month, but between the *cupola* and her coma, I haven't had a moment to give it to her. Better locate Cruz fast, or she'll be ravaging some of the guests. And even though a faerie revel wouldn't be the same without an orgy, I feel like Cruz wouldn't be pleased if he weren't at least present."

Angelina glowed like an angel, a gorgeous angel. Dawson had been right, she was incredible, dazzling even. I reached out to touch her arm, but Ace strapped his fingers around my wrist and hauled me over his big shoulder.

"Perhaps I should've saved some for her *duobosi*," Angelina said with a little laugh that sounded like butterfly wings, like dandelion florets, like—

I was suddenly airborne.

I yelped as Ace hurtled up the grandiose stairway. But then I closed my eyes, and smelled the wind, the fire, the spice, and turned blissfully languid. I trailed my fingers up Ace's back, over the stiff fabric of his blue tunic, then rolled up the hem to feel his hot skin.

"Stop it, Cat."

"Why? Don't you like this?"

His arms hardened around me. "Fuck. *Fuck*."

Exactly what I wanted.

As I drew my nails up his spine, he flew faster. Goosebumps broke out over his golden skin. He flipped me, and I squealed with delight as I slid into his arms, as my swollen breasts pressed against his sculpted, heaving chest.

As though realizing the position gave me more access to him, he flipped me again. New, exquisite sensations exploded over my back. He grumbled as he readjusted his hold so that I wasn't flattened against him, but hung like a ragdoll against the band of his rigid forearms.

I whimpered a little, not out of fear for the violet void, but from the lack of contact. I ran my hands around his forearms, stroked the long sinew, the strong bones covered by the softest skin.

He muttered something and heaved me back against him, and even though in some recess of my mind, the sound seemed outrageous, I purred.

54

ACE AND ME

*A*ce soared so high I thought we would reach a *lustrium*. I extended my hand to stroke the glittery cluster of stars that illumined Neverra at night, but he swooped toward the apex of a *calimbor* instead.

He dove toward a platform identical to the one in front of Cruz's home, then kicked open a door and carried me inside, cursing the entire time. He released me and I stumbled, catching myself on the thick edge of a clear guardrail that gave onto a sprawling bedroom. A four-poster bed made up of stone-colored sheets, silver fur pelts, and a medley of silken taupe pillows beckoned to me.

I turned back toward Ace, walked over to where he stood, and reached for him. He jerked away.

I blinked as a jumble of emotions twisted through my pulsating body. I wanted to cry, yell, laugh, touch, take, give. I settled on pouting. "I want you."

His eyes shut tight, the only movement on his rigid body. "Cat, you're not you right now. Angelina drugged—"

I approached him and ran my nose along the straight line of his jaw. He smelled like pleasure and safety and happiness and everything I'd ever desired. "I know what she did." Like smoke, desire expanded from my navel to every single one of my limbs. It erased the sharp lines of my bones and bloated my blood vessels; it softened my muscles and electrified my skin.

His eyes flew open, and his voice swelled like sails fed by wind. "You'll regret this."

"Not in this lifetime." My hands trekked over his arms, up the loose sleeves of his tunic, and wrapped around his biceps. "And if there's a next one, then not in that one either."

"Cat . . . no." He shook me off. "Daneelie scales are the equivalent of ten faeries using *captis* on you. You. Are. Not. Yourself. And you'd hate me for taking advantage of you."

My pulse tripped, and then my eyes filled with tears. *Shame.* "Don't you want me?"

He cocooned my cheeks with his palms. "More than anything, but not under the influence of a drug."

My lips wobbled. "I'm sorry."

"You have *nothing* to be sorry about."

Tears cascaded down my cheeks.

"I'm the one who's sorry." He swiped his thumbs over the wetness. "For not protecting you from my world. For what Cruz made you do. For doubting you. I'm sorry for not having been there for you when you needed me the most. I'm sorry for coming into your life and—"

Drawing a sharp breath, I slapped him. "Don't ever say that."

His eyes flared.

"I've been miserable without you."

His forehead pressed against mine. "But if I'd kept my distance, if—" His hot, erratic breaths hit my trembling lips.

"I'd still be here." I dragged one of his hands off my face and settled it over my pounding heart. "My pulse may beat faster because of a potion, but it beats for you."

His lashes rose and fell, then rose again.

I waited him out. Waited for him to say no again. I wasn't sure where this inner calmness stemmed from, for all of me was ache and need and want. I swept my hand over the soft bristles of his hair, down his warm, corded neck, then back up again.

His Adam's apple bobbed in his throat. I kissed it, and then I kissed the side of his neck and the ridge of his jaw.

A groan left his lips. "Cat—"

"I need you, Ace. Just like I needed you yesterday and I'll need you tomorrow."

His pupils danced in his magnificent eyes.

Like a current, my hunger pulled at me, dragging me away from shore and sweeping me into its magnificent depths. "Don't make me beg. Please don't make me beg."

His hand slid off my heart, but didn't leave my body. It cupped my breast, crumpled the fabric over it. Both my nipples tightened, even though only one was being touched.

His other hand gripped the back of my neck. I gasped as my necklace's metal and stones imprinted into my skin. He drew away, hunted my eyes, and then he dipped his head and kissed the swell of my breasts. His hands tracked over my ribcage and to the back of my dawn-gray dress. He muttered as he searched for the ribbon holding the tight bodice in place.

I would've helped him seek it, but my hands were too busy racing over the jagged knobs of his spine.

I realized he'd found the ribbon when his tongue touched skin instead of fabric.

Another ribbon and the rest of the dress slid off my hips and pooled on the floor.

He leaned away and gazed. His breath caught as his eyes roved over my bared body. "Skies, you are beautiful."

Only a tiny scrap of fabric still covered me. Too much fabric covered him, though. I stepped toward him and pushed the hem of his tunic up. He raised his arms, and I rolled it up and off. My gaze dipped to the waistband of his pants that held with a strip of knotted leather. I tunneled a finger into the loose knot and tugged.

The pants slid off his hips and he sprang out. I almost purred again as I grazed his jutting hipbones with my fingernails, raising goosebumps on his fiery skin as I trailed my fingers lower, lower.

He was all smooth skin and male perfection. "How am I supposed to refuse you?"

"You're not."

Growling, he scooped me up and soared over the glass guardrail, landing in a crouch on his bed. With heartbreaking gentleness, he set me down. I reached out for him, but he bunched my wrists in one of his hands and pushed my arms away, locking them over my head the same way he'd done in that strange tavern atop a bale of hay.

"Let me touch you," I whispered as he slanted his head and kissed the spot where my neck connected with my ear.

"Tonight's not about me." His silky stiffness trailed over my stomach, over my navel, over the fabric of my underwear.

His free hand followed the hot trail, his fingers rough as they caressed my skin. He drew his tongue over my collarbone and down the seam of my ribs, then released my wrists and traced the sides of my body and the indents of my waist with his fingertips. He dragged one of his hands over my navel, then lower, settling it beneath the lace waistband of my underwear.

He stroked the bundle of nerves that ached for his touch, teasing me until my body arched into him, wanting more . . . and more . . . and more.

He pushed my thighs apart with his broad shoulders and hooked one finger underneath the fabric, then pulled it away. I knew my mind was muddled with the potion, because I didn't blush and I didn't try coaxing him back up.

I watched him watch me. Watched him glide one long finger inside of me. My hips bucked. He splayed his free hand over my hip, pinning me in place, then dipped another finger inside. His gaze climbed up to mine as he brought both fingers to his mouth.

I trembled as need, loneliness, love, hope, and sadness rained over me like a shower of arrows, pinning me underneath this remarkable, prodigious man.

He pushed my underwear aside and lazily swirled both fingers against me before plunging them back inside. My breathing grew shallower as his deep strokes intensified. My thighs clenched against his shoulders as I tightened around his fingers. When my release came, it came so violently, I cried out in surprise.

Surprise and ecstasy.

But ecstasy shunted the surprise.

He kept stroking me as breakers turned into waves that turned into slow surges and finally ripples.

When my underwear settled back over my sensitive skin, I shivered.

Ace climbed back the length of my body, his face a map of mixed emotions, but it was his frown that made my heart hold still.

"Did I hurt you?"

"Hurt me?" I croaked.

His voice was hoarse. "You're crying."

I swiped my palms over my wet cheeks, hands trembling. All of me trembled. "No, Ace." I cupped his face with my shaky hands.

As though not believing me, as though a little distance would help him see more clearly, he flattened his palms on either side of my face and pushed himself up.

I raised my hands to his broad shoulders, keeping him anchored to me in case he decided he needed to add even more distance.

His gaze swept over my face, over and over, just as his fingers had swept over me. The memory had me clenching my thighs. His eyes darted down to where our bodies still connected, to where our legs tangled. I shifted my hips until he was aligned with me.

He closed his eyes and groaned.

I rocked, and he growled. "Cat—" His voice broke off, but not his restraint. He didn't move. He didn't even twitch.

I locked my hands around his neck and tugged him to me, but he wouldn't bend. I wrapped my legs around his back.

Greedy.

I was greedy for more.

More of him.

All of him.

Finally, he ground his powerful hips into mine. A short cry tore through my lips as he moved against me. I clawed his shoulders, drew him closer with my hooked legs. With an almost feral growl, he ripped off my underwear.

His mouth found mine, his teeth clashed against mine, his tongue twisted around mine. With one swift thrust, he was inside me, and then further inside, and further still. When he touched the end of me, he glided back out, paused, then impaled me again. I gasped against his lips and dug my fingers into his back.

He drew back out, stilled, and I broke the kiss because I knew he wasn't done. So why had he stopped?

He was gazing down at me. "Catori Price, when you wake tomorrow, when the potion wears off, don't be angry with me for having no willpower. And remember one thing, and one thing alone . . ." He pushed into me and stilled there. "I . . ."

Every inch of me burned and tightened and throbbed.

He drew out, teasing me with his idle strokes and slow words.

I panted, pulse feverish. "You what?"

He smiled and thrust back in so deep, I arched and whimpered. " . . . love . . ." He didn't move as he murmured the very last word. "You."

I embraced him then, wishing I could weld my body to his, not just for one night, but for always.

"This might scare the hell out of you, Cat, but I've never felt this way about anyone."

Yeah, it scared the hell out of me. But it also thrilled the hell out of me.

He drew back out, then sheathed himself inside of me with such force that I broke, splintering around him into a billion, blissful, beautiful fragments.

AFTERSHOCK

I woke up to bright light slanting over my face and a heavy arm draped over my waist. For a second, I held my breath and ran through all that happened the night before. When it all slotted into place, I smiled and slowly . . . slowly, turned to face the man who'd told me he'd loved me.

Loved me.

I grazed his jaw, and his eyelashes fluttered. I trailed my fingers over his skin again, awed that I was lying next to such a glorious man.

His lids lifted, and his magnificent blue eyes settled on my black ones.

"I didn't mean to wake you," I whispered.

"Yes, you did." It came out as a grumble, but half of his mouth tipped up.

I smiled. "Thank you for putting up with me last night."

He closed his eyes and tucked me closer.

"Did you mean it?"

His eyes opened, and his grin disappeared. "Did I mean what?"

"That—" My cheeks colored. Had I heard him wrong? Had my muddled mind made it up? "That you loved me?" It came out thinly.

"Nah. That was just to get you naked."

My ratcheting heart settled back into a steady rhythm, and I touched the tip of his nose. "If I remember correctly, I was already naked at that point."

He rolled me onto my back, and I yelped.

Pinning me underneath him, he said in a rough voice, "If I remember correctly, you never said it back."

The heady scent of him laced around me, and I raised a brazen smile. "Was I supposed to?"

His features tripped over each other as a frown touched his brow. "No. I mean—"

"Ace Wood, if I weren't already engaged, and you too for that matter, I'd most probably ask you to marry me right now."

He snorted. "Wanting to marry me is not the same as loving me." He brushed away a lock of hair from my forehead. "So? Do you?"

"No."

He tensed against me.

"I—" I pressed my lips to the groove beneath his eyebrows. He didn't move. Didn't breathe. "Adore." I kissed the corner of his motionless mouth. "You." I stamped the other corner with another chaste kiss. And then I lay back and watched as my words sank in, as his features realigned and smoothed. "You know what . . . I'm not sure *adore* is even the right word. Is there a term that means my heart belongs to you?"

He growled and brought his mouth down hard on mine. After long, delicious seconds, he pulled back. "You're vicious."

I gripped his shoulders, then hooked my legs around his back. "I thought I was supremely sexy and powerfully addictive."

He chuckled.

Even though I ached from last night, I wanted him again, and from the heavy feel of him, I knew he wanted me too. "I don't regret last night." I tugged him down until he was aligned with me. "No. Actually, I do." I raked my hands down his spine. "I regret that you thought I wanted you because of a damn aphrodisiac. I regret that it took us so long to get *here*." I tipped my head to the bed. "I regret that you thought you'd hurt me." I dug my nails into his skin, driving him down until every warm, throbbing inch of him was inside me.

His neck bent and his forehead pressed against the pillow, and a deep groan rumbled out of him. It rolled over my skin, where it scattered goosebumps.

"But most of all," I murmured, "I regret that you went to sleep thinking I might not love you back."

WHEN ACE DROPPED me off at Cruz's house with a damaged necklace—
I didn't remember it breaking, even though I remembered almost
everything from the night before—a badly tied dress, and a noticeable
limp—I hurt as much as my first time, or more—I prayed neither Cruz
nor Veroli would be home.

My flight of shame had been shameful enough when we'd crossed
paths with Silas on our way over. I'd asked Ace if he was spying on us,
and he'd said no with such aplomb that I hadn't doubted him, even
though I had wondered what a faerie guard was doing flitting around
the top of a *calimbor*.

My prayers to find the apartment empty weren't answered. I
supposed too many had been answered last night.

Cruz *was* home, sitting in an armchair, wearing such a grim expression that I backed up straight into Ace when my fiancé's eyes landed on
mine.

"We've got a problem."

My cheeks flooded with heat.

"Gregor made more *lucionaga*."

Oh. So his problem wasn't with me. Which should've reassured the
heck out of me. But considering the actual problem, it didn't. If
anything, I almost regretted the problem wasn't that I'd spent the night
with Ace.

"How many more?" Ace asked, as his big hands wrapped around the
top of my arms.

I didn't know if he touched me to offer me support or to keep
himself upright.

"He tripled them. Now a fleet is posted around the *Hareni*, and
another fleet is guarding the portals. I fear he senses something is
brewing."

"He can't," I found myself saying.

Cruz cocked an eyebrow. "Why can't he?"

"Because . . . because . . ." Because Lyoh hadn't read my thoughts and
informed him. I realized how dumb it sounded. Lyoh and Gregor
could've had spies listening to us. "Do they know what I . . . am?"

"Hopefully not, but it may be wiser to believe they do." He rose from the chair and walked over to us. "On another note, I heard Angelina fed you Daneelie scales last night."

I gulped.

"Silas came to fetch me in the middle of the meeting to tell me Ace had kindly whisked my future bride away before she could make a fool of herself at the party."

My face flamed.

"And just so you know, Ace, Linus offered to relieve Catori of her *itch*, but I told him that she preferred his younger version. And I also told him I wouldn't be pressing charges against you. That I didn't have time to pleasure my fiancée what with the *forma* attacking our mist, so I was actually thankful you took it upon yourself to *help*."

Ace's fingers dug into my burning flesh.

"Anyway, I hope you two had a pleasant night, because mine was shit." He raked a hand through his hair. "Years it took me to plan, and in minutes, it's crumbling. I'm starting to doubt we'll even get a shot at bringing change."

"The best generals always doubt themselves before an attack," I offered.

Cruz snorted.

"It's true."

"Well, that doesn't help."

I racked my brain for something that would help, but the only thing that came up was a reel of thigh-clenching images from last night. *Whoa. Not now, brain.*

Actually . . .

"I have an idea."

And I told them.

And although their first reaction was to say absolutely not, it was demented and I couldn't possibly be serious, the idea took root.

The moment Cruz changed his mind, I saw it in his eyes, and the moment Ace accepted it, I felt it in his fingers.

56

THE ELDER

*A*fter Ace left, Cruz informed me that our *duobosi* was scheduled for that very evening.

"No." My pulse flattened. "I won't do it. Tell them I won't do it. Tell them it's against hunter culture. Tell them I'll call off the wedding. Tell them . . ."

He gripped my trembling shoulders. "Shh . . ."

"Don't tell me to shush, Cruz! This might mean nothing to you, but to me . . ." I pressed the back of my hand against my mouth. I was going to be sick.

"Don't you think I've given this some thought?"

Slowly, I lowered my hand.

His green eyes flashed. "Give me a little credit."

"How are we—"

"The *duobosi* was enforced to test the male's virility, but it's become a spectacle. It doesn't affect the oath we've made to the Cauldron in any way, so technically, it's unnecessary. I told Linus that if he made me debase myself in front of his courtiers by bedding a huntress, I would disclose the parentage of Angelina's son to my mother. Even though Linus denies the boy is his, he came to the conclusion that since our marriage is a caste alliance, he could overlook the *duobosi* this one time."

"Thank the Great Spirit."

"The Great Spirit, huh?" His mouth cocked in a wry grin. "He didn't have much to do with getting you off the hook."

Right! "Thank *you*."

"You don't have to thank me, Catori. I know you think I have no scruples about sex like most of the other Seelies, but I do, and I wouldn't want to be with someone who didn't want me."

He turned his gaze to the large window. In the distance, faeries glided across the lavender sky. Some carried *runas*, some journeyed in little clusters, some traveled alone. I envied their power, especially now that I knew flying would never be a possibility for me.

"Can I ask you something?"

He swung his gaze back toward me.

"I know you once told me you considered Lily a little sister, but did you ever see her as more?"

"I never allowed myself to see her as more."

Not a yes, but not a no . . . "What if I broke up with you before we're bonded in matrimony, and then you ask her to marry you again? Or she asks you? Would the Cauldron accept her back into Neverra then?"

"First, she'd have to come back inside Neverra, because the Cauldron can't travel out of Neverra."

"Which she might be able to do thanks to Ley's book."

A splinter of sunlight fell across his face. "Have you considered that if you break our bond, then *you'll* be the one locked out forever?"

"I can survive on Earth."

"Ace can't."

"He can return to Neverra, refuel, then return to me."

"He would outlive you."

"Maybe he would outlive me even if I were to stay in Neverra. Once people know what I am—"

"You'd age quicker than him."

That shut me up. Well, for a minute it did. "Nothing lasts forever."

"I just want you to be aware of all you'd be giving up. Besides, maybe the Cauldron won't let me bond with Lily again. If Lily even accepts me back."

"She knows that what you did wasn't out of spite. She still loves you."

"Does she?" He heaved a weighty sigh.

I patted Cruz's shoulder. "Why don't we find out if it's a possibility first? Who would know?"

"An elder perhaps. I'd have to seek one out." Hope stained his voice, brightened his tone.

"Go."

He went.

57

BLUE MAGIC

*A*fter Cruz left, I dressed in my jeans, T-shirt, and sneakers, and did something I had never done before. I headed down the spirals.

Unlike mornings or evenings, the middle of the day was calm in Neverra. Few sky-dwellers swooped through the grove of *calimbors*. And only a handful of marsh-dwellers climbed the spirals.

Without exception, the *calidum* I passed flattened themselves against the trunk and blinked frenetically at me. In my still limited Faeli, I greeted them. Hearing me speak their tongue simply intensified their shock.

The younger ones said *hi* back, though, and some even smiled, but the older ones flinched as though engaging with me would send them straight into a *cupola*, like Ingrid. I shuddered as her haggard face materialized in my mind.

I replaced images of her with images of Blake and our tree house. What would he have thought of Neverra? Would he have been fascinated by the housing here? Probably. It was hard not to be mesmerized by it. I lifted my eyes and looked up at the periwinkle sky streaked with thick, sinuous branches and hanging footbridges.

Even though I'd been brought to this strange isle against my will, was I truly ready to leave it forever?

Could I miss a place that wasn't home?

No . . . it was the people I would miss. Veroli. Dawson.

I thought of Cass then, thought of how she would love it here. Thinking of my friend made me smile, but it also drilled a hole in my chest. I missed her. Like I missed my father. Like I missed Kajika. And Lily.

The Gottwas called Neverra a *baseetogan*—a bubble—and it described this place so well. This was a bubble. A delicate, airtight, magical world, that deserved to be rid of the cloying ribbon of mist.

If I failed to displace it though, which was a real possibility—it wasn't as though I'd had any opportunities to practice displacing it— would Cruz ask Aylen for help? Or one of her twins?

I couldn't see the ground beneath the thick net of clouds, but I could smell it—cold mud and green earth. The temperature had dropped, and although my muscles were warm from the brisk descent, my skin broke out in goosebumps. I quickened my pace, hoping the effort would heat my extremities, before coming to an abrupt halt several feet above the mist.

Curious gazes struck me from other spirals. I kept my eyes locked on the mist. The vast gray-white sea stretched far and wide. In the distance rose the flat tops of the blue cliffs I'd seen the day I'd run to the glades.

A filament of mist broke away from the white clumps and snaked around my fingers. I jolted. Had I gotten closer, or was the mist reacting to me? I pressed away from the thick vine banister, and in the shadow between my body and the handrail, I checked my hands. They sparkled, not copper, but blue. I squeezed my fingers into fists.

A soft gasp sounded from the *calimbor* across from me, which set off my heart, which in turn lit up my brand.

Certain that someone had somehow seen my glowing hands, I looked across the misty expanse, in the direction of the sound. People were bent over the vine railing. I jolted my gaze to where they pointed. The hazy fabric had torn. Not a huge hole, but large enough to see the ground, which was closer than I'd expected.

Had I done that?

Had *I* torn the mist?

"Oh, skies, the Cauldron is answering our prayers!" someone exclaimed somewhere below me.

Heart knocking against my ribs, I spread my fingers and the

tendrils of mist rushed to cover the hole, which elicited more excitement, more pointing.

"Did you see that?" someone squealed beside me.

Was their question for me? Sticking my hands in my jeans' pockets, I turned to find a child peering down below.

A child I knew. *Ranka*. Sarsay's son. "The mist moved."

"Did it?" I asked, trying to still my pounding heart.

He nodded, copper hair juddering around his ears that stuck out from his round face. "I need to tell Mudder."

He was already racing down. Soon his little body was swallowed by the mist. I turned back to find someone standing so close to me, I jerked and slapped a hand over my heart.

Ace was leaning over the banister. "The mist moved, did it?"

"Don't sneak up on me."

"I don't sneak, just like I don't flit." He gave me that cocky grin of his that made indecent thoughts parade through my brain. "I fly soundlessly." Ace's gaze slid from my face to my hand, which was still pressed against my heart. "Your hand, Cat." His tone was quiet, but brusque.

I thrust my hand back down and away from prying eyes.

"Let's put some distance between you and"—he nodded toward the mist—"that."

I thought he might offer to fly me back up, but instead, we walked. In silence at first, then, "Did you descend the spirals by foot or did Dawson bring you here?"

"I walked."

If people had flattened themselves for me, they melted into the tree at the sight of Ace, vanishing through doors if there were any available and unlocked.

"I don't think people like me much," I told him.

"You scare them."

"Me?"

"Your blood could kill them in an instant."

"Your dust would kill them quicker."

"Because your dust couldn't?"

I rubbed my neck, but then remembered the blue threads of magic pulsing in my fingers and quickly lowered my hand.

"Your skin's back to normal," he murmured, "but you're going to have wear gloves from now on. Opaque ones. I'll tell Veroli."

"Won't she ask why?"

"Tell her your hands get cold fast. Which is true." He grabbed my hand and rubbed heat into it.

We stayed silent for a little while longer. "Did Cruz tell you about my idea?"

"He did."

"And? Did he find an elder?"

Ace's Adam's apple jostled in his throat. "He did."

"Is it possible?"

"He said no one had ever been able to return to Neverra to test such a theory."

"So no one knows?"

Ace lowered his gaze to the rising wooden steps and shook his head.

"Did the elder say anything else?"

Dappled sunlight glanced over his bent head and glinted off his cropped hair.

"Ace?"

He looked up. "What?"

"Did the elder say anything about the Cauldron that could be useful?"

A turquoise beetle landed on his shoulder then fluttered off, leaving behind a delicate trail of musk.

"So?"

His gaze was so intense it felt heavy on my skin, like the fur pelt he'd given me during Middle Month.

"What did he say?"

His lids snapped shut over his eyes, then lifted almost instantly. "Nothing. He said nothing."

"Liar."

He grinned. "You should talk."

I blushed. "I lied to protect you."

He wound an arm around my waist and tucked me against his side. "I know." His fingers slid beneath the cotton hem of my T-shirt and settled over my skin. He kissed the top of my head.

And even though curious passersby stared, I didn't care what they thought of my relationship with their prince.

58

THE TRIM

a day later, while Cruz met with his mother, Gregor, and Linus to discuss the strategic placement of *lucionaga* on the Night of Mist, Ace flew me to the glades.

"Will it hurt?" I asked him, as I stared into the shiny, inky depths.

"Honestly, I don't know."

We stood on a floating shell, enclosed by a circle of *volitors* that afforded us some privacy. The mist was so low it clung to my hair when I was standing. Like the last time I'd passed through the mist, my skin glimmered strangely, but it was nothing next to the blue threads of magic stirring in my hands.

Ace stroked the water's surface, and it rippled like the mist rippled when I combed my fingers through it.

"We should . . ." He tipped his head toward the water, then turned his gaze upward to scan the cloud-heavy sky. "We should hurry." . . .

Swallowing a gulp of courage, I knelt next to him.

He produced a velvet pouch from his pocket. Then his palm ignited with ribbons of dust that frolicked over his palm before knotting into tiny shears. "Ready when you are."

I dipped my hand in the glade all the way up to my elbow and waited. It took almost a full minute for my skin to react. Once it broke out into what felt like a gazillion goosebumps, I lifted my arm out and propped it in Ace's outstretched palm.

I shivered, which made Ace look up. "We don't have to do this."

"I know. But I want to." When he brought the sharp tip of the shears to my small copper scales, I closed my eyes and turned my face away.

Metal clinked against metal as he squeezed the cutters. I gritted my teeth to hold back my hiss.

Excruciating.

That's what it was.

Like he'd sliced off a piece of skin.

"Cat?" His anxious tone had me opening my eyes. Concern leached off him. "We're not doing this."

"We only need a few more."

He pushed my arm away. "No."

"If you don't do it, I'll do it myself."

He glared at me, lips pressed tightly together.

"Please, Ace? Think of the edge this will give us."

He grumbled, but brought the shears back to my arm. He clipped, and I saw stars. He clipped again, and perspiration broke out over my upper lip. *Clip.* Sweat beaded down my neck. *Clip.* My eyesight blurred with pain. *Clip.* My ears buzzed. *Clip.* Black and white dots scrambled my sight. *Clip.* Only darkness remained.

I WOKE up on Ace's bed. Unlike last time, he wasn't spooning me. This time, he was standing with his arms tied so tightly in front of him, his biceps bulged underneath the sleeves of his tunic.

"That was stupid."

I sat up, putting pressure on the arm he'd carved up. I hissed as pain radiated all the way down to the bone. A long strip of gauze was wrapped around my forearm. Blood had seeped into the white bandage.

"I tried repairing your skin with fire, but it didn't do crap!"

I unwrapped it slowly to see the extent of the damage. My skin was pockmarked with nine seeping wounds that resembled popped blisters.

"It's not so bad." My arm hurt like hell, but I wouldn't admit this to Ace. He was sufficiently angry already. "Do we have enough?"

He huffed before answering. "Yes."

I slotted my fingers around his forearms and pulled to untangle them.

"How exactly are we going to explain your arm, huh?"

"No one will see anything through gloves." I tugged on him again, and he sat heavily on the bed.

"You passed out," he said, his voice hoarse.

"I know."

"From pain. You passed out. For an entire night!"

"I know. But I'm awake now."

He rubbed the sides of his face. "I'm going to have nightmares about this for a long time."

"Do I owe you?"

"What?" His hands fell against his thighs like dumbbells.

"I asked you to do something, and you did it. Do I owe you? A *gajoï*."

He grunted. "No. It was my choice to help. Fuck. Never ask me to hurt you again."

I touched the back of his hand. "I won't."

"Can we be done hurting each other?"

"We can be done." I kissed his jaw, felt a nerve jump there. "Thank you. For going along with this."

He side-eyed me, still very pissed. "Uh-huh."

I climbed on his lap and locked my arms around his neck, trying not to cringe when my raw skin skimmed his shoulder. He splayed his palms on my waist and held me as I leaned in to kiss him.

The mere contact of his lips made my heart thrash with lust instead of pain. It wasn't until we broke free to breathe that I felt the sting. So I kissed him again and drowned my pain in pleasure.

59

RED

*T*he following evening, as the sky darkened and filled with *lustriums,* anticipation rippled through Neverra. People spoke louder. I could hear them through the glass of Ace's room, where I'd remained holed up. I wasn't awaited anywhere else. Fireflies spangled the raisin-colored sky as they patrolled. The *Hareni* would open its gates and release the Unseelies in a matter of minutes.

The Night of Mist was upon us.

After midnight, I would be married.

After midnight, I would fight to rid the faerie isle of its rising silver mist.

The enormity of the task stiffened my body to the point where my bones felt fused together.

Like a starting pistol, the door shut upstairs. Its nerve-crackling sound resonated inside my skull, making my molars grind together. "Catori, it's Veroli. It's time, sweetheart."

I'd hoped it would be Ace, but he'd left to stand by Cruz's side to greet the Unseelies.

I turned away from the window. Veroli was peering down at me from the glass guardrail. If she was surprised to find me at Ace's instead of Cruz's, she didn't mention it. Over her arm was draped a blood-red gown—my wedding dress.

Brides marry in red, she'd told me the night we met.

She walked over to the staircase along the wall and descended toward the bed, over which she draped the dress. Next to it, she laid out gloves, and on the floor, satin slippers in the same shade as the dress.

I wasn't sure why, but it appeased me that the dress wasn't white.

White would've felt like a real wedding.

"I'll go run you a bath." Tonight, she'd traded her green tunic for a white one. I wondered if it was Neverrian tradition for guests to dress in white, but didn't ask because my vocal cords felt crafted of hard plastic, unable to produce sound.

Veroli observed me through deeply-lined eyes—surely Cruz's doing. Unless it was my wedding that caused her the strain. When she vanished inside Ace's black marble bathroom, I looked out at Neverra and wondered if Ley's book would allow the Unseelies out of their gilded prison? Would they all leave? Were there enough pages for that to happen? Cruz had a page safely stowed away for Lily.

Cruz hadn't told me the specifics of tonight's plan. All I knew was that I had to go through with the ceremony; I had to dip my hand in the Cauldron again.

"The bath is ready."

On numb legs, I walked toward the bathroom that smelled of musk and patchouli and steam. No longer prudish around Veroli, I pulled Ace's tunic top off, slipped off my undergarment, and lowered myself into his colossal bath.

Veroli worked soap over my skin, then wet my hair and massaged my scalp with lavender-scented oil, rinsed, and rubbed shampoo through my long tresses. The only part of my body she avoided was my battered arm.

"Ace told me to bring gloves, but he failed to tell me why. What happened to your arm, Catori?"

"Bug bites. They itched, so I scratched my skin raw."

If she didn't believe me, she kept quiet. Once I was clean, she wrapped a fluffy warm towel around me and swiped her palms over my hair. Once her fire had dried it, she drew a comb through the black mass to untangle it and kept brushing long after it fell in a silky curtain to my waist. The rhythmic, gentle strokes did little to soothe me, but perhaps they soothed her.

"Instead of taking from you, the Cauldron will give tonight." She speared two ruby barrettes on either side of my face to keep my hair back.

I frowned.

"When you become engaged, the Cauldron takes from you, wends your essence with all of the essences of Neverra to bond you, not only with your fiancé, but also with the marsh, the moss, the trees, the water, with all of Neverra's creatures." She dabbed glittery cream over my cheekbones, then lined my eyes with kohl, swiped mascara over my lashes, and applied a coat of see-through gloss to my lips. "On wedding nights, the Cauldron slides your essence back into your veins, as well as the essence of your husband, and that of Neverra. For months, you will be more powerful, stronger, healthier, more fertile, and more beautiful." She smiled, a small, gentle smile. "Although I'm not sure how you could be any more beautiful."

More powerful. Those were the only two words that stayed with me as she led me back into the bedroom and eased the gown over my head.

My nerves sizzled like high-voltage power lines, and spots of blackness flecked my vision. I blinked to dispel them.

Veroli laced the gossamer redness until it compressed my chest and hugged my waist so closely I had to gasp for breath. Air shot down my throat, burning as it snuck into my squashed lungs. I pulled the gloves on and then the slippers.

A knock rasped on the door, then a voice. "Mom, I'm here."

Dawson had arrived.

In spite of the gloves, my fingers felt cold and numb. All of me felt cold and numb. Veroli draped a cape made of white mink over my shoulders and hooked it around my neck with a diamond-encrusted brooch. She dipped all ten of her fingertips inside a pouch filled with gold powder, then positioned her fingers over my eyebrows and pressed gently.

I frowned.

"The mark of a bride," she explained.

As I turned to leave, I caught sight of my reflection in Ace's window. Even though my skin scintillated as wildly as the brooch nestled in the hollow of my collarbone, and my flame-colored dress blazed bright, my eyes were as dark and murky as Lake Michigan on a moonless night.

"I'll come pick you up after I drop Catori off," Dawson told his mother.

"Veroli—" My voice cracked, so I started again. "Veroli, don't come. Please."

She stared into my face a long moment without speaking. "And leave my children alone on the most important night of their life?"

I grabbed her hands. "Please. Stay up here."

"No." She squeezed my trembling fingers once, then let them go.

Let me go.

60

FIRST ENCOUNTER

*D*uring the entire ride down, Dawson's eyes needled me. As we flew lower, it was no longer only his eyes watching me. Thousands of sets gleamed in the night.

Votive candles lined the spirals of the *calimbors,* while currant-colored paper lanterns hovered and dipped over the crowd below.

Everyone in Neverra had come it seemed. Even though *caligosupra* stood on the misty ground, they didn't mix with the *caligosubi.* It was their clothes and jewels that set the castes apart. Where the courtiers had worn their usual multi-hued finery, the people living below the mist had traded their green uniforms for white tunics.

Again, I wondered if it was a tradition. But if it was, why weren't the *caligosupra* in white, too?

Concentrating on outfits made me momentarily forget the attention hobbling me. Unfortunately, the moment passed, and I was back to gnawing on the inside of my cheek.

Dawson's face uncrinkled once he landed on the floor of fog that blanketed the ground like fresh snow. Linus advanced toward the *runa* and extended his palm to help me out. Even though I didn't want to touch him, or the ground for that matter, I placed my hand atop his and descended as graciously as possible from the *runa.* Tendrils of mist wrapped around my ankles like dewy spider webs, snaking up the folds of my dress.

"You look dazzling, my dear," he said, as Dawson took flight again.

Don't come back, Dawson. Don't get your mother. Stay safe.

"Catori, child of ours," whispered a voice that sent a chill down my spine. As though the mist had risen, cold threads now enveloped my cheeks.

I blinked as I realized it wasn't the mist that had skated over my cheeks, but hands . . . fingers made of glimmering smoke. My heart pitched as I stared into a face that was more skull than face.

A wispy, dark skull.

I gulped.

Living over a cemetery had not prepared me for this.

61

THE NIGHT OF MIST

*T*he Unseelie slid its misty hand down my neck. Its insubstantial limb separated from its body, then reattached.

I clamped my fingers over Linus's hand, who chuckled from my death grip. "You're intimidating our bride, Rafi."

The Unseelie—Rafi—turned his—or was it a her?—head toward Linus and scowled. For a skull made of smoke, it possessed an extensive palette of expressions.

"Shall we?" Linus asked me.

As though I had a choice in my destination.

As though I could say no.

As though I could go home instead.

He led me toward an arched trellis covered in thin green vines dripping with white blossoms. Candlelight flickered between the petals and leaves like shards of fallen stars. A single soprano voice as clear as the violet night trickled over the silent crowd—mesmerizing, hypnotic.

As the Unseelie's wispy arm wound and unwound around my gloved forearm, I tried not to flinch. My dust shifted, as wild and jumpy as I was. The ghost's empty black orbs turned toward the hunter tattoo wreathing my neck.

As my feet carried me nearer to the end of the floral tunnel, I inhaled the dark scent of twilight. A dais as translucent as an ice floe rose before me. It couldn't have been made of ice, or it would've melted from the heat of the faeries standing upon it.

Ace, Cruz, Lyoh, and Gregor were all there, waiting. All in black except for Gregor, who wore white.

Dusky shadows billowed in the space between their bodies. Not shadows. Unseelies. Many more wafted around the clear dais, limbs disconnecting and reconnecting as they craned their skulls to watch me walk past them and climb up the crystal steps.

There were so many of them that I wondered if any had left Neverra.

Cruz had said I wouldn't be alone, but I'd thought he'd meant he and Ace would be there. Had he meant the Unseelies would add their numbers to our modest ranks?

Had they stayed to help us, or had the pages of Ley's book not let them pass through the portals?

Once I reached Cruz's side, Linus released my hand and went to stand next to his grim-faced *wariff*. As though sensing my arrival, the Cauldron appeared.

Cruz dipped his face toward mine. Slowly, he kissed my cheek. As he kissed the other, his breath carried quiet words into my ears. "Our allies wear white."

I blinked at him as he pulled away and faced the Cauldron. The aria that had accompanied my walk came to an end, and in the silence that settled over the land, my deep heartbeats rivaled the sound of the bubbling Cauldron.

"Neverrians!" Linus's voice boomed through the still air like a canon.

I jumped, and my pulse scattered. Ace's palm glowed. Through my red glove, the top of my hand lit up too. A low hiss rose from the Unseelies closest to us.

The king lifted a gold goblet from a white marble platter. In time with him, the crowd below lifted gleaming goblets that twinkled in the obscurity like lighter flames during concerts. Soon Lyoh, Gregor, and Ace also clutched goblets, but didn't raise theirs.

Cruz and I weren't offered drinks. The Unseelies held no drinks, either. The strange fabric of their bodies probably didn't allow them to hold on to anything, much less ingest anything.

"Tonight, a period of great peace is upon us!" Linus announced.

"Tonight, our essences will join in the Cauldron of Life and forever bind us—Seelie and Unseelie—as one people.

"In the history of our world, never has there been such a momentous union, but let us hope it will be the first of countless others. Too many wars have torn us apart, and although a mist fashioned by our common enemies still separates us, tonight we set aside our differences. We push away the mist and stand united to welcome these two brave souls into our hearths and hearts."

The Cauldron's glow cast ripples of blue light over Linus's satisfied face. He raised his goblet higher as he turned his attention to Cruz and me.

"Cruz, Catori, we thank you for your tremendous courage and sacrifice. May the skies bless you. May the skies bless all of our Neverrian souls."

He drank his sweet wine in long, wet gulps.

In waves, everyone drank. Everyone but Ace and Gregor. They pretended to, but their Adam's apples stayed still.

Over the lip of his goblet, Gregor's eyes flashed to mine, but flashed away almost as rapidly.

Had he worn white by mistake, or was the man who'd tortured me truly an ally?

I swept my gaze over the crowd.

So many wore white.

I swallowed the emotion ratcheting up my throat and gazed back at the faeries standing beside me, found Lyoh studying me, cup clutched in front of her chin. She raised it to her mouth, but didn't tip it back. As though she suspected the drink was laced with some drug, she brought it back down and curled her lips into a knowing smile.

Keeping my face blank, I lowered my gaze to the Cauldron. Metal clanked against stone as goblets were collected and disposed of. Another stretch of silence filled the darkness.

"May the joining ceremony begin!" Linus's voice was fringed with delight and something else . . . something hot and slick that lacquered his wandering irises.

Energy crackled from the crowd below. Like smoke, it rose in wispy, pheromone-heavy puffs.

"Catori." Cruz nodded to the Cauldron.

I concentrated on him again, on the sharp slant of his eyebrows.

I unglued my arm from my side and began reaching into the sputtering pit, when he said, "Your glove."

I jerked my hand back, and white noise rushed between my ears. Pulling in a quivering breath, I rolled off my glove and let it drop.

"Both," he instructed.

I cocked my head to the side and searched his face, wondering why he wanted me to reveal my tattered arm. Slowly, I removed the second glove, exposing my pockmarked skin. Lyoh's eyes traced each one of my cuts as though trying to make sense of them, as though combing for a pattern. When her lids lifted a fraction of an inch higher, my nerves rattled as brashly as maladjusted piano keys.

I swung my gaze back to Cruz, searched his face again. Again I found nothing.

He wasn't paying attention to his mother. His sole focus was Ace, who stood across the Cauldron from us.

Was it my imagination, or had Ace moved closer to it?

"Are you ready?" Cruz's quiet voice lashed my eardrums.

No.

I was not ready.

62

BECOMING ONE

*A*s I plunged my hand into the Cauldron, the world turned hazy, faces blurred, flowers dissolved, lights grayed, sounds faded. It was as though the mist had risen and cloaked every living thing.

The gluey tangle of essences wrapped around my fingers like wet hair. It slithered and slinked and snarled, irrevocably anchoring my fingers inside.

Another hand sank into the hissing pit, its fingers twining around mine. The contact was so intimate I jerked my head up, and my gaze collided with Ace's.

Had he—

Was it—

I swung my gaze toward Cruz, whose eyesight had sharpened to a point, a spikey point directed at the hand ensconcing mine. Unsure if this was planned, I tried to yank my fingers out, but the Cauldron didn't let go. Fear that it would kill us sliced through me like a warm knife.

Something brushed the top of my knuckles. It took me a second to realize it was Ace's thumb. How could he move if I couldn't? Was it because it wasn't supposed to be his hand inside the Cauldron?

What would it do to him?

To Cruz?

To Angelina?

Would the Cauldron reject our hands or would it plait our essences together?

My blood sloshed through my veins like an engorged stream. And my heart . . . my poor, poor heart clattered like the hooves of a thousand wild horses.

"What have you done, my boy?" Linus roared.

He walked tipsily, tripping over Gregor's foot. The *wariff* caught the king's arm and steadied him. Linus tugged on Ace's black tunic sleeve, grabbed his arm and pulled hard. Either my ground scales had syphoned off his strength, or the Cauldron had moored his son's hand, but Linus was incapable of tearing it out.

A powerful murmur rumbled around us. Lyoh barked at her son in Faeli, then turned to Gregor and screeched at him. He tipped his head toward the sky and let out a strange whistling sound that summoned a cloud of glowing *lucionaga*.

The vaporous bodies of the Unseelies levitated and eddied like a swarm of angered wasps around Gregor's sentries. The momentum of the churning bodies kicked up my long hair and sent it flying around my face, strafing my eyesight.

The Cauldron flashed, and its green magic coiled around my wrists and forearms, slid beneath the fur cape, spread into my shoulder blades, and dripped down my spine. My muscles thrummed as they contracted, absorbing the magic they were being fed, and my bones hardened, as though they were being cast from steel instead of collagen.

When the magic reached my heart, even though chaos reigned around me, I stared deep into Ace's eyes, and it felt like I was wading on the calmest of oceans, the gentlest of seas. His lips tipped into a quiet, conspiratorial smile, a smile that told me he wasn't in pain, that he knew what he was doing.

As swiftly as the magic infused my body, it receded. Its glittery threads peeled off my skin, flowed back through the grid of my veins, and plunged into the faerie vessel. Unlike the last time, my skin didn't prickle. It thrummed, sang, quivered with residual magic.

The Cauldron puffed a contented sigh, then vanished into oblivion.

For several seconds, I watched the empty space, not daring to breathe, not daring to move.

It hadn't killed us.

I lowered my gaze to my hand, still linked with Ace's.

Instinct, or perhaps desire, made me move toward him. Arms banded around both his shoulders, dragged him back, ripped his fingers from mine.

Fear snapped around my belly like a snare. "NO!" Cruz would know what to do. Cruz had a plan.

I sought him out, but he was neither beside me, nor in the dense mesh of bodies below the dais. "Cruz!"

I spun, squinted, yelled. Ace was still struggling against the *lucionaga*, growling as they tightened their hold on his writhing form.

A murky skull hit my face, breathing words that smelled like cold smoke into my ear. "They've arrived."

I jerked backward and would've fallen into the chaos below, were it not for Gregor's hand. He heaved me back up and steadied me.

"Wh-Who arrived?" I stuttered.

The skull turned toward Gregor before realigning with its ethereal body and soaring away.

The king's elbow knocked into me as he stumbled off the dais. Two *lucionaga* dove for him, but white-robed men caught him, tossed ropes around his neck.

Unseelies and *lucionaga* flew overhead, spinning like a children's top, like an iridescent tornado.

"Cruz!" I yelled.

Pushing hair off my face, I scanned the crowd for the red-robed boy I'd been supposed to marry, but found only the one I had married. Ace's eyes were turned upward, toward the enormous black creature soaring toward us, a golden cage rocking in its elongated fangs.

Terror gripped my spine and twisted it . . . twisted it.

Why was the *draca* bringing a *cupola*?

For whom was she bringing it?

Her large leathery wings beat the panic-filled air, displacing Unseelie bodies. The mass of spectators began scattering, legs pumping. Some took flight but face-planted before they could get enough air between their feet and the marsh.

Had my scales done that?

I bit the inside of my mouth and tasted blood. Gregor was still holding me. I ripped my arm from his clutches and ran at Ace and the guards.

"Stay back, Cat," Ace hissed.

"No." My voice cracked. What the hell was happening? Where was Cruz?

Still clutching Ace, Silas and the other guard soared up toward the cage. "Cruz!" I yelled again, and suddenly he was there. In front of me. I waited for his orders.

His lips parted, but his command wasn't for me. "Lock Ace in the *cupola*. Teach the prince he cannot take what is mine."

63

ARROWS AND DUST

a scream reverberated inside my ears.

My scream.

I spun toward Cruz. "You . . . you . . . I trusted *you!*" There was a throbbing at the base of my skull that made the world narrow to a single point.

Cruz was that single point.

I threw myself on him, but he whooshed off the dais. My slippered feet slid and my body went airborne. I squeezed my eyes shut as I went down.

Arms caught me. A bearded man I didn't know. He wore white.

I was supposed to trust people in white, but that advice had come from a man who'd deceived me.

"I got you, princess," the man said.

I clawed his hands off of me, crawled away from him as best I could in my impractical gown, my nails clawing at the soggy earth.

A tortured howl pierced the night, echoing over the screams and grunts of the belligerent crowd. I flung my head up and found Ace kneeling in the cage, gripping his head. The cage hovered on its own now. The *draca* was gone.

The white-robed man crouched next to me and tried to help me up, or maybe he was trying to keep me down. I jerked up to my feet and cowered away, holding my hands out in front of me. "DON'T TOUCH

ME!" Blue sparks flickered underneath my skin. I ripped my hands down and a scrap of mist broke from the dense quilt.

The man eyed the missing section, then his lips moved, but I couldn't hear what he was saying over the dizzying pounding at my temples.

"Ace! Help Ace!" I shouted at the man.

Ace screamed again.

The man's mouth opened and moved. I shook my head. "I can't hear you!" I couldn't hear anything over Ace's keening pain. "Help him." My voice broke. "Help *him*."

The man tried to approach me, but I stepped back, bumping into a hard form. I spun, and my eyes went wide as they climbed the length of the body, taking in the hard angles of the man's face, the silky black hair, the whorls of ink on the bare, muscled forearms, the deep-set dark eyes.

I knew this man.

His picture was in Ley's book.

It was Gwenelda's mate.

Kajika's brother.

Menawa.

He ducked and spun as a *lucionaga* dove for him, and then a rope of iron chain curled out of his hands like a lasso and wrapped around the faerie guard. The sentinel screeched as he thudded against the earth.

Menawa dug an arrow out of his pack, nicked his skin, then held it over the screaming sentry's chest. "Where is the *draca*?" His voice . . . his voice sent shivers skating over my skin. It was so much like Kajika's, as rumbling and rough as the deepest of grottos.

If the guard gave him an answer, I didn't hear it, because a shrill cry struck my eardrums. And then a body slammed into mine. Angelina's. Her face was pale, her eyes wild and slick, her hair a tangle of vines and bruised petals, her rounded belly smeared with ochre mud. She screamed, and it raised the small hairs on the nape of my neck.

Shadows moved around us. Unseelies. "Give her to us, Catori," they whispered.

"No," Angelina cried, clinging to my battered arm so hard that blood trickled out of my cuts and stained her fingers like cherry juice.

"Let us take her," the Unseelie breathed into my ear.

Angelina was my enemy.

I should give her to them.

But . . . but I couldn't.

"She's harmless," I rasped. "Break the *cupola*. Free Ace!"

The vaporous bodies swirled once around us before sliding upward toward the cage. What could they do without solid fingers, though?

The bearded man was before me again. "Princess . . ."

"Take her to safety."

The man's eyes slid to Angelina, and his forehead creased.

"Please," I begged.

Angelina was squeezing my arm so hard. "No. Don't let him take me. He'll kill me. Catiri, please. Don't leave me."

Her pupils ate up her irises.

"He won't hurt you."

She shook with terror.

"He won't," I promised, even though it was an empty promise. I could only hope he didn't harm her.

I pared her clinging fingers off my arm. Her fingers were wet with my blood. I almost told her she held the greatest weapon, but I didn't. I may have been gracious, but I would most definitely not offer her a weapon with which to hurt people.

With which to kill them.

I pushed her into the man's arms, and although she screeched, he picked her up and ran through the thrashing crowd.

Ace. I needed to get to Ace.

I looked for the *cupola*.

It had drifted toward the palace, a great distance from where I stood. I started running, but my speed was hampered by my mud-soaked fur cape. Without stopping, I scrabbled to unhook it, tugging on the diamond brooch.

Stuck.

Gritting my teeth, I yanked, and this time, the metal pin sprang open, and the burdensome fur tumbled off my shoulders.

To my left, Dawson was herding bloodied, muddied, white-robed *calidum* into his *runa*. One was cradling her forearm. Where her hand should've been was only torn flesh and dripping blood. Bile rose in my throat at the sight of her missing hand. A growl ripped through the darkness, and then a courtier in a navy tunic was upon them, a golden orb clutched between his palms, lighting up his wild expression.

A chill seeped down my spine. When the man dragged his arm back, I screeched Dawson's name. He swiveled his head toward me just as an arrow slid into the courtier's chest.

The man gasped, and his ball of dust disintegrated. He tried to grab the arrow, but his hands paled and grayed, burst into a thousand flecks like the rest of him. Only his tunic remained. It drooped emptily onto the carpet of mist.

Across the murky field stood a young girl with a bow. Her dark eyes flashed to mine, and then, in one swift motion, she grabbed another arrow from her quiver, twirled, nocked it, and let it fly. A *lucionaga* plummeted from the sky.

The sky.

Ace . . .

My pulse ratcheted as I searched the darkness for the cage.

Please, let him be alive.

I located the gilt monstrosity over the floating palace garden.

Ace was kneeling inside, face pressed against the bars, looking straight at me. Could he see me or was his mind showing him something else . . . something terrifying?

I pumped my legs. The ground suctioned off my shoes, then sucked at my feet, but adrenaline and months of training compensated for the pull. I blurred past scuffling faeries, past crouched forms, jumped over fallen bodies.

I lunged through the pink arch, then latched onto the roots of a mallow tree, and biting back the pain radiating in the bone of my bleeding arm, I swung from a root to a vine to a root again until I managed to reach the spongy edge of the garden.

Digging my fingers into the earth, abdominals on fire, molars jammed tight, I clawed my way up, then threw my leg over and rolled. My maimed arm screamed in pain and my raging lungs burned, but I scrambled to my feet and sprinted over rock and moss and vapor, nicking the soles of my feet.

"Ace!"

He looked down. And then his bone-white face turned a shade paler. "Cat!"

He was conscious.

As though his mind grasped what I was about to do, his hands shot through the bars of the cage.

The cage coasted away from the garden.

Focusing on his extended hands, I leaped off the edge.

If I missed, if I fell, my body would shatter against the mist-soaked marsh below.

I caught the bottom rung of the *cupola*, which seesawed from my weight.

Ace's body banged against the bars of his prison. He blinked.

My clammy fingers skidded over the metal. "Ace!"

The cage tipped again, and one of my hands slid off. The fingers of my good arm remained curled around the metal bars. Cringing, I clenched them tighter as the cage ascended into the sky.

I wouldn't survive the fall.

The cage shook, and my fingers almost slid off.

But they didn't.

They didn't.

Ace curled his fingers around my hand. "Cat, watch out!"

A *lucionaga* was hurtling straight for me, hands stretched in front of him, ribbons of dust dancing over his palms.

I thought about my own dust, and lifted my palm to my neck, but I didn't have time to extricate it before he tossed his at me.

I squeezed my eyes, plugged my nose, and squashed my lips, praying he'd miss, praying a hunter would shoot him before he could fly into me. But that didn't happen.

The guard hit me, hard, and the blow tore my fingers out from Ace's.

"NO!" Ace's roar accompanied my fall, his petrified blue eyes my beacon in the darkest of nights.

I flailed as I fell away from the man I loved.

64

RAGE

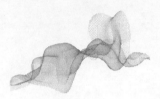

I hadn't been able to save Ace.

I hadn't been able to save anyone.

I hadn't been able to save myself.

If only fire burned inside my veins.

If only . . .

In midair, I stopped falling.

A glittery navy cloud had caught me, cushioned me, and now carried me delicately back down to the foggy ground.

Spectral voices murmured my name, murmured words that didn't sound like any I knew.

Unseelie bodies had knit together, had crafted substance where there was none.

They rested me gently onto the marsh floor, then rose and formed a wall around me to fend off more attacks.

None came.

I pressed my weight onto my forearms, then, teeth grinding, I lurched onto to my hands and knees. My red gown spilled around me like fresh blood. Legs trembling, I bit down on my lip as I pushed myself onto my feet.

Feet that were so cold and numb, they barely kept me upright.

I felt broken.

Devastated.

A howling wail surged from the cage.

I lifted my gaze. Found Ace's starlit face pressed against the golden bars, lips hitched, teeth bared.

Anger swelled behind my breastbone. My blood roiled, my hands itched, and my fingers glowed with blue light. Magic rushed through me like a cresting wave, pounded into my skin, and then . . .

And then it finally broke loose.

Like an earthquake, the ground around me shook. The mist rippled away, carrying off the bodies of unsuspecting faeries.

Another wave cracked out of me like a whip.

The ground shook harder as I pulled the mist from under the stone palace like magicians wrenched tablecloths from underneath laden tables.

The stone arch creaked as it tipped, buckled, and burst into a thousand brilliant pink shards around me.

I sped away as a column ripped from the massive white stone facade and punched the ground I'd been standing on. Moss peeled off the collapsing turrets, then pummeled the scattering crowd with clumps of tawny-green sludge. The rose quartz orbs that crowned the palace rocketed toward the crowd like cannon balls.

The garden held, but the windows sparkled like sequins as they cracked and sprayed the land. The colossal golden doors ripped from their thick hinges and banged onto the wreckage like leaden butterfly wings.

Another surge of magic, and the mist scurried farther.

Away from the ruined castle.

Away from the fringe of giant *calimbors*.

Away from the field of tinkling *adamans*.

I dragged air into my burning lungs and sent my magic hurtling out of me again.

My body formed ferocious waves of magic that splashed against my bones and escaped through the barrier of my luminescent skin.

Relentlessly, they struck the isle. If only one of those waves could carry me skyward, if only one of them could fracture Ace's cage, but my magic wasn't made for the skies.

It was made for the ground and the water and the cloying, shifting mist.

65

QUIESCENCE

*W*hen the waves of my anger ebbed, a terrible silence draped over the land.

Over the people who sat huddled in clumps over the debris of my marriage.

Some brave souls moved around, lifting the fallen, feeling for pulses on the bodies that hadn't disintegrated into smoke.

Metal chains clanked. A shadowy group of men and women not dressed in Neverrian fashion looked my way.

I met Gwenelda's familiar stare, and although she'd never been my favorite person, I had the urge to run to her and throw myself into her arms.

I didn't.

I was too spent, too shell-shocked to move.

Next to Gwen stood her tall, broad-bodied mate, whose path I'd crossed on the battlefield. He nodded to me, then went back to coiling a length of iron chain.

I looked for Kajika, but he wasn't among them. I scanned the cleared land for his tall frame but found only faeries hobbling or hovering. Some wore torn gowns, others wore soiled white tunics. The chill of the chaos I'd unleashed deepened inside my bones, numbed my core, and froze my beating heart.

Tears pooled behind my gummy lids. I wiped them away as I

searched the night for the golden cage. It sat on the ground, door swung open. I searched for a body but found none.

Had he—

Had his fire—

The gut-wrenching thought cleaved a hole so large in my chest, my heart threatened to lurch out and crumble onto the sodden ground like the grand, spoiled palace.

"Cat." A voice brushed my bare shoulder, sliding against the shell of my ear.

Holding my breath, I spun, and when I stopped, my head was still spinning.

Before me, against the violet sky frosted with stars, stood the man I'd fought so hard to save.

I ran my hands over his jaw, his eyes, his hair, his neck, to make sure he was real.

Really standing in front of me.

Not an illusion cast by my desperate mind to ease the chasm of pain blooming within me.

Ace grabbed the sides of my face, a smile curving his beautiful mouth. A mouth that could still pull in lungfuls of air, that could still create words, that could still show feelings. "You did it."

Did it? A harsh breath snuck through my teeth. I let my hands tumble away from his face. "How did you . . . how did you get out?"

"The door wasn't locked. My imprisonment, it wasn't real."

Tears flowed down my cheeks, streamed around his pulsing fingers, and steamed between his face and mine. "But Cruz locked you—" My voice broke. "He locked you in the . . ." I couldn't get myself to pronounce the word.

"It wasn't real," he repeated.

I blinked. Just blinked.

"We needed to get you angry."

My brow crumpled, and I stepped back, breaking his hold on my face.

He approached me, and began raising his hands, but I slapped both away, and then I slapped him.

The smack echoed in the abysmal night.

"Do you know . . ." My chest constricted with violent breaths. "What it did to me . . . to see you . . . in there?"

"I'm sorry, Cat. I'm so sorry."

A sob broke from my mouth as I sank to my knees and pressed my hands against my face. Emotions tumbled through me like dirty laundry. I was humiliated. Angry. Terrorized. Pained.

Cold mud slopped against my bare forearms when Ace dropped to his knees and wrenched my hands off my face. "Shh . . ."

I wanted to hit him again, but he held my wrists back, his grip gentle yet unyielding.

"I was so . . . so scared," I cried.

"I'm sorry, sweetheart. So fucking sorry." He gathered me in his arms and dragged me against his chest. His tattered nerves thudded against my ear in the form of a raging pulse, a mirror of my own heartbeat.

He scrubbed his broad palm against my back until my sobs slowed and subsided, until I could almost catch my breath again. Then his fingers thumbed the slope of my neck and tangled in my windblown, mud-clumped hair, pulling it away from my face.

"*Massin*," someone called to him. "You are needed for—"

"Not now." Ace's gaze didn't leave my face as he answered.

"*Massin?* You are— Your father is . . .?"

He nodded, not even a hint of sadness slickening his eyes. "You were incredible tonight. Fierce. Strong. Magnificent."

I felt his declaration in my stomach, under my ribs.

"My extraordinary wife."

Wife.

I was Ace's wife.

I craned my neck, lifted my heavy eyelashes, and hunted his face with my swollen eyes.

He cupped my jaw. Gazed down at me adoringly. My blood felt laced with mallow. His features swirled and blurred. He kissed my salted lips, but then I pressed him away.

"Where is Cruz?"

My answer came in the form of a feral roar.

I whipped around. Cruz was crouched over the fallen *draca*, his back to me. For a moment, I didn't move. And then my feet were covering ground almost as fast as they'd sprinted to get to Ace's cage. As though he sensed me approach, he turned.

I punched him in the chest, right at the spot where his heart beat.

Where it was supposed to beat if he had one.

Instead of a scowl, amusement flickered over his features.

"You asshole!"

That got people talking. Three different languages buzzed and tangled around me. Cruz's gaze moved to someone behind me. I knew it was Ace without having to turn around. His scent was imprinted in me.

Ace let out a low chuckle. "Only fair you get a beating too."

"Yes, but I'm sure you got a kiss to make it all better."

How could they joke about this?

Someone called out my name. *Gwenelda.* Her hair hung in a thick braid against her shoulder, speared through with yellow feathers—Mom's favorite color. Gwen smiled. And it was arresting, because I was almost certain it was the first time I'd ever seen her smile.

The man who resembled Kajika towered over her. Her mate.

He dipped his head. "Catori. It is an honor to meet you."

I recoiled from the word *honor*. And then I wondered if perhaps he'd absorbed a human with a strange way of speaking. But that made me wince, so I banished the thought.

Someone pushed past him, a slender girl with cheekbones as high as mine, hair as black as mine but cut just below her ears, and skin as sun-kissed as my own. "I am Magena."

The huntress I'd dreamed about.

The one who'd chased after a bluebird.

Ishtu's oldest sister.

Had she communicated with me from her coffin, or had the vision of her come from the Unseelie locked in Negongwa's body?

Her eyes were shiny, but crinkled with a smile. Blake used to say I had feline eyes because they tipped up on the side. Magena had the same eyes.

"It is true. Your resemblance to Ishtu"—she fingered the wide suede strap holding her quiver—"is astonishing."

Someone squeezed my hand. Ace. He knew how much it bothered me to be compared to the huntress Lyoh Vega had ruthlessly killed. I closed my fingers around his, then sought out the heinous murderer's gaze. Found her elongated green pupils on me. Thin plumes of smoke wafted from her nostrils.

"Why is she still alive?"

"Because I'm trying to decide how to kill her," Cruz said.

66

THE FACEOFF

*G*regor and Silas and a handful of *lucionaga* in human form stood around the fallen dragon. Their expressions were guarded, wary, as they took in Cruz's cool, calculating gaze.

Around me, Ace and Cruz formed two solid walls.

"Ace," Cruz said.

I swung my head between the two. Was Cruz asking Ace to kill the *draca*?

Ace crouched and pressed his hand against the *draca*'s chest. Magic quivered around his fingers and made his hand spark a striking white. And then bones cracked, animal hide turned into skin, fangs shrank, and claws receded.

Hand still aglow, he rose and turned toward the *lucionaga* with the ponytail—Silas—and placed his hand on the man's chest, right over his heart. Threads of light frolicked around his fingers and penetrated through the black cloth, into the muscled chest.

Silas threw his head back, closed his eyes, and gritted his teeth. When Ace removed his hand, Silas dropped to one knee and bowed deeply. Spoke words in Faeli. Probably a pledge of loyalty to the new sovereign. And then he turned toward Gregor and repeated similar words.

When Ace rose again, I whispered, "You made Silas *draca*?"

"Remember how I told you I had two friends in Neverra?" His voice was so low, it was barely audible. "The first was Pietro. The second is Silas."

"What about . . . what about Cruz?"

"Cruz is more than a friend. He's my brother, Cat."

"That's not what I meant. Why didn't you make him *draca*?"

"Because I have no such ambition," Cruz responded.

The scent of charred flesh wafted sickeningly in the air. Although Lyoh gritted her human teeth, she bore the pain of the iron chains in silence.

Ace tipped his face toward a small man framed by two Unseelies. "Negongwa's back, Cruz."

Negongwa.

The father of hunters.

I took in the brown, crosshatched face and the salt-and-pepper-colored hair held back in a queue. My oldest living ancestor. The man who'd been made, who'd then made a tribe of powerful beings.

"Catori . . . extraordinary Catori. *Nilwa nockwad*. Defeater of the mist." His voice, his words gave me shivers. He raised both his palms, then lowered them slowly. "Blessed child of mine."

Goosebumps scampered over my arms, over my chest, *inside* my chest.

Along with the Unseelies whose skulls tipped low, Negongwa dipped his head in a bow. Why were they bowing to me? It felt wrong. I didn't deserve to be bowed to.

"Please . . ." I started, but stopped. Would asking them not to bow embarrass them? "I never thought we'd have the pleasure to meet, Negongwa."

He smiled, and it crinkled every swatch of leathery skin. "Never underestimate the resilience of a Gottwa mixed with an Unseelie."

"Excuse my candor. I am still learning."

"And so you shall never stop. Wisdom is acquired until the day one passes into the next realm."

I bit my lip, then released it. I really didn't feel like dwelling on death, so I asked, "Where's Kajika?"

"He stayed in Rowan," Gwen answered, her eyes flashing to Ace's. "To ensure Lily Wood's safety."

"Lily couldn't— The book didn't get her through?"

Thick shadows obliterated all the light from Cruz's face. I knew, without him having to speak, that it hadn't worked. Still he confirmed it in a quiet voice. "It did not let her pass."

A deep tremble seized my bones.

"Hey . . . it's going to be all right." He touched my arm.

All right? Lily was stuck outside Neverra. How was that *all right?* The only way to get her back in would be for him to die. How was *that* all right?

I felt anger simmer beneath my skin. Blue sparks crackled in my fingers. Two *lucionaga* stepped back.

Scared.

They were scared of *me.* I would've laughed had I not been so anguished about Lily's situation.

"Breathe," Ace said.

And so I did. And the magic receded. "Will you return to Rowan now?" I asked Gwenelda.

Paper rustled between Negongwa's knobby fingers—pages from Ley's book. "We cannot."

"The pages do not unlock the Neverrian portals, Father?" Gwen asked.

He shook his weathered face.

I blanched.

Negongwa rested a papery hand on my forearm. "But we knew it was a possibility, Catori."

"What about a portal stamp?" I suggested.

"They don't take on hunter skin." Ace's mouth was set in a grim line. "Gregor tried."

I thought about Kajika then. He'd just gotten his family back and now they'd left him again. I needed to return to Rowan fast, so I could take his place at Lily's side, so he could be free to join his tribe.

"The bluffs over the *Hareni* are yours until we find the lock," Ace said.

"Thank you, *Massin,*" Negongwa inclined his head. "You are most generous."

I craned my neck to take in the rocky blue cliffs surrounded by water, under which had sprawled the *Hareni.* Was it still there, under the liquefied mist?

"And they shall stay yours even after the lock is unearthed," Ace said slowly. "Neverra belongs to faeries, *all* faeries. Seelie, Unseelie, and Daneelie."

No one added the word *hunters* to the list, which meant they all knew what they were . . . which meant Kajika knew. I wondered how he'd reacted to that.

"Will the portal stamp take to my skin?" I asked.

"You are Daneelie," Ace said, "so it should."

"*Mishipeshu.*" Gwen smiled as she shook her head. "Incredible. Simply incredible."

Metal clanged as Lyoh managed to toss one of the chains off her body. Before I could blink, Menawa was crouched and tethering the other restraints, even though too much iron crisscrossed her limbs for her to escape.

"Menawa, remove the chains," Cruz said.

I hiked an eyebrow. "I thought you were going to kill her."

"What honor would there be in killing a person who is already down?" Cruz's head was bent toward his mother's prostrate form. "I will give you a ten-second head start."

My heart thudded. He was going to fight her. What if he missed? What if Lyoh—

"Silas, shift," Ace ordered.

The large man growled as black smoke cloaked his human form, as his web of bones reassembled, as his muscles swelled, as his skin blackened. Hunters, Unseelies, and *lucionaga* moved out of his way. He roared and stretched out his fibrous wings. They were broader than Lyoh's had been. All of him was larger than she'd been.

"You have five minutes, Cruz," Ace said. "And if you haven't finished her off by then, Silas will fly."

Cruz nodded just as the hunters lifted all the chains at once. Lyoh scrambled backward, mud squishing beneath her lacerated body, head swinging left and right.

"Ten . . . nine . . ." Cruz started counting.

"You think you've made the world better, don't you?" she snarled at us. "I welcome death, for I have no desire to live in a world where order and laws have been banished. Your system will fail."

" . . . eight . . . seven . . ." Cruz continued.

"You say you want to rule differently, Ace, but if you make a show of my death, how does that set you apart from your father?"

"I would take to the sky, Lyoh." Ace's voice was pleasant, but sharp, like spikes covered in silk. "Unless you'd rather die in a *cupola*. That could also be arranged."

I cringed at the word.

" . . . six . . . five . . ."

"You soil the Wood name."

"Do I?" Ace grinned. "Yet I am the last male carrying the name not mixed into the soil."

" . . . four . . . three . . ."

Even though she was no longer a dragon, she chuffed and pushed off the ground, rocketing toward the copse of *calimbors*.

" . . . two . . ." On *one*, Cruz was airborne.

My neck cracked as I followed his ascent.

Lyoh spun as her son approached. Waited. Dust glittered in her hands.

"You didn't confiscate her dust!" I yelled at Gregor.

He side-eyed Ace. "Cruz wanted a fair fight."

I turned my attention back to the two soaring faeries.

A body swung from Lyoh's hands. The head bent at a terrible angle. A scream rose out of me as I scanned the crowd.

Who'd she taken?

Who'd she killed?

Ace brushed a hand over my cold cheek. "It's an illusion, Cat."

Cruz froze in midair as he faced the swinging body. Even though they were high up, I swore I could detect a smile curling over Lyoh's lips.

Whose body had she fashioned with her dust?

The answer came to me as violently as the current that had traversed Cruz's body in the glades. *Jacobiah*. It had to be Cruz's father. The body crumbled, and her dust changed form. It became a sword. She flew toward her still stunned son. I felt Ace stand taller next to me, felt his spine straighten, felt a jolt go through his bones.

"Move," I whispered underneath my breath. *Move.*

Cruz wasn't moving.

Why wasn't he moving?

"Cruz!" I yelled.

My scream must've awakened him from his stupor, because he flung his body sideways and dropped several feet just as Lyoh's blade pierced the piece of air in which he'd been hovering. I watched his hands, waiting for him to gather his dust.

"Why isn't he shaping a weapon?" My voice was blistered with worry.

"I don't know." Ace's gaze clung to his friend's bobbing figure.

What was he doing up there? Talking?

Fuck their five-minute rule. If Cruz didn't fight, he wouldn't last a human minute up there.

A chill went through me.

Was that his plan? To sacrifice himself to get Lily back inside? He knew Ace or Silas would finish off Lyoh, whatever happened to him.

The second the theory hit my mind, it took unshakable roots.

I whipped my face around the crowd. I needed a weapon. Or could I send my dust that high up? I didn't have the luxury of time to experiment. The quiver strapped to Magena's back held a bow and arrows. I lurched toward the huntress and filched her bow and a single arrow.

She let out a little gasp that broke people from the spell of the terrible show overhead. I raced toward the nearest *calimbor* and raced up the spirals. I climbed so fast, the stairs blurred underneath my feet. Splinters pierced my bare soles. Instead of slowing me, the pain propelled me forward.

Mother and son moved, dipped, twirled, rose higher. When their voices became clear, I stopped, positioned the bow, and nocked the arrow.

Maybe I should've taken more than one, but I doubted I'd get more than one shot.

Lyoh and Cruz hadn't noticed me in their faceoff. His hands were still bare of dust, while hers gripped her gleaming sword that seemed to have grown longer, sharper.

I closed one eye, pulled my arm back.

My muscles sang as the string strained.

I shut out the world.

Inhaled a breath.

And then I waited.

My shaking fingers stilled.

My eyesight narrowed to a single point.

I should've taken Lily up on her idea of training on moving targets. It would've come in handy.

A dark smile curved my lips as I raised the bow a fraction of an inch higher.

I let the arrow fly.

67

THE LAST BARGAIN

*M*y arrow soared through the silent, violet air, its tip gleaming in the starlight.

Cruz blinked at it. Then at me.

Sensing her son's faltering attention, Lyoh shoved her sword toward his chest.

Before it could breach Cruz's skin, my arrow met its mark.

The sword melted into shimmery ribbons as the iron arrow tip speared Lyoh's back, right between those sharp shoulder blades that had once transformed into monstrous wings.

She fell.

Fell.

Fell.

And then she hit solid ground so hard that a body made of anything but fire would've shattered.

"I'm not letting you die. Not today. Not tomorrow," I yelled at Cruz.

He didn't answer, but he understood.

"I didn't dip the arrow in my blood. But help me God, skies, and Great Spirits, if you don't finish her off right now, *I* will."

"You still owe me a *gajoï.*"

"I'm not letting her live."

"That's not what I was going to claim . . ."

I sucked in a breath. "Don't you dare. Don't you fucking dare ask me to kill you *or* to stand by you while you take your own life."

He was now so close I could see his pupils throb. "Lily won't be able to come back if—"

I took a step back from the wooden handrail. "She still has three months. We'll find a way."

Cruz pinned a silent, sullen gaze on me.

Below us, the crowd had shifted and were circling Lyoh's prostrate body. Ace's face was turned upward. He didn't take to the skies, but I felt him ready to spring.

"Fine." Cruz's word had me lifting my head back up. "But if you don't find a solution, know that I *will* end my life. With or without your help."

CRUZ FLEW ME BACK DOWN.

Only then did I realize how high I'd climbed. How quickly I'd moved. Ley had once told me I would have to make a choice between my two natures on a Blue Moon, but she'd lied.

I needn't choose.

I was both.

I felt it in the marrow of my spine that I was as much Unseelie as I was Daneelie. I felt it like I now felt the blistering pain on the bottom of my feet. I didn't have to look down to know they were as bloodied as my arm.

Once we landed, Cruz walked toward his mother.

The rowan wood arrow had skewered her chest. Smoke whooshed from the wound.

I didn't move. Couldn't.

My feet. My poor feet.

"May the skies damn you, Catori Wood," she hissed.

Her curse startled me less than the name she'd given me: Catori Wood.

An arm wrapped around my waist. "Don't worry, our skies cannot hear her anymore." Ace kissed my temple.

"That's not—" I didn't finish my sentence.

As understanding dawned on him, his irises churned. He didn't say anything. Just studied my face. Studied what the name did to me.

When I winced, hurt thinned his lips.

"My feet," I whispered.

He crouched and made me show him my shredded soles. He shook his head, then scooped me into his arms.

"Thank you." I leaned my cheek against his chest and sighed a thousand sighs rolled into one.

His arms tightened around me.

In silence, we all watched Cruz kneel next to his mother. "I will never forget you, mother. Never forget the way you tormented so many innocents. Never forget how you murdered my father. Never forget how you abandoned me with Borgo because I was too much of a hindrance. I will never forget how I tried so desperately to make you take notice of me, to make you proud. I am sorry that I was such a disappointment."

Lyoh's eyes were on the skies above and her lips immobile. If she was listening to her son, she didn't let it show. Maybe she was in too much pain to hear him.

"I don't know what happened to make you so cruel, but I hope that if there is an afterlife, you will get to start over and become a better person." Ribbons of dust danced over Cruz's palm. He shaped them into a long strip of silken fabric.

Her recessed eyes finally rolled up to her son's puckered brow, and my heartbeat slowed.

Would he have the courage to end her life?

Was it cruel to let him do it alone?

Cruz wadded the dust-made fabric into a ball, pried Lyoh's mouth open, and delicately stuffed it inside.

Her eyelashes fluttered higher, and then, slowly, they closed over the windows to her murky soul.

Silence enveloped the forest, buffeted the moss, the branches, the leaves.

It seemed like it took hours for her fire to burn out. Perhaps it only took minutes. Time was strange in Neverra.

A small rumble escaped Cruz when the breeze began combing away her grayed body, whisking her away, layer after layer. He unfurled his hunched body, and head lowered, he walked away, his dust reeling back into his closed fist.

I watched him recede across the dark land, torn between letting him grieve on his own and going to him.

But how could I go to him when I couldn't even walk?

Ace called Negongwa. The ancient hunter came to us.

Ace nodded to my arm. "My fire cannot heal her wounds. Maybe your blood will work?"

Negongwa smiled, then pulled an arrow from his quiver and sliced his palm with the iron tip. As he pressed his hand against my tattered soles, his creased face, Ace's solid arms, the forest of giant trees, the hushed conversations, my broken body . . . they all vanished into a soundless, lightless chasm.

68

THE IMPOSTOR

I came to as violently as a child ripped from her mother's womb, as brutally as a person awakening from a nightmare.

Had last night been a nightmare?

I crushed the bedsheets between my fingers as I lurched off the bed, stumbling on legs that felt as flimsy as a newborn foal's. Surprisingly, they carried me to the enormous curved pane of glass that leaked sunlight over Ace's apartment.

My feet didn't hurt. I lifted them and stared at the unblemished skin.

Had I imagined last night?

I pressed my palms to the window and gazed out over Neverra. The land looked different without the mist—greener, browner, bluer. I sought out the ruined palace, but found no trace of it. The faeries must've burned it away during the night. A large square moved.

The floating garden.

The desire to destroy it thumped against my breastbone, but I'd destroyed enough last night. "Why didn't you fall like the castle?" I whispered to it.

"Because its soil is made of ground *volitor* fronds," said a deep voice.

I spun.

Ace soared off the glass guardrail and sank through the air toward me. He was clean and golden and . . . happy. A smile glinted off his teeth, blinding like the sunlight now warming my back.

"Last night . . ." I licked my lips. "It was real?"

His smile grew, jeweled his eyes. "It was." He approached on noiseless footsteps, then slid a hand beneath my loose hair that felt smooth and clean, that smelled of musk and lavender. Someone had washed me. I lowered my gaze to my forearm, remembering the blood that had dripped from it.

My breath snagged, and I flung my gaze back up to Ace's, whose smile turned a little crooked, or maybe it was the world that was turning crooked, tipping like it had last night.

Ace rubbed the new whorls of ink decorating my forearm. The skin felt tender even though the little slices had been healed.

"How—"

"How did we patch you up, or how did you get the new tattoo?"

"Both."

He traced the shifting navy dust with the tip of his forefinger. "Negongwa spread his blood over your cuts. As to how you got the new tattoo . . ." He dragged in a heavy breath. "Remember when you were clinging to my cage?" His eyes darkened, shifting from aquamarine to cobalt. "A *lucionaga* attacked you with his dust, and you captured it."

The memory jolted through me like an electrical current.

"He's dead. Silas caught him after"—he swallowed hard—"after he knocked you off."

Ace was still tracing my new tattoo, and his gentle touch dotted my skin. I removed my arm from his reach and nursed it against me.

He cocked his head to the side, but didn't try to bridge the distance I'd put between our bodies.

"I'm still mad about the cage," I said.

"I know."

"Don't ever do that to me again. *Ever.* I have so many other sources of anger inside of me that making me fear for your life was cruel."

"Sweetheart. Please forgive me. Forgive me." He cupped my trembling jaw and fit his mouth to mine. Perhaps it was to ease the tremble, or perhaps it was to reassure me, or perhaps it was just to kiss me.

My heart and mind were a mess of emotions, but I kissed him back, my fingers crushing the fabric of his black tunic.

After a long moment, I pulled away, and we breathed each other's ragged breaths in silence.

Ace watched me like a hawk as Veroli returned with my jeans and a long-sleeved black top. She'd tried to make me wear a dress, but I refused the unsubstantial bands of fabric. I wanted something solid and simple.

A cloth for mourning. Not a cloth for rejoicing.

Besides, I was returning to Rowan today. I needed human clothes, not a fancy gown.

"I still don't see why you can't wear a dress. You are the—"

Ace's hard gaze stopped Veroli midsentence.

"What am I?"

Ace's jaw worked. Nerves ticked. Finally, he said, "The savior."

"People died because of me," I deadpanned. "I am a killer, but I am no savior."

Veroli gasped. But not Ace. His mouth stayed perfectly still. As still as his gaze.

After she'd tied my hair in a low ponytail and supplied me with my sneakers, she left to find Gregor.

"He wore white last night." It wasn't a question.

"He did."

"He was on our side?"

"He's the one who called all the *lucionaga* away from the portals right after the Cauldron bound us. That's how the hunters managed to get in."

"With the pages from the book?"

He nodded.

"We're really married?"

Another nod.

"And you're the king?"

He tipped his head in assent.

"What about your mother?"

"She's alive but she abdicated. Left us in charge."

I lowered my gaze to the rippling expanse beyond the window. *Us .. .* "I can't be queen."

"Why not?"

"Because I'm . . . I'm . . ."

"You're what?"

I whipped my gaze toward him. "Because I'm human."

The corners of his stiff lips finally budged. "And here I thought I'd married a girl who was half Daneelie and half Unseelie."

"And half human."

"I'm no math whiz, but I do believe that's one too many halves." His smile had broadened.

I tossed my hands in the air. "Oh. You know what I mean."

"No." He grew serious. "I don't think I do know what you mean."

"Ace, look at me. I'm not queen material."

"I'm looking at you, like I looked at you last night, like I plan on looking at you for the rest of my life. Never has a woman deserved to be queen more than you, Catori Wood."

The tips of my ears flushed bright as he stepped closer, gripped the back of my head, and angled my face toward his.

"I feel like an impostor." My chest swelled with heartbeats. "Our marriage was a ruse. It wasn't real."

Emotion lanced behind his luminous irises. "It was real."

"I'm twenty, Ace. I can't be married at twenty. How will I explain it to my father?"

"Were you planning on going home and pretending none of this happened?"

My breath caught in my throat, which felt suddenly as tight as a wire.

He spun my rigid body toward the window and gestured below. "These people rely on you now. They are *your* people." He banded his arms around my stomach. "Neverra needs you. *I* need you."

69

A NEW ORDER

*G*regor and Silas arrived soon after.

As Ace met with the new *draca* in the loft to discuss something, Gregor joined me by the window. He pressed his hand over my skin, and I jolted from the searing heat.

"Pain means the portal stamp is taking. Consider yourself lucky, Catori. If you'd been only Unseelie—"

"I heard." Breathing through the unpleasant sensation, I asked, "When did you pick our side?"

"When Lily Wood disclosed our little secret to her brother."

My jaw flushed.

"I may not seem like I care about much, Catori, but Faith is my only child, and unlike Linus and Lyoh, I've protected her my entire life. That's why I kept Stella close. She was unfit to be a mother, but she was still the mother of my little girl."

My skin tickled now, as though Gregor were dragging a compass point over it. "Will you bring her here?"

"Should I?"

"Yes."

A crooked smile touched those rigid lips of his. "Are you suggesting this to get rid of her in Rowan?"

"Believe it or not, I've come to . . . *appreciate* Faith."

"I am aware of that."

"How?"

"I have my sources." He lifted his hand from my arm. "It might even have contributed to lessening your sentence. Besides, I enjoy youth. I enjoy its vivacity. Its tempestuousness. Its sentimentality. Its desire to revolutionize the world."

A circle slashed by five uneven lines now graced my wrist. My key to both worlds. "Has she had her baby?" I asked Gregor, without looking away from the new symbol.

"Not yet."

"When will you bring her?"

"After her daughter is born. A child born on Earth will always have two homes. A child born in Neverra cannot survive outside of it."

I frowned at him.

"For us Seelies, that is. If the child is born with only fire in its veins, it could never survive anywhere else." His hazel eyes fixed my face. "At least not for long."

Although neither of us uttered her name, Lily's face flickered in the air between us.

"I need to— I should go."

"Of course." Gregor inclined his head. "Keep my daughter safe, and I will keep your kingdom safe while you are gone."

My kingdom.

As he soared to the loft, he winked at me. Ace must've caught the wink, because the second Gregor and Silas were gone, he growled, "He better not have hit on you."

I almost snorted. "I don't think anyone would dare."

He watched the loft as though he feared Gregor were still there.

"Do you trust him?"

"No. And you shouldn't either." He scraped a finger over my wrist, over my newest marking. "It worked."

I nodded. "I am free to come and go as I please."

He smiled slowly. "I hope you plan on coming more than you plan on going."

I sighed and leaned into him. "After we get Lily home, I'll come more than I'll leave."

He stroked my hair. "Before we leave, Cat, I have something I want to give you."

He lowered himself to one knee, then swiped his tongue over his lips. "I know you're only twenty, and that we met six months ago, and that I might not have been your first choice of husband, and that technically the Cauldron already bound us"—he opened his hand, and a ring shaped like a crown, made up of a stunning web of rose-cut diamonds, twinkled wildly—"but will you marry me again, on Earth this time, so that your dad and Aylen and Cass—"

I bent over and kissed him.

As he rose to his feet, he asked, "Was that a yes?"

I peeled my left hand off his chest, off his thundering heart, and held it out before him. "Yes."

As though part of him had expected me to refuse, he blinked. But then he latched on to my hand and fit the small crown around my ring finger.

I nestled my chin in the crook of his neck and shut my eyes while he ran his palm down my spine. "*Ti ama ut Rowan e retri.*"

His hands stilled on my back, and then his voice vibrated against my hair. "Who taught you to say that?"

"I taught myself. Is it wrong?"

"No. It's right," he said slowly. "I was just worried."

"Worried?"

"Worried someone had said it to *you.*"

"Few people love me, Ace Wood."

"That's not true."

"It is. Why do you think I accepted your proposal?" I pressed away from him. "It might be the only one I ever get."

He smiled a dark smile full of bright teeth, and then he dragged those teeth along my jaw as his hands tugged me to him. "Shall I remind you that you're already married anyway?"

Right. I was married . . . "When did you know it would work?"

"The elder you sent us to meet. He told us that during the first bonding ceremony, the Cauldron takes your essence, but doesn't wrap it around another until the final ceremony. That at that point, it could mix two untethered essences as long as both were already in the Cauldron."

"When did you decide to switch with Cruz?"

"When we were walking up the spirals." His hands slid underneath my tunic to caress my skin. "I wanted to ask your permission. I hated taking the decision away from you."

For a few long heartbeats, we were both quiet . . . both motionless . . . both concentrated on the momentous impact of what the Cauldron had done to us.

"I thought marriage didn't mean anything to you."

His face set in a look of such deep concentration that a furrow formed between his eyebrows. I touched the spot with the tip of my finger, and then I pressed onto my tiptoes and kissed him there. I felt his eyelashes flutter against my jaw, felt his heated breaths pulse against my chin, felt his fingers dig deeper into my skin.

"I thought so too," he finally said. "But then I met this girl. In a police station of all places, and after being exceptionally rude to me"—I flicked him, and he smiled gently, caught my hand, enveloped my fingers—"she showed me there were other options in this life besides the ones I'd been given. And then she became one of those options."

My heart thundered. He touched his mouth to mine, smiled against my lips, and I saw stars as dazzling and wondrous as the diamonds around my finger. "About the name . . ."

"What about the name?"

"Maybe . . . maybe I should keep my maiden name."

"Why? You don't like mine?"

"It's . . . it's not that. But it's . . ."

"You don't want people to know that you're mine?"

"*Yours?*" I whispered softly.

"Yes. *Mine.*"

The four-letter word was a brand, this time on my heart.

EPILOGUE

*a*t sunset, after an endless afternoon of meetings, Ace returned to the apartment. We would leave for Rowan together. While he would have to return to Neverra every day, I would remain in Michigan until the winter . . . or until we found a solution for Lily.

Whichever came first.

I would return with Ace from time to time, to attend functions and be at his side to help rebuild and restructure Neverra, socially and politically.

And then there would be the coronation ceremony. Ace promised it would be painless, even though the Cauldron would be involved. Until then I was still Catori from Earth.

Not Queen Catori of Neverra.

I shuddered at the title, which felt fraudulent, which felt like it should belong to another. A woman worthy and desirous of power, who'd harbored dreams of being a princess since childhood at the very least.

I would have a few weeks to come to terms with all of this.

Until then, Lily was my only priority.

When we landed on the magical round doorway that was as thin as a knife blade, I stared at the violet-cloaked immensity surrounding me, at the bustling, fire-lit marketplace down below where celebrations were under way, at the *lustrium*-filled sky up above, and then I performed a slow pirouette to take in the forest of *calimbors*, the silver glades with their bobbing *volitors*, the *Hareni* now entirely submerged by the liquefied mist, and the steel-blue cliffs beyond that.

Two vaporous bodies crested over the cliff, glittery limbs swirling and knitting as they plunged down the steep rock walls.

"Are the Unseelies very disappointed?"

"Some of them are. Some had no plans of leaving."

Regret still had me pursing my lips.

Ace tucked a strand of hair behind my ear. "You gave them their freedom, Cat. They're so thankful for that."

"But they wanted bodies."

"And I'm certain they'll get them. The hunters are working on it."

I frowned.

"I charged your tribe with a great mission: finding the lock of the portals so we can alter the combination."

I sighed. "An impossible mission."

"An impossibly *long* mission, but possible. It's somewhere." Ace stared around him. "Silas and some of the *lucionaga* will be working with them."

"That should be interesting."

Ace smirked. "Sure you don't want to stay and oversee the task?"

"However tempting, I'd really like to get back to my old life. For a short while at least."

"Come on then. Take us back."

"Me?"

He smiled.

"But I don't know how to—"

"Press your hand to the silver surface. When your stamp lights up, the portal will soften and let us through."

I swallowed, then crouched and followed Ace's instructions. In seconds, the circle on my wrist activated and the portal rippled, and then it pulled us both under, into its starless darkness.

It was night in Rowan, too.

The boathouse was deserted. The lingering scent of wet sand and warm bodies clung to the navy air like a second skin. I closed my eyes and inhaled deeply.

Home.

I was home.

Fingers brushed my cheeks.

I opened my eyes to find Ace's face millimeters from my own. He placed a chaste kiss on my mouth, slotted his fingers through mine, then tugged me outside.

The moon was full and burning brightly over the inky lake. And the stars . . . there were so many of them, but they were scattered throughout the sky, unlike in Neverra where they streaked the darkness in thickets.

I turned to Ace, whose face glowed again. I blinked in surprise, but also in understanding. "It's the moon."

"What's the moon?"

"What gives me sight. It's the moon. In Neverra, you don't glow, and the ink is invisible."

He turned pensive eyes toward the Earth's satellite.

Laughter and music broke me out of my considerations. In the distance, tiki torches spilled firelight over a makeshift picnic table. The charred scent of meat had my stomach growling.

"Catori!"

I jolted and squinted in the direction of the familiar voice. A girl with wild bangs careened into me, ripping my hand out of Ace's and tackling me to the sand.

"You're back!"

My ears rang from the shrillness of Cass's voice.

"How was Africa? The pictures you sent were amazeballs. I so wanted to come and visit, but airfare was *so* expensive." She bit her lip. "Are you crying?"

I was. "I'm just happy to see you."

"Aw." She hugged me tight. "Honey."

That made me cry even harder.

After another squeeze, she said, "I need to get something from my car. I'll meet you over there." She tipped her head toward the picnic table and dashed off.

I got up and dusted my palms on the back of my jeans, trying to make out who else was at the picnic table. When I caught sight of two really tall men and a diminutive blonde, my breaths jumbled in my lungs.

"They're all here?" I squeaked.

Ace nodded.

"How did they—"

"I might've sent someone to inform them of your imminent arrival."

He extended his hand, and I took it, but then I remembered that no one knew about us, so I slid my hand back out and walked alongside him.

He cocked his head. "The world found out Angelina's baby wasn't mine, so we had a public breakup. It was in all the magazines."

"Even so, if you show up with a new girlfriend—"

"Fiancée."

"That's even worse."

He stuck his hands into the pockets of his jeans and gave me a crooked smile.

"What?" I asked.

"Nothing."

"I can tell you're thinking something."

"Can you? What a shame you can't tell what it is, though."

"Oh my God, you told them!"

"I did no such thing," he said but kept smiling.

I side-eyed him, trying to figure out what he'd done, because he'd definitely done something . . .

Suddenly a body lurched from the darkness and rocketed into Ace's arms. A body with a golden mane of hair.

Lily.

He spun her around. "Hey, little sis. Long time no see."

She grinned, then hopped off him, and startled *me* with a hug. She pressed away, and then her hands moved.

"Yes. Cat did it," Ace said, his voice limned with such pride, it made my chest prickle.

Her hands fluttered quickly.

"Mom's safe. So are Dawson and Veroli."

Another sign.

"Dad didn't make it."

Lily sucked in a breath, and then her gray eyes silvered with tears.

Ace wrapped an arm around her. "Don't, Lily. Don't waste any emotion on that man."

Her shoulders still shook with silent sobs.

"Cat, baby, is that you?"

I looked past Lily. Standing over a compact barbecue was my father. Tanned and healthier than I'd left him, well cared for.

My heart pounced with joy. "Hey, Daddy."

The tongs slid out of his hand and landed on the sand. He lunged toward me, and then his arms were around me, his grip bone-crushing.

"How I've missed you," he said, smoothing my hair back with his big hands. He held me and held me. "My baby girl is finally home." He pressed me away and looked at me. Really looked at me. As though to ascertain I was really there, really me. And then, as though one hug hadn't sufficed, he gathered me to his chest once more and squashed me against him.

"Was it fun? It looked fun."

"It was . . . difficult," I said, stepping out of Dad's embrace.

"I'm really sorry I never made it out there. I was all booked to go, but then Lily got sick, and well, you know the rest since you were so understanding about it all."

I cast a glance at Lily, who gave me a sheepish grin. "Glad to see you're all better."

"It took her almost a month to recover!" Dad exclaimed.

"You don't say . . ." I smiled at Lily, knowing full well that she hadn't been sick. Before leaving Neverra, Cruz had stopped by to return my phone and fill me in on all the lies that he and Lily had fed my father to keep him from making a trip out to Rwanda.

Behind Lily and Ace, a shadow detached itself from the darkness. Kajika. I smiled at him, but he didn't return my smile. His gaze darted to the boathouse beyond me, as though expecting others to step out of it, but no one else was coming. At least, not the people he was holding out for.

I walked over to the hunter and hugged him. "I'm really glad to see you." He didn't hug me back, but I wasn't expecting him to. I released him, then in a soft voice, I answered his unasked question. "It's a one-way ticket."

A nerve ticked in his jaw.

Voice still low, I added, "Gwen wanted me to tell you that they're all well. But now that I'm here, why don't you go find out for yourself?" I smiled as I tipped my head toward the boathouse.

"Why would I go to them?"

My smile faltered. "Don't you want to be with your family?"

His gaze darted to Lily, but darted away almost as quickly. "Someone has to stay in Rowan to keep an eye on the *pahans*."

The pahans or one pahan in particular? "I'm back, Kajika."

"But for how long?"

I looked at Lily, who was smiling at something Dad was telling Ace. "For long enough."

Kajika folded his arms. "Until they find a way out of the *baseetogan*, I will stay here."

Although his reasoning sounded sensible, I couldn't help but suspect there was more to him wanting to stay in Rowan. Perhaps I was wrong. Perhaps Lyoh had planted a seed of doubt in my mind that had no reason to germinate. Perhaps there was nothing more than a mental bond between Lily and him.

"Thank you. For everything you taught me. Believe it or not, it came in handy."

His amber eyes flickered.

"I have so much to tell you."

An arm swung over my shoulder. "Correction. You have so much to tell all of us." Cass was back. "But first. Here." She shoved something into my hands.

"What's this?"

"Your birthday present, silly."

Delicately, I tore the paper open and extricated a booklet. *Dictionary* was stamped in bold gold lettering atop a highlighter-pink canvas cover. I held my breath as I flipped through it.

"Do you love it?" Cass asked. "I arranged all the words alphabetically." Cass had typed up every single Gottwa and Faeli word and their definition. "You're not mad I took it from your bedroom? I put it back. I just thought, you know, that typing it up would preserve it better. I know how much your ancestors' books mean to you."

I made a little sound at the back of my throat. "It's perfect. I love it."

Lily signed something.

"You want one too?" Cass asked.

I blinked at Cass. "You understand sign language now?"

"Lily's been teaching me." Cass grinned. "Is it okay if I make her a copy?"

"Sure. Maybe Kajika wants one too?" I suggested.

He grunted. "I am well versed in our tribal languages."

Dad was wiping the sand off the tongs with a wet dishrag. "Maybe I should learn too."

I shot my gaze to his face. "Uh . . ."

"That's a great idea," Ace said, smiling.

My heart picked up its pace. "It is?"

"Oh my God, what is that?" Cass grabbed my left hand.

The blood drained from my face. My brand was flaring. *Crap. Crap. And triple crap.*

"You got engaged?" she squealed.

"Oh. Uh." Sweat beaded on my upper lip. I licked it off as I snuck a glance at Ace, whose arms were folded and whose lips were curved in a sly smile. *Shoot.* I lowered my gaze to the ring. I suddenly wished Cass had noticed my brand instead.

"Oh my God, you did! You *so* did!" she all but shrieked. "And you didn't tell me! Is it someone you met in Africa?"

Even though the glow of the tiki torches was low, I was pretty sure my face was the deepest shade of red ever. I combed my hand through my hair as I considered lying about it, passing the ring off as a present I'd bought myself in Africa.

"I got to hand it to you, son," Dad said. "I wasn't certain she'd say yes."

I gulped. "What?"

"You didn't think I'd ask for your hand in marriage without your father's consent, did you?" Ace asked.

Oh.

Great.

Freaking.

Spirit.

Ace had talked to my father about this! Which was surely why he'd been grinning like an idiot earlier.

Sand, swallow me up. Lake, sweep me away.

Neither the sand nor the lake listened.

Cass's gaze ripped off the ring and landed on Ace. "You"—I was pretty sure she was about to have an aneurism—"you asked her to marry you?"

Ace smiled. "I did."

Both Lily and Kajika frowned, which told me they hadn't been looped in.

Cass blinked at him and then she put her hands on her hips, and looked squarely at me. "I better be your maid of honor."

I was starting to recover, but it was slow. *Really slow.* My hand no longer glowed. "Who else would I ask?" I finally said, which made Cass's face split with a grin.

As she explained to Lily that we'd talked about each other's weddings since we were little—which was not exactly true . . . whereas Cass had everything except the groom picked out, I'd never given it much thought—I asked Dad, "Are you mad?"

"Mad? I was a little surprised. Especially since I thought Ace was already engaged and about to be a father. But then he explained that Angelina's baby wasn't his, that he'd known since the beginning but had stayed with her out of duty, and well, when he told me he was in love with my little girl"—Dad took my hand and clasped it between both of his—"when he told me he'd never felt this way before, that you were his Nova"—his eyes misted over at the mention of Mom, as did mine—"I told him not to waste a minute, for you never know how many of those you'll have." He smiled. "But I have to admit, I didn't think you would accept." His eyes shone so bright, with tears but also with tenderness. "You'll never cease to surprise me."

"Your approval means the world to me, you know that, right?"

"I would hope so."

Emotion ruffled my heart.

"So when is the mating ceremony?" Kajika's question had me turning horror-stricken eyes on him.

"Mating ceremony? You mean, wedding?" Cass rolled her eyes. "Geez, what century are you from?"

I coughed while Lily laughed and Ace smirked.

"But yeah, when's the wedding?" Cass asked.

Ace snuck his arm around my waist and tucked me against his side, where I stood rigid as an ironing board. "We haven't decided yet."

"Well, we should discuss it over dinner," Cass proposed.

Kajika cleared his throat. "Lily suggests doing it before she leaves Rowan. She would like to be there."

Ace's arms stiffened around me.

"Or they could do it after your backpacking trip, Lily," Dad suggested.

Was that what we were calling it? *A backpacking trip.*

"Backpacking trip?" Ace said. "You're not going on any backpacking trip."

Lily pressed her lips together.

"Ah. *Finally.* Someone reasonable," Dad said. "To think your parents agreed to let her go off on her own." He shook his head.

"Or . . . we could all go with Lily!" Cass said. "Except you, Derek. You're too old."

Dad gave her a lopsided grin. "Well thanks for that, Cass."

She winked at him. "Seriously, I always dreamed of going backpacking. And it could be a neat bonding experience. Plus Kajika knows so much about nature and stuff, and Ace is very resourceful, not to mention responsible, and Cat's almost a doctor, so that'll come in handy if anything goes wrong. And as for me, I'm an awesome conversationalist." She laughed, and it lifted some of the gloom from Ace's face.

"I have to admit," I said, "I agree with Cass. Either we all go. Or none of us go."

Lily narrowed her gaze at me.

I linked my arm around Ace's waist. "And I know exactly where we should go."

"Really?" Cass asked.

"Yeah. It's this place called Neverra. I read about it on a travel blog. Apparently it was rated one of the places to see before you die."

Lily gasped softly while Kajika's eyes gleamed.

Ace kissed my temple. "I'm on board with that trip."

"Neverra, huh?" Dad said, returning to the grill. "Never heard of it. Is it a region?"

"Sort of. It's not on any map, though," I added, because Cass had already started scrolling on her phone.

"Like Atlantis?" she asked.

"Atlantis isn't real, honey," Dad said.

I smiled, and that smile loosened months of tension. I looked up at Ace to find his eyes already on mine. He smiled back, and I swear the sand vanished from underneath my feet for a moment. The beach too. My father. My friends. Everyone and everything vanished.

But just for a moment.

A beautiful moment.

UP NEXT: LILY AND KAJIKA'S STORY.
RAGING RIVAL HEARTS

WHAT TO READ NEXT

Ready for Lily and Kajika's love story?

IN THE MOOD FOR ANOTHER PARANORMAL ADVENTURE?

If you enjoy enemies-to-lovers stories with alpha males and heroines
who know their own mind, then you'll love my wolves.

Start *The Boulder Wolves* series with
A PACK OF BLOOD AND LIES.

How about a witchy, slow-burn romance? Travel to the coldest and mistiest town in France with a ragtag crew tasked with bringing magic back to the world in **OF WICKED BLOOD.**

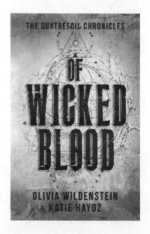

Or head over to the City of Lights with my angels in FEATHER for a modern and darkly romantic *Romeo & Juliet* retelling.

ACKNOWLEDGMENTS

There are so many people I'd like to thank for this book...for this series. First and foremost, you, my reader. You gave me the desire and drive to see Catori's story through. Well, Cat's and Ace's, and their family and friends. Although I'm sad to leave Rowan and Neverra behind (for now...I'll travel back there soon, and I'm taking you with me), I have many new projects planned. The latest is a werewolf trilogy, A PACK OF BLOOD & LIES.

To my extraordinary beta readers—Astrid Arditi, Theresea Barrett, and Katie Hayoz—you make each one of my stories better. You are all at once my pit crew, my wing women, and my muses.

To my editors, Jessica Nelson, I love working with you. You get the kinks out of my writing and smooth out my prose. Josiah Davis, thank you for cleaning up my manuscript. You made me realize I had the terrible habit of chaining clauses without using an "and."

To my cover designer, Alessia Casali, you are so talented and so patient, an absolute pleasure to work with.

To my parents, thank you for the loving childhood you've given me.

To my children, I know Mommy's attached to the hip with her laptop, but I do love you more than my computer. A lot more. "Megamuch more."

To my husband, the most patient, charming, generous man, I love you to Neverra and back. In case you're not aware of this, Neverra is very *very* far away.

ALSO BY OLIVIA WILDENSTEIN

PARANORMAL ROMANCE

The Lost Clan series

ROSE PETAL GRAVES

ROWAN WOOD LEGENDS

RISING SILVER MIST

RAGING RIVAL HEARTS

RECKLESS CRUEL HEIRS

The Boulder Wolves series

A PACK OF BLOOD AND LIES

A PACK OF VOWS AND TEARS

A PACK OF LOVE AND HATE

A PACK OF STORMS AND STARS

Angels of Elysium series

FEATHER

CELESTIAL

STARLIGHT

The Quatrefoil Chronicles series

OF WICKED BLOOD

OF TAINTED HEART

CONTEMPORARY ROMANCE

GHOSTBOY, CHAMELEON & THE DUKE OF GRAFFITI

NOT ANOTHER LOVE SONG

ROMANTIC SUSPENSE

Cold Little Games series

COLD LITTLE LIES

COLD LITTLE GAMES

COLD LITTLE HEARTS

ABOUT THE AUTHOR

USA TODAY bestselling author Olivia Wildenstein grew up in New York City, the daughter of a French father with a great sense of humor, and a Swedish mother whom she speaks to at least three times a day. She chose Brown University to complete her undergraduate studies and earned a bachelor's in comparative literature. After designing jewelry for a few years, Wildenstein traded in her tools for a laptop computer and a very comfortable chair. This line of work made more sense, considering her college degree.

When she's not writing, she's psychoanalyzing everyone she meets (Yes. Everyone), eavesdropping on conversations to gather material for her next book, baking up a storm (that she actually eats), going to the gym (because she eats), and attempting not to be late at her children's school (like she is 4 out of 5 mornings, on good weeks).

Wildenstein lives with her husband and three children in Geneva, Switzerland, where she's an active member of the writing community.

oliviawildenstein.com
Olivia@wildenstein.com

Made in the USA
Columbia, SC
06 November 2021

48449660R10250